Nora Roberts is the *New York Times* bestselling author of more than two hundred novels. A born storyteller, she creates a blend of warmth, humour and poignancy that speaks directly to her readers and has earned her almost every award for excellence in her field. The youngest of five children, Nora Roberts lives in western Maryland. She has two sons.

Visit her website at www.noraroberts.com

Nora Roberts

Coming Home to the Winter Wonderland

MILLS & BOON

Mills & Boon
An imprint of HarperCollins*Publishers* Ltd
1 London Bridge Street
London SE1 9GF

This paperback edition 2020

First published in Great Britain by Mills & Boon,
an imprint of HarperCollins*Publishers* Ltd 2020

ISBN: 978-0-263-27652-7

MIX
Paper from
responsible sources
FSC™ C007454

A Will and a Way

For my family members, who, fortunately,
aren't as odd as the relatives in this book.

Chapter 1

One hundred fifty million dollars was nothing to sneeze at. No one in the vast, echoing library of Jolley's Folley would have dared. Except Pandora. She did so with more enthusiasm than delicacy into a tattered tissue. After blowing her nose, she sat back, wishing the antihistamine she had taken would live up to its promise of fast relief. She wished she'd never caught the wretched cold in the first place. More, she wished she were anywhere else in the world.

Surrounding her were dozens of books she'd read and hundreds more she'd never given a thought to, though she'd spent hours and hours in the library. The scent of the leather-bound volumes mixed with the lighter, homier scent of dust. Pandora preferred either to the strangling fragrance of lilies that filled three stocky vases.

In one corner of the room was a marble-and-ivory chess set, where she'd lost a great many highly disputed matches. Uncle Jolley, bless his round, innocent face and pudgy fingers, had been a compulsive and skilled cheat. Pandora had never taken a loss in stride. Maybe that's why he'd so loved to beat her, by fair means or foul.

Through the three arching windows the light shone dull and a little gloomy. It suited her mood and, she thought, the proceedings. Uncle Jolley had loved to set scenes.

When she loved—and she felt this emotion for a select few who'd touched her life—she put everything she had into it. She'd been born with boundless energy. She'd developed iron-jawed stubbornness. She'd loved Uncle Jolley in her uninhibited, expansive fashion, acknowledging then accepting all of his oddities. He might have been ninety-three, but he'd never been dull or fussy.

A month before his death, they'd gone fishing—poaching actually—in the lake that was owned and stocked by his neighbor. When they'd caught more than they could eat, they'd sent a half-dozen trout back to the owner, cleaned and chilled.

She was going to miss Uncle Jolley with his round cherub's face, high, melodious voice and wicked humors. From his ten-foot, extravagantly framed portrait, he looked down at her with the same little smirk he'd worn whether he'd been making a million-dollar merger or handing an unsuspecting vice-president a drink in a dribble glass. She missed him already. No one else in her far-flung, contrasting family understood and accepted her with the same ease. It had been one more reason she'd adored him.

Miserable with grief, aggravated by a head cold, Pandora listened to Edmund Fitzhugh drone on, and on, with the preliminary technicalities of Uncle Jolley's will. Maximillian Jolley McVie had never been one for brevity. He'd always said if you were going to do something, do it until the steam ran out. His last will and testament bore his style.

Not bothering to hide her disinterest in the proceedings, Pandora took a comprehensive survey of the other occupants of the library.

To have called them mourners would have been just the sort of bad joke Jolley would have appreciated.

There was Jolley's only surviving son, Uncle Carlson, and his wife. What was her name? Lona—Mona? Did it matter? Pandora saw them sitting stiff backed and alert in matching shades of black. They made her think of crows on a telephone wire just waiting for something to fall at their feet.

Cousin Ginger—sweet and pretty and harmless, if rather vacuous. Her hair was Jean Harlow blond this month. Good old Cousin Biff was there in his black Brooks Brothers suit. He sat back, one leg crossed over the other as if he were watching a polo match. Pandora was certain he wasn't missing a word. His wife—was it Laurie?—had a prim, respectful look on her face. From experience, Pandora knew she wouldn't utter a word unless it were to echo Biff. Uncle Jolley had called her a silly, boring fool. Hating to be cynical, Pandora had to agree.

There was Uncle Monroe looking plump and successful and smoking a big cigar despite the fact that his sister, Patience, waved a little white handkerchief in front of her nose. Probably because of it, Pandora corrected. Uncle Monroe liked nothing better than to make his ineffectual sister uncomfortable.

Cousin Hank looked macho and muscular, but hardly more than his tough athletic wife, Meg. They'd hiked the Appalachian Trail on their honeymoon. Uncle Jolley had wondered if they stretched and limbered up before lovemaking.

The thought caused Pandora to giggle. She stifled it halfheartedly with the tissue just before her gaze wandered over to cousin Michael. Or was it second cousin Michael? She'd never been able to get the technical business straight. It seemed a bit foolish when you weren't talking blood relation anyway. His mother had been Uncle Jolley's niece by Jolley's son's second marriage. It was a complicated state of affairs, Pandora thought. But then Michael Donahue was a complicated man.

They'd never gotten along, though she knew Uncle Jolley had favored him. As far as Pandora was concerned, anyone who made his living writing a silly television series that kept people glued to a box rather than doing something worthwhile was a materialistic parasite. She had a momentary flash of pleasure as she remembered telling him just that.

Then, of course, there were the women. When a man

dated centerfolds and showgirls it was obvious he wasn't interested in intellectual stimulation. Pandora smiled as she recalled stating her view quite clearly the last time Michael had visited Jolley's Folley. Uncle Jolley had nearly fallen off his chair laughing.

Then her smile faded. Uncle Jolley was gone. And if she was honest, which she was often, she'd admit that of all the people in the room at that moment, Michael Donahue had cared for and enjoyed the old man more than anyone but herself.

You'd hardly know that to look at him now, she mused. He looked disinterested and slightly arrogant. She noticed the set, grim line around his lips. Pandora had always considered Donahue's mouth his best feature, though he rarely smiled at her unless it was to bare his teeth and snarl.

Uncle Jolley had liked his looks, and had told Pandora so in his early stages of matchmaking. A hobby she'd made sure he'd given up quickly. Well, he hadn't given it up precisely, but she'd ignored it all the same.

Being rather short and round himself, perhaps Jolley had appreciated Donahue's long lean frame, and the narrow intense face. Pandora might have liked it herself, except that Michael's eyes were often distant and detached.

At the moment he looked like one of the heroes in the action series he wrote—leaning negligently against the wall and looking just a bit out of place in the tidy suit and tie. His dark hair was casual and not altogether neat, as though he hadn't thought to comb it into place after riding with the top down. He looked bored and ready for action. Any action.

It was too bad, Pandora thought, that they didn't get along better. She'd have liked to have reminisced with someone about Uncle Jolley, someone who appreciated his whimsies as she had.

There was no use thinking along those lines. If they'd elected to sit together, they'd have been picking little pieces out of each other by now. Uncle Jolley, smirking down from his portrait, knew it very well.

With a half sigh she blew her nose again and tried to listen to Fitzhugh. There was something about a bequest to whales. Or maybe it was whalers.

Another hour of this, Michael thought, and he'd be ready to chew raw meat. If he heard one more *whereas*... On a long breath, Michael drew himself in. He was here for the duration because he'd loved the crazy old man. If the last thing he could do for Jolley was to stand in a room with a group of human vultures and listen to long rambling legalese, then he'd do it. Once it was over, he'd pour himself a long shot of brandy and toast the old man in private. Jolley had had a fondness for brandy.

When Michael had been young and full of imagination and his parents hadn't understood, Uncle Jolley had listened to him ramble, encouraged him to dream. Invariably on a visit to the Folley, his uncle had demanded a story then had settled himself back, bright-eyed and eager, while Michael wove on. Michael hadn't forgotten.

When he'd received his first Emmy for *Logan's Run*, Michael had flown from L.A. to the Catskills and had given the statuette to his uncle. The Emmy was still in the old man's bedroom, even if the old man wasn't.

Michael listened to the dry impersonal attorney's voice and wished for a cigarette. He'd only given them up two days before. Two days, four hours and thirty-five minutes. He'd have welcomed the raw meat.

He felt stifled in the room with all these people. Every one of them had thought old Jolley was half-mad and a bit of a nuisance. The one-hundred-fifty-million-dollar estate was different. Stocks and bonds were extremely sane. Michael had seen several assessing glances roaming over the library furniture. Big, ornate Georgian might not suit some of the streamlined life-styles, but it would liquidate into very tidy cash. The old man, Michael knew, had loved every clunky chair and oversize table in the house.

He doubted if any of them had been to the big echoing house in the past ten years. Except for Pandora, he admitted grudgingly. She might be an annoyance, but she'd adored Jolley.

At the moment she looked miserable. Michael didn't believe he'd ever seen her look unhappy before—furious, disdainful, infuriated, but never unhappy. If he hadn't known better, he'd have gone to sit beside her, offer some comfort, hold her hand. She'd probably chomp it off at the wrist.

Still, her shockingly blue eyes were red and puffy. Almost as red as her hair, he mused, as his gaze skimmed over the wild curly mane that tumbled, with little attention to discipline or style, around her shoulders. She was so pale that the sprinkling of freckles over her nose stood out. Normally her ivory-toned skin had a hint of rose in it—health or temperament, he'd never been sure.

Sitting among her solemn, black-clad family, she stood out like a parrot among crows. She'd worn a vivid blue dress. Michael approved of it, though he'd never say so to Pandora. She didn't need black and crepe and lilies to mourn. That he understood, if he didn't understand her.

She annoyed him, periodically, with her views on his life-style and career. When they clashed, it didn't take long for him to hurl criticism back at her. After all, she was a bright, talented woman who was content to play around making outrageous jewelry for boutiques rather than taking advantage of her Master's degree in education.

She called him materialistic, he called her idealistic. She labeled him a chauvinist, he labeled her a pseudo-intellectual. Jolley had sat with his hands folded and chuckled every time they argued. Now that he was gone, Michael mused, there wouldn't be an opportunity for any more battles. Oddly enough, he found it another reason to miss his uncle.

The truth was, he'd never felt any strong family ties to anyone but Jolley. Michael didn't think of his parents very often. His father was somewhere in Europe with his fourth wife, and his mother had settled placidly into Palm Springs society with husband number three. They'd never understood their son who'd opted to work for a living in something as bourgeois as television.

But Jolley had understood and appreciated. More, much more important to Michael, he'd enjoyed Michael's work.

A grin spread over his face when he heard Fitzhugh drone out the bequest for whales. It was so typically Jolley. Several impatient relations hissed through their teeth. A hundred fifty thousand dollars had just spun out of their reach. Michael glanced up at the larger-than-life-size portrait of his uncle. You always said you'd have the last word, you old fool. The only trouble is you're not here to laugh about it.

'To my son, Carlson...' All the quiet muttering and whispers died as Fitzhugh cleared his throat. Without much interest Pandora watched her relatives come to attention. The charities and servants had their bequests. Now it was time for the big guns. Fitzhugh glanced up briefly before he continued. 'Whose—aaah—mediocrity was always a mystery to me, I leave my entire collection of magic tricks in hopes he can develop a sense of the ridiculous.'

Pandora choked into her tissue and watched her uncle turn beet red. First point Uncle Jolley, she thought and prepared to enjoy herself. Maybe he'd left the whole business to the A.S.P.C.A.

'To my grandson, Bradley, and my granddaughter by marriage, Lorraine, I leave my very best wishes. They need nothing more.'

Pandora swallowed and blinked back tears at the reference to her parents. She'd call them in Zanzibar that evening. They would appreciate the sentiment even as she did.

'To my nephew Monroe who has the first dollar he ever made, I leave the last dollar I made, frame included.

To my niece, Patience, I leave my cottage in Key West without much hope she'll have the gumption to use it.'

Monroe chomped on his cigar while Patience looked horrified.

'To my grand-nephew, Biff, I leave my collection of matches, with the hopes that he will, at last, set the world on fire. To my pretty grand-niece, Ginger, who likes equally pretty things, I leave the sterling silver mirror purported to have been owned by Marie Antoinette. To my grand-nephew, Hank, I leave the sum of 3528. Enough, I believe, for a lifetime supply of wheat germ.'

The grumbles that had begun with the first bequest continued and grew. Anger hovered on the edge of outrage. Jolley would have liked nothing better. Pandora made the mistake of glancing over at Michael. He didn't seem so distant and detached now, but full of admiration. When their gazes met, the giggle she'd been holding back spilled out. It earned her several glares.

Carlson rose, giving new meaning to the phrase controlled outrage. 'Mr. Fitzhugh, my father's will is nothing more than a mockery. It's quite obvious that he wasn't in his right mind when he made it, nor do I have any doubt that a court will overturn it.'

'Mr. McVie.' Again Fitzhugh cleared his throat. The sun began to push its way through the clouds but no one seemed to notice. 'I understand perfectly your sentiments in this matter. However, my client was perfectly well and lucid when this will was drawn. He may have worded it against my advice, but it is legal and binding. You are, of course, free to consult with your own counsel. Meanwhile, there's more to be read.'

'Hogwash.' Monroe puffed on his cigar and glared at everyone. 'Hogwash,' he repeated while Patience patted his arm and chirped ineffectually.

'Uncle Jolley liked hogwash,' Pandora said as she balled her tissue. She was ready to face them down, almost hoped she'd have to. It would take her mind off her grief. 'If he wanted to leave his money to the Society for the Prevention of Stupidity, it was his right.'

'Easily said, my dear.' Biff polished his nails on his lapel. The gold band of his watch caught a bit of the sun and gleamed. 'Perhaps the old lunatic left you a ball of twine so you can string more beads.'

'You haven't got the matches yet, old boy.' Michael spoke lazily from his corner, but every eye turned his way. 'Careful what you light.'

'Let him read, why don't you?' Ginger piped up, quite pleased with her bequest. Marie Antoinette, she mused. Just imagine.

'The last two bequests are joint,' Fitzhugh began before there could be another interruption. 'And, a bit unorthodox.'

'The entire document's unorthodox,' Carlson tossed out, then harrumphed. Several heads nodded in agreement.

Pandora remembered why she always avoided family gatherings. They bored her to death. Quite deliberately, she waved a hand in front of her mouth and yawned.

'Could we have the rest, Mr. Fitzhugh, before my family embarrasses themselves any further?'

She thought, but couldn't be sure, that she saw a quick light of approval in the fusty attorney's eyes. 'Mr. McVie wrote this portion in his own words.' He paused a moment, either for effect or courage. 'To Pandora McVie and Michael Donahue,' Fitzhugh read. 'The two members of my family who have given me the most pleasure with their outlook on life, their enjoyment of an old man and old jokes, I leave the rest of my estate, in entirety, all accounts, all business interests, all stocks, bonds and trusts, all real and personal property, with all affection. Share and share alike.'

Pandora didn't hear the half-dozen objections that sprang out. She rose, stunned and infuriated. 'I can't take his money.' Towering over the family who sat around her, she strode straight up to Fitzhugh. The lawyer, who'd anticipated attacks from other areas, braced for the unexpected. 'I wouldn't know what to do with it. It'd just clutter up my life.' She waved a hand at the papers on the desk as if they were a minor annoyance. 'He should've asked me first.'

'Miss McVie…'

Before the lawyer could speak again, she whirled on Michael. 'You can have it all. You'd know what to do with it, after all. Buy a hotel in New York, a condo in L.A., a club in Chicago and a plane to fly you back and forth, I don't care.'

Deadly calm, Michael slipped his hands in his pockets. 'I appreciate the offer, cousin. Before you pull the trigger, why don't we wait until Mr. Fitzhugh finishes before you embarrass yourself any further?'

She stared at him a moment, nearly nose to nose with him in heels. Then, because she'd been taught to do so at an early age, she took a deep breath and waited for her temper to ebb. 'I don't want his money.'

'You've made your point.' He lifted a brow in the cynical, half-amused way that always infuriated her. 'You're fascinating the relatives by the little show you're putting on.'

Nothing could have made her find control quicker. She angled her chin at him, hissed once, then subsided. 'All right then.' She turned and stood her ground. 'I apologize for the interruption. Please finish reading, Mr. Fitzhugh.'

The lawyer gave himself a moment by taking off his glasses and polishing them on a big white handkerchief. He'd known when Jolley had made the will the day would come when he'd be forced to face an enraged family. He'd argued with his client about it, cajoled, reasoned, pointed out the absurdities. Then he'd drawn up the will and closed the loopholes.

'I leave all of this,' he continued, 'the money, which is a small thing, the stocks and bonds, which are necessary but boring, the business interests, which are interesting weights around the neck. And my home and all in it, which is everything important to me, the memories made there, to Pandora and Michael because they understood and cared. I leave this to them, though it may annoy them, because there is no one else in my family I can leave what is important to me. What was mine is

Pandora and Michael's now, because I know they'll keep me alive. I ask only one thing of each of them in return.'

Michael's grip relaxed, and he nearly smiled again. 'Here comes the kicker,' he murmured.

'Beginning no more than a week after the reading of this document, Pandora and Michael will move into my home in the Catskills, known as Jolley's Folley. They will live there together for a period of six months, neither one spending more than two nights in succession under another roof. After this six-month period, the estate reverts to them, entirely and without encumbrance, share and share alike.

'If one does not agree with this provision, or breaks the terms of this provision within the six-month period, the estate, in its entirety, will be given over to all my surviving heirs and the Institute for the Study of Carnivorous Plants in joint shares.

'You have my blessing, children. Don't let an old, dead man down.'

For a full thirty seconds there was silence. Taking advantage of it, Fitzhugh began straightening his papers.

'The old bastard,' Michael murmured. Pandora would've taken offense if she hadn't agreed so completely. Because he judged the temperature in the room to be on the rise, Michael pulled Pandora out, down the hall and into one of the funny little parlors that could be found throughout the house. Just before he closed the door, the first explosion in the library erupted.

Pandora drew out a fresh tissue, sneezed into it, then

plopped down on the arm of a chair. She was too flab-bergasted and worn-out to be amused. 'Well, what now?'

Michael reached for a cigarette before he remembered he'd quit. 'Now we have to make a couple of decisions.'

Pandora gave him one of the long lingering stares she'd learned made most men stutter. Michael merely sat across from her and stared back. 'I meant what I said. I don't want his money. By the time it's divided up and the taxes dealt with, it's close to fifty million apiece. Fifty million,' she repeated, rolling her eyes. 'It's ridiculous.'

'Jolley always thought so,' Michael said, and watched the grief come and go in her eyes.

'He only had it to play with. The trouble was, every time he played, he made more.' Unable to sit, Pandora paced to the window. 'Michael, I'd suffocate with that much money.'

'Cash isn't as heavy as you think.'

With something close to a sneer, she turned and sat on the window ledge. 'You don't object to fifty million or so after taxes I take it.'

He'd have loved to have wiped that look off her face. 'I haven't your fine disregard for money, Pandora, prob-ably because I was raised with the illusion of it rather than the reality.'

She shrugged, knowing his parents existed, and al-ways had, mainly on credit and connections. 'So, take it all then.'

Michael picked up a little blue glass egg and tossed it from palm to palm. It was cool and smooth and worth several thousand. 'That's not what Jolley wanted.'

With a sniff, she snatched the egg from his hand. 'He wanted us to get married and live happily ever after. I'd like to humor him....' She tossed the egg back again. 'But I'm not that much of a martyr. Besides, aren't you engaged to some little blond dancer?'

He set the egg down before he could heave it at her. 'For someone who turns their pampered nose up at television, you don't have the same intellectual snobbery about gossip rags.'

'I *adore* gossip,' Pandora said with such magnificent exaggeration Michael laughed.

'All right, Pandora, let's put down the swords a minute.' He tucked his thumbs in his pockets and rocked back on his heels. Maybe they could, if they concentrated, talk civilly with each other for a few minutes. 'I'm not engaged to anyone, but marriage wasn't a term of the will in any case. All we have to do is live together for six months under the same roof.'

As she studied him a sense of disappointment ran through her. Perhaps they'd never gotten along, but she'd respected him if for nothing more than what she'd seen as his pure affection for Uncle Jolley. 'So, you really want the money?'

He took two furious steps forward before he caught himself. Pandora never flinched. 'Think whatever you like.' He said it softly, as though it didn't matter. Oddly enough, it made her shudder. 'You don't want the money, fine. Put that aside a moment. Are you going to stand by and watch this house go to the clan out there or a bunch of scientists studying Venus's-flytraps? Jolley loved this place and everything in it. I always thought you did, too.'

'I do.' The others would sell it, she admitted. There wasn't one person in the library who wouldn't put the house on the market and run with the cash. It would be lost to her. All the foolish, ostentatious rooms, the ridiculous archways. Jolley might be gone, but he'd left the house like a dangling carrot. And he still held the stick.

'He's trying to run our lives still.'

Michael lifted a brow. 'Surprised?'

With a half laugh, Pandora glanced over. 'No.'

Slowly she walked around the room while the sun shot through the diamond panes of glass and lit her hair. Michael watched her with a sense of detached admiration. She'd look magnificent on the screen. He'd always thought so. Her coloring, her posture. Her arrogance. The five or ten pounds the camera would add couldn't hurt that too angular, bean-pole body, either. And the fire-engine-red hair would make a statement on the screen while it was simply outrageous in reality. He'd often wondered why she didn't do something to tone it down.

At the moment he wasn't interested in any of that—just in what was in her brain. He didn't give a damn about the money, but he wasn't going to sit idly by and watch everything Jolley had had and built go to the vultures. If he had to play rough with Pandora, he would. He might even enjoy it.

Millions. Pandora cringed at the outrageousness of it. That much money could be nothing but a headache, she was certain. Stocks, bonds, accountants, trusts, tax shelters. She preferred a simpler kind of living. Though no one would call her apartment in Manhattan primitive.

She'd never had to worry about money and that was just the way she liked it. Above or below a certain income level, there were nothing but worries. But if you found a nice, comfortable plateau, you could just cruise. She'd nearly found it.

It was true enough that a share of this would help her tremendously professionally. With a buffer sturdy enough, she could have the artistic freedom she wanted and continue the life-style that now caused a bit of a strain on her bank account. Her work was artistic and critically acclaimed but reviews didn't pay the rent. Outside of Manhattan, her work was usually considered too unconventional. The fact that she often had to create more mainstream designs to keep her head above water grated constantly. With fifty or sixty thousand to back her, she could...

Furious with herself, she blocked it off. She was thinking like Michael, she decided. She'd rather die. He'd sold out, turned whatever talent he had to the main chance, just as he was ready to turn these circumstances to his own financial advantage. She would think of other areas. She would think first of Jolley.

As she saw it, the entire scheme was a maze of problems. How like her uncle. Now, like a chess match, she'd have to consider her moves.

She'd never lived with a man. Purposely. Pandora liked running by her own clock. It wasn't so much that she minded sharing *things*, she minded sharing space. If she agreed, that would be the first concession.

Then there was the fact that Michael was attractive, attractive enough to be unsettling if he hadn't been so annoying. Annoying and easily annoyed, she recalled with a flash of amusement. She knew what buttons to push. Hadn't she always prided herself on the fact that she could handle him? It wasn't always easy; he was too sharp. But that made their altercations interesting. Still, they'd never been together for more than a week at a time.

But there was one clear, inarguable fact. She'd loved her uncle. How could she live with herself if she denied him a last wish? Or a last joke.

Six months. Stopping, she studied Michael as he studied her. Six months could be a very long time, especially when you weren't pleased with what you were doing. There was only one way to speed things up. She'd enjoy herself.

'Tell me, cousin, how can we live under the same roof for six months without coming to blows?'

'We can't.'

He'd answered without a second's hesitation, so she laughed again. 'I suppose I'd be bored if we did. I can tidy up loose ends and move in in three days. Four at the most.'

'That's fine.' When his shoulders relaxed, he realized he'd been tensed for her refusal. At the moment he didn't want to question why it mattered so much. Instead he held out a hand. 'Deal.'

Pandora inclined her head just before her palm met

his. 'Deal,' she agreed, surprised that his hand was hard and a bit callused. She'd expected it to be rather soft and limp. After all, all he did was type. Perhaps the next six months would have some surprises.

'Shall we go tell the others?'

'They'll want to murder us.'

Her smile came slowly, subtly shifting the angles of her face. It was, Michael thought, at once wicked and alluring. 'I know. Try not to gloat.'

When they stepped out, several griping relatives had spilled out into the hallway. They did what they did best together. They argued.

'You'd blow your share on barbells and carrot juice,' Biff said spitefully to Hank. 'At least I know what to do with money.'

'Lose it on horses,' Monroe said, and blew out a stream of choking cigar smoke. 'Invest. Tax deferred.'

'You could use yours to take a course in how to speak in complete sentences.' Carlson stepped out of the smoke and straightened his tie. 'I'm the old man's only living son. It's up to me to prove he was incompetent.'

'Uncle Jolley had more competence than the lot of you put together.' Feeling equal parts frustration and disgust, Pandora stepped forward. 'He gave you each exactly what he wanted you to have.'

Biff drew out a flat gold cigarette case as he glanced over at his cousin. 'It appears our Pandora's changed her mind about the money. Well, you worked for it, didn't you, darling?'

Michael put his hand on Pandora's shoulder and

squeezed lightly before she could spring. 'You'd like to keep your profile, wouldn't you, cousin?'

'It appears writing for television's given you a taste for violence.' Biff lit his cigarette and smiled. If he'd thought he could get in a blow below the belt… 'I think I'll decline a brawl,' he decided.

'Well, I think it's fair.' Hank's wife came forward, stretching out her hand. She gave both Pandora and Michael a hearty shake. 'You should put a gym in this place. Build yourself up a little. Come on, Hank.'

Silent, and his shoulders straining the material of his suit, Hank followed her out.

'Nothing but muscles between the head,' Carlson mumbled. 'Come, Mona.' He strode ahead of his wife, pausing long enough to level a glare at Pandora and Michael. The inevitable line ran though Michael's mind before Carlson opened his mouth and echoed it. 'You haven't heard the last of this.'

Pandora gave him her sweetest smile. 'Have a nice trip home, Uncle Carlson.'

'Probate,' Monroe said with a grunt, and waddled his way out behind them.

Patience fluttered her hands. 'Key West, for heaven's sake. I've never been south of Palm Beach. My, oh my.'

'Oh, Michael.' Fluttering her lashes, Ginger placed a hand on his arm. 'When do you think I might have my mirror?'

He glanced down into her perfectly lovely, heart-shaped face. Her eyes were as pure a blue as tropical waters. He thanked God Jolley hadn't asked that he spend six months with Cousin Ginger. 'I'm sure Mr. Fitzhugh will have it shipped to you as soon as possible.'

'Come along, Ginger, we'll give you a ride to the airport.' Biff pulled Ginger's hand through his arm, patted it and smiled down at Pandora. 'I'd be worried if I didn't know you better. You won't last six days with Michael much less six months. Beastly temper,' he said confidentially to Michael. 'The two of you'll murder each other before a week's out.'

'Don't spend the old man's money yet,' Michael warned. 'We'll make the six months if for no other reason than to spite you.' He smiled when he said it, a chummy, well-meaning smile that took the arrogance from Biff's face.

'We'll see who wins the game.' Straight backed, Biff turned toward the door. His wife walked out behind him without having said a word since she'd walked in.

'Biff,' Ginger began as they walked out. 'What are you going to do with all those matches?'

'Burn his bridges, I hope,' Pandora muttered. 'Well, Michael, though I can't say there was a lot of love before, there's nearly none lost now.'

'Are you worried about alienating them?'

With a shrug of her shoulders, she walked toward a bowl of roses, then gave him a considering look. 'Well, I've never had any trouble alienating you. Why is that, do you suppose?'

'Jolley always said we were too much alike.'

'Really?' Haughty, she lifted a brow. 'I find myself

disagreeing with him again. You and I, Michael Donahue, have almost nothing in common.'

'If that's so we have six months to prove it.' On impulse he moved closer and put a finger under her chin. 'You know, darling, you might've been stuck with Biff.'

'I'd've given the place to the plants first.'

He grinned. 'I'm flattered.'

'Don't be.' But she didn't move away from him. Not yet. It was an interesting feeling to be this close without snarling. 'The only difference is you don't bore me.'

'That's enough,' he said with a hint of a smile. 'I'm easily flattered.' Intrigued, he flicked a finger down her cheek. It was still pale, but her eyes were direct and steady. 'No, we won't bore each other, Pandora. In six months we might experience a lot of things, but boredom won't be one of them.'

It might be an interesting feeling, she discovered, but it wasn't quite a safe one. It was best to remember that he didn't find her appealing as a woman but would, for the sake of his own ego, string her along if she permitted it. 'I don't flatter easily. I haven't decided exactly what your reasons are for going through with this farce, but I'm doing it only for Uncle Jolley. I can set up my equipment here quite easily.'

'And I can write here quite easily.'

Pandora plucked a rose from the bowl. 'If you can call those implausible scripts writing.'

'The same way you call the bangles you string together art.'

Color came back to her cheeks and that pleased him.

'You wouldn't know art if it reached up and bit you on the nose. My jewelry expresses emotion.'

His smile showed pleasant interest. 'How much is lust going for these days?'

'I would have guessed you'd be very familiar with the cost.' Pandora fumbled for a tissue, sneezed into it, then shut her bag with a click. 'Most of the women you date have price tags.'

It amused him, and it showed. 'I thought we were talking about work.'

'My profession is a time-honored one, while yours— yours stops for commercial breaks. And furthermore—'

'I beg your pardon.'

Fitzhugh paused at the doorway of the library. He wanted nothing more than to be shed of the McVie clan and have a quiet, soothing drink. 'Am I to assume that you've both decided to accept the terms of the will?'

Six months, she thought. It was going to be a long, long winter.

Six months, he thought. He was going to have the first daffodil he found in April bronzed.

'You can start counting the days at the end of the week,' he told Fitzhugh. 'Agreed, cousin?'

Pandora set her chin. 'Agreed.'

Chapter 2

It was a pleasant trip from Manhattan along the Hudson River toward the Catskills. Pandora had always enjoyed it. The drive gave her time to clear her mind and relax. But then, she'd always taken it at her own whim, her own pace, her own convenience. Pandora made it a habit to do everything just that way. This time, however, there was more involved than her own wants and wishes. Uncle Jolley had boxed her in.

He'd known she'd have to go along with the terms of the will. Not for the money. He'd been too smart to think she could be lured into such a ridiculous scheme with money. But the house, her ties to it, her need for the continuity of family. That's what he'd hooked her with.

Now she had to leave Manhattan behind for six months. Oh, she'd run into the city for a few hours here and there, but it was hardly the same as living in the center of things. She'd always liked that—being in the center, surrounded by movement, being able to watch and become involved whenever she liked. Just as she'd always liked long weekends in the solitude of Jolley's Folley.

She'd been raised that way, to enjoy and make the most of whatever environment she was in. Her parents were gypsies. Wealth had meant they'd traveled first class instead of in covered wagons. If there'd been campfires, there had also been a servant to gather kindling, but the spirit was the same.

Before she'd been fifteen, Pandora had been to more than thirty countries. She'd eaten sushi in Tokyo, roamed the moors in Cornwall, bargained in Turkish markets. A succession of tutors had traveled with them so that by her calculations, she'd spent just under two years in a classroom environment before college.

The exotic, vagabond childhood had given her a taste for variety—in people, in foods, in styles. And oddly enough the exposure to widely diverse cultures and mores had formed in her an unshakable desire for a home and a sense of belonging.

Though her parents liked to meander through countries, recording everything with pen and film, Pandora had missed a central point. Where was home? This year in Mexico, next year in Athens. Her parents made a name for themselves with their books and articles on the unusual, but Pandora wanted roots. She'd discovered she'd have to find them for herself.

She'd chosen New York, and in her way, Uncle Jolley.

Now, because her uncle and his home had become her central point, she was agreeing to spend six months living with a man she could hardly tolerate so that she could inherit a fortune she didn't want or need. Life, she'd discovered long ago, never moved in straight lines.

Jolley McVie's ultimate joke, she thought as she turned up the long drive toward his Folley. Well, he could throw them together, but he couldn't make them stick.

Still, she'd have felt better if she'd been sure of Michael. Was it the lure of the millions of dollars, or an affection for an old man that would bring him to the Catskills? She knew his *Logan's Run* was in its very successful fourth year, and that he'd had other lucrative ventures in television. But money was a seduction itself. After all, her Uncle Carlson had more than he could ever spend, yet he was already taking the steps for a probate of the will.

That didn't worry her. Uncle Jolley had believed in hiring the best. If Fitzhugh had drawn up the will, it was air-tight. What worried her was Michael Donahue.

Because of the trap she'd fallen into, she'd found herself thinking of him a great deal too much over the past couple of days. Ally or enemy, she wasn't sure. Either way, she was going to have to live with him. Or around him. She hoped the house was big enough.

By the time she arrived, she was worn-out from the drive and the lingering head cold. Though her equipment and supplies had been shipped the day before, she still had three cases in the car. Deciding to take one at a time, Pandora popped the trunk, then simply looked at Jolley's Folley.

He'd built it when he'd been forty, so the house was already over a half century old. It went in all directions at once, as if he'd never been able to decide where he wanted to start and where he wanted to finish. The truth about Jolley, she admitted, was that he'd never wanted to finish. The project, the game, the puzzle, was always more interesting to him before the last pieces were in place.

Without the wings, it might have been a rather somber and sedate late-nineteenth-century mansion. With them, it was a mass of walls and corners, heights and widths. There was no symmetry, yet to Pandora it had always seemed as sturdy as the rock it had been built on.

Some of the windows were long, some were wide, some of them were leaded and some sheer. Jolley had made up his mind then changed it again as he'd gone along.

The stone had come from one of his quarries, the wood from one of his lumberyards. When he'd decided to build a house, he'd started his own construction firm. McVie Construction, Incorporated was one of the five biggest companies in the country.

It struck her suddenly that she owned half of Jolley's share in the company and her mind spun at how many others. She had interests in baby oil, steel mills, rocket engines and cake mix. Pandora lifted the case and set her teeth. What on earth had she let herself in for?

From the upstairs window, Michael watched her. The jacket she wore was big and baggy with three vivid col-

ors, blue, yellow and pink, patched in. The wind caught
at her slacks and rippled them from thigh to ankle. She
wasn't looking teary-eyed and pale this time, but grim
and resigned. So much the better. He'd been tempted to
comfort her during their uncle's funeral. Only the knowledge that too much sympathy for a woman like Pandora
was fatal had prevented him.

He'd known her since childhood and had considered
her a spoiled brat from the word go. Though she'd often
been off for months at a time on one of her parents' jour-
nalistic safaris, they'd seen enough of each other to feed a
mutual dislike. Only the fact that she had cared for Jolley
had given Michael some tolerance for her. And the fact,
he was forced to admit, that she had more honesty and
humanity in her than any of their other relations.

There had been a time, he recalled, a brief time, during
late adolescence that he'd felt a certain...stirring for her.
A purely shallow and physical teenage hunger, Michael
assured himself. She'd always had an intriguing face; it
could be unrelentingly plain one moment and striking the
next, and when she'd hit her teens...well, that had been a
natural enough reaction. And it had passed without incident. He now preferred a woman with more subtlety,
more gloss and femininity—and shorter fangs.

Whatever he preferred, Michael left the arranging of
his own office to wander downstairs.

'Charles, did my shipment come?' Pandora pulled off
her leather driving gloves and dropped them on a little
round table in the hall. Since Charles was there, the an-

cient butler who had served her uncle since before she was born, she felt a certain pleasure in coming.

'Everything arrived this morning, miss.' The old man would have taken her suitcase if she hadn't waved him away.

'No, don't fuss with that. Where did you have them put everything?'

'In the garden shed in the east yard, as you instructed.'

She gave him a smile and a peck on the cheek, both of which pleased him. His square bulldog's face grew slightly pink. 'I knew I could count on you. I didn't tell you before how happy I was that you and Sweeney are staying. The place wouldn't be the same without you serving tea and Sweeney baking cakes.'

Charles managed to pull his back a bit straighter. 'We wouldn't think about going anywhere else, miss. The master would have wanted us to stay.'

But made it possible for them to go, Pandora mused. Leaving each of them three thousand dollars for every year of service. Charles had been with Jolley since the house was built, and Sweeney had come some ten years later. The bequest would have been more than enough for each to retire on. Pandora smiled. Some weren't made for retirement.

'Charles, I'd love some tea,' she began, knowing if she didn't distract him, he'd insist on carrying her bags up the long staircase.

'In the drawing room, miss?'

'Perfect. And if Sweeney has any of those little cakes…'

'She's been baking all morning.' With only the slightest of creaks, he made his way toward the kitchen.

Pandora thought of rich icing loaded with sugar. 'I wonder how much weight a person can gain in six months.'

'A steady diet of Sweeney's cakes wouldn't hurt you,' Michael said from above her head. 'Men are generally more attracted to flesh than bone.'

Pandora spun around, then found herself in the awkward position of having to arch her neck back to see Michael at the top of the stairs. 'I don't center my life around attracting men.'

'I'd be the last one to argue with that.'

He looked quite comfortable, she thought, feeling the first stirrings of resentment. And negligently, arrogantly attractive. From several feet above her head, he leaned against a post and looked down on her as though he was the master. She'd soon put an end to that. Uncle Jolley's will had been very clear. Share and share alike.

'Since you're already here and settled in, you can come help me with the rest of my bags.'

He didn't budge. 'I always thought the one point we were in perfect agreement on was feminism.'

Pandora paused at the door to toss a look over her shoulder. 'Social and political views aside, if you don't help me up with them before Charles comes back, he'll insist on doing it himself. He's too old to do it and too proud to be told he can't.' She walked back out and wasn't surprised when she heard his footsteps on the gravel behind her.

She took a deep breath of crisp autumn air. All in all, it was a lovely day. 'Drive up early?'

'Actually, I drove up late last night.'

Pandora turned at the open trunk of her car. 'So eager to start the game, Michael?'

If he hadn't been determined to start off peacefully, he'd have found fault with the tone of her voice, with the look in her eyes. Instead he let it pass. 'I wanted to get my office set up today. I was just finishing it when you drove in.'

'Work, work, work,' she said with a long sigh. 'You must put in slavish hours to come up with an hour of chase scenes and steam a week.'

Peace wasn't all that important. As she reached for a suitcase, he closed a hand over her wrist. Later he'd think about how slim it was, how soft. Now he could only think how much he wished she were a man. Then he could've belted her. 'The amount of work I do and what I produce is of absolutely no concern to you.'

It occurred to Pandora, oddly, she thought, just how much she enjoyed seeing him on the edge of temper. All of her other relatives were so bland, so outwardly civilized. Michael had always been a contrast, and therefore of more interest. Smiling, she allowed her wrist to stay limp.

'Did I indicate that it was? Nothing, I promise you, could be further from the truth. Shall we get these in and have that tea? It's a bit chilly.'

He'd always admired, grudgingly, how smoothly she could slip into the lady-of-the-manor routine. As a writer who wrote for actors and for viewers, he appreciated natural talent. He also knew how to set a scene to his best advantage. 'Tea's a perfect idea.' He hauled one case out and left the second for her. 'We'll establish some guidelines.'

'Will we?' Pandora pulled out the case, then let the trunk shut quietly. Without another word, she started back toward the house, holding the front door open for him, then breezing by the suitcase she'd left in the main hall. Because she knew Michael was fond of Charles, she hadn't a doubt he'd pick it up and follow.

The room she always took was on the second floor in the east wing. Jolley had let her decorate it herself, and she'd chosen white on white with a few startling splashes of color. Chartreuse and blazing blue in throw pillows, a long horizontal oil painting, jarring in its colors of sunset, a crimson waist-high urn stuffed with ostrich plumes.

Pandora set her case by the bed, noted with satisfaction that a fire had been laid in the small marble fireplace, then tossed her jacket over a chair.

'I always feel like I'm walking into *Better Homes*,' he commented as he let her cases drop.

Pandora glanced down at them briefly, then at him. 'I'm sure you're more at home in your own room. It's more—*Field and Stream*. I expect tea's ready.'

He gave her a long, steady survey. Her jacket had concealed the trim cashmere sweater tucked into the narrow waist of her slacks. It reminded Michael quite forcibly just what had begun to attract him all those teenage years ago. For the second time he found himself wishing she were a man.

Though they walked abreast down the stairs, they didn't speak. In the drawing room, amid the Mideast opulence Jolley had chosen there, Charles was setting up the tea service.

'Oh, you lit the fire. How lovely.' Pandora walked over and began warming her hands. She wanted a moment, just a moment, because for an instant in her room she thought she'd seen something in Michael's eyes. And she thought she'd felt the same something in response. 'I'll pour, Charles. I'm sure Michael and I won't need another thing until dinner.'

Casually she glanced around the room, at the flowing drapes, the curvy brocade sofas, the plump pillows and brass urns. 'You know, this has always been one of my favorite rooms.' Going to the tea set, she began to fill cups. 'I was only twelve when we visited Turkey, but this room always makes me remember it vividly. Right down to the smells in the markets. Sugar?'

'No.' He took the cup from her, plopped a generous slice of cake on a dish, then chose a seat. He preferred the little parlor next door with its tidy English country air. This was the beginning, he thought, with the old butler and plump cook as witnesses. Six months from today, they'd all sign a document swearing that the terms of the will had been adhered to and that would be that. It was the time in between that concerned him.

'Rule number one,' Michael began without preamble. 'We're both in the east wing because it makes it easier for Charles and Sweeney. But—' he paused, hoping to emphasize his point '—both of us will, at all times, respect the other's area.'

'By all means.' Pandora crossed her legs and sipped her tea.

'Again, because of the staff, it seems fair that we eat at the same time. Therefore, in the interest of survival, we'll keep the conversations away from professional matters.'

Pandora smiled at him and nibbled on cake. 'Oh yes, let's do keep things personal.'

'You're a nasty little package—'

'See, we're off to a perfect start. Rule number two. Neither of us, no matter how bored or restless, will disturb the other during his or her set working hours. I generally work between ten and one, then again between three and six.'

'Rule number three. If one of us is entertaining, the other will make him or herself scarce.'

Pandora's eyes narrowed, only for a moment. 'Oh, and I so wanted to meet your dancer. Rule number four. The first floor is neutral ground and to be shared equally unless specific prior arrangements are made and agreed upon.' She tapped her finger against the arm of the chair. 'If we both play fair, we should manage.'

'I don't have any trouble playing fair. As I recall, you're the one who cheats.'

Her voice became very cool, her tone very rounded. 'I don't know what you're talking about.'

'Canasta, poker, gin.'

'That's absurd and you have absolutely no proof.' Rising, she helped herself to another cup of tea. 'Besides, cards are entirely different.' Warmed by the fire, soothed by the tea, she smiled at him. As Michael recalled, that particular smile was lethal. And stunning. 'Are you still holding a grudge over that five hundred I won from you?'

'I wouldn't if you'd won it fairly.'

'I won it,' she countered. 'That's what counts. If I cheated and you didn't catch me, then it follows that I cheated well enough for it to be legal.'

'You always had a crooked sense of logic.' He rose as well and came close. She had to admire the way he moved. It wasn't quite a swagger because he didn't put the effort into it. But it was very close. 'If we play again, whatever we play, you won't cheat me.'

Confident, she smiled at him. 'Michael, we've known each other too long for you to intimidate me.' She reached a hand up to pat his cheek and found her wrist captured a second time. And a second time she saw and felt that same dangerous something she'd experienced upstairs.

There was no Uncle Jolley as a buffer between them now. Perhaps they'd both just begun to realize it. Whatever was between them that made them snarl and snap would have a long, cold winter to surface.

Perhaps neither one of them wanted to face it, but both were too stubborn to back down.

'Perhaps we're just beginning to know each other,' Michael murmured.

She believed it. And didn't like it. He wasn't a posturing fool like Biff nor a harmless hulk like Hank. He might be a cousin by marriage only, but the blood between them had always run hot. There was violence in him. It showed sometimes in a look in his eyes, in the way he held himself. As though he wouldn't ward off a blow but counter it. Pandora recognized it because there was violence in her, as well. Perhaps that was why she always felt compelled to shoot darts at him, just to see how many he could boomerang back at her.

They stood as they were a moment, gauging each other, reassessing. The wise thing to do was for each to acknowledge a hit and step aside. Pandora threw up her chin. Michael set for the volley. 'We'll go to the mat another time, Michael. At the moment, I'm a bit tired from the drive. If you'll excuse me?'

'Rule number five,' he said without releasing her. 'If one of us takes potshots at the other, they'll damn well pay the consequences.' When he freed her arm, he went back for his cup. 'See you at dinner, cousin.'

Pandora awoke just past dawn fully awake, rested and bursting with energy. Whether it had been the air in the mountains or the six hours of deep sleep, she was ready and eager to work. Breakfast could wait, she decided as she showered and dressed. She was going out to the garden shed, organizing her equipment and diving in.

The house was perfectly quiet and still dim as she made her way downstairs. The servants would sleep another hour or two, she thought as she stuck her head in the pantry and chose a muffin. As she recalled, Michael might sleep until noon.

They had made it through dinner without incident. Perhaps they'd been polite to each other because of Charles and Sweeney or perhaps because both of them had been too tired to snipe. Pandora wasn't sure herself.

They'd dined under the cheerful lights of the big chandelier and had talked, when they'd talked, about the weather and the food.

By nine they'd gone their separate ways. Pandora to read until her eyes closed and Michael to work. Or so he'd said.

Outside the air was chill enough to cause Pandora's skin to prickle. She hunched up the collar of her jacket and started across the lawn. It crunched underfoot with the early thin frost. She liked it—the absolute solitude, the lightness of the air, the incredible smell of mountain and river.

In Tibet she'd once come close to frostbite because she hadn't been able to resist the snow and the swoop of rock. She didn't find this slice of the Catskills any less fascinating. The winter was best, she'd always thought, when the snow skimmed the top of your boots and your voice came out in puffs of smoke.

Winter in the mountains was a time for the basics. Heat, food, work. There were times Pandora wanted only the basics. There were times in New York she'd argue for hours over unions, politics, civil rights because the fact was, she loved an argument. She wanted the stimulation of an opposing view over broad issues or niggling ones. She wanted the challenge, the heat and the exercise for her brain. But...

There were times she wanted nothing more than a quiet sunrise over frost-crisped ground and the promise of a warm drink by a hot fire. And there were times, though she'd rarely admit it even to herself, that she wanted a shoulder to lay her head against and a hand to hold. She'd been raised to see independence as a duty, not a choice. Her parents had the most balanced of relationships, equal to equal. Pandora saw them as something rare in a world where the scales tipped this way or that too often. At age eighteen, Pandora had decided she'd never settle for less than a full partnership. At age twenty, she decided marriage wasn't for her. Instead she put all her passion, her energy and imagination into her work.

Straight-line dedication had paid off. She was successful, even prominent, and creatively she was fulfilled. It was more than many people ever achieved.

Now she pulled open the door of the utility shed. It was a big square building, as wide as the average barn, with hardwood floors and paneled walls. Uncle Jolley hadn't believed in the primitive. Hitting the switch, she flooded the building with light.

As per her instructions, the crates and boxes she'd shipped had been stacked along one wall. The shelves where Uncle Jolley had kept his gardening tools during his brief, torrid gardening stage had been packed away. The plumbing was good, with a full-size stainless-steel sink and a small but more than adequate bath with shower enclosed in the rear. She counted five workbenches. The light and ventilation were excellent.

It wouldn't take her long, Pandora figured, to turn the shed into an organized, productive workroom.

It took three hours.

Along one shelf were boxes of beads in various sizes—jet, amethyst, gold, polished wood, coral, ivory. She had trays of stones, precious and semiprecious, square cut, brilliants, teardrops and chips. In New York, they were kept in a safe. Here, she never considered it. She had gold, silver, bronze, copper. There were solid and hollow drills, hammers, tongs, pliers, nippers, files and clamps. One might have thought she did carpentry. Then there were scribes and drawplates, bottles of chemicals, and miles of string and fiber cord.

The money she'd invested in these materials had cost her every penny of an inheritance from her grandmother, and a good chunk of savings she'd earned as an apprentice. It had been worth it. Pandora picked up a file and tapped it against her palm. Well worth it.

She could forge gold and silver, cast alloys and string impossibly complex designs with the use of a few beads or shells. Metals could be worked into thin, threadlike strands or built into big bold chunks. Pandora could do as she chose, with tools that had hardly changed from those used by artists two centuries earlier.

It was and always had been both the sense of continuity and the endless variety that appealed to her. She never made two identical pieces. That, to her, would have been manufacturing rather than creating. At times, her pieces were elegantly simple, classic in design. Those pieces sold well and allowed her a bit of artistic freedom. At other times, they were bold and brash and exaggerated. Mood guided Pandora, not trends. Rarely, very rarely, she would agree to create a piece along specified lines. If the lines, or the client, interested her.

She turned down a president because she'd found his ideas too pedestrian but had made a ring at a new father's request because his idea had been unique. Pandora had been told that the new mother had never taken the braided gold links off. Three links, one for each of the triplets she'd given birth to.

At the moment, Pandora had just completed drafting the design for a three-tiered necklace commissioned to her by the husband of a popular singer. Emerald. That was her name and the only requirement given to Pandora. The man wanted lots of them. And he'd pay, Pandora mused, for the dozen she'd chosen just before leaving New York. They were square, three karats apiece and of the sharp, sharp green that emeralds are valued for.

This was, she knew, her big chance, professionally and, most importantly, artistically. If the necklace was a success, there'd not only be reviews for her scrapbook, but acceptance. She'd be freer to do more of what she wanted without compromise.

The trick would be to fashion the chain so that it held like steel and looked like a cobweb. The stones would hang from each tier as if they'd dripped there.

For the next two hours, she worked in gold.

Between the two heaters at each end of the shed and the flame from her tools, the air became sultry. Sweat rolled down under her sweater, but she didn't mind. In fact, she barely noticed as the gold became pliable. Again and again, she drew the wire through the drawplate, smoothing out the kinks and subtly, slowly, changing the shape and size. When the wire looked like angel hair she began working it with her fingers, twisting and braiding until she matched the design in her head and on her drawing paper.

It would be simple—elegantly, richly simple. The emeralds would bring their own flash when she attached them.

Time passed. After careful, meticulous use of drawplate, flame and her own hands, the first thin, gold tier formed.

She'd just begun to stretch out the muscles in her back when the door of the shed opened and cool air poured in. Her face glowing with sweat and concentration, she glared at Michael.

'Just what the hell do you think you're doing?'

'Following orders.' He had his hands stuffed in his jacket pockets for warmth, but hadn't buttoned the front. Nor, she noticed, had he bothered to shave. 'This place smells like an oven.'

'I'm working.' She lifted the hem of the big apron she wore and wiped at her brow. It was being interrupted that annoyed her, Pandora told herself. Not the fact that he'd walked in on her when she looked like a steelworker. 'Remember rule number three?'

'Tell that to Sweeney.' Leaving the door ajar, he wandered in. 'She said it was bad enough that you skipped breakfast, but you're not getting away with missing lunch.' Curious, he poked his finger into a tray that held brilliant colored stones. 'I have orders to bring you back.'

'I'm not ready.'

He picked up a tiny sapphire and held it to the light. 'I had to stop her from tramping out here herself. If I go back alone, she's going to come for you. Her arthritis is acting up again.'

Pandora swore under her breath. 'Put that down,' she ordered, then yanked the apron off.

'Some of this stuff looks real,' he commented. Though he put the sapphire back, he picked up a round, winking diamond.

'Some of this stuff is real.' Pandora crouched to turn the first heater down.

The diamond was in his hand as he scowled down at her head. 'Why in hell do you have it sitting out like candy? It should be locked up.'

Pandora adjusted the second heater. 'Why?'

'Don't be any more foolish than necessary. Someone could steal it.'

'Someone?' Straightening, Pandora smiled at him. 'There aren't many someones around. I don't think Charles and Sweeney are a problem, but maybe I should worry about you.'

He cursed her and dropped the diamond back. 'They're your little bag of tricks, cousin, but if I had several thousand dollars sitting around that could slip into a pocket, I'd be more careful.'

Though under most circumstances she fully agreed, Pandora merely picked up her jacket. After all, they weren't in Manhattan but miles away from anyone or anything. If she locked everything up, she'd just have to unlock it again every time she wanted to work. 'Just one of the differences between you and me, Michael. I suppose it's because you write about so many dirty deeds.'

'I also write about human nature.' He picked up the sketch of the emerald necklace she had drawn. It had the sense of scale that would have pleased an architect and the flair and flow that would appeal to an artist. 'If you're so into making bangles and baubles, why aren't you wearing any?'

'They get in the way when I'm working. If you write about human nature, how come the bad guy gets caught every week?'

'Because I'm writing for people, and people need heroes.'

Pandora opened her mouth to argue, then found she agreed with the essence of the statement. 'Hmm,' was all she said as she turned out the lights and went out ahead of him.

'At least lock the door,' Michael told her.

'I haven't a key.'

'Then we'll get one.'

'*We* don't need one.'

He shut the door with a snap. '*You* do.'

Pandora only shrugged as she started across the lawn. 'Michael, have I mentioned that you've been more crabby than usual?'

He pulled a piece of hard candy out of his pocket and popped it into his mouth. 'Quit smoking.'

The candy was lemon. She caught just a whiff. 'So I noticed. How long?'

He scowled at some leaves that skimmed across the lawn. They were brown and dry and seemed to have a life of their own. 'Couple weeks. I'm going crazy.'

She laughed sympathetically before she tucked her arm into his. 'You'll live, darling. The first month's the toughest.'

Now he scowled at her. 'How would you know? You never smoked.'

'The first month of anything's the toughest. You just have to keep your mind occupied. Exercise. We'll jog after lunch.'

'We?'

'And we can play canasta after dinner.'

He gave a quick snort but brushed the hair back from her cheek. 'You'll cheat.'

'See, your mind's already occupied.' With a laugh, she turned her face up to his. He looked a bit surly, but on him, oddly, it was attractive. Placid, good-natured good looks had always bored her. 'It won't hurt you to give up one of your vices, Michael. You have so many.'

'I like my vices,' he grumbled, then turned his head to look down at her. She was giving him her easy, friendly smile, one she sent his way rarely. It always made him forget just how much trouble she caused him. It made him forget he wasn't attracted to dramatically bohemian women with wild red hair and sharp bones. 'A woman who looks like you should have several of her own.'

Her mouth was solemn, her eyes wicked. 'I'm much too busy. Vices take up a great deal of time.'

'When Pandora opened the box, vices popped out.'

She stopped at the back stoop. 'Among other miseries. I suppose that's why I'm careful about opening boxes.'

Michael ran a finger down her cheek. It was the sort of gesture he realized could easily become a habit. She was right, his mind was occupied. 'You have to lift off the lid sooner or later.'

She didn't move back, though she'd felt the little tingle of tension, of attraction, of need. Pandora didn't believe in moving back, but in plowing through. 'Some things are better off locked up.'

He nodded. He didn't want to release what was in their private box any more than she did. 'Some locks aren't as strong as they need to be.'

They were standing close, the wind whistling lightly between them. Pandora felt the sun on her back and the chill on her face. If she took a step nearer, there'd be heat. That she'd never doubted and had always avoided. He'd use whatever was available to him, she reminded herself. At the moment, it just happened to be her. She let her breath come calmly and easily before she reached for the doorknob.

'We'd better not keep Sweeney waiting.'

Chapter 3

The streets are almost deserted. A car turns a corner and disappears. It's drizzling. Neon flashes off puddles. It's garish rather than festive. There's a gray, miserable feel to this part of the city. Alleyways, cheap clubs, dented cars. The small, neatly dressed blonde walks quickly. She's nervous, out of her element, but not lost. Close-up on the envelope in her hands. It's damp from the rain. Her fingers open and close on it. Tires squeal offscreen and she jolts. The blue lights of the club blink off and on in her face as she stands outside. Hesitates. Shifts the envelope from hand to hand. She goes in. Slow pan of the street. Three shots and freeze.

Three knocks sounded at the door of Michael's office. Before he could answer, Pandora swirled in. 'Happy anniversary, darling.'

Michael looked up from his computer. He'd been up most of the night working the story line out in his mind. It was nine in the morning, and he'd only had one cup of coffee to prime him for the day. Coffee and cigarettes together were too precious a memory. The scene that had just jelled in his mind dissolved.

'What the hell are you talking about?' He reached his hand into a bowl of peanuts and discovered he'd already eaten all but two.

'Two full weeks without any broken bones.' Pandora swooped over to him, clucked her tongue at the disorder, then chose the arm of a chair. It was virtually the only free space. She brushed at the dust on the edge of the table beside her and left a smear. 'And they said it wouldn't last.'

She looked fresh with her wild mane of red pulled back from her face, comfortable in sweater and slacks that were too big for her. Michael felt like he'd just crawled out of a cave. His sweatshirt had ripped at the shoulder seam two years before, but he still favored it. A few weeks before, he'd helped paint a friend's apartment. The paint smears on his jeans showed her preference for baby pink. His eyes felt as though he'd slept facedown in the sand.

Pandora smiled at him like some bright, enthusiastic kindergarten teacher. She had a fresh, clean, almost woodsy scent. 'We have a rule about respecting the other's work space,' he reminded her.

'Oh, don't be cranky.' It was said with the same positive smile. 'Besides, you never gave me any schedule.

From what I've noticed in the past couple of weeks, this is early for you.'

'I'm just starting the treatment for a new episode.'

'Really?' Pandora walked over and leaned over his shoulder. 'Hmm,' she said, though she wondered who had shot whom. 'Well, I don't suppose that'll take long.'

'Why don't you go play with your beads?'

'Now you're being rude when I came up here to invite you to go with me into town.' After brushing off the sleeve of her sweater, she sat on the edge of the desk. She didn't know exactly why she was so determined to be friendly. Maybe it was because the emerald necklace was nearly finished and was exceeding even her standards. Maybe it was because in the past two weeks she'd found a certain enjoyment in Michael's company. Mild enjoyment, Pandora reminded herself. Nothing to shout about.

Suspicious, Michael narrowed his eyes. 'What for?'

'I'm going in for some supplies Sweeney needs.' She found the turtle shell that was his lampshade intriguing, and ran her fingers over it. 'I thought you might like to get out for a while.'

He would. It had been two weeks since he'd seen anything but the house and grounds. He glanced back at the page on his computer. 'How long will you be?'

'Oh, two, three hours I suppose.' She moved her shoulders. 'It's an hour's round trip to begin with.'

He was tempted. Free time and a change of scene. But the half-blank page remained on his computer. 'Can't. I have to get this fleshed out.'

'All right.' Pandora rose from the desk a bit surprised

by the degree of disappointment she felt. Silly, she thought. She loved to drive alone with the radio blaring. 'Don't strain your fingers.'

He started to growl something at her back, then because his bowl of nuts was empty, thought better of it. 'Pandora, how about picking me up a couple pounds of pistachios?'

As she stopped at the door, she lifted a brow. 'Pistachios?'

'Real ones. No red dye.' He ran a hand over the bristle on his chin and wished for a pack of cigarettes. One cigarette. One long deep drag.

She glanced at the empty bowl and nearly smiled. The way he was nibbling, he'd lose that lean, rangy look quickly. 'I suppose I could.'

'And a copy of the *New York Times*.'

Her brow rose. 'Would you like to make me a list?'

'Be a sport, will you? Next time Sweeney needs supplies, I'll go in.'

She thought about it a moment. 'Very well then, nuts and news.'

'And some pencils,' he called out.

She slammed the door smartly.

Nearly two hours passed before Michael decided he deserved another cup of coffee. The story line was bumping along just as he'd planned, full of twists and turns. The fans of *Logan's Run* expected the gritty with occasional bursts of color and magic. That's just the way it was panning out.

Critics of the medium aside, Michael enjoyed writing

for the small screen. He liked knowing his stories would reach literally millions of people every week and that for an hour, they could involve themselves with the character he had created.

The truth was, Michael liked Logan—the reluctant but steady heroism, the humor and the flaws. He'd made Logan human and fallible and reluctant because Michael had always imagined the best heroes were just that.

The ratings and the mail proved he was on target. His writing for Logan had won him critical acclaim and awards, just as the one-act play he'd written had won him critical acclaim and awards. But the play had reached a few thousand at best, the bulk of whom had been New Yorkers. *Logan's Run* reached the family of four in Des Moines, the steelworkers in Chicago and the college crowd in Boston. Every week.

He didn't see television as the vast wasteland but as the magic box. Michael figured everyone was entitled to a bit of magic.

Michael switched off the laptop so that the screen died. For a moment he sat in silence. He'd known he could work at the Folley. He'd done so before, but never long-term. What he hadn't known was that he'd work so well, so quickly or be so content. The truth was, he'd never expected to get along half so well with Pandora. Not that it was any picnic, Michael mused, absently running the stub of a pencil between his fingers.

They fought, certainly, but at least they weren't taking chunks out of each other. Or not very big ones. All in all he enjoyed the evenings when they played cards if for no other reason than the challenge of trying to catch her cheating. So far he hadn't.

Also true was the odd attraction he felt for her. That hadn't been in the script. So far he'd been able to ignore, control or smother it. But there were times... There were times, Michael thought as he rose and stretched, when he'd like to close her smart-tongued mouth in a more satisfactory way. Just to see what it'd be like, he told himself. Curiosity about people was part of his makeup. He'd be interested to see how Pandora would react if he hauled her against him and kissed her until she went limp.

He let out a quick laugh as he wandered to the window. Limp? Pandora? Women like her never went soft. He might satisfy his curiosity, but he'd get a fist in the gut for his trouble. Even that might be worth it....

She wasn't unmoved. He'd been sure of that since the first day they'd walked back together from her workshop. He'd seen it in her face, heard it, however briefly in her voice. They'd both been circling around it for two weeks. Or twenty years, Michael speculated.

He'd never felt about another woman exactly the way he felt about Pandora McVie. Uncomfortable, challenged, infuriated. The truth was that he was almost always at ease around women. He liked them—their femininity, their peculiar strengths and weaknesses, their style. Perhaps that was the reason for his success in relationships, though he'd carefully kept them short-term.

If he romanced a woman, it was because he was interested in her, not simply in the end result. True enough he was interested in Pandora, but he'd never considered romancing her. It surprised him that he'd caught himself once or twice considering seducing her.

Seducing, of course, was an entirely different matter than romancing. But all in all, he didn't know if attempting a casual seduction of Pandora would be worth the risk.

If he offered her a candlelight dinner or a walk in the moonlight—or a mad night of passion—she'd come back with a sarcastic remark. Which would, inevitably, trigger some caustic rebuttal from him. The merry-go-round would begin again.

In any case, it wasn't romance he wanted with Pandora. It was simply curiosity. In certain instances, it was best to remember what had happened to the intrepid cat. But as he thought of her, his gaze was drawn toward her workshop.

They weren't so very different really, Michael mused. Pandora could insist from dawn to dusk that they had nothing in common, but Jolley had been closer to the mark. They were both quick-tempered, opinionated and passionately protective of their professions. He closed himself up for hours at a time with a laptop. She closed herself up with tools and torches. The end result of both of their work was entertainment. And after all, that was...

His thoughts broke off as he saw the shed door open. Odd, he hadn't thought she was back yet. His rooms were on the opposite end of the house from the garage, so he wouldn't have heard her car, but he thought she'd drop off what she'd picked up for him.

He started to shrug and turn away when he saw the

figure emerge from the shed. It was bundled deep in a coat and hat, but he knew immediately it wasn't Pandora. She moved fluidly, unselfconsciously. This person walked with speed and wariness. Wariness, he thought again, that was evident in the way the head swiveled back and forth before the door was closed again. Without stopping to think, Michael dashed out of the room and down the stairs.

He nearly rammed into Charles at the bottom. 'Pandora back?' he demanded.

'No, sir.' Relieved that he hadn't been plowed down, Charles rested a hand on the rail. 'She said she might stay in town and do some shopping. We shouldn't worry if—'

But Michael was already halfway down the hall.

With a sigh for the agility he hadn't had in thirty years, Charles creaked his way into the drawing room to lay a fire.

The wind hit Michael the moment he stepped outside, reminding him he hadn't stopped for a coat. As he began to race toward the shed, his face chilled and his muscles warmed. There was no one in sight on the grounds. Not surprising, he mused as he slowed his pace just a bit. The woods were close at the edge, and there were a half a dozen easy paths through them.

Some kid poking around? he wondered. Pandora would be lucky if he hadn't pocketed half her pretty stones. It would serve her right.

But he changed his mind the minute he stood in the doorway of her workshop.

Boxes were turned over so that gems and stones and

beads were scattered everywhere. Balls of string and twine had been unraveled and twisted and knotted from wall to wall. He had to push some out of his way to step inside. What was usually almost pristine in its order was utter chaos. Gold and silver wire had been bent and snapped, tools lay where they'd been carelessly tossed to the floor.

Michael bent down and picked up an emerald. It glinted sharp and green in his palm. If it had been a thief, he decided, it had been a clumsy and shortsighted one.

'Oh, God!' Pandora dropped her purse with a thud and stared.

When Michael turned, he saw her standing in the doorway, ice pale and rigid. He swore, wishing he'd had a moment to prepare her. 'Take it easy,' he began as he reached for her arm.

She shoved him aside forcibly and fought her way into the shed. Beads rolled and bounced at her feet. For a moment there was pure shock, disbelief. Then came a white wall of fury. 'How could you?' When she turned back to him she was no longer pale. Her color was vivid, her eyes as sharp as the emerald he still held.

Because he was off guard, she nearly landed the first blow. The air whistled by his face as her fist passed. He caught her arms before she tried again. 'Just a minute,' he began, but she threw herself bodily into him and knocked them both against the wall. Whatever had been left on the shelves shuddered or fell off. It took several moments, and a few bruises on both ends, before he managed to pin her arms back and hold her still.

'Stop it.' He pressed her back until she glared up at him, dry-eyed and furious. 'You've a right to be upset, but putting a hole in me won't accomplish anything.'

'I knew you could be low,' she said between her teeth. 'But I'd never have believed you could do something so filthy.'

'Believe whatever the hell you want,' he began, but he felt her body shudder as she fought for control. 'Pandora,' and his voice softened. 'I didn't do this. Look at me,' he demanded with a little shake. 'Why would I?'

Because she wanted to cry, her voice, her eyes were hard. 'You tell me.'

Patience wasn't one of his strong points, but he tried again. 'Pandora, listen to me. Try for common sense a minute and just listen. I got here a few minutes before you. I saw someone coming out of the shed from my window and came down. When I got here, this is what I found.'

She was going to disgrace herself. She felt the tears backing up and hated them. It was better to hate him. 'Let go of me.'

Perhaps he could handle her anger better than her despair. Cautiously Michael released her arms and stepped back. 'It hasn't been more than ten minutes since I saw someone coming out of here. I figured they cut through the woods.'

She tried to think, tried to clear the fury out of her head. 'You can go,' she said with deadly calm. 'I have to clean up and take inventory.'

Something hot backed up in his throat at the casual dismissal. Remembering his own reaction when he'd opened the shed door, he swallowed it. 'I'll call the police if you like, but I don't know if anything was stolen.' He opened his palm and showed her the emerald. 'I can't imagine any thief leaving stones like this behind.'

Pandora snatched it out of his hand. When her fingers closed over it, she felt the slight prick of the hoop she'd fastened onto it only the day before. The emerald seemed to grow out of the braided wire.

Her heart was thudding against her ribs as she walked to her worktable. There was what was left of the necklace she'd been fashioning for two weeks. The deceptively delicate tiers were in pieces, the emeralds that had hung gracefully from them, scattered. Her own nippers had been used to destroy it. She gathered up the pieces in her hands and fought back the urge to scream.

'It was this, wasn't it?' Michael picked up the sketch from the floor. It was stunning on paper—at once fanciful and bold. He supposed what she had drawn had some claim to art. He imagined how he'd feel if someone took scissors to one of his scripts. 'You'd nearly finished.'

Pandora dropped the pieces back on the table. 'Leave me alone.' She crouched and began to gather up stones and beads.

'Pandora.' When she ignored him, Michael grabbed her by the shoulders and shook. 'Dammit, Pandora, I want to help.'

She sent him a long, cold look. 'You've done enough, Michael. Now leave me alone.'

'All right, fine.' He released her and stormed out.

Anger and frustration carried him halfway across the lawn. Michael stopped, swore and wished bitterly for a cigarette. She had no right to accuse him. Worse, she had no right to make him feel responsible. The guilt he was experiencing was nearly as strong as it would have been if he'd actually vandalized her shop. Hands in his pockets, he stood staring back at the shed and cursing her.

She really thought he'd done that to her. That he was capable of such meaningless, bitter destruction. He'd tried to talk to her, soothe her. Every offer of help had been thrown back at him. Just like her, he thought with his teeth gritted. She deserved to be left alone.

He nearly started back to the house again when he remembered just how shocked and ill she'd looked in the doorway of the shed. Calling himself a fool, he went back.

When he opened the door of the shed again, the chaos was just as it had been. Sitting in the middle of it on the floor by her workbench was Pandora. She was weeping quietly.

He felt the initial male panic at being confronted with feminine tears and surprise that they came from Pandora who never shed them. Yet he felt sympathy for someone who'd been dealt a bull's-eye blow. Without saying a word, he went to her and slipped his arms around her.

She stiffened, but he'd expected it. 'I told you to go away.'

'Yeah. Why should I listen to you?' He stroked her hair.

She wanted to crawl into his lap and weep for hours. 'I don't want you here.'

'I know. Just pretend I'm someone else.' He drew her against his chest.

'I'm only crying because I'm angry.' With a sniff, she turned her face into his shirt.

'Sure.' He kissed the top of her head. 'Go ahead and be angry for a while. I'm used to it.'

She told herself it was because she was weakened by shock and grief, but she relaxed against him. The tears came in floods. When she cried, she cried wholeheartedly. When she was finished, she was done.

Tears dry, she sat cushioned against him. Secure. She wouldn't question it now. Along with the anger came a sense of shame she was unaccustomed to. She'd been filthy to him. But he'd come back and held her. Who'd have expected him to be patient, or caring? Or strong enough to make her accept both. Pandora let out a long breath and kept her eyes shut for just a moment. He smelled of soap and nothing else.

'I'm sorry, Michael.'

She was soft. Hadn't he just told himself she wouldn't be? He let his cheek brush against her hair. 'Okay.'

'No, I mean it.' When she turned her head her lips skimmed across his cheek. It surprised them both. That kind of contact was for friends—or lovers. 'I couldn't think after I walked in here. I—' She broke off a moment, fascinated by his eyes. Wasn't it strange how small the world could become if you looked into someone's eyes? Why hadn't she ever noticed that before? 'I need to sort all this out.'

'Yeah.' He ran a fingertip down her cheek. She was soft. Softer than he'd let himself believe. 'We both do.'

It was so easy to settle herself in the crook of his arm. 'I can't think.'

'No?' Her lips were only an inch from his—too close to ignore, too far to taste. 'Let's both not think for a minute.'

When he touched his mouth to hers, she didn't draw away but accepted, experimented with the same sense of curiosity that moved through him. It wasn't an explosion or a shock, but a test for both of them. One they'd both known would come sooner or later.

She tasted warm, and her sweetness had a bite. He'd known her so long, shouldn't he have known that? Her body felt primed to move, to act, to race. Soft, yes, she was soft, but not pliant. Perhaps he'd have found pliancy too easy. When he slipped his tongue into her mouth hers met it teasingly, playfully. His stomach knotted. She made him want more, much more of that unapologetically earthy scent, the taut body. His fingers tangled in her hair and tightened.

He was as mysterious and bold as she'd always thought he would be. His hands were firm, his mouth giving. Sometimes she'd wondered what it would be like to meet him on these terms. But she'd always closed her mind before any of the answers could slip through. Michael Donahue was dangerous simply because he was Michael Donahue. By turns he'd attracted and alienated her since they'd been children. It was more than any other man had been able to do for more than a week.

Now, as her mouth explored his, she began to understand why. He was different, for her. She didn't feel altogether safe in his arms, and not completely in control. Pandora had always made certain she was both those things when it came to a man. The scrape of his unshaved cheek didn't annoy her as she'd thought it would. It aroused. The discomfort of the hard floor seemed suitable, as was the quick rush of cold air through the still-open door.

She felt quietly and completely at home. Then the quick nip of his teeth against her lip made her feel as though she'd just stepped on uncharted land. New territory was what she'd been raised on, and yet, in all her experience, she'd never explored anything so unique, so exotic or so comfortable.

She wanted to go on and knew she had to stop.

Together they drew away.

'Well.' She scrambled for composure as she folded her hands in her lap. Be casual, she ordered herself while her pulse thudded at her wrists. Be careless. She couldn't afford to say anything that might make him laugh at her. 'That's been coming for a while, I suppose.'

He felt as though he'd just slid down a roller coaster without a cart. 'I suppose.' He studied her a moment, curious and a bit unnerved. When he saw her fingers twist together he felt a small sense of satisfaction. 'It wasn't altogether what I'd expected.'

'Things rarely are.' Too many surprises for one day, Pandora decided, and rose unsteadily to her feet. She made the mistake of looking around and nearly sunk to the floor again.

'Pandora—'

'No, don't worry.' She shook her head as he rose. 'I'm not going to fall apart again.' Concentrating on breathing evenly, she took one long look at her workshop. 'It looks like you were right about the locks. I suppose I should be grateful you haven't said I told you so.'

'Maybe I would if it applied.' Michael picked up the emeralds scattered on her table. 'I'm no expert, cousin, but I'd say these are worth a few thousand.'

'So?' She frowned as her train of thought began to march with his. 'No thief would've left them behind.' Reaching down, she picked up a handful of stones. Among them were two top-grade diamonds. 'Or these.'

As was his habit, he began to put the steps together in a sort of mental scenario. Action and reaction, motive and result. 'I'd wager once you've inventoried, you won't be missing anything. Whoever did this didn't want to risk more than breaking and entering and vandalism.'

With a huff, she sat down on her table. 'You think it was one of the family.'

"They said it wouldn't last," he quoted, and stuck his hands in his pockets. 'You may've had something there, Pandora. Something neither of us considered when we were setting out the guidelines. None of them believed we'd be able to get through six months together. The fact is, we've gotten through the first two weeks without a hitch. It could make one of them nervous enough to want to throw in a complication. What was your first reaction when you saw all this?'

She dragged her hand through her hair. 'That you'd

done it for spite. Exactly what our kith and kin would expect me to think. Dammit, I hate to be predictable.'

'You outsmarted them once your mind cleared.'

She sent him a quick look, not certain if she should thank him or apologize again. It was best to do neither. 'Biff,' Pandora decided with relish. 'This sort of low-minded trick would be just up his alley.'

'I'd only vote for Biff if you find a few rocks missing.' Michael rocked back on his heels. 'He'd never be able to resist picking up a few glitters that could be liquidated into nice clean cash.'

'True enough.' Uncle Carlson—no, it seemed a bit crude for his style. Ginger would've been too fascinated with the sparkles to have done any more than fondle. Pulling a hand through her hair, she tried to picture one of her bland, civilized relations wielding a pair of nippers. 'Well, I don't suppose it matters a great deal which one of them did it. They've put me two weeks behind on my commission.' Again she picked up pieces of thin gold. 'It'll never be quite the same,' she murmured. 'Nothing is when it's done over.'

'Sometimes it's better.'

With a shake of her head, she walked over to a heater. If he gave her any more sympathy now, she wouldn't be able to trust herself. 'One way or the other I've got to get started. Tell Sweeney I won't make it in for lunch.'

'I'll help you clean this up.'

'No.' She turned back when he started to frown. 'No, really, Michael, I appreciate it. I need to be busy. And alone.'

He didn't like it, but understood. 'All right. I'll see you at dinner.'

'Michael…' He paused at the doorway and looked back. Amid the confusion she looked strong and vivid. He nearly closed the door and went back to her. 'Maybe Uncle Jolley was right.'

'About what?'

'You may have one or two redeeming qualities.'

He smiled at her then, quick and dashing. 'Uncle Jolley was always right, cousin. That's why he's still pulling the strings.'

Pandora waited until the door shut again. Pulling the strings he was, she mused. 'But you're not playing matchmaker with my life,' she mumbled. 'I'm staying free, single and unattached. Just get that through your head.'

She wasn't superstitious, but Pandora almost thought she heard her uncle's high, cackling laugh. She rolled up her sleeves and got to work.

Chapter 4

Because after a long, tedious inventory Pandora discovered nothing missing, she vetoed Michael's notion of calling in the police. If something had been stolen, she'd have seen the call as a logical step. As it was, she decided the police would poke and prod around and lecture on the lack of locks. If the vandal had been one of the family—and she had to agree with Michael's conclusion there—a noisy, official investigation would give the break-in too much importance and undoubtedly too much publicity.

Yes, the press would have a field day. Pandora had already imagined the headlines. 'Family vs. family in the battle of eccentric's will.' There was, under her independent and straightforward nature, a prim part of her that felt family business was private business.

If one or more of the members of the family were keeping an eye on Jolley's Folley and the goings-on there, Pandora wanted them to think that she'd brushed off the vandalism as petty and foolish. As a matter of pride, she didn't want anyone to believe she'd been dealt a stunning blow. As a matter of practicality, she didn't want anyone to know that she had her eyes open. She was determined to find out who had broken into her shop and how they'd managed to pick such a perfect time for it.

Michael hadn't insisted on calling the police because his thoughts had run along the same lines as Pandora's. He'd managed, through a lot of maneuvering and silence, to keep his career totally separate from his family. In his business, he was known as Michael Donahue, award-winning writer, not Michael Donahue, relative of Jolley McVie, multimillionaire. He wanted to keep it that way.

Stubbornly, each had refused to tell the other of their reasons or their plans for some personal detective work. It wasn't so much a matter of trust, but more the fact that neither of them felt the other could do the job competently. So instead, they kept the conversation light through one of Sweeney's four-star meals and let the vandalism rest. More important, they carefully avoided any reference that might trigger some remark about what had happened on a more personal level in Pandora's workshop.

After two glasses of wine and a generous portion of chicken fricassee, Pandora felt more optimistic. It would have been much worse if any of her stock or tools had been taken. That would have meant a trip into Manhattan and days, perhaps weeks of delay. As it was, the worst crime that she could see was the fact that she'd been spied on. Surely that was the only explanation for the break-in coinciding so perfectly with her trip to town. And that would be her first order of business.

'I wonder,' Pandora began, probing lightly, 'if the Saundersons are in residence for the winter.'

'The neighbors with the pond.' Michael had thought of the Saunderson place himself. There were certain points on that property where, with a good set of binoculars, someone could watch the Folley easily. 'They spend a lot of time in Europe, don't they?'

'Hmm.' Pandora toyed with her chicken. 'He's in hotels, you know. They tend to pop off here or there for weeks at a time.'

'Do they ever rent the place out?'

'Oh, not that I know of. I'm under the impression that they leave a skeleton staff there even when they fly off. Now that I think of it, they were home a few months ago.' The memory made her smile. 'Uncle Jolley and I went fishing and Saunderson nearly caught us. If we hadn't scrambled back to the cabin—' She broke off as the thought formed.

'Cabin.' Michael picked up where she'd left off. 'That old two-room wreck Jolley was going to use as a hunting lodge during his eat-off-the-land stage? I'd forgotten all about it.'

Pandora shrugged as though it meant nothing while her mind raced ahead. 'He ended up eating more beans than game. In any case, we caught a bundle of trout, ate like pigs and sent the rest along to Saunderson. He never sent a thank-you note.'

'Poor manners.'

'Well, I've heard his grandmother was a barmaid in Chelsea. More wine?'

'No, thanks.' He thought it best to keep a clear head if he was going to carry out the plans that were just beginning to form. 'Help yourself.'

Pandora set the bottle down and sent him a sweet smile. 'No, I'm fine. Just a bit tired really.'

'You're entitled.' It would clear his path beautifully if he could ship her off to bed early. 'What you need is a good night's sleep.'

'I'm sure you're right.' Both of them were too involved with their own moves to notice how excruciatingly polite the conversation had become. 'I'll just skip coffee tonight and go have a bath.' She feigned a little yawn. 'What about you? Planning to work late?'

'No—no, I think I'll get a fresh start in the morning.'

'Well then.' Pandora rose, still smiling. She'd give it an hour, she calculated, then she'd be out and gone. 'I'm going up. Good night, Michael.'

'Good night.' Once the light in her room was off, he decided, he'd be on his way.

Pandora sat in her darkened room for exactly fifteen minutes and just listened. All she had to do was get outside without being spotted. The rest would be easy. Opening her door a crack, she held her breath, waited and listened a little longer. Not a sound. It was now or never, she decided and bundled into her coat. Into the deep pockets, she shoved a flashlight, two books of matches and a small can of hair spray. As good as mace, Pandora figured, if you ran into something unfriendly. She crept out into the hall and started slowly down the stairs, her back to the wall.

An adventure, she thought, feeling the familiar pulse of excitement and anxiety. She hadn't had one since Uncle Jolley died. As she let herself out one of the side doors, she thought how much he'd have enjoyed this one. The moon was only a sliver, but the sky was full of stars. The few clouds that spread over them were hardly more than transparent wisps. And the air—she took a deep breath—was cool and crisp as an apple. With a quick glance over her shoulder at Michael's window, she started toward the woods.

The starlight couldn't help her there. Though the trees were bare, the branches were thick enough to block out big chunks of sky. She dug out her flashlight and, turning it side to side, found the edges of the path. She didn't hurry. If she rushed, the adventure would be over too soon. She walked slowly, listened and imagined.

There were sounds—the breeze blew through pine needles and scattered the dry leaves. Now and again there was a skuttle in the woods to the right or left. A fox, a raccoon, a bear not quite settled down to hibernate? Pandora liked not being quite certain. If you walked through the woods alone, in the dark, and didn't have some sense of wonder, it was hardly worth the trip.

She liked the smells—pine, earth, the hint of frost that would settle on the ground before morning. She liked the sense of being alone, and more, of having something up ahead that warranted her attention.

The path forked, and she swung to the left. The cabin wasn't much farther. She stopped once, certain she'd heard something move up ahead that was too big to be considered a fox. For a moment she had a few uncomfortable thoughts about bears and bobcats. It was one thing to speculate and another to have to deal with them. Then there was nothing. Shaking her head, Pandora went on.

What would she do if she got to the cabin, and it wasn't dusty and deserted? What would she do if she actually found one of her dear, devoted relatives had set up housekeeping? Uncle Carlson reading the *Wall Street Journal* by the fire? Aunt Patience fussing around the rocky wooden table with a dust cloth? The thought was almost laughable. Almost, until Pandora remembered her workshop.

Drawing her brows together, she walked forward. If someone was there, they were going to answer to her. In moments, the shadow of the cabin loomed up before her. It looked as it was supposed to look, desolate, deserted, eerie. She kept her flashlight low as she crept toward the porch, then nearly let out a scream when her own weight caused the narrow wooden stair to creak. She held a hand to her heart until it no longer felt as though it would break her ribs. Then slowly, quietly, stealthily, she reached for the doorknob and twisted it.

The door moaned itself open. Wincing at the sound, Pandora counted off ten seconds before she took the next step. With a quick sweep of her light, she stepped in.

When the arm came around her neck, she dropped the flashlight with a clatter. It rolled over the floor, sending an erratic beam over the log walls and brick fireplace. Even as she drew the breath to scream, she reached in her pocket for the hair spray. After she was whirled around, she found herself face-to-face with Michael. His fist was poised inches from her face, her can inches from his. Both of them stood just as they were.

'Dammit!' Michael dropped his arm. 'What are you doing here?'

'What are you doing here?' she tossed back. 'And what do you mean by grabbing me that way? You may've broken my flashlight.'

'I almost broke your nose.'

Pandora shook back her hair and walked over to retrieve her light. She didn't want him to see her hands tremble. 'Well, I certainly think you should find out who someone is before you throw a headlock on them.'

'You followed me.'

She sent him a cool, amused look. It helped to be able to do so when her stomach was still quaking. 'Don't flatter yourself. I simply wanted to see if something was going on out here, and I didn't want you to interfere.'

'Interfere.' He shone his own light directly in her face so that she had to throw up a hand in defense. 'And what the hell were you going to do if something was going on? Overpower them?'

She thought of how easily he'd taken her by surprise. It only made her lift her chin higher. 'I can take care of myself.'

'Sure.' He glanced down at the can she still held. 'What have you got there?'

Having forgotten it, Pandora looked down herself, then had to stifle a chuckle. Oh, how Uncle Jolley would've appreciated the absurdity. 'Hair spray,' she said very precisely. 'Right between the eyes.'

He swore, then laughed. He couldn't have written a scene so implausible. 'I guess I should be glad you didn't get a shot off at me.'

'I look before I pounce.' Pandora dropped the can back into her pocket. 'Well, since we're here, we might as well look around.'

'I was doing just that when I heard your catlike approach.' She wrinkled her nose at him, but he ignored her. 'It looks like someone's been making themselves at home.' To prove his point, Michael shone his light at the fireplace. Half-burnt logs still smoldered.

'Well, well.' With her own light, Pandora began to walk around the cabin. The last time she'd been there, the chair with the broken rung had been by the window. Jolley had sat there himself, keeping a lookout for Saunderson while she'd opened a tin of sardines to ward off starvation. Now the chair was pulled up near the fire. 'A vagrant, perhaps.'

Watching her, Michael nodded. 'Perhaps.'

'But not likely. Suppose they'll be back?'

'Hard to say.' The casual glance showed nothing out of place. The cabin was neat and tidy. Too tidy. The floor and table surfaces should have had a film of dust. Everything had been wiped clean. 'It could be they've done all the damage they intend to do.'

Disgruntled, Pandora plopped down on the bunk and dropped her chin in her hands. 'I'd hoped to catch them.'

'And what? Zap them with environmentally safe hair spray?'

She glared up at him. 'I suppose you had a better plan.'

'I think I might've made them a bit more uncomfortable.'

'Black eyes and broken noses.' She made an impatient sound. 'Really, Michael, you should try to get your mind out of your fists.'

'I suppose you just wanted to talk reasonably with whichever member of our cozy family played search and destroy with your workshop.'

She started to snap, caught herself, then smiled. It was the slow, wicked smile Michael could never help admiring. 'No,' she admitted. 'Reason wasn't high on my list. Still, it appears we've both missed our chance for brute force. Well, you write the detective stories—so to speak—shouldn't we look for clues?'

His lips curved in something close to a sneer. 'I didn't think to bring my magnifying glass.'

'You can almost be amusing when you put your mind to it.' Rising, Pandora began to shine her light here and there. 'They might've dropped something.'

'A name tag?'

'Something,' she muttered, and dropped to her knees to look under the bunk. 'Aha!' Hunkering down, she grabbed at something.

'What is it?' Michael was beside her before she'd straightened up.

'A shoe.' Feeling foolish and sentimental, she held it in both hands. 'It's nothing. It was Uncle Jolley's.'

Because she looked lost, and more vulnerable than he'd expected, Michael offered the only comfort he knew. 'I miss him, too.'

She sat a moment, the worn sneaker in her lap. 'You know, sometimes it's as though I can almost feel him. As though he's around the next corner, in the next room, waiting to pop up and laugh at the incredible joke he's played.'

With a quick laugh, Michael rubbed a hand over her back. 'I know what you mean.'

Pandora looked at him, steady, measuring. 'Maybe you do,' she murmured. Briskly she set the sneaker on the bunk and rose. 'I'll have a look in the cupboards.'

'Let me know if you find any cookies.' He met the look she tossed over her shoulder with a shrug. 'In the early stages of nonsmoking, you need a lot of oral satisfaction.'

'You ought to try chewing gum.' Pandora opened a cupboard and shone her light over jars and cans. There was peanut butter, chunky, and caviar, Russian. Two of Jolley's favorite snacks. She passed over taco sauce and jumbo fruit cocktail, remembering that her ninety-three-year-old uncle had had the appetite of a teenager. Then reaching in, she plucked out a can and held it up.

'Aha!'

'Again?'

'Tuna fish,' Pandora announced waving the can at Michael. 'It's a can of tuna.'

'Right you are. Any mayo to go with it?'

'Don't be dense, Michael. Uncle Jolley hated tuna.'

Michael started to say something sarcastic, then stopped. 'He did, didn't he?' he said slowly. 'And he never kept anything around he didn't like.'

'Exactly.'

'Congratulations, Sherlock. Now which of the suspects has an affection for canned fish?'

'You're just jealous because I found a clue and you didn't.'

'It's only a clue,' Michael pointed out, a little annoyed at being outdone by an amateur, 'if you can do something with it.'

He'd never give her credit, she thought, for anything, not her craft, her intelligence and never her womanhood. There was an edge to her voice when she spoke again. 'If you're so pessimistic, why did you come out here?'

'I was hoping to find someone.' Restless, Michael moved his light from wall to wall. 'As it is all we've done is prove someone was here and gone.'

Pandora dropped the can of tuna in disgust. 'A waste of time.'

'You shouldn't've followed me out.'

'I didn't follow you out.' She shone her light back at him. He looked too male, too dangerous in the shadows. She wished, only briefly, that she had the spectacular build and stunning style that would bring him whimpering to his knees. Their breath came in clouds and merged together. 'For all I know, you followed me.'

'Oh, I see. That's why I was here first.'

'Beside the point. If you'd planned to come out here tonight, why didn't you tell me?'

He came closer. But if he came too close to her, he discovered, he began to feel something, something like an itch along the skin. Try to scratch it, he reminded himself, and she'd rub you raw in seconds. 'For the same reason you didn't tell me. I don't trust you, cousin. You don't trust me.'

'At least we can agree on something.' She started to brush by him and found her arm captured. In one icy movement, she tilted her head down to look at his hand, then up to look at his face. 'That's a habit you should try to break, Michael.'

'They say when you break one habit, you pick up another.'

The ice in Pandora's voice never changed, but her blood was warming. 'Do they?'

'You're easier to touch than I'd once thought, Pandora.'

'Don't be too sure, Michael.' She took a step back, not in retreat, she told herself. It was a purely offensive move. Still, he moved with her.

'Some women have trouble dealing with physical attraction.'

The temper that flared in her eyes appealed to him as much as the passion he'd seen there briefly that afternoon. 'Your ego's showing again. This dominant routine might work very well with your centerfolds, but—'

'You've always had an odd fascination with my sex life.' Michael grinned at her, pleased to see frustration flit over her face.

'The same kind of educated fascination one has with the sex lives of lower mammals.' It infuriated her that her heart was racing. And not from anger. She was too honest to pretend it was anger. She'd come looking for an adventure, and she'd found one. 'It's getting late,' she said, using the tone of a parochial schoolteacher to a disruptive student. 'You'll have to excuse me.'

'I've never asked about your sex life.' When she took another step away, he boxed her neatly into a corner. Pandora's hand slipped into her pocket and rested on the can of hair spray. 'Let me guess. You prefer a man with a string of initials after his name who philosophizes about sex more than he acts on it.'

'Why, you pompous, arrogant—'

Michael shut her mouth the way he'd once fantasized. With his own.

The kiss was no test this time, but torrid, hot, edging toward desperate. Whatever she might feel, she'd dissect later. Now she'd accept the experience. His mouth was warm, firm, and he used it with the same cocky male confidence that would have infuriated her at any other time. Now she met it with her own.

He was strong, insistent. For the first time Pandora felt herself body to body with a man who wouldn't treat her delicately. He demanded, expected and gave a completely uninhibited physicality. Pandora didn't have to think her way through the kiss. She didn't have to think at all.

He'd expected her to rear back and take a swing at him. Her instant and full response left him reeling. Later Michael would recall that nothing as basic and simple as a kiss had made his head spin for years.

She packed a punch, but she did it with soft lips. If she knew just how quickly she'd knocked him out, would she gloat? He wouldn't think of it now. He wouldn't think of anything now. Without a moment's hesitation, he buried his consciousness in her and let the senses rule.

The cabin was cold and dark without even a single stream of moonlight for romance. It smelled of dying smoke and settling dust. The wind had kicked up enough to moan grumpily at the windows. Neither of them noticed. Even when they broke apart, neither of them noticed.

He wasn't steady. That was something else he'd think about later. At least he had the satisfaction of seeing she wasn't steady, either. She looked as he felt, stunned, off balance and unable to set for the next blow. Needing some equilibrium, he grinned at her.

'You were saying?'

She wanted to slug him. She wanted to kiss him again until he didn't have the strength to grin. He'd expect her to fall at his feet as other women probably did. He'd expect her to sigh and smile and surrender so he'd have one more victory. Instead she snapped, 'Idiot.'

'I love it when you're succinct.'

'Rule number six,' Pandora stated, aiming a killing look. 'No physical contact.'

'No physical contact,' Michael agreed as she stomped toward the doorway, 'unless both parties enjoy it.'

She slammed the door and left him grinning.

When two people are totally involved in their own projects, they can live under the same roof for days at a time and rarely see each other. Especially if the roof is enormous and the people very stubborn. Pandora and Michael brushed together at meals and otherwise left each other alone. This wasn't out of any sense of politeness or consideration. It was simply because each of them was too busy to heckle the other.

Separately, however, each felt a smug satisfaction when the first month passed. One down, five to go.

When they were into their second month, Michael drove into New York for a day to handle a problem with a script that had to be dealt with personally. He left, cross as a bear and muttering about imbeciles. Pandora prepared to enjoy herself tremendously in his absence. She wouldn't have to keep up her guard or share the Folley for hours. She could do anything she wanted without worrying about anyone coming to look over her shoulder or make a caustic remark. It would be wonderful.

She ended up picking at her dinner, then watching for his car through the heavy brocade drapes. Not because she missed *him*, she assured herself. It was just that she'd become used to having someone in the house.

Wasn't that one of the reasons she'd never lived with anyone before? She wanted to avoid any sense of dependence. And dependence, she decided, was natural when you shared the same space—even when it was with a two-legged snake.

So she waited, and she watched. Long after Charles and Sweeney had gone to bed, she continued to wait and watch. She wasn't concerned, and certainly not lonely. Only restless. She told herself she didn't go to bed herself because she wasn't tired. Wandering the first floor, she walked into Jolley's den. Game room would have been a more appropriate name. The decor was a cross between video arcade and disco lounge with its state-of-the-art components and low, curved-back sofas.

She turned on the huge, fifty-four-inch television, then left it on the first show that appeared. She wasn't going to *watch* it. She just wanted the company.

There were two pinball tables where she passed nearly an hour trying to beat the high scores Jolley had left behind. Another legacy. Then there was an arcade-size video game that simulated an attack on the planet Zarbo. Under her haphazard defense system, the planet blew up three times before she moved on. There was computerized chess, but she thought her mind too sluggish to take it on. In the end she stretched out on the six-foot sofa in front of the television. Just to rest, not to watch.

Within moments, she was hooked on the late-night syndication of a cop show. Squealing tires and blasting bullets. Head pillowed on her arms, one leg thrown over the top of the sofa, she relaxed and let herself be entertained.

When Michael came to the doorway, she didn't notice him. He'd had a grueling day and had hit some nasty traffic on the drive back. The fact was he'd considered staying in the city overnight—the sensible thing to do. He'd found himself making a dozen weak excuses why he had to go back instead of accepting the invitation of the assistant producer—a tidily built brunette with big brown eyes.

He'd intended to crawl upstairs, fall into his bed and sleep until noon, but he'd seen the lights and heard the racket. Now, here was Pandora, self-proclaimed critic of the small screen, sprawled on a sofa watching reruns at one in the morning. She looked suspiciously as though she were enjoying herself.

Not a bad show, Michael mused, recognizing the series. In fact, he'd written a couple of scripts for it in his early days. The central character had a sly sort of wit and a fumbling manner that caused the perpetrator to spill out enough information for an arrest by the end of the show.

Michael watched Pandora as she shifted comfortably on the couch. He waited until the commercial break. 'Well, how the mighty have fallen.'

She nearly did, rolling quickly to look back toward the doorway. She sat up, scowled and searched her mind for a plausible excuse. 'I couldn't sleep,' she told him, which was true enough. She wouldn't add it was because he hadn't been home. 'I suppose television is made for the insomniac. Valium for the mind.'

He was tired, bone tired, but he realized how glad he was she'd had a comeback. He came over, plopped down beside her and propped his feet on a coffee table made out of a fat log. 'Who done it?' he asked, and sighed. It was good to be home.

'The greedy business partner.' She was too pleased to have him back to be embarrassed. 'There's really very little challenge in figuring out the answers.'

'This show wasn't based on the premise of figuring out who did the crime, but in how the hero maneuvers them into betraying themselves.'

She pretended she wasn't interested, but shifted so that she could still see the screen. 'So, how did things go in New York?'

'They went.' Michael pried off one shoe with the toe of the other. 'After several hours of hair tearing and blame casting, the script's intact.'

He looked tired. Really tired, she realized, and unbent enough to take off his other shoe. He merely let out a quick grunt of appreciation. 'I don't understand why people would get all worked up about one silly hour a week.'

He opened one eye to stare at her. 'It's the American way.'

'What's there to get so excited about? You have a crime, the good guys chase the bad guys and catch them before the final credits. Seems simple enough.'

'I can't thank you enough for clearing that up. I'll point it out at the next production meeting.'

'Really, Michael, it seems to me things should run fairly smoothly, especially since you've been on the air with this thing for years.'

'Know anything about ego and paranoia?'

She smiled a little. 'I've heard of them.'

'Well, multiply that with artistic temperament, the ratings race and an escalating budget. Don't forget to drop in a good dose of network executives. Things haven't run smoothly for four years. If *Logan* goes another four, it still won't run smoothly. That's show biz.'

Pandora moved her shoulders. 'It seems a foolish way to make a living.'

'Ain't it just,' Michael agreed, and fell sound asleep.

She let him doze for the next twenty minutes while she watched the sly, fumbling cop tighten the ropes on the greedy business partner. Satisfied that justice had been done, Pandora rose to switch off the set and dim the lights.

She could leave him here, she considered as she watched Michael sleep. He looked comfortable enough at the moment. She thought about it as she walked over to brush his hair from his forehead. But he'd probably wake up with a stiff neck and a nasty disposition. Better get him upstairs into bed, she decided, and shook his shoulder.

'Michael.'

'Mmm?'

'Let's go to bed.'

'Thought you'd never ask,' he mumbled, and reached halfheartedly for her.

Amused, she shook him harder. 'Never let your reach exceed your grasp. Come on, cousin, I'll help you upstairs.'

'The director's a posturing idiot,' he grumbled as she dragged him to his feet.

'I'm sure he is. Now, see if you can put one foot in front of the other. That's the way. Here we go.' With an arm around his waist, she began to lead him from the room.

'He kept screwing around with my script.'

'Of all the nerve. Here come the steps.'

'Said he wanted more emotional impact in the second act. Bleaches his hair,' Michael muttered as she half pulled him up the steps. 'Lot he knows about emotional impact.'

'Obviously a mental midget.' Breathlessly she steered him toward his room. He was heavier than he looked. 'Here we are now, home again.' With a little strategy and a final burst of will, she shoved him onto the bed. 'There now, isn't that cozy?' Leaving him fully dressed, she spread an afghan over him.

'Aren't you going to take my pants off?'

She patted his head. 'Not a chance.'

'Spoilsport.'

'If I helped you undress this late at night, I'd probably have nightmares.'

'You know you're crazy about me.' The bed felt like heaven. He could've burrowed in it for a week.

'You're getting delirious, Michael. I'll have Charles bring you some warm tea and honey in the morning.'

'Not if you want to live.' He roused himself to open his eyes and smile at her. 'Why don't you crawl in beside me? With a little encouragement, I could show you the time of your life.'

Pandora leaned closer, closer, until her mouth was inches from his. Their breath mixed quickly, intimately.

She hovered there a moment while her hair fell forward and brushed his cheek. 'In a pig's eye,' she whispered.

Michael shrugged, yawned and rolled over. "Kay.'

In the dark, Pandora stood for a moment with her hands on her hips. At least he could've acted insulted. Chin up, she walked out—making sure she slammed the door at her back.

Chapter 5

Tier by painstaking tier, Pandora had completed the emerald necklace. When it was finished, she was pleased to judge it perfect. This judgment pleased her particularly because she was her own toughest critic. Pandora didn't feel emotionally attached or creatively satisfied by every piece she made. With the necklace, she felt both. She examined it under a magnifying glass, held it up in harsh light, went over the filigree inch by inch and found no flaws. Out of her own imagination she'd conceived it, then with her own skill created it. With a kind of regret, she boxed the necklace in a bed of cotton. It wasn't hers any longer.

With the necklace done, she looked around her workshop without inspiration. She'd put so much into that one piece, all her concentration, her emotion, her skill.

She hadn't made a single plan for the next project. Restless, wanting to work, she picked up her pad and began to sketch.

Earrings perhaps, she mused. Something bold and chunky and ornate. She wanted a change after the fine, elegant work she'd devoted so much time to. Circles and triangles, she thought. Something geometric and blatantly modern. Nothing romantic like the necklace.

Romantic, she mused, and sketched strong, definite lines. She'd been working with a romantic piece; perhaps that's why she'd nearly made a fool of herself with Michael. Her emotions were involved with her work, and her work had been light and feminine and romantic. It made sense, she decided, satisfied. Now, she'd work with something strong and brash and arrogant. That should solve the problem.

There shouldn't be a problem in the first place. Teeth gritted, she flipped a page and started over. Her feelings for Michael had always been very definite. Intolerance. If you were intolerant of someone, it went against the grain to be attracted to him.

It wasn't real attraction in any case. It was more some sort of twisted…curiosity. Yes, curiosity. The word satisfied her completely. She'd been curious, naturally enough, to touch on the sexuality of a man she'd known since childhood. Curious, again naturally, to find out what it was about Michael Donahue that attracted all those poster girls. She'd found out.

So he had a way of making a woman feel utterly a woman, utterly involved, utterly willing. It wasn't something that had happened to her before nor something she'd looked for. As Pandora saw it, it was a kind of skill. She decided he'd certainly honed it as meticulously as any craftsman. Though she found it difficult to fault him for that, *she* wasn't about to fall in with the horde. If he knew, if he even suspected, that she'd had the same reaction to him that she imagined dozens of other women had, he'd gloat for a month. If he guessed that from time to time she'd wished—just for a moment—that he'd think of her the way he thought of those dozens of other women, he'd gloat for twice as long. She wouldn't give him the pleasure.

Individuality was part of her makeup. She didn't want to be one of his women, even if she could. Now that her curiosity had been satisfied, they'd get through the next five months without any more...complications.

Just because she'd found him marginally acceptable as a human being, almost tolerable as a companion wouldn't get in the way. It would, if anything, make the winter pass a bit easier.

And when she caught herself putting the finishing touches on a sketch of Michael's face, she was appalled. The lines were true enough, though rough. She'd had no trouble capturing the arrogance around the eyes or the sensitivity around the mouth. Odd, she realized; she'd sketched him to look intelligent. She ripped the sheet from her pad, crumpled it up in a ball and tossed it into the trash. Her mind had wandered, that was all. Pandora picked up her pencil again, put it down, then dug the sketch out again. Art was art, after all, she told herself as she smoothed out Michael's face.

He wasn't having a great deal of success with his own work. Michael sat at his desk and typed like a maniac for five minutes. Then he stared into space for fifteen. It wasn't like him. When he worked, he worked steadily, competently, smoothly until the scene was set.

Leaning back in his chair, he picked up a pencil and ran his fingers from end to end. Whatever the statistics said, he should never have given up smoking. That's what had him so edgy. Restless, he pushed away from the desk and wandered over to the window. He stared down at Pandora's workshop. It looked cheerful under a light layer of snow that was hardly more than a dusting. The windows were blank.

That's what had him so edgy.

She wasn't what he'd expected. She was softer, sweeter. Warmer. She was fun to talk to, whether she was arguing and snipping and keeping you on the edge of temper, or whether she was being easy and companionable. There wasn't an overflow of small talk with Pandora. There weren't any trite conversations. She kept your mind working, even if it was in defense of her next barb.

It wasn't easy to admit that he actually enjoyed her company. But the weeks they'd been together at the Folley had gone quickly. No, it wasn't easy to admit he liked being with her, but he'd turned down an interesting invitation from his assistant producer because… Because, Michael admitted on a long breath, he hadn't wanted to spend the night with one woman when he'd known his thoughts would have been on another.

Just how was he going to handle this unwanted and unexpected attraction to a woman who'd rather put on the gloves and go a few rounds than walk in the moonlight?

Romantic women had always appealed to him because he was, unashamedly, a romantic himself. He enjoyed candlelight, quiet music, long, lonely walks. Michael courted women in old-fashioned ways because he felt comfortable with old-fashioned ways. It didn't interfere with the fact that he was, and had been since college, a staunch feminist. Romance and sociopolitical views were worlds apart. He had no trouble balancing equal pay for equal work against offering a woman a carriage ride through the park.

And he knew if he sent Pandora a dozen white roses, she'd complain about the thorns.

He wanted her. Michael was too much a creature of the senses to pretend otherwise. When he wanted something, he worked toward it in one of two ways. First, he planned out the best approach, then took the steps one at a time, maneuvering subtly. If that didn't work, he tossed out subtlety and went after it with both hands. He'd had just as much success the first way as the second.

As he saw it, Pandora wouldn't respond to patience and posies. She wouldn't go for being swept off her feet, either. With Pandora, he might just have to toss his two usual approaches and come up with a whole new third.

An interesting challenge, Michael decided with a slow smile. He liked nothing better than arranging and rearranging plot lines and shifting angles. And hadn't he always thought Pandora would make a fascinating character? So, he'd work it like a screenplay.

Hero and heroine living as housemates, he began. Attracted to each other but reluctant. Hero is intelligent, charming. Has tremendous willpower. Hadn't he given up smoking—five weeks, three days and fourteen hours ago? Heroine is stubborn and opinionated, often mistakes arrogance for independence. Hero gradually cracks through her brittle shield to their mutual satisfaction.

Michael leaned back in his chair and grinned. He might just make it a play. A great deal of the action would be ad-lib, of course, but he had the general theme. Satisfied, and looking forward to the opening scene, Michael went back to work with a vengeance.

Two hours breezed by with Michael working steadily. He answered the knock at his door with a grunt.

'I beg your pardon, Mr. Donahue.' Charles, slightly out of breath from the climb up the stairs, stood in the doorway.

Michael gave another grunt and finished typing the paragraph. 'Yes, Charles?'

'Message for you, sir.'

'Message?' Scowling, he swiveled around in the chair. If there was a problem in New York—as there was at least once a week—the phone was the quickest way to solve it. 'Thanks.' He took the message, but only flapped it against his palm. 'Pandora still out in her shop?'

'Yes, sir.' Grateful for the chance to rest, Charles expanded a bit. 'Sweeney is a bit upset that Miss McVie missed lunch. She intends to serve dinner in an hour. I hope that suits your schedule.'

Michael knew better than to make waves where Sweeney was concerned. 'I'll be down.'

'Thank you, sir, and if I may say, I enjoy your television show tremendously. This week's episode was particularly exciting.'

'I appreciate that, Charles.'

'It was Mr. McVie's habit to watch it every week in my company. He never missed an episode.'

'There probably wouldn't have been a *Logan's Run* without Jolley,' Michael mused. 'I miss him.'

'We all do. The house seems so quiet. But I—' Charles reddened a bit at the thought of overstepping his bounds.

'Go ahead, Charles.'

'I'd like you to know that both Sweeney and I are pleased to remain in your service, yours and Miss McVie's. We were glad when Mr. McVie left you the house. The others...' He straightened his back and plunged on. 'They wouldn't have been suitable, sir. Sweeney and I had both discussed resigning if Mr. McVie had chosen to leave the Folley to one of his other heirs.' Charles folded his bony hands. 'Will there be anything else before dinner, sir?'

'No, Charles. Thank you.'

Message in hand, Michael leaned back as Charles went out. The old butler had known him since childhood. Michael could remember distinctly when Charles had stopped calling him Master Donahue. He'd been sixteen and visiting the Folley during the summer months.

Charles had called him Mr. Donahue and Michael had felt as though he'd just stepped from childhood, over adolescence and into adulthood.

Strange how much of his life had been involved with the Folley and the people who were a part of it. Charles had served him his first whisky—with dignity if not approval on his eighteenth birthday. Years before that, Sweeney had given him his first ear boxing. His parents had never bothered to swat him and his tutors wouldn't have dared. Michael still remembered that after the sting had eased, he'd felt like part of a family.

Pandora had been both bane and fantasy during his adolescence. Apparently that hadn't changed as much as Michael had thought. And Jolley. Jolley had been father, grandfather, friend, son and brother.

Jolley had been Jolley, and Michael had spoken no less than the truth when he'd told Charles he missed the old man. In some part of himself, he always would. Thinking of other things, Michael tore open the message.

Your mother is gravely ill. The doctors are not hopeful. Make arrangements to fly to Palm Springs immediately. L. J. KEYSER.

Michael stared at the message for nearly a minute. It wasn't possible; his mother was never ill. She considered it something of a social flaw. He felt a moment's disbelief, a moment's shock. He was reaching for the phone before either had worn off.

When Pandora walked by his room fifteen minutes

later, she saw him tossing clothes into a bag. She lifted a brow, leaned against the jamb and cleared her throat. 'Going somewhere?'

'Palm Springs.' He tossed in his shaving kit.

'Really?' Now she folded her arms. 'Looking for a sunnier climate?'

'It's my mother. Her husband sent me a message.'

Instantly she dropped her cool, sarcastic pose and came into the room. 'Is she ill?'

'The message didn't say much, but it doesn't sound good.'

'Oh, Michael, I'm sorry. Can I do anything? Call the airport?'

'I've already done it. I've got a flight in a couple of hours. They're routing me through half a dozen cities, but it was the best I could do.'

Feeling helpless, she watched him zip up his bag. 'I'll drive you to the airport if you like.'

'No, thanks anyway.' He dragged a hand through his hair as he turned to face her. The concern was there, though he realized she'd only met his mother once, ten, perhaps fifteen years before. The concern was for him and unexpectedly solid. 'Pandora, it's going to take me half the night to get to the coast. And then I don't know—' He broke off, not able to imagine his mother seriously ill. 'I might not be able to make it back in time—not in forty-eight hours.'

She shook her head. 'I don't want you to think about it. I'll call Fitzhugh and explain. Maybe he'll be able to do something. After all, it's an emergency. If he can't, he can't.'

He was taking a step that could pull millions of dollars out from under her. Millions of dollars and the home she loved. Torn, Michael went to her and rested his hands on her shoulders. She was so slender. He'd forgotten just how fragile a strong woman could be. 'I'm sorry, Pandora. If there was any other way...'

'Michael, I told you I didn't want the money. I meant it.'

He studied her a moment. Yes, the strength was there, the stubbornness and the basic goodness he often overlooked. 'I believe you did,' he murmured.

'As for the rest, well, we'll see. Now go ahead before you miss your plane.' She waited until he'd grabbed his bag then walked with him to the hall. 'Call me if you get the chance and let me know how your mother is.'

He nodded, started for the stairs, then stopped. Setting his bag down, he came back and pulled her against him. The kiss was hard and long, with hints of a fire barely banked. He drew her away just as abruptly. 'See you.'

'Yeah.' Pandora swallowed. 'See you.'

She stood where she was until she heard the front door slam.

She had a long time to think about the kiss, through a solitary dinner, during the hours when she tried to read by the cheery fire in the parlor. It seemed to Pandora that there'd been more passion concentrated in that brief contact than she'd experienced in any of her carefully structured relationships. Was it because she'd always been able to restrict passion to her temper, or her work?

It might have been because she'd been sympathetic, and Michael had been distraught. Emotions had a way of feeding emotions. But for the second time she found herself alone in the house, and to her astonishment, lonely. It was foolish because the fire was bright, the book entertaining and the brandy she sipped warming.

But lonely she was. After little more than a month, she'd come to depend on Michael's company. Even to look forward to it, as strange as that may have been. She liked sitting across from him at meals, arguing with him. She especially liked watching the way he fought, exploding when she poked pins in his work. Perverse? she wondered with a sigh. Perhaps she was, but life was so boring without a bit of friction. No one seemed to provide it more satisfactorily than Michael Donahue.

She wondered when she'd see him again. And she wondered if now they'd have to forgo spending the winter together. If the terms of the will were broken, there would be no reason for them to stay on together. In fact, they'd have no right to stay at the Folley at all. They'd both go back to New York where, due to separate life-styles, they never saw one another. Not until now, when it was a possibility, did Pandora fully realize how much she didn't want it to happen.

She didn't want to lose the Folley. There were so many memories, so many important ones. Wouldn't they begin to fade if she couldn't walk into a room and bring them back? She didn't want to lose Michael. His companionship, she amended quickly. It was more satisfying than she'd imagined to have someone near who could meet you head to head. If she lost that daily challenge, life would be terribly flat. Since it was Michael who was adding that certain spark to the days, it was only natural to want him around. Wasn't it?

With a sigh, Pandora shut the book and decided an early night would be more productive than idle speculation. Just as she reached over to shut out the lamp, it went out on its own. She was left with the glow of the fire.

Odd, she thought and reached for the switch. After turning it back and forth, she rose, blaming a defective bulb. But when she walked into the hall she found it in darkness. The light she'd left burning was out, along with the one always left on at the top of the stairs. Again Pandora reached for a switch and again she found it useless.

Power failure, she decided but found herself hesitating in the dark. There was no storm. Electricity at the Folley went out regularly during snow and thunderstorms, but the back-up generator took over within minutes. Pandora waited, but the house remained dark. It occurred to her as she stood there hoping for the best, that she'd never really considered how dark dark could be. She was already making her way back into the parlor for a candle when the rest occurred to her. The house was heated with electricity, as well. If she didn't see about the power soon, the house was going to be very cold as well as very dark before too long. With two people in their seventies in the house, she couldn't let it go.

Annoyed, she found three candles in a silver holder

and lit them. It wasn't any use disturbing Charles's sleep and dragging him down to the basement. It was probably only a faulty fuse or two. Holding the candles ahead of her, Pandora wound her way through the curving halls to the cellar door.

She wasn't bothered about going down into the cellar in the dark. So she told herself as she stood with her hand on the knob. It was, after all, just another room. And one, if memory served, which was full of the remains of several of Uncle Jolley's rejected hobbies. The fuse box was down there. She'd seen it when she'd helped her uncle cart down several boxes of photographic equipment after he'd decided to give up the idea of becoming a portrait photographer. She'd go down, check for faulty fuses and replace them. After the lights and heat were taken care of, she'd have a hot bath and go to bed.

But she drew in a deep breath before she opened the door.

The stairs creaked. It was to be expected. And they were steep and narrow as stairs were in any self-respecting cellar. The light from her candles set the shadows dancing over the crates and boxes her uncle had stored there. She'd have to see if she could talk Michael into helping her sort through them. On some bright afternoon. She was humming nervously to herself before she reached the bottom stair.

Pandora held the candles high and scanned the floor as far as the light circled. She knew mice had an affection for dark, dank cellars and she had no affection for them. When nothing rushed across the floor, she skirted around two six-foot crates and headed for the fuse box. There was the motorized exercise bike that Uncle Jolley had decided took the fun out of staying fit. There was a floor-to-ceiling shelf of old bottles. He'd once been fascinated by a ten-dollar bottle cutter. And there, she saw with a sigh of relief, was the fuse box. Setting the candles on a stack of boxes, she opened the big metal door and stared inside. There wasn't a single fuse in place.

'What the hell's this?' she muttered. Then as she shifted to look closer, her foot sent something rattling over the concrete floor. Jolting, she stifled a scream and the urge to run. Holding her breath, she waited in the silence. When she thought she could manage it, she picked up the candles again and crouched. Scattered at her feet were a dozen fuses. She picked one up and let it lie in her palm. The cellar might have its quota of mice, but they weren't handy enough to empty a fuse box.

She felt a little shudder, which she ignored as she began to gather up the fuses. Tricks, she told herself. Just silly tricks. Annoying, but not as destructive as the one played in her workshop. It wasn't even a very clever trick, she decided, as it was as simple to put fuses back as it had been to take them out.

Working quickly, and trying not to look over her shoulder, Pandora put the fuses back in place. Whoever had managed to get into the basement and play games had wasted her time, nothing more.

Finished, she went over to the stairs, and though she hated herself, ran up them. But her sigh of relief was premature. The door she'd carefully left open was closed tightly. For a few moments she simply refused to believe it. She twisted the knob, pushed, shoved and twisted again. Then she forgot everything but the fear of being closed in a dark place. Pandora beat on the door, shouted, pleaded, then collapsed half sobbing on the top step. No one would hear her. Charles and Sweeney were on the other side of the house.

For five minutes she gave in to fear and self-pity. She was alone, all alone, locked in a dark cellar where no one would hear her until morning. It was already cold and getting colder. By morning…her candles would go out by then, and she'd have no light at all. That was the worst, the very worst, to have no light.

Light, she thought, and called herself an idiot as she wiped away tears. Hadn't she just fixed the lights? Scrambling up, Pandora hit the switch at the top of the stairs. Nothing happened. Holding back a scream, she held the candles up. The socket over the stairs was empty.

So, they'd thought to take out the bulbs. It had been a clever trick after all. She swallowed fresh panic and tried to think. They wanted her to be incoherent, and she refused to give them the satisfaction. When she found out which one of her loving family was playing nasty games…

That was for later, Pandora told herself. Now she was going to find a way out. She was shivering, but she told herself it was anger. There were times it paid to lie to yourself. Holding the candles aloft, she forced herself to go down the steps again when cowering at the top seemed so much easier.

The cellar was twice the size of her apartment in New York, open and barnlike without any of the ornate decorating Uncle Jolley had been prone to. It was just dark and slightly damp with concrete floors and stone walls that echoed. She wouldn't think about spiders or things that scurried into corners right now. Slowly, trying to keep calm, she searched for an exit.

There were no doors, but then she was standing several feet underground. Like a tomb. That particular thought didn't soothe her nerves so she concentrated on other things. She'd only been down in the cellar a handful of times and hadn't given a great deal of thought to the setup. Now she had to think about it—and pretend her palms weren't clammy.

She eased by a pile of boxes as high as her shoulders, then let out a scream when she ran into a maze of cobwebs. More disgusted than frightened, she brushed and dragged at them. It didn't sit well with her to make a fool out of herself, even if no one was around to see it. Someone was going to pay, she told herself as she fought her way clear.

Then she saw the window, four feet above her head and tiny. Though it was hardly the size of a transom, Pandora nearly collapsed in relief. After setting the candles on a shelf, she began dragging boxes over. Her muscles strained and her back protested, but she hauled and stacked against the wall. The first splinter had her swearing. After the third, she stopped counting. Out of breath, streaming with sweat, she leaned against her makeshift ladder. Now all she had to do was climb it. With the candles in one hand, she used the other to haul herself up. The light shivered and swayed. The boxes groaned and teetered a bit. The thought passed through her mind that if she fell, she could lie there on the frigid concrete with broken bones until morning. She pulled herself high and refused to think at all.

When she reached the window, she found the little latch rusted and stubborn. Swearing, praying, she balanced the candles on the box under her and used both hands. She felt the latch give, then stick again. If she'd only thought to find a tool before she'd climbed up. She considered climbing back down and finding one, then made the mistake of looking behind her. The stack of boxes looked even more rickety from up there.

Turning back to the window, she tugged with all the strength she had. The latch gave with a grind of metal against metal, the boxes swayed from the movement. She saw her candles start to tip and grabbed for them. Out of reach, they slid from the box and clattered to the concrete, their tiny flames extinguished as they hit the ground. She almost followed them, but managed to fight for balance. Pandora found herself perched nine feet off the floor in pitch-darkness.

She wouldn't fall, she promised herself as she gripped the little window ledge with both hands. Using her touch to guide her, she pulled the window out and open, then began to ease herself through. The first blast of cold air made her almost giddy. After she'd pushed her shoulders through she gave herself a moment to breathe and adjust to the lesser dark of starlight. From somewhere to the west, she heard a hardy night bird call twice and fall silent. She'd never heard anything more beautiful.

Grabbing the base of a rhododendron, she pulled herself through to the waist. When she heard the crash of boxes behind her, she laid her cheek against the cold grass. Inch by inch, she wiggled her way out, ignoring the occasional rip and scratch. At last, she was flat on her back, looking up at the stars. Cold, bruised and exhausted, she lay there, just breathing. When she was able, Pandora dragged herself up and walked around to the east terrace doors.

She wanted revenge, but first, she wanted a bath.

After three layovers and two plane changes, Michael arrived in Palm Springs. Nothing, as far as he could see, had changed. He never came to the exclusive little community but that he came reluctantly. Now, thinking of his mother lying ill, he was swamped with guilt.

He rarely saw her. True, she was no more interested in seeing him than he was her. Yet, she was still his mother. They had been on a different wavelength since the day he'd been born, but she'd taken care of him. At least, she'd hired people to take care of him. Affection, Michael realized, didn't have to enter into a child's feelings for his parent. The bond was there whether or not understanding followed it.

With no more than a flight bag, he bypassed the crowd at baggage claim and hailed a cab. After giving his mother's address, he sat back and checked his watch, subtracting time zones. Even with the hours he'd gained, it was probably past visiting hours. He'd get around that, but first he had to know what hospital his mother was in. If he'd been thinking straight, he would have called ahead and checked.

If his mother's husband wasn't in, one of the servants could tell him. It might not be as bad as the message made it sound. After all, his mother was still young. Then it struck Michael that he didn't have the vaguest idea how old his mother was. He doubted his father knew, and certainly not her current husband. At another time, it might have struck him as funny.

Impatient, he watched as the cab glided by the gates and pillars of the elite. His career had caused him to stay in California for extended lengths of time, but he preferred L.A. to Palm Springs. There, at least, was some action, some movement, some edge. But he liked New York best of all; the pace matched his own and the streets were tougher.

He thought of Pandora. Both of them lived in New York, but they never saw each other unless it was miles north of the city at the Folley. The city could swallow you. Or hide you. It was another aspect Michael appreciated.

Didn't he often use it to hide—from his stifling upbringing, from his recurring lack of faith in the human race? It was at the Folley that he felt the easiest, but it was in New York that he felt the safest. He could be anonymous there if he chose to be. There were times he wanted nothing more. He wrote about heroes and justice, sometimes rough but always human. He wrote, in his own fashion, about basic values and simple rights.

He'd been raised with the illusions and hypocrisy of wealth and with values that were just as unstable. He'd broken away from that, started on his own. New York had helped make it possible because in the city backgrounds were easily erased. So easily erased, Michael mused, that he rarely thought of his.

The cab cruised up the long semicircle of macadam, under the swaying palms, toward the towering white house where his mother had chosen to live. Michael remembered there was a lily pond in the back with goldfish the size of groupers. His mother refused to call them carp.

'Wait,' he told the driver, then dashed up two levels of stairs to the door. The butler who answered was new. It was his mother's habit to change the staff regularly, before, as she put it, they got too familiar. 'I'm Michael Donahue, Mrs. Keyser's son.'

The butler glanced over his shoulder at the waiting cab, then back at Michael's disheveled sweater and unshaven face. 'Good evening, sir. Are you expected?'

'Where's my mother? I want to go to the hospital directly.'

'Your mother isn't in this evening, Mr. Donahue. If you'll wait, I'll see if Mr. Keyser's available.'

Intolerant, as always, of cardboard manners, he stepped inside. 'I know she's not in. I want to go see her tonight. What's the name of the hospital?'

The butler gave a polite nod. 'What hospital, Mr. Donahue?'

'Jackson, where did that cab come from?' Wrapped in a deep-rose smoking jacket, Lawrence Keyser strolled downstairs. He had a thick cigar between the fingers of one hand and a snifter of brandy in the other.

'Well, Lawrence,' Michael began over a wave of fury. 'You look comfortable. Where's my mother?'

'Well, well, it's—ah, it's Matthew.'

'It's Michael.'

'Michael, of course. Jackson, pay off Mr. ah, Mr. Donavan's cab.'

'No, thanks, Jackson.' Michael held up a hand. Another time, he'd have been amused at his stepfather's groping for his name. 'I'll use it to get to the hospital. Wouldn't want to put you out.'

'No trouble at all, not at all.' Big, round and only partially balding, Keyser gave Michael a friendly grin. 'Veronica will be pleased to see you, though we didn't know you were coming. How long are you in town?'

'As long as I'm needed. I left the minute I got the message. You didn't mention the name of the hospital. Since you're home and relaxing,' he said with only the slightest trace of venom, 'should I assume that my mother's condition's improved?'

'Condition?' Keyser gave a jovial laugh. 'Well now, I don't know how she'd take to that term, but you can ask her yourself.'

'I intend to. Where is she?'

'Playing bridge at the Bradleys'. She'll be coming along in about an hour. How about a brandy?'

'Playing bridge!' Michael stepped forward and grabbed his surprised stepfather by the lapels. 'What the hell do you mean she's playing bridge?'

'Can't stomach the game myself,' Keyser began warily. 'But Veronica's fond of it.'

It came to Michael, clear as a bell. 'You didn't send me a message about Mother?'

'A message?' Keyser patted Michael's arm, and hoped Jackson stayed close. 'No need to send you a message about a bridge game, boy.'

'Mother's not ill?'

'Strong as a horse, though I wouldn't let her hear me say so just that way.'

Michael swore and whirled around. 'Someone's going to pay,' he muttered.

'Where are you going?'

'Back to New York,' Michael tossed over his shoulder as he ran down the steps.

Relieved, Keyser opted against the usual protests about his departure. 'Is there a message for your mother?'

'Yeah.' Michael stopped with a hand on the door of the cab. 'Yeah, tell her I'm glad she's well. And I hope she wins—in spades.' Michael slammed the door shut behind him.

Keyser waited until the cab shot out of sight. 'Odd boy,' Keyser grumbled to his butler. 'Writes for television.'

Chapter 6

Pandora, sleeping soundly, was awakened at seven in the morning when Michael dropped on her bed. The mattress bounced. He snuggled his head into the pillow beside her and shut his eyes.

'Sonofabitch,' he grumbled.

Pandora sat up, remembered she was naked and grabbed for the sheets. 'Michael! You're supposed to be in California. What are you doing in my bed?'

'Getting horizontal for the first time in twenty-four hours.'

'Well, do that in your own bed,' she ordered, then saw the lines of strain and fatigue. 'Your mother.' Pandora grabbed for his hand. 'Oh, Michael, is your mother—'

'Playing bridge.' He rubbed his free hand over his face. Even to him it felt rough and seedy. 'I bounced across country, once in a tuna can with propellers, to find out she was sipping sherry and trumping her partner's ace.'

'She's better then?'

'She was always better. The message was a hoax.' He yawned, stretched and settled. 'God, what a night.'

'You mean…' Pandora tugged on the sheets and glowered. 'Well, the rats.'

'Yeah. I plotted out several forms of revenge when I was laid over in Cleveland. Maybe our friend who stomped through your workshop figured it was my turn. Now we each owe them one.'

'I owe 'em two.' Pandora leaned back against the headboard with the sheets tucked under her arms. Her hair fell luxuriously over her naked shoulders. 'Last night while you were off on your wild-goose chase, I was locked in the cellar.'

Michael's attention shot away from the thin sheet that barely covered her. 'Locked in? How?'

Crossing one ankle over the other, Pandora told him what happened from the time the lights went out.

'Climbed up on boxes? To that little window? It's nearly ten feet.'

'Yes, I believe I noticed that at the time.'

Michael scowled at her. The anger he'd felt at being treated to a sleepless night doubled. He could picture her groping her way around in the dank cellar all too well. Worse, he could see her very clearly climbing on shaky boxes and crates. 'You could've broken your neck.'

'I didn't. What I did do was rip my favorite pair of slacks, scratch both knees and bruise my shoulder.'

Michael managed to hold back his fury. He'd let it go, he promised himself, when the time was right. 'It could've been worse,' he said lightly, and thought of what he'd do to whoever had locked her in.

'It was worse,' Pandora tossed back, insulted. 'While you were sipping Scotch at thirty thousand feet, I was locked in a cold, damp cellar with mice and spiders.'

'We might reconsider calling the police.'

'And do what with them? We can't prove anything. We don't even know whom we can't prove anything against.'

'New rule,' Michael decided. 'We stick together. Neither of us leaves the house overnight without the other. At least until we find out which of our devoted relations is playing games.'

Pandora started to protest, then remembered how frightened she'd been, and before the cellar, before the fear, how lonely. 'Agreed. Now…' With one hand hanging onto the sheet, she shifted toward him. 'I vote for Uncle Carlson on this one. After all, he knows the house better than any of the others. He lived here.'

'It's as good a guess as any. But it's only a guess.' Michael stared up at the ceiling. 'I want to know. Biff stayed here for six weeks one summer when we were kids.'

'That's right.' Pandora frowned at the ceiling herself. The mirror across the room reflected them lying companionably, hip to hip. 'I'd forgotten about that. He hated it.'

'He's never had a sense of humor.'

'True enough. As I recall he certainly didn't like you.'

'Probably because I gave him a black eye.'

Pandora's brow lifted. 'You would.' Then, because the

image of Biff with a shiner wasn't so unappealing, she added: 'Why did you? You never said.'

'Remember the frogs in your dresser?'

Pandora sniffed and smoothed at the sheets. 'I certainly do. It was quite immature of you.'

'Not me. Biff.'

'Biff?' Astonished, she turned toward him again. 'You mean that little creep put the frogs in my underwear?' The next thought came, surprisingly pleasing. 'And you punched him for it?'

'It wasn't hard.'

'Why didn't you deny it when I accused you?'

'It was more satisfying to punch Biff. In any case, he knows the house well enough. And I imagine if we checked up, we'd find most of our happy clan has stayed here, at least for a few days at a time. Finding a fuse box in the cellar doesn't take a lot of cunning. Think it through, Pandora. There are six of them, seven with the charity added on. Split a hundred fifty million seven ways and you end up with plenty of motive. Every one of them has a reason for wanting us to break the terms of the will. None of them, as far as I'm concerned, is above adding a little pressure to help us along.'

'Another reason the money never appealed to me,' she mused. 'They haven't done anything but vandalize and annoy, but, dammit, Michael, I want to pay them back.'

'The ultimate payback comes in just under five months.' Without thinking about it, Michael put his arm around her shoulders. Without thinking about it, Pandora settled against him. A light fragrance clung to her skin.

'Can't you see Carlson's face when the will holds up and he gets nothing but a magic wand and a trick hat?'

His shoulder felt more solid than she'd imagined. 'And Biff with three cartons of matchbooks.' Comfortable, she chuckled. 'Uncle Jolley's still having the last laugh.'

'We'll have it with him in a few months.'

'It's a date. And you've got your shoes on my sheets.'

'Sorry.' With two economical movements, he pried them off.

'That's not exactly what I meant. Don't you want to wander off to your own room now?'

'Not particularly. Your bed's nicer than mine. Do you always sleep naked?'

'No.'

'My luck must be turning then.' He shifted to press his lips to a bruise on her shoulder. 'Hurt?'

She shrugged and prayed it came off as negligent. 'A little.'

'Poor little Pandora. And to think I always thought you were tough-skinned.'

'I am—'

'Soft,' he interrupted, and skimmed his fingers down her arm. 'Very soft. Any more bruises?' He brushed his lips over the curve of her neck. They both felt her quick, involuntary shudder.

'Not so you'd notice.'

'I'm very observant.' He rolled, smoothly, so that his body pressed more intimately into hers as he looked down on her. He was tired. Yes, he was tired and more than a little punchy with jet lag, but he hadn't forgotten he wanted her. Even if he had, the way her body yielded, the way her face looked rosy and soft with sleep, would've jogged his memory. 'Why don't I look for myself?' He ran his fingers down to where the sheet lay, neat, prim and arousing, at her breast.

She sucked in her breath, incredibly moved by his lightest touch. She couldn't let it show…could she? She couldn't reach out for something that was only an illusion. He wasn't stable. He wasn't real. He was with her now because she was here and no one else was. Why was it becoming so hard to remember that?

His face was close, filling her vision. She saw the little things she'd tried not to notice over the years. The way a thin ring of gray outlined his irises, the straight, almost aristocratic line of his nose that had remained miraculously unbroken through countless fistfights. The soft, sculpted, somehow poetic shape of his mouth. A mouth, she remembered, that was hot and strong and inventive when pressed against hers.

'Michael…' The fact that she hesitated, then fumbled before she reached down to take his hand both pleased and unnerved him. She wasn't as cool and self-contained as she'd always appeared. And because she wasn't, he could slip his way under her skin. But he might not slip out again so easily.

Be practical, she told herself. Be realistic. 'Michael, we have almost five months more to get through.'

'Good point.' He needed the warmth. He needed the woman. Maybe it was time to risk the consequences. He lowered his head and nibbled at her mouth. 'Why waste it?'

She let herself enjoy him. For just a moment, she promised herself. For only a moment. He was warm and his hands were easy. The night had been long and cold and frightening. No matter how much she hated to admit it, she'd needed him. Now, with the sun pouring through the tiny square panes in the windows, falling bright and hard on the bed, she had him. Close, secure, comforting.

Her lips opened against his.

He'd had no plan when he'd come into her room. He'd simply been drawn to her; he'd wanted to lie beside her and talk to her. Passion hadn't guided him. Desire hadn't pushed him. There'd only been the basic need to be home, to be home with her. When she'd snuggled against him, hair tousled, eyes heavy, it had been so natural that the longing had snuck up on him. He wanted nothing more than to stay where he was, wrapped around her, slowly heating.

And for her, passion didn't bubble wildly, but easily, like a brew that had been left to simmer through the day while spices were added. One sample, then another, and the taste changed, enriched, deepened. With Michael, there the flavors were only hinted at, an aroma to draw in and savor. She could have gone on, and on, hour after hour, until what they made between them was perfected. She wanted to give in to the need, the beginnings of greed. If she did, everything would change. It was a change she couldn't predict, couldn't see clearly, could only anticipate. So she resisted him and herself and what could happen between them.

'Michael...' But she let her fingers linger in his hair for just a minute more. 'This isn't smart.'

He kissed her eyes closed. It was something no one had done before. 'It's the smartest thing either of us has done in years.'

She wanted to agree, felt herself on the edge of agreeing. 'Michael, things are complicated enough. If we were lovers and things went wrong, how could we manage to go on here together? We've made a commitment to Uncle Jolley.'

'The will doesn't have a damn thing to do with you and me in this bed.'

How could she have forgotten just how intense he could look when he was bent on something? How was it she'd never noticed how attractive it made him? She'd have to make a stand now or go under. 'The will has everything to do with you and me in this house. If we go to bed together and our relationship changes, then we'll have to deal with all the problems and complications that go with it.'

'Name some.'

'Don't be amusing, Michael.'

'Giving you a laugh wasn't my intention.' He liked the way she looked against the pillow—hair spread out like wildfire, cheeks a bit flushed, her mouth on the edge of forming a pout. Strange he'd never pictured her this way before. It didn't take any thought to know he'd picture her like this again and again. 'I want you, Pandora. There's nothing amusing about it.'

No, that wasn't something she could laugh or shrug off, not when the words brushed over her skin and made her muscles limp. He didn't mean it. He couldn't mean it. But she wanted to believe it. If she couldn't laugh it off, she had to throw up a guard and block it. 'Becoming lovers is something that takes a lot of thought. If we're going to discuss it—'

'I don't want to discuss it.' He pressed his lips against hers until he felt her body soften. 'We're not making a corporate merger, Pandora, we're making love.'

'That's just it.' She fought back an avalanche of longing. Be practical. It was her cardinal rule. 'We're business partners. Worse, we're family business partners, at least for the next few months. If we change that now it could—'

'If,' he interrupted. 'It could. Do you always need guarantees?'

Her brows drew together as annoyance competed with desire. 'It's a matter of common sense to look at all the angles.'

'I suppose you have any prospective lover fill out an application form.'

Her voice chilled. It was, in a distorted way, close to the truth. 'Don't be crude, Michael.'

Pushed to the limit, he glared down at her. 'I'd rather be crude than have your brand of common sense.'

'You've never had any brand of common sense,' she tossed back. 'Why else would every busty little blonde you've winked at be public knowledge? You don't even have the decency to be discreet.'

'So that's it.' Shifting, Michael drew her into a sitting position. There was no soft yielding now. She faced him with fire in her eyes. 'Don't forget the brunettes and the redheads.'

She hadn't. She promised herself she wouldn't. 'I don't want to discuss it.'

'You brought it up, and we'll finish it. I've gone to bed with women. So put me in irons. I've even enjoyed it.'

She tossed her hair behind her shoulder. 'I'm sure you have.'

'And I haven't had a debate with every one of them beforehand. Some women prefer romance and mutual enjoyment.'

'Romance?' Her brows shot up under her tousled hair. 'I've always had another word for it.'

'You wouldn't recognize romance if it dropped on your head. Do you consider it discreet to take lovers and pretend you don't? To pledge undying fidelity to one person while you're looking for another? What you want to call discretion, I call hypocrisy. I'm not ashamed of any of the women I've known, in bed or out.'

'I'm not interested in what you are or aren't ashamed of. I'm not going to be your next mutual enjoyment. Keep your passion for your dancers and starlets and chorus girls.'

'You're as big a snob as the rest of them.'

That hit home and had her shoulders stiffening. 'That's not true. I've simply no intention of joining a crowd.'

'You flatter me, cousin.'

'There's another word for that, too.'

'Think about this.' He gave her a shake, harder than he'd intended. 'I've never made love with a woman I didn't care for and respect.' Before he cut loose and did more than shake her, he got up and walked to the door while she sat in the middle of the bed clutching sheets and looking furious.

'It appears you give respect easily.'

He turned back to study her. 'No,' he said slowly. 'But I don't make people jump through hoops for it.'

A cold war might not be as stimulating as an active battle, but with the right participants, it could be equally destructive. For days Pandora and Michael circled around each other. If one made a sarcastic comment, the other reached into the stockpile and used equal sarcasm. Neither drew out the red flag for full-scale attack, instead they picked and prodded at each other while the servants rolled their eyes and waited for bloodshed.

'Foolishness,' Sweeney declared as she rolled out the crust for two apple pies. 'Plain foolishness.' She was a sturdy, red-faced woman, as round as Charles was thin. In her pragmatic, no-nonsense way, she'd married and buried two husbands, then made her way in the world by cooking for others. Her kitchen was always neat and tidy, all the while smelling of the sinfully rich food she prepared. 'Spoiled children,' she told Charles. 'That's what they are. Spoiled children need the back of the hand.'

'They've over four months to go.' Charles sat gloomily

at the kitchen table, hunched over a cup of tea. 'They'll never make it.'

'Hah!' Sweeney slammed the rolling pin onto a fresh ball of dough. 'They'll make it. Too stubborn not to. But it's not enough.'

'The master wanted them to have the house. As long as they do, we won't lose it.'

'What'll we be doing in this big empty house when both of them go back to the city? How often will either of them be visiting with the master gone?' Sweeney turned the crust into a pan and trimmed it expertly. 'The master wanted them to have the house, true enough. And he wanted them to have each other. The house needs a family. It's up to us to see it gets one.'

'You didn't hear them over breakfast.' Charles sipped his tea and watched Sweeney pour a moist apple mixture into the crust.

'That has nothing to do with it. *I've* seen the way they look at each other when they think the other one's not noticing. All they need's a push.'

With quick, economic movements, she filled the second crust. 'We're going to give 'em one.'

Charles stretched out his legs. 'We're too old to push young people.'

Sweeney gave a quick grunt as she turned. Her hands were thick, and she set them on her hips. 'Being old's the whole trick. You've been feeling poorly lately.'

'No, to tell you the truth, I've been feeling much better this week.'

'You've been feeling poorly,' Sweeney repeated, scowling at him. 'Now here's our Pandora coming in for lunch. Just follow my lead. Look a little peaked.'

Snow had come during the night, big fat flakes that piled on the ground and hung in the pines. As she walked, Pandora kicked it up, pleased with herself. Her work couldn't have been going better. The earrings she'd finally fashioned had been unique, so unique, she'd designed a necklace to complement them. It was chunky and oversize with geometric shapes of copper and gold. Not every woman could wear it, but the one who could wouldn't go unnoticed.

It was, to Pandora, a statement of the strong, disciplined woman. She was just as pleased with the shoulder-brushing earrings she was making with jet and silver beads. They had been painstakingly strung together and when finished would be elegantly flirtatious. Another aspect of woman. If her pace kept steady, she'd have a solid inventory to ship off to the boutique she supplied. In time for the Christmas rush, she reminded herself smugly.

When she opened the kitchen door, she was ravenously hungry and in the best of moods.

'…if you're feeling better in a day or two,' Sweeney said briskly, then turned as if surprised to see Pandora inside. 'Oh, time must've got away from me. Lunch already and I'm just finishing up the pies.'

'Apple pies?' Grinning, Pandora moved closer. But Sweeney saw with satisfaction that Pandora was already studying Charles. 'Any filling left?' she began, and started to dip her fingers into the bowl. Sweeney smacked them smartly.

'You've been working with those hands. Wash them up in the sink, and you'll have your lunch as soon as I can manage it.'

Obediently, Pandora turned on a rush of water. Under the noise, she murmured to Sweeney. 'Is Charles not feeling well?'

'Bursitis is acting up. Cold weather's a problem. Just being old's a problem in itself.' She pushed a hand at the small of her back as though she had a pain. 'Guess we're both slowing down a bit. Aches and pains,' Sweeney sighed and cast a sidelong look at Pandora. 'Just part of being old.'

'Nonsense.' Concerned, Pandora scrubbed her hands harder. She told herself she should have been keeping a closer eye on Charles. 'You just try to do too much.'

'With the holidays coming…' Sweeney trailed off and made a business out of arranging a top crust. 'Well, decorating the house is a lot of work, but it's its own reward. Charles and I'll deal with the boxes in the attic this afternoon.'

'Don't be silly.' Pandora shut off the water and reached for a towel. 'I'll bring the decorations down.'

'No, now, missy, there're too many boxes and most of them are too heavy for a little girl like you. That's for us to see to. Isn't that right, Charles?'

Thinking of climbing the attic stairs a half-dozen times, Charles started to sigh. A look from Sweeney stopped him. 'Don't worry, Miss McVie, Sweeney and I will see to it.'

'You certainly will not.' Pandora hung the towel back

on the hook. 'Michael and I will bring everything down this afternoon, and that's that. Now I'll go tell him to come to lunch.'

Sweeney waited until the door swung shut behind Pandora before she grinned.

Upstairs, Pandora knocked twice on Michael's office door, then walked in. He kept on typing. Putting her pride on hold, Pandora walked over to his desk and folded her arms. 'I need to talk to you.'

'Come back later. I'm busy.'

Abuse rose up in her throat. Remembering Sweeney's tired voice, she swallowed it. 'It's important.' She ground her teeth on the word, but said it. 'Please.'

Surprised, Michael stopped typing in midword. 'What? Has one of the family been playing games again?'

'No, it's not that. Michael, we have to decorate the house for Christmas.'

He stared at her a moment, swore and turned back to his machine. 'I've got a twelve-year-old boy kidnapped and being held for a million-dollar ransom. That's important.'

'Michael, will you put away fantasyland for a moment? This is real.'

'So's this. Just ask my producer.'

'Michael!' Before he could stop her, Pandora grabbed the laptop. He was halfway out of his chair to retaliate. 'It's Sweeney and Charles.'

It stopped him, though he snatched the computer back from her. 'What about them?'

'Charles's bursitis is acting up again, and I'm sure Sweeney's not feeling well. She sounded, well, old.'

'She is old.' But Michael tossed the paper on the desk. 'Think we should call in a doctor?'

'No, they'd be furious.' She swung around his desk, trying to pretend she wasn't reading part of his script. 'I'd rather just keep an eye on them for a few days and make sure they don't overdo. That's where the Christmas decorations come in.'

'I figured you'd get to them. Look, if you want to deck the halls, go ahead. I haven't got time to fool with it today.'

'Neither do I.' She folded her arms in a manner that amused him. 'Sweeney and Charles have it in their heads that it has to be done. Unless we want them dragging up and down the attic stairs, we have to take care of it.'

'Christmas is three weeks away.'

'I know the date.' Frustrated, she strode to the window then back. 'They're old and they're set on it. You know Uncle Jolley would've had them up the day after Thanksgiving. It's traditional.'

'All right, all right.' Trapped, Michael rose. 'Let's get started.'

'Right after lunch.' Satisfied she'd gotten her way, Pandora swept out.

Forty-five minutes later, she and Michael were pushing open the attic door. The attic was, in Jolley's tradition, big enough to house a family of five. 'Oh, I'd forgotten what a marvelous place this is.' Forgetting herself, Pandora grabbed Michael's hand and pulled him in. 'Look at this table, isn't it horrible?'

It was. Old and ornate with curlicues and cupids, it had been shoved into a corner to hold other paraphernalia Jolley had discarded. 'And the bird cage out of Popsicle sticks. Uncle Jolley said it took him six months to finish it, then he didn't have the heart to put a bird inside.'

'Lucky for the bird,' Michael muttered, but found himself, as always, drawn to the dusty charm of the place. 'Spats,' he said, and lifted a pair from a box. 'Can't you see him in them?'

'And this hat.' Pandora found a huge circular straw hat with a garden of flowers along the brim. 'Aunt Katie's. I've always wished I'd met her. My father said she was just as much fun as Uncle Jolley.'

Michael watched Pandora tip the brim over her eyes. 'If that was her hat, I believe it. How about this?' He found a black derby and tilted it rakishly.

'It's you,' Pandora told him with her first easy laugh in days. 'All you need's a high white collar and a walking stick. Look.' She pulled him in front of a tall cheval mirror that needed resilvering. Together, they studied themselves.

'An elegant pair,' Michael decided, though his sweater bagged over his hips, and she already had dust on her nose. 'All you need is one of those slim little skirts that sweep the floor and a lace blouse with padded shoulders.'

'And a cameo on a ribbon,' she added as she tried to visualize herself. 'No, I probably would've worn bloomers and picketed for women's rights.'

'The hat still suits you.' He turned to adjust it just a bit. 'Especially with your hair long and loose. I've always liked it long, though you looked appealingly lost and big-eyed when you had it all chopped short.'

'I was fifteen.'

'And you'd just come back from the Canary Islands with the longest, brownest legs I'd ever seen in my life. I nearly ate my saucer when you walked into the parlor.'

'You were in college and had some cheerleader hanging on your arm.'

Michael grinned. 'You had better legs.'

Pandora pretended little interest. She remembered the visit perfectly, but was surprised, and pleased, that he did. 'I'm surprised you noticed or remembered.'

'I told you I was observant.'

She acknowledged the thrust with a slight nod. There were times when it was best to pad quietly over danger-ous ground. 'We'd better start digging out the decora-tions. Sweeney said the boxes were back along the left and clearly marked.' Without waiting for agreement, she turned and began to look. 'Oh good grief.' She stopped again when she saw the stacks of boxes, twenty, perhaps twenty-five of them. Michael stood at her shoulder and stuck his hands in his pockets.

'Think we can hire some teamsters?'

Pandora blew out a breath. 'Roll up your sleeves.'

On some trips, they could pile two or three boxes apiece and maneuver downstairs. On others, it took both of them to haul one. Somewhere along the way they'd stopped arguing. It was just too much effort.

Grimy and sweaty, they dropped the last boxes in the parlor. Ignoring the dust on her slacks, Pandora collapsed in the nearest chair. 'Won't it be great fun hauling them all up again after New Year's?'

'Couldn't we've settled on a plastic Santa?'

'It'll be worth it.' Drumming up the energy, she knelt on the floor and opened the first box. 'Let's get started.'

Once they did, they went at it with a vengeance. Boxes were opened, garland strewed and bulbs tested. They squabbled good-naturedly about what looked best where and the proper way to drape lights at the windows. When the parlor, the main hall and the staircase were finished, Pandora stood at the front door and took a long look.

The garland was white and silver, twisting and twining down the banister. There were bright red bells, lush green ribbon and tiny lights just waiting for evening.

'It looks good,' she decided. 'Really good. Of course, Sweeney and Charles will want to decorate the servants' quarters and that entire box goes into the dining room, but it's a wonderful start.'

'Start?' Michael sat on the stairs. 'We're not entering a contest, cousin.'

'These things have to be done right. I wonder if my parents will make it home for Christmas. Well…' She brushed that off. They always considered wherever they were home. 'I'd say we're ready for the tree. Let's go find one.'

'You want to drive into town now?'

'Of course not.' Pandora was already pulling coats out

of the hall closet. 'We'll go right out in the woods and dig one up.'

'We?'

'Certainly. I hate it when people cut trees down and then toss them aside after the new year. The woods are loaded with nice little pines. We'll dig one up, then replant it after the holidays.'

'How handy are you with a shovel?'

'Don't be a spoilsport.' Pandora tossed his coat to him, then pulled on her own. 'Besides, it'll be nice to spend some time outside after being in that stuffy attic. We can have some hot buttered rum when we're finished.'

'Heavy on the rum.'

They stopped at the toolshed for a shovel. Michael picked two and handed one to Pandora. She took it without a blink, then together they walked through the ankle-high snow to the woods. The air had a bite and the scent of pine was somehow stronger in the snow.

'I love it when it's like this.' Pandora balanced the shovel on her shoulder and plowed through the woods. 'It's so quiet, so—separated. You know, sometimes I think I'd rather live here and visit the city than the other way around.'

He'd had the same thought, but was surprised to hear it from her. 'I always thought you liked the bright lights and confusion.'

'I do. But I like this, too. How about this one?' She paused in front of a spruce. 'No, the trunk's too crooked.' She walked on. 'Besides, I wonder if it wouldn't be more exciting to go into the city for a week now and again and know you had someplace like this to come back to. I seem to work better here. Here's one.'

'Too tall. We're better off digging up a young one. Wouldn't it put a crimp in your social life?'

'What?' She studied the tree in question and was forced to agree with him. 'Oh. My social life isn't a priority, my work is. In any case, I could entertain here.'

He had a picture of her spending long, cozy weekends with flamboyant, artsy types who read Keats aloud. 'You don't have to come all the way to the Catskills to play house.'

Pandora merely lifted a brow. 'No, I don't. This one looks good.' She stopped again and took a long study of a four-and-a-half-foot spruce. Behind her, Michael worked hard to keep his mouth shut. 'It's just the right size for the parlor.'

'Fine.' Michael stuck his shovel into the ground. 'Put your back into it.'

As he bent over to dig, Pandora scooped up a shovelful of snow and tossed it into his face. 'Oh, sorry.' She smiled and batted her eyes. 'Looks like my aim's off.' Digging with more effort, she began to hum.

He let it go, probably because he appreciated the move and wished he'd thought of it himself. Within fifteen minutes, they had the hole dug.

'There now.' Only a little out of breath, Pandora leaned on her shovel. 'The satisfaction of a job well done.'

'We only have to carry it back to the house, set it up and...damn, we need something to wrap the roots and dirt in. There was burlap in the shed.'

They eyed each other blandly.

'All right,' he said after a moment. 'I'll go get it, then you have to sweep up the needles and dirt we trail on the floor.'

'Deal.'

Content, Pandora turned away to watch a cardinal when a snowball slapped into the back of her head. 'Sorry.' Michael gave her a companionable smile. 'Aim must be off.' He whistled as he walked back to the shed.

Pandora waited until he was out of sight, then smiling smugly, knelt down to ball snow. By the time he got back, she calculated, she could have an arsenal at hand. He wouldn't have a chance. She took her time, forming and smoothing each ball into a sophisticated weapon. Secure in her advantage, she nearly fell on her face when she heard a sound behind her. She had the ball in her hand and was already set to throw as she whirled. No one was there. Narrowing her eyes, she waited. Hadn't she seen a movement back in the trees? It would be just like him to skirt around and try to sneak up on her. She saw the cardinal fly up again as if startled and heard the quiet plop of snow hitting snow as it was shaken from branches.

'All right, Michael, don't be a coward.' She picked up a ball in her left hand, prepared to bombard.

'Guarding your flank?' Michael asked so that this time when she whirled back around, she slid onto her bottom. He grinned at her and dropped the burlap sack in her lap.

'But weren't you...' She trailed off and looked behind her again. How could he be here if he was there? 'Did you circle around?'

'No, but from the looks of that mound of balls, I should've. Want to play war?'

'It's just a defense system,' she began, then looked over her shoulder again. 'I thought I heard you. I would've sworn there was someone just beyond the trees there.'

'I went straight to the shed and back.' He looked beyond her. 'You saw something out there?'

'Michael, if you're playing tricks—'

'No.' He cut her off and reached down to pull her to her feet. 'No tricks. Let's have a look.'

She moved her shoulders but didn't remove her hand from his as they walked deeper into the trees. 'Maybe I was a bit jumpy.'

'Or expecting me to be sneaky?'

'That, too. It was probably just a rabbit.'

'A rabbit with big feet,' he murmured as he looked down at the tracks. They were clear enough in the snow, tracks leading to and away from the spot ten yards behind where they'd dug up the tree. 'Rabbits don't wear boots.'

'So, we still have company. I was beginning to think they'd given the whole business up.' She kept her voice light, but felt the uneasiness of anyone who'd been watched. 'Maybe it's time we talked to Fitzhugh, Michael.'

'Maybe, in the meantime—' The sound of an engine cut him off. He was off in a sprint with Pandora at his heels. After a five-minute dash, they came, clammy and out of breath, to what was hardly more than a logging trail. Tire tracks had churned up the snow and blackened it. 'A Jeep, I'd guess.' Swearing, Michael stuck his hands in his pockets. If he'd started out right away, he might have caught someone or at least have caught a glimpse of someone.

Pandora let out an annoyed breath. Racing after someone was one thing, being outmaneuvered another. 'Whoever it is is only wasting his time.'

'I don't like being spied on.' He wanted physical contact. Longed for it. Frustrated, he stared at the tracks that led back to the main road. 'I'm not playing cat and mouse for the next four months.'

'What are we going to do?'

His smile spread as he looked at the tracks. 'We'll spread the word through Fitzhugh that we've been bothered by trespassers. Being as there's any number of valuables on the premises, we've decided to haul out one of Jolley's old .30-.30's.'

'Michael! They may be a nuisance, but they're still family.' Unsure, she studied him. 'You wouldn't really shoot at anyone.'

'I'd rather shoot at family than strangers,' he countered, then shrugged. 'They're also fond of their own skin. I can't think of one of them who wouldn't hesitate to play around if they thought they might be picking buckshot out of embarrassing places.'

'I don't like it. Guns, even the threat of guns, are trouble.'

'Got a better idea?'

'Let's buy a dog. A really big, mean dog.'

'Great, then we can let him loose and have him sink

his teeth into one of our favorite relatives. They'd like that a lot better than buckshot.'

'He doesn't have to be that mean.'

'We'll compromise and do both.'

'Michael—'

'Let's call Fitzhugh.'

'And take his advice?' Pandora demanded.

'Sure…if I like it.'

Pandora started to object, then laughed. It was all as silly as a plot of one of his shows. 'Sounds reasonable,' she decided, then tucked her arm through his. 'Let's get the tree inside first.'

Chapter 7

'I know it's Christmas Eve, Darla.' Michael picked up his coffee cup, found it empty and lifted the pot from his hot plate. Dregs. He bit off a sigh. The trouble with the Folley was that you had to hike a half a mile to the kitchen whenever the pot ran dry. 'I know it'll be a great party, but I can't get away.'

That wasn't precisely true, Michael mused as he listened to Darla's rambles about a celebration in Manhattan. *Everyone*, according to her estimate, was going to be there. That meant a loud, elbow-to-elbow party with plenty of booze. He could have taken a day and driven into the city to raise a glass or two with friends. He was well ahead of schedule. So far ahead, he could have taken off a week and not felt the strain. The precise truth was, he didn't want to get away.

'I appreciate that…you'll just have to tell everyone Merry Christmas for me. No, I like living in the country, Darla. Weird? Yeah, maybe.' He had to laugh. Darla was a top-notch dancer and a barrel of laughs, but she didn't believe life went on outside of the island of Manhattan. 'New Year's if I can manage it. Okay, babe. Yeah, yeah, *ciao.*'

More than a little relieved, Michael hung up. Darla was a lot of fun, but he wasn't used to being clung to by a woman, especially one he'd only dated casually. The truth was, she was just as attracted to the influence he had with certain casting agents as she was interested in him. He didn't hold it against her. She had ambition and talent, a combination that could work in the tough-edged business of entertaining if a dash of luck was added. After the holidays he'd make a few calls and see what he could do.

From the doorway, Pandora watched as Michael ran a hand along the back of his neck. Darla, she repeated silently. She imagined the women his taste leaned toward had names like Darla, or Robin and Candy. Sleek, smooth, sophisticated and preferably empty-headed.

'Popularity's such a strain, isn't it, darling?'

Michael turned in his chair to give her a long, narrowed look. 'Eavesdropping's so rude, isn't it, darling?'

She shrugged but didn't come in. 'If you'd wanted privacy, you should've closed your door.'

'Around here you have to nail it shut for privacy.'

One brow raised, head slightly inclined, Pandora looked as aloof as royalty. 'Your phone conversations have absolutely no interest for me. I only came up as a favor to Charles. You've a package downstairs.'

'Thanks.' He didn't bother to hide amusement at her tone. If he knew Pandora, and he did, she'd listened to every word. 'I thought these were your sacred working hours.'

'Some of us schedule our work well enough that we can take some time off during the holidays. No, no, let's not bicker,' she decided abruptly before he could retaliate. 'It is nearly Christmas after all, and we've had three weeks of peace from our familial practical jokers. Truce,' Pandora offered with a smile Michael wasn't sure he should trust. 'Or a moratorium if you prefer.'

'Why?'

'Let's just say I'm a sucker for holly and ivy. Besides, I'm relieved we didn't have to buy a big drooling dog or a supply of buckshot.'

'For now.' Not completely satisfied, Michael tipped back in his chair. 'Fitzhugh's notion of notifying the local police of trespassers and spreading the rumor of an official investigation might be working temporarily. Or maybe our friends and family are just taking a holiday break themselves. Either way I'm not ready to relax.'

'You'd rather break someone's nose than solve things peaceably,' Pandora began, then waved a hand. 'Never mind. I, for one, am going to enjoy the holidays and not give any of our dear family a thought.' She paused a moment, toying with her braided chain of gold and amethyst. 'I suppose Darla was disappointed.'

Michael watched the way the stones caught the thin winter light and made sparks from it. 'She'll pull through.'

Pandora twisted the chain one way, twisted it back, then let it go. It was the sort of nervous gesture Michael hadn't expected from her. 'Michael, you know you don't have to stay. I really will be fine if you want to run into New York for the holiday.'

'Rule number six,' he reminded her. 'We stick together, and you've turned down a half-dozen invitations for the holidays yourself.'

'My choice.' She reached for the chain again, then dropped her hands. 'I don't want you to feel obligated—'

'My choice,' he interrupted. 'Or have you suddenly decided I'm chivalrous and unselfish?'

'Certainly not,' she tossed back, but smiled. 'I prefer thinking you're just too lazy to make the trip.'

He shook his head, but his lips curved in response. 'I'm sure you would.'

She hesitated in the doorway until he lifted a brow in question. 'Michael, would you become totally obnoxious if I told you I'm glad you're staying?'

He studied her as she stood, looking slim and neat in the doorway, her hair a riotous contrast to the trim sweater and stovepipe pants. 'I might.'

'Then I won't tell you.' Without another word, she slipped out of the doorway and disappeared.

Contrary woman, Michael thought. He was close to being crazy about her. And crazy was the perfect word. She baited him or, he admitted, he baited her at every possible opportunity. He could imagine no two people less inclined to peaceful coexistence, much less harmony. And yet...and yet he was close to being crazy about her. Knowing better than to try to go back to work, he rose and followed her downstairs.

He found her in the parlor, rearranging packages under the tree. 'How many have you shaken?'

'All of them,' she said easily. But she didn't turn because he might have seen how pleased she was he'd come downstairs with her. 'I don't want to show any preference. Thing is,' she added, poking at an elegantly wrapped box, 'I seem to have missed my present from you.'

Michael gave her a bland smile. 'Who says I got you anything?'

'You would have been terribly rude and insensitive otherwise.'

'Yep. In any case, you seem to've done well enough.' He crouched down to study the stacks of boxes under the tree. 'Who's Boris?' Idly he picked up a small silver box with flowing white ribbon.

'A Russian cellist who defected. He admires my...gold links.'

'I bet. And Roger?'

'Roger Madison.'

His mouth dropped open, but only for a moment. 'The Yankee shortstop who batted .304 last year?'

'That's right. You may've noticed the silver band he wears on his right wrist. I made that for him last March. He seems to think it straightened out his bat or something.' She lifted the blue-and-gold box and shook it gently. 'He tends to be very generous.'

'I see.' Michael took a comprehensive study of the boxes. 'There don't seem to be a great many packages here for you from women.'

'Really?' Pandora took a scan herself. 'It appears you make up for that with your pile. Chi-Chi?' she asked as she picked up a box with a big pink bow.

'She's a marine biologist,' Michael said with his tongue in his cheek.

'Fascinating. And I imagine Magda's a librarian.'

'Corporate attorney,' he said blandly.

'Hmm. Well, whoever sent this one's obviously shy.' She picked up a magnum of champagne with a glittering red ribbon. The tag read 'Happy Holidays, Michael,' and nothing more.

Michael scanned the label with approval. 'Some people don't want to advertise their generosity.'

'How about you?' She tilted her head. 'After all, it is a magnum. Are you going to share?'

'With whom?'

'I should've known you'd be greedy.' She picked up a box with her name on it. 'Just for that I'm eating this entire box of imported chocolates myself.'

Michael eyed the box. 'How do you know they're chocolates?'

She only smiled. 'Henri always gives me chocolate.'

'Imported?'

'Swiss.'

Michael put out a hand. 'Share and share alike.'

Pandora accepted it. 'I'll chill the wine.'

* * *

Hours later when there was starlight on the snow and a fire in the hearth, Pandora lit the tree. Like Michael, she didn't miss any of the crowded, frenzied parties in the city. She was where she wanted to be. It had taken Pandora only a matter of weeks to discover she wasn't as attached to the rush of the city as she'd once thought. The Folley was home. Hadn't it always been? No, she no longer thought of going back to Manhattan in the spring. But what would it be like to live in the Folley alone?

Michael wouldn't stay. True, he'd own half of the Folley in a few months, but his life—including his active social life—was in the city. He wouldn't stay, she thought again, and found herself annoyed with her own sense of regret. Why should he stay? she asked herself as she wandered over to poke at the already crackling fire. How could he stay? They couldn't go on living together indefinitely. Sooner or later she'd have to approach him about her decision to remain there. To do so, she'd have to explain herself. It wouldn't be easy.

Still, she was grateful to Jolley for doing something she'd once resented. Boxing her in. She may have been forced into dealing with Michael on a day-to-day level, but in the few months she'd done so, her life had had more energy and interest than in the many months before. It was that, Pandora told herself, that she hated to give up.

She'd dealt with her attraction to him semisuccessfully. The fact was, he was no more her type than she was his. She jammed hard at a log. From all the many reports, Michael preferred a more flamboyant, exotic sort of woman.

Actresses, dancers, models. And he preferred them in droves. She, on the other hand, looked for more intellectual men. The men she spent time with could discuss obscure French novelists and appreciate small, esoteric plays. Most of them wouldn't have known if *Logan's Run* was a television show or a restaurant in SoHo.

The fact that she had a sort of primitive desire for Michael was only a tempest in a teapot. Pandora smiled as she replaced the poker. She couldn't deny she enjoyed a tempest now and again.

When a small one erupted behind her, Pandora turned in disbelief. A little white dog with oversize feet scrambled into the room, slid on the Aubusson carpet and rammed smartly into a table. Barking madly, it rolled over twice, righted itself, then dashed at Pandora to leap halfheartedly and loll its tongue. Entertained, Pandora crouched down and was rewarded when the puppy sprang onto her lap and licked her face.

'Where'd you come from?' Laughing, and defending herself as best she could, Pandora found the card attached to the red bow around the puppy's neck. It read:

My name is Bruno. I'm a mean, ugly dog looking for a lady to defend.

'Bruno, huh?' Laughing again, Pandora stroked his unfortunately long ears. 'How mean are you?' she asked as he contented himself with licking her chin.

'He especially likes to attack discontented relatives,' Michael announced as he wheeled in a tray carrying an ice bucket and champagne. 'He's been trained to go after anyone wearing a Brooks Brothers suit.'

'We might add Italian loafers.'

'That's next.'

Moved, incredibly moved, she concentrated on the puppy. She hadn't the least idea how to thank Michael without making a fool of herself. 'He isn't really ugly,' she murmured.

'They promised me he would be.'

'They?' She buried her face in the puppy's fur a moment. 'Where did you get him?'

'Pound.' Watching her, Michael ripped the foil from the champagne. 'When we went into town for supplies last week and I deserted you in the supermarket.'

'And I thought you'd gone off somewhere to buy pornographic magazines.'

'My reputation precedes me,' he said half to himself. 'In any case, I went to the pound and walked through the kennels. Bruno bit another dog on the—on a sensitive area in order to get to the bars first. Then he grinned at me with absolutely no dignity. I knew he was the one.'

The cork came out with a bang and champagne sprayed up and dripped onto the floor. Bruno scrambled out of Pandora's lap and greedily licked it up. 'Perhaps his manners are lacking a bit,' Pandora observed. 'But his taste is first class.' She rose, but waited until Michael had poured two glasses. 'It was a lovely thing to do, dammit.'

He grinned and handed her a glass. 'You're welcome.'

'It's easier for me when you're rude and intolerable.'

'I do the best I can.' He touched his glass to hers.

'When you're sweet, it's harder for me to stop myself from doing something foolish.'

He started to lift his glass, then stopped. 'Such as?'

'Such as.' Pandora set down her champagne, then took Michael's and set it on the table as well. Watching him, only him, she put her arms around his neck. Very slowly—unwise acts done slowly often take on a wisdom of their own—she touched her mouth to his.

It was, as she'd known it would be, warm and waiting. His hands came to her shoulders, holding her without pressure. Perhaps they'd both come to understand that pressure would never hold her. When she softened, when she gave, she gave through her own volition, not through seduction, not through demand. So it was Pandora who moved closer, Pandora who pressed body to body, offering hints of intimacy with no submission.

It wasn't submission he wanted. It wasn't submission he looked for, though it was often given to him. He didn't look for matching strength, but strength that meshed. In Pandora, where he'd never thought to search for it, he found it. Her scent twisted around him, heightening emotions her taste had just begun to stir. Under his hands, her body was firm with the underlying softness women could exploit or be exploited by. He thought she'd do neither, but would simply be. By being alone, she drew him in.

She didn't resist his touch, not when his hands slipped down to her hips or skimmed up again. It seemed he'd done so before, though only in dreams she'd refused to acknowledge. If this was the time for acceptance, she'd accept. If this was the time for pleasure, she'd take it.

If she found both with him, she wouldn't refuse. Even questions could come later. Maybe tonight was a night without questions.

She drew back, but only to smile at him. 'You know, I don't think of you as a cousin when I'm kissing you.'

'Really?' He nipped at her lips. She had an incredibly alluring mouth—full and pouty. 'What do you think of me as?'

She cocked a brow. His arms surrounded her, but didn't imprison. Pandora knew she'd have to analyze the difference later. 'I haven't figured that out yet.'

'Then maybe we should keep working it out.' He started to pull her back, but she resisted.

'Since you've broken tradition to give me my Christmas present a few hours early, I'll do the same.' Going to the tree, Pandora reached down and found the square, flat box. 'Happy Christmas, Michael.'

He sat down on the arm of a chair to open it while Pandora picked up her glass of champagne. She sipped, watching a bit nervously for his reaction. It was only a token after all, she told herself, as she played with the stem of her glass. When he ripped off the paper then said nothing, she shrugged. 'It's not as inventive as a guard dog.'

Michael stared down at the pencil sketch of their uncle without any idea what to say. The frame she'd made herself, he knew. It was silver and busily ornate in a style Jolley would have appreciated. But it was the sketch that held him silent. She'd drawn Jolley as Michael remembered him best, standing, a bit bent forward from the waist as though he were ready to pop off on a new tangent. What thin hair he'd had left was mussed. His cheeks were stretched out in a big, wide-open grin. It had been drawn with love, talent and humor, three qualities Jolley had possessed and admired. When Michael looked up, Pandora was still twisting the stem of the glass in her hands.

Why, she's nervous, he realized. He'd never expected her to be anything but arrogantly confident about her work. About herself. The secrets he was uncovering were just as unnerving to him as they were to her. A man tended to get pulled into a woman who had soft spots in unexpected places. If he was pulled in, how would he work his way out again? But she was waiting, twisting the stem of her glass in her hand.

'Pandora. No one's ever given me anything that's meant more.'

The line between her brows smoothed out as her smile bloomed. The ridiculous sense of pleasure was difficult to mask. 'Really?'

He held a hand out to her. 'Really.' He glanced down at the sketch again and smiled. 'It looks just like him.'

'It looks like I remember him.' She let her fingers link with Michael's. Pandora could tell herself it was Jolley who drew them together, and nothing else. She could nearly believe it. 'I thought you might remember him that way, too. The frame's a bit gaudy.'

'And suitable.' He studied it with more care. The silver shone dully, set off with the deep curls and lines she'd etched. It could, he realized, be put in an antique shop and pass for an heirloom. 'I didn't know you did this sort of thing.'

'Now and again. The boutique carries a few of them.'

'Doesn't fit in the same category as bangles and beads,' he mused.

'Doesn't it?' Her chin tilted. 'I thought about making you a big gold collar with rhinestones just to annoy you.'

'It would have.'

'Maybe next year then. Or perhaps I'll make one for Bruno.' She glanced around. 'Where'd he go?'

'He's probably behind the tree gnawing on presents. During his brief stay in the garage, he ate a pair of golf shoes.'

'We'll put a stop to that,' Pandora declared, and went to find him.

'You know, Pandora, I'd no idea you could draw like this.' Michael settled against the back of the chair to study the sketch again. 'Why aren't you painting?'

'Why aren't you writing the Great American Novel?'

'Because I enjoy what I'm doing.'

'Exactly.' Finding no sign of the puppy around the tree, Pandora began to search under the furniture. 'Though certainly a number of painters have toyed with jewelry design successfully enough—Dali for one—I feel... Michael!'

He set his untouched champagne back down and hurried over to where she knelt by a divan. 'What is it?' he demanded, then saw for himself. Eyes closed, breathing fast and heavy, the puppy lay half under the divan.

Even as Pandora reached for him, Bruno whimpered and struggled to stand.

'Oh, Michael, he's sick. We should get him to a vet.'

'It'll be midnight before we get to town. We won't find a vet at midnight on Christmas Eve.' Gently Michael laid a hand on Bruno's belly and heard him moan. 'Maybe I can get someone on the phone.'

'Do you think it's something he ate?'

'Sweeney's been supervising his feeding like a new mother.' On cue Bruno struggled and shuddered and relieved himself of what offended his stomach. Exhausted from the effort, he lay back and dozed fitfully. 'Something he drank,' Michael murmured.

Pampering and soothing, Pandora stroked the dog. 'That little bit of champagne shouldn't have made him ill.' Because the dog was already resting easier, she relaxed a bit. 'Charles isn't going to be pleased Bruno cast up his accounts on the carpet. Maybe I should—' She broke off as Michael grabbed her arm.

'How much champagne did you drink?'

'Only a sip. Why—' She broke off again to stare. 'The champagne. You think something's wrong with it?'

'I think I'm an idiot for not suspecting an anonymous present.' He grabbed her by the chin. 'Only a sip. You're sure? How do you feel?'

Her skin had gone cold, but she answered calmly enough. 'I'm fine. Look at my glass, it's still full.' She turned her head to look at it herself. 'You—you think it was poisoned?'

'We'll find out.'

Logic seeped through, making her shake her head. 'But, Michael, the wine was corked. How could it have been tampered with?'

'The first season on *Logan* I used a device like this.' He thought back, remembering how he'd tested the theory by adding food coloring to a bottle of Dom Perignon. 'The killer poisoned champagne by shooting cyanide through the cork with a hypodermic.'

'Fiction,' Pandora claimed, and fought a shiver. 'That's just fiction.'

'Until we find out differently, we're going to treat it as fact. The rest of the bottle's going into New York to Sanfield Labs for testing.'

Shaky, Pandora swallowed. 'For testing,' she said on an unsteady breath. 'All right, I suppose we'll both be easier when we're sure. Do you know someone who works there?'

'We own Sanfield.' He looked down at the sleeping puppy. 'Or we will own it in a matter of months. That's just one of the reasons someone might've sent us some doctored champagne.'

'Michael, if it was poisoned…' She tried to imagine it and found it nearly impossible. 'If it was poisoned,' she repeated, 'this wouldn't just be a game anymore.'

He thought of what might have happened if they hadn't been distracted from the wine. 'No, it wouldn't be a game.'

'It doesn't make any sense.' Uneasy and fighting to calm herself, Pandora rose. 'Vandalism I can see, petty annoyances I can understand, but I just can't attribute something like this to one of the family. We're probably overreacting. Bruno's had too much excitement. He could very well have picked up something in the pound.'

'I had him sent to the vet for his shots before he was delivered here yesterday.' Michael's voice was calm, but his eyes were hot. 'He was healthy, Pandora, until he lapped up some spilled champagne.'

One look at him told her rationalizing was useless. 'All right. The wine should be tested in any case so we can stop speculating. We can't do anything about it until day after tomorrow. In the meantime, I don't want to dwell on it.'

'Pulling the blinds down, Pandora?'

'No.' She picked up Bruno, who whimpered and burrowed into her breast. 'But until it's proven, I don't want to consider that a member of my family tried to kill me. I'll fix him something warm to drink, then I'm going to take him upstairs. I'll keep an eye on him tonight.'

'All right.' Fighting a combination of frustration and fury, Michael stood by the fire.

Long after midnight when he couldn't sleep, couldn't work, Michael looked in on her. She'd left a light burning low across the room so that the white spreads and covers took on a rosy hue. Outside snow was falling again in big, festive flakes. Michael could see her, curled in the wide bed, the blankets up to her chin. The fire was nearly out. On the rug in front of it, the puppy snored. She'd put a mohair throw over him and had set a shallow bowl filled with what looked like tea nearby. Michael crouched beside the dog.

'Poor fella,' he murmured. As he stroked, Bruno stirred, whimpered, then settled again.

'I think he's better.'

Glancing over, Michael saw the light reflected in Pandora's eyes. Her hair was tousled, her skin pale and soft. Her shoulders, gently sloped, rose just above the covers pooled around her. She looked beautiful, desirable, arousing. He told himself he was mad. Pandora didn't fit into his carefully detailed notion of beauty. Michael looked back at the dog.

'Just needs to sleep it off. You could use another log on this fire.' Needing to keep busy, Michael dug in the woodbox, then added a log to the coals.

'Thanks. Can't sleep?'

'No.'

'Me, either.' They sat in silence a moment, Pandora in the big bed, Michael on the hearth rug. The fire crackled greedily at the fresh log and flickered light and shadow. At length, she drew her knees up to her chest. 'Michael, I'm frightened.'

It wasn't an easy admission. He knew it cost her to tell him. He stirred at the fire a moment, then spoke lightly as he replaced the screen. 'We can leave. We can drive into New York tomorrow and stay there. Forget this whole business and enjoy the holidays.'

She didn't speak for a minute, but she watched him carefully. His face was turned away toward the fire so that she had to judge his feelings by the way he held himself. 'Is that what you want to do?'

He thought of Jolley, then he thought of Pandora. Every muscle in his body tightened. 'Sure.' He tossed it off like a shrug. 'I've got to think about myself.' He said it as if to remind himself it had once been true.

'For someone who earns his living by making up stories, you're a lousy liar.' She waited until he turned to face her. 'You don't want to go back. What you want is to gather all our relatives together and beat them up.'

'Can you see me pounding Aunt Patience?'

'With a few exceptions,' Pandora temporized. 'But the last thing you want is to give up.'

'All right, that's me.' He rose and, hands in pockets, paced back and forth in front of the fire. He could smell the woodsmoke mixed with some light scent from one of the bottles on Pandora's dresser. 'What about you? You didn't want to hassle with this whole business from the beginning. I talked you into it. I feel responsible.'

For the first time in hours she felt her humor return. 'I hate to dent your ego, Michael, but you didn't talk me into anything. No one does. And I'm completely responsible for myself. I don't want to quit,' she added before he could speak. 'I said I didn't want the money, and that was true. I also said I didn't need it, and that's not precisely true. Over and above that, there's pride. I'm frightened, yes, but I don't want to quit. Oh, stop pacing around and come sit down.' The order was cross and impatient, nearly making him smile. He came over and sat on the bed.

'Better?'

She gave him a long, steady look that had the hint of a smile fading. 'Yes. Michael, I've been lying here for hours thinking this thing through. I've realized a few things. You called me a snob once, and perhaps you were right in a way. I've never thought much about money. Never allowed myself to. When Uncle Jolley cut everyone out, I thought of it as a cross between a joke and a slap on the wrist. I figured they'd grumble and complain certainly, but that was all.' She lifted her hand palm up. 'It was only money, and every one of them has their own.'

'Ever heard of greed or the lust for power?'

'That's just it, I didn't think. How much do I know about any of those people? They bore or annoy me from time to time, but I've never thought about them as individuals.' Now she ran the hand through her hair so that the blankets fell to her waist. 'Ginger must be about the same age as I am, and I can't think of two things we have in common. I'd probably pass Biff's wife on the street without recognizing her.'

'I have a hard time remembering her name,' Michael put in, and earned a sigh from Pandora.

'That's my point. We don't really know them. The family, in a group, is a kind of parlor joke. Separately, who are they and what are they capable of? I've just begun to consider it. It's not a joke, Michael.'

'No, it's not.'

'I want to fight back, but I don't know how.'

'The surest way is by staying. And maybe,' he added, and took her hand. It was cool and soft. 'Add a little psychological warfare.'

'Such as?'

'What if we sent each one of our relatives a nice bottle of champagne?'

Her smile came slowly. 'A magnum.'

'Naturally. It'd be interesting to see what sort of reaction we get.'

'It would be a nasty gesture, wouldn't it?'

'Uh-hmm.'

'Maybe I haven't given your creative brain enough credit.' She fell silent as he wound her hair around his finger. 'I suppose we should get some sleep.'

'I suppose.' But his fingers skimmed down her shoulders.

'I'm not very tired.'

'We could play canasta.'

'We could.' But she made no move to stop him when he nudged the thin straps of her chemise from her shoulders. 'There's always cribbage.'

'That, too.'

'Or...' It was her decision, they both understood that. 'We might finish playing out the hand we started downstairs earlier.'

He lifted her hand and pressed his lips to the palm. 'Always best to finish what you start before going on. As I recall, we were...here.' He lowered his mouth to hers. Slowly, on a sigh, she wound her arms around his neck.

'That seems about right.'

Holding fast, they sunk into the bed together.

Perhaps it was because they knew each other well. Perhaps it was because they'd already waited a lifetime, but each moved slowly. Desire, for the moment, was comfortable, easy to satisfy with a touch, a taste. Passion curled inside him then unwound with a sigh. There was inch after inch of her to explore with his fingertips, with his lips. He'd waited too long, wanted too long, to miss any part of what they could give to each other.

She was more generous than he'd imagined, less inhibited, more open. She didn't ask to be coaxed, she didn't pretend to need persuasion. She ran her hands over him with equal curiosity. Her mouth took from him and gave again. When his lips parted from hers, her eyes were on him, clouded with desire, dark with amusement of a shared joke. They were together, Michael thought as he buried his face in her hair. About to become lovers. The joke was on both of them.

Her hands were steady when she pulled his sweatshirt over his head, steady still as she ran them over his chest. Her pulse wasn't. She'd avoided this, refused this. Now she was accepting it though she knew there would be consequences she couldn't anticipate.

The fire crackled steadily. The soft light glowed. Consequences were for more practical times.

Her skin slid over his with each movement. Each movement enticed. With his heartbeat beginning to hammer in his head, he journeyed lower. With openmouthed kisses he learned her body in a way he'd only been able to imagine. Her scent was everywhere, subtle at the curve of her waist, stronger at the gentle underside of her breasts. He drew it in and let it swim in his head.

He felt the instant her lazy enjoyment darkened with

power. When her breath caught on a moan, he took her deeper. They reached a point where he no longer knew what they did to each other, only that strength met need and need became desperation.

His skin was damp. She tasted the moistness of it and craved more. So this was passion. This was the trembling, churning hunger men and women longed for. She'd never wanted it. That's what she told herself as her body shuddered. Pleasure and pain mixed, needs and fears tangled. Her mind was as swamped with sensations as her flesh—heat and light, ecstasy and terror. The vulnerability overwhelmed her though her body arched taut and her hands clung. No one had ever brushed back her defenses so effortlessly and taken. Taken and taken.

Breathless and desperate, she dragged his mouth back to hers. They rolled over the bed, rough, racing. Neither had had enough. While she tugged and pulled at his jeans, Michael drove her higher. He'd wanted the madness, for himself and for her. Now he felt the wild strength pouring out of her. No thought here, no logic. He rolled on top of her again, reveling in her frantic breathing.

She curled around him, legs and arms. When he plunged into her, they watched the astonishment on each other's faces. Not like this—it had never been like this. They'd come home. But home, each discovered, wasn't always a peaceful place.

There was silence, stunned, awkward silence. They lay tangled in the covers as the log Michael had set to fire broke apart and showered sparks against the screen. They knew each other well, too well to speak of what had happened just yet. So they lay in silence as their skin cooled and their pulses leveled. Michael shifted to pull the spread up over them both.

'Merry Christmas,' he murmured.

With a sound that was both sigh and laugh, Pandora settled beside him.

Chapter 8

They left the Folley in the hard morning light the day after Christmas. Sun glared off snow, melting it at the edges and forming icicles down branches and eaves. It was a postcard with biting wind.

After a short tussle they'd agreed that Pandora would drive into the city and Michael would drive back. He pushed his seat back to the limit and managed to stretch out his legs. She maneuvered carefully down the slushy mountain road that led from the Folley. They didn't speak until she'd reached clear highway.

'What if they don't let us in?'

'Why shouldn't they?' Preferring driving to sitting, Michael shifted in his seat. For the first time he was impatient with the miles of road between the Folley and New York.

'Isn't that like counting your chickens?' Pandora turned the heat down a notch and loosened the buttons of her coat. 'We don't own the place yet.'

'Just a technicality.'

'Always cocky.'

'You always look at the negative angles.'

'Someone has to.'

'Look...' He started to toss back something critical, then noticed how tightly she gripped the wheel. All nerves, he mused. Though the scenery was a print by Currier and Ives, it wasn't entirely possible to pretend they were off on a holiday jaunt. He was running on nerves himself, and they didn't all have to do with doctored champagne. How would he have guessed he'd wake up beside her in the cool light of dawn and feel so involved? So responsible. So hungry.

He took a deep breath and watched the scenery for another moment. 'Look,' he began again in a lighter tone. 'We may not own the lab or anything else at the moment, but we're still Jolley's family. Why should a lab technician refuse to do a little analysis?'

'I suppose we'll find out when we get there.' She drove another ten miles in silence. 'Michael, what difference is an analysis going to make?'

'I have this odd sort of curiosity. I like to know if someone's tried to poison me.'

'So we'll know if, and we'll know why. We still won't know who.'

'That's the next step.' He glanced over. 'We can invite them all to the Folley for New Year's and take turns grilling them.'

'Now you're making fun of me.'

'No, actually, I'd thought of it. I just figure the time's not quite right.' He waited a few minutes. In thin leather gloves, her fingers curled and uncurled on the wheel. 'Pandora, why don't you tell me what's really bothering you?'

'Nothing is.' Everything was. She hadn't been able to think straight for twenty-four hours.

'Nothing?'

'Nothing other than wondering if someone wants to kill me.' She tossed it off arrogantly. 'Isn't that enough?'

He heard the edge under the sarcasm. 'Is that why you hid in your room all day yesterday?'

'I wasn't hiding.' She had enough pride to sound brittle. 'I was tending to Bruno. And I was tired.'

'You hardly ate any of that enormous goose Sweeney slaved over.'

'I'm not terribly fond of goose.'

'I've had Christmas dinner with you before,' he corrected. 'You eat like a horse.'

'How gallant of you to point it out.' For no particular reason, she switched lanes, pumped the gas and passed another car. 'Let's just say I wasn't in the mood.'

'How did you manage to talk yourself into disliking what happened between us so quickly?' It hurt. He felt the hurt, but it didn't mean he had to let it show. His voice, as hers had been, was cool and hard.

'I haven't. That's absurd.' Dislike? She hadn't been able

to think of anything else, feel anything else. It scared her to death. 'We slept together.' She managed to toss it off with a shrug. 'I suppose we both knew we would sooner or later.'

He'd told himself precisely the same thing. He'd lost count of the number of times. He'd yet to figure out when he'd stopped believing. For himself. 'And that's it?'

The question was deadly calm, but she was too preoccupied with her own nerves to notice. 'What else?' She had to stop dwelling on a moment of impulse. Didn't she? She couldn't go on letting her common sense be overrun by an attraction that would lead nowhere. Could she? 'Michael, there's no use blowing what happened out of proportion.'

'Just what is that proportion?'

The car felt stuffy and close. Pandora switched off the heat and concentrated on the road. 'We're two adults,' she began, but had to swallow twice.

'And?'

'Dammit, Michael, I don't have to spell it out.'

'Yes, you do.'

'We're two adults,' she said again, but with temper replacing nerves. 'We have normal adult needs. We slept together and satisfied them.'

'How practical.'

'I am practical.' Abruptly, and very badly, she wanted to weep. 'Much too practical to weave fantasies about a man who likes his women in six packs. Too practical,' she went on, voice rising, 'to picture myself emotionally involved with a man I spent one night with. And too practical to romanticize what was no more than an exchange of normal and basic lust.'

'Pull over.'

'I will not.'

'Pull over to the shoulder, Pandora, or I'll do it for you.'

She gritted her teeth and debated calling his bluff. There was just enough traffic on the road to force her hand. With only a slight squeal of tires, Pandora pulled off to the side of the road. Michael turned off the key then grabbed her by the lapels and pulled her half into his seat. Before she could struggle away, he closed his mouth over hers.

Heat, anger, passion. They seemed to twist together into one emotion. He held her there as cars whizzed by, shaking the windows. She infuriated him, she aroused him, she hurt him. In Michael's opinion, it was too much for one man to take from one woman. As abruptly as he'd grabbed her, he released her.

'Make something practical out of that,' he challenged.

Breathless, Pandora struggled back into her own seat. In a furious gesture, she turned the key, gunning the motor. 'Idiot.'

'Yeah.' He sat back as she pulled back onto the highway. 'We finally agree on something.'

It was a long ride into the city. Longer still when you sat in a car in tense silence. Once they entered Manhattan, Pandora was forced to follow Michael's directions to the lab.

'How do you know where it is?' she demanded after

they left the car in a parking garage. The sidewalk was mobbed with people hurrying to exchange what had been brightly boxed and wrapped the day before. As they walked, Pandora held her coat closed against the wind.

'I looked the address up in Jolley's files yesterday.' Michael walked the half block hatless, his coat flapping open, clutching the box with the champagne under one arm. He wasn't immune to the cold but found it a relief after the hot tension of the drive. With a brisk gesture to Pandora, he pushed through revolving doors and entered the lobby of a steel-and-glass building. 'He owned the whole place.'

Pandora looked across the marble floor. It sloped upward and widened into a crowded, bustling area with men and women carrying briefcases. 'This whole place?'

'All seventy-two floors.'

It hit her again just how complicated the estate was. How many companies operated in the building? How many people worked there? How could she possibly crowd her life with this kind of responsibility? If she could get her hands on Uncle Jolley—Pandora broke off, almost amused. How he must be enjoying this, she thought.

'What am I supposed to do with seventy-two floors in midtown?'

'There are plenty of people to do it for you.' Michael gave their names to the guard at the elevators. With no delay, they were riding to the fortieth floor.

'So there are people to do it for us. Who keeps track of them?'

'Accountants, lawyers, managers. It's a matter of hiring people to look after people you hire.'

'That certainly clears that up.'

'If you're worried, think about Jolley. Having a fortune didn't seem to keep him from enjoying himself. For the most part, he looked at the whole business as a kind of hobby.'

Pandora watched the numbers above the door. 'A hobby.'

'Everyone should have a hobby.'

'Tennis is a hobby,' she muttered.

'The trick is to keep the ball moving. Jolley tossed it in our court, Pandora.'

She folded her arms. 'I'm not ready to be grateful for that.'

'Look at it this way then.' He put a hand on her shoulder and squeezed lightly. 'You don't have to know how to build a car to own one. You just have to drive steady and follow the signs. If Jolley didn't think we could follow the signs, he wouldn't have given us the keys.'

It helped to look at it that way. Still it was odd to consider she was riding on an elevator she would own when the six months were up. 'Do we know whom to go to?' Pandora glanced at the box Michael held, which contained the bottle of champagne.

'A man named Silas Lockworth seems to be in charge.'

'You did your homework.'

'Let's hope it pays off.'

When the elevator stopped, they walked into the reception area for Sanfield Laboratories. The carpet was pale rose, the walls lacquered in cream. Two huge split-leaf philodendrons flanked the wide glass doors that slid open at their approach. A woman behind a gleaming desk folded her hands and smiled.

'Good morning. May I help you?'

Michael glanced at the computer terminal resting on an extension of her desk. Top of the line. 'We'd like to see Mr. Lockworth.'

'Mr. Lockworth's in a meeting. If I could have your names, perhaps his assistant can help you.'

'I'm Michael Donahue. This is Pandora McVie.'

'McVie?'

Pandora saw the receptionist's eyebrows rise. 'Yes, Maximillian McVie was our uncle.'

Already polite and efficient, the receptionist became gracious. 'I'm sure Mr. Lockworth would have greeted you himself if we'd known you were coming. Please have a seat. I'll ring through.'

It took under five minutes.

The man who strode out into reception didn't look like Pandora's conception of a technician or scientist. He was six-three, lean as a gymnast with blond hair brushed back from a tanned, lantern-jawed face. He looked, Pandora thought, more like a man who'd be at home on the range than in a lab with test tubes.

'Ms. McVie.' He walked with an easy rolling gait, hand outstretched. 'Mr. Donahue. I'm Silas Lockworth. Your uncle was a good friend.'

'Thank you.' Michael accepted the handshake. 'I apologize for dropping in unannounced.'

'No need for that.' Lockworth's smile seemed to mean it. 'We never knew when Jolley was going to drop in on us. Let's go back to my office.'

He led them down the corridor. Lockworth's office was the next surprise. It was plush enough, with curvy chairs and clever lithographs, to make you think of a corporate executive. The desk was piled high with enough files and papers to make you think of a harried clerk. It carried the scent from the dozens of leather-bound books on a floor-to-ceiling shelf. Built into one wall was a round aquarium teeming with exotic fish.

'Would you like coffee? I can guarantee it's hot and strong.'

'No.' Pandora was already twisting her gloves in her hands. 'Thank you. We don't want to take too much of your time.'

'It's my pleasure,' Lockworth assured her. 'Jolley certainly spoke often of both of you,' Lockworth went on as he gestured to chairs. 'There was never a doubt you were his favorites.'

'And he was ours,' Pandora returned.

'Still you didn't come to pass the time.' Lockworth leaned back on his desk. 'What can I do for you?'

'We have something we'd like analyzed,' Michael began. 'Quickly and quietly.'

'I see.' Silas stopped there, brow raised. Lockworth was a man who picked up impressions of people right away. In Pandora he saw nerves under a sheen of politeness. In Michael he saw violence, not so much buried as thinly coated. He thought he detected a bond between them though they hadn't so much as looked at each other since entering the room.

Lockworth could have refused. His staff was slimmed down during the holidays, and work was backlogged. He was under no obligation to either of them yet. But he never forgot his obligation to Jolley McVie. 'We'll try to accommodate you.'

In silence, Michael opened the box and drew out the bottle of champagne. 'We need a report on the contents of this bottle. A confidential report. Today.'

Lockworth took it and examined the label. His lips curved slightly. 'Seventy-two. A good year. Were you thinking of starting a vineyard?'

'We need to know what's in there other than champagne.'

Rather than showing surprise, Lockworth leaned back on the desk again. 'You've reason to think there is?'

Michael met the look. 'We wouldn't be here otherwise.'

Lockworth only inclined his head. 'All right. I'll run it through the lab myself.'

With a quick scowl for Michael's manners, Pandora rose and offered her hand. 'We appreciate the trouble, Mr. Lockworth. I'm sure you have a great many other things to do, but the results are important to Michael and me.'

'No problem.' He decided he'd find out why it was important after he'd analyzed the wine. 'There's a coffee shop for the staff. I'll show you where it is. You can wait for me there.'

'There was absolutely no reason to be rude.' Pandora settled herself at a table and looked at a surprisingly varied menu.

'I wasn't rude.'

'Of course you were. Mr. Lockworth was going out of his way to be friendly, and you had a chip on your shoulder. I think I'm going to have the shrimp salad.'

'I don't have a chip on my shoulder. I was being cautious. Or maybe you think we should spill everything to a total stranger.'

Pandora folded her hands and smiled at the waitress. 'I'd like the shrimp salad and coffee.'

'Two coffees,' Michael muttered. 'And the turkey platter.'

'I've no intention of spilling, as you put it, everything to a total stranger.' Pandora picked up her napkin. 'However, if we weren't going to trust Lockworth, we'd have been better off to buy a chemistry set and try to handle it ourselves.'

'Drink your coffee,' Michael muttered, and picked up his own the moment the waitress served it.

Pandora frowned as she added cream. 'How long do you think it'll take?'

'I don't know. I'm not a scientist.'

'He didn't look like one, either, did he?'

'Bronc rider.' Michael sipped his black coffee and found it as strong as Lockworth had promised.

'What?'

'Looks like a bronc rider. I wonder if Carlson or any of the others have any interest in this building.'

Pandora set her coffee down before she tasted it. 'I hadn't thought of that.'

'As I remember, Jolley turned over Tristar Corporation to Monroe about twenty-five years ago. I remember my parents talking about it.'

'Tristar. Which one is that?'

'Plastics. I know he gave little pieces of the pie out here and there. He told me once he wanted to give all his relatives a chance before he crossed them off the list.'

After a moment's thought, she shrugged and picked up her coffee again. 'Well, if he did give a few shares of Sanfield to one of them, what difference does it make?'

'I don't know how much we should trust Lockworth.'

'You'd have felt better if he'd been bald and short with Coke-bottle glasses and a faint German accent.'

'Maybe.'

'See?' Pandora smiled. 'You're just jealous because he has great shoulders.' She fluttered her lashes. 'Here's your turkey.'

They ate slowly, drank more coffee, then passed more time with pie. After an hour and a half, both of them were restless and edgy. When Lockworth came in, Pandora forgot to be nervous about the results.

'Thank God, here he comes.'

After maneuvering around chairs and employees on lunch break, Lockworth set a computer printout on the table and handed the box back to Michael. 'I thought you'd want a copy.' He took a seat and signaled for coffee. 'Though it's technical.'

Pandora frowned down at the long, chemical terms printed out on the paper. It meant little more than nothing to her, but she doubted trichloroethanol or any of the other multisyllabic words belonged in French champagne. 'What does it mean?'

'I wondered that myself.' Lockworth reached in his pocket and drew out a pack of cigarettes. Michael looked at it for a moment with longing. 'I wondered why anyone would put rose dust in vintage champagne.'

'Rose dust?' Michael repeated. 'Pesticide. So it was poisoned.'

'Technically, yes. Though there wasn't enough in the wine to do any more than make you miserably ill for a day or two. I take it neither one of you had any?'

'No.' Pandora looked up from the report. 'My puppy did,' she explained. 'When we opened the bottle, some spilled and he lapped it up. Before we'd gotten around to drinking it, he was ill.'

'Luckily for you, though I find it curious that you'd jumped to the conclusion that the champagne had been poisoned because a puppy was sick.'

'Luckily for us, we did.' Michael folded the report and slipped it into his pocket.

'You'll have to pardon my cousin,' Pandora said. 'He has no manners. We appreciate you taking time out to do this for us, Mr. Lockworth. I'm afraid it isn't possible to fully explain ourselves at this point, but I can tell you that we had good reason to suspect the wine.'

Lockworth nodded. As a scientist he knew how to theorize. 'If you find you need a more comprehensive report, let me know. Jolley was an important person in my life. We'll call it a favor to him.'

As he rose, Michael stood with him. 'I'll apologize for myself this time.' He held out a hand.

'I'd be a bit edgy myself if someone gave me pesticide disguised as Moët et Chandon. Let me know if I can do anything else.'

'Well,' Pandora began when they were alone. 'What next?'

'A little trip to the liquor store. We've some presents to buy.'

They sent, first-class, a bottle of the same to each of Jolley's erstwhile heirs. Michael signed the cards simply, 'One good turn deserves another.' After it was done and they walked outside in the frigid wind, Pandora huffed and pulled on her gloves.

'An expensive gesture.'

'Look at it as an investment,' Michael suggested.

It wasn't the money, she thought, but the sudden futility she felt. 'What good will it do really?'

'Several bottles'll be wondered over, then appreciated. But one,' Michael said with relish. 'One makes a statement, even a threat.'

'An empty threat,' Pandora returned. 'It's not as if we'll be there when everyone gets one to gauge reactions.'

'You're thinking like an amateur.'

Michael was halfway across the street when Pandora grabbed his arm. 'Just what does that mean?'

'When an amateur plays a practical joke, he thinks he has to be in on the kill.'

Ignoring the people who brushed by them, Pandora

held her ground. 'Since when is pesticide poisoning a practical joke?'

'Revenge follows the same principle.'

'Oh, I see. And you're an expert.'

The light changed. Cars started for them, horns blaring. Gritting his teeth, Michael grabbed her arm and pulled her to the curb. 'Maybe I am. It's enough for me to know someone's going to look at the bottle and be very nervous. Someone's going to look at it and know we intend to give as good as we get. Your trouble is you don't like to let your emotions loose long enough to appreciate revenge.'

'Leave my emotions alone.'

'That's the plan,' he said evenly, and started walking again.

In three strides she'd caught up with him. Her face was pink from the wind, the anger in her voice came out in thin wisps. 'You're not annoyed with Lockworth or about the champagne or over differing views on revenge. You're mad because I defined our relationship in practical terms.'

He stared at her as her phrasing worked on both his temper and his humor. 'Okay,' he declared, turning to walk on. Patience straining, he turned back when Pandora grabbed his arm. 'You want to hash this out right here?'

'I won't let you make me feel inadequate just because I broke things off before you had a chance to.'

'Before I had a chance to?' He took her by the coat. With the added height from the heels on her boots, she looked straight into his eyes. Another time, another place, he might have considered her magnificent. 'I barely had the chance to recover from what happened before you were shoving me out. I wanted you. Dammit, I still want you. God knows why.'

'Well, I want you, too, and I don't like it, either.'

'Looks like that puts us in the same fix, doesn't it?'

'So what're we going to do about it?'

He looked at her and saw the anger. But he looked closely enough to see confusion, as well. One of them had to make the first move. He decided it was going to be him. Taking her hand, he dragged her across the street.

'Where are we going?'

'The Plaza.'

'The Plaza Hotel? Why?'

'We're going to get a room, put the chain on the door and make love for the next twenty-four hours. After that, we'll decide how we want to handle it.'

There were times, Pandora decided, when it was best to go along for the ride. 'We don't have any luggage.'

'Yeah. My reputation's about to be shattered.'

She made a sound that might have been a laugh. When they walked into the elegant lobby, the heat warmed her skin and stirred up her nerves. It was all impulse, she told herself. She knew better than to make any important decision on impulse. He could change everything. That was something she hadn't wanted to admit but had known for years. When she started to draw away, his hand locked on her arm.

'Coward,' he murmured. He couldn't have said anything more perfectly designed to make her march forward.

'Good afternoon.' Michael smiled at the desk clerk. Pandora wondered briefly if the smile would have been so charming if the clerk had been a man. 'Checking in.'

'You have a reservation?'

'Donahue. Michael Donahue.'

The clerk punched some buttons and stared at her computer screen. 'I'm afraid I don't show anything under Donahue for the twenty-sixth.'

'Katie,' Michael said on a breath of impatience. He sent Pandora a long suffering look. 'I should never have trusted her to handle this.'

Catching the drift, Pandora patted his hand. 'You're going to have to let her go, Michael. I know she's worked for your family for forty years, but when a person gets into their seventies...' She trailed off and let Michael take the ball.

'We'll decide when we get home.' He turned back to the desk clerk. 'Apparently there's been a mix-up between my secretary and the hotel. We'll only be in town overnight. Is anything available?'

The clerk went back to her buttons. Most people in her experience raised the roof when there was a mix-up in reservations. Michael's quiet request touched her sympathies. 'You understand there's a problem because of the holiday.' She punched more buttons, wanting to help. 'We do have a suite available.'

'Fine.' Michael took the registration form and filled it out. With the key in his hand, he sent the clerk another smile. 'I appreciate the trouble.' Noting the bellhop hovering at his elbow, he handed him a bill. 'We'll handle it, thanks.'

The clerk looked at the twenty in his palm and the lack of luggage. 'Yes, sir!'

'He thinks we're having an illicit affair,' Pandora murmured as they stepped onto the elevator.

'We are.' Before the doors had closed again, Michael grabbed her to him and locked her in a kiss that lasted twelve floors. 'We don't know each other,' he told her as they stepped into the hallway. 'We've just met. We don't have mutual childhood memories or share the same family.' He put the key in the lock. 'We don't give a damn what the other does for a living nor do we have any longstanding opinions about each other.'

'Is that supposed to simplify things?'

Michael drew her inside. 'Let's find out.'

He didn't give her a chance to wonder, a chance to debate. The moment the door was shut behind them, he had her in his arms. He took questions away. He took choice away. For once, she wanted him to. In a fury of passions, of hungers, of cravings, they came together. Each fought to draw more, still more out of the other, to touch faster, to possess more quickly. They forgot what they knew, what they thought and reveled in what they felt.

Coats, still chill from the wind, were pushed to the floor. Sweaters and shirts followed. Hardly more than a foot inside the door, they slid to the carpet.

'Damn winter,' Michael muttered as he fought with her boots.

Laughing, Pandora struggled with his, then moaned when he pressed his lips to her breast.

It was a race, part warring, part loving. Neither gave the other respite. When their clothes were shed, they sprinted ahead, hands reaching, lips arousing. There was none of the dreamy déjà vu they'd experienced the first time. This was new. The fingers tracing her skin had never been felt before. The lips, hot and searing, had never been tasted. Fresh, erotically fresh, their mouths met and clung.

Her heart had never beat so fast. She was sure of it. Her body had never ached and pulsed so desperately. She'd never wanted it to. Now she wanted more, everything. Him. She rolled so that she could press quick, hungry kisses over his face, his neck, his chest. Everywhere.

His mind was teeming with her, with every part of her that he could touch or taste or smell. She was wild in a way he'd never imagined. She was demanding in a way any man would desire. His body seemed to fascinate her, every curve, every angle. She exploited it until he was half mad, then he groped for her.

She'd never known a man could give so much. Racked with sensations, she arched under him. Hot and ready, she offered. But he was far from through. The taste of her thighs was subtle, luring him toward the heat. He found her, drove her and kept her helplessly trapped in passion. Helplessly. The sensation shivered over her. She'd never known what it had meant to be truly vulnerable to another. He could have taken anything from her then, asked anything and she couldn't have refused. But he didn't ask, he gave.

She crested wave after wave. Between heights and depths she pinwheeled, delighting in the spin. On the rug with the afternoon light streaming through the windows, she was locked in blinding darkness without any wish to see. *Make me feel,* her mind seemed to shout. More. Again. Still.

And he was inside her, joined, melded. She found there was more. Impossibly more.

They stayed where they were, sprawled on scattered clothes. Gradually Pandora found her mind swimming back to reality. She could see the pastel walls, the sunlight. She could smell the body heat that was a mix of hers and his. She could feel Michael's hair brushing over her cheek, the beat of his heart, still fast, against her breast.

It happened so fast, she thought. Or had it taken hours? All she was certain of was that she'd never experienced anything like it. Never permitted herself to, she amended. Strange things could happen to a woman who lifted the lid from her passion. Other things could sneak in before the top closed again. Things like affection, understanding. Even love.

She caught herself stroking Michael's hair and let her hand fall to the carpet. She couldn't let love in, not even briefly. Love took as well as gave. That she'd always known. And it didn't always give and take in equal shares. Michael wasn't a man a woman could love practically, and certainly not wisely. That she understood. He wouldn't follow the rules.

She'd be his lover, but she wouldn't love him. Though there would be no pretending they could live with each other for the next three months platonically, she wouldn't risk her heart. For an instant Pandora thought she felt it break, just a little. Foolishness, she told herself. Her heart was strong and unimpaired. What she and Michael had together was a very basic, very uncomplicated arrangement. Arrangement, she thought, sounded so much more practical than romance.

But her sigh was quiet, and a little wistful.

'Figure it all out?' He shifted a little as he spoke, just enough so that he could brush his lips down her throat.

'What do you mean?'

'Have you figured out the guidelines for our relationship?' Lifting his head, he looked down at her. He wasn't smiling, but Pandora thought he was amused.

'I don't know what you're talking about.'

'I can almost hear the wheels turning. Pandora, I can see just what's going on in your head.'

Annoyed that he probably could, she lifted a brow. 'I thought we'd just met.'

'I'm psychic. You're thinking....' He trailed off to nibble at her lips. 'That there should be a way to keep our... relationship on a practical level. You're wondering how you'll keep an emotional distance when we're sleeping together. You've decided that there'll be absolutely no romantic overtones to any arrangement between us.'

'All right.' He made her feel foolish. Then he ran a

hand over her hip and made her tremble. 'Since you're so smart, you'll see that I've only been using common sense.'

'I like it better when your skin gets hot, and you haven't any sense at all. But—' he kissed her before she could answer '—we can't stay in bed all the time. I don't believe in practical affairs, Pandora. I don't believe in emotional distance between lovers.'

'You've had a great deal of experience there.'

'That's right.' He sat up, drawing her with him. 'And I'll tell you this. You can wall up your emotions all you want. You can call whatever we have here by any practical term you can dream up. You can turn up your nose at candlelight dinners and quiet music. It's not going to make any difference.' He gathered her hair in his hand and pulled her head back. 'I'm going to get to you, cousin. I'm going to get to you until you can't think of anything, anyone but me. If you wake up in the middle of the night and I'm not there, you'll wish I were. And when I touch you, any time I touch you, you're going to want me.'

She had to fight the shudder. She knew, as well as she'd ever known anything, that he was right. And she knew, perhaps they both did, that she'd fight it right down to the end. 'You're arrogant, egocentric and simpleminded.'

'True enough. And you're stubborn, willful and perverse. The only thing we can be sure of at this point is that one of us is going to win.'

Sitting on the pile of discarded clothes, they studied each other. 'Another game?' Pandora murmured.

'Maybe. Maybe it's the only game.' With that, he stood and lifted her into his arms.

'Michael, I don't need to be carried.'

'Yes, you do.'

He walked across the suite toward the bedroom. Pandora started to struggle, then subsided. Maybe just this once, she decided, and relaxed in his arms.

Chapter 9

January was a month of freezing wind, pelting snow and gray skies. Each day was as bitterly cold as the last, with tomorrow waiting frigidly in the wings. It was a month of frozen pipes, burst pipes, overworked furnaces and stalled engines. Pandora loved it. The frost built up on the windows of her shop, and the inside temperature always remained cool even with the heaters turned up. She worked until her fingers were numb and enjoyed every moment.

Throughout the month, the road to the Folley was often inaccessible. Pandora didn't mind not being able to get out. It meant no one could get in. The pantry and freezer were stocked, and there was over a cord of wood stacked beside the kitchen door. The way she looked at it, they had everything they needed. The days were short and productive, the nights long and relaxing. Since the incident of the champagne, it had been a quiet, uneventful winter.

Uneventful, Pandora mused, wasn't precisely the right term. With quick, careful strokes, she filed the edges of a thick copper bracelet. It certainly wasn't as though nothing had happened. There'd been no trouble from outside sources, but… Trouble, as she'd always known, was definitely one of Michael Donahue's greatest talents.

Just what was he trying to pull by leaving a bunch of violets on her pillow? She was certain a magic wand would have been needed to produce the little purple flowers in January. When she'd questioned him about them, he'd simply smiled and told her violets didn't have thorns. What kind of an answer was that? Pandora wondered, and examined the clasp of the bracelet through a magnifying glass. She was satisfied with the way she'd designed it to blend with the design.

Then, there'd been the time she'd come out of the bath to find the bedroom lit with a dozen candles. When she'd asked if there'd been a power failure, Michael had just laughed and pulled her into bed.

He did things like reaching for her hand at dinner and whispering in her ear just before dawn. Once he'd joined her in the shower uninvited and silenced her protests by washing every inch of her body himself. She'd been right. Michael Donahue didn't follow the rules. He'd been right. He was getting to her.

Pandora removed the bracelet from the vise, then absently began to polish it. She'd made a half a dozen others in the last two weeks. Big chunky bracelets, some had gaudy stones, some had ornate engraving. They suited her mood—daring, opinionated and a bit silly. She'd learned to trust her instincts, and her instincts told her they'd sell faster than she could possibly make them—and be copied just as quickly.

She didn't mind the imitations. After all, there was only one of each type that was truly a Pandora McVie. Copies would be recognized as copies because they lacked that something special, that individuality of the genuine.

Pleased, she turned the bracelet over in her hand. No one would mistake any of her work for an imitation. She might often use glass instead of precious or semiprecious stones because glass expressed her mood at the time. But each piece she created carried her mark, her opinion and her honesty. She never gave a thought to the price of a piece when she crafted it or its market value. She created what she needed to create first, then after it was done, her practical side calculated the profit margin. Her art varied from piece to piece, but it never lied.

Looking down at the bracelet, Pandora sighed. No, her art never lied, but did she? Could she be certain her emotions were as genuine as the jewelry she made? A feeling could be imitated. An emotion could be fraudulent. How many times in the past few weeks had she pretended? Not pretended to feel, Pandora thought, but pretended not to feel. She was a woman who'd always prided herself on her honesty. Truth and independence went hand in hand with Pandora's set of values. But she'd lied—over and over again—to herself, the worst form of deception.

It was time to stop, Pandora told herself. Time to face the truth of her feelings if only in the privacy of her own heart and mind.

How long had she been in love with Michael? She had to stand and move around the shop as the question formed in her mind. Weeks? Months? Years? It wasn't something she could answer because she would never be sure. But she was certain of the emotion. She loved. Pandora understood it because she loved only a few people, and when she did, she loved boundlessly. Perhaps that was the biggest problem. Wasn't it a sort of suicide to love Michael boundlessly?

Better to face it, she told herself. No problem resolved itself without being faced first and examined second. However much a fool it made her, she loved Michael. Pandora rubbed at the steam on the windows and looked out at the snow. Strange, she'd really believed once she accepted it she'd feel better. She didn't.

What options did she have? She could tell him. And have him gloat, Pandora thought with a scowl. He would, too, before he trotted off to his next conquest. *She* certainly wasn't fool enough to think he'd be interested in a long-term relationship. Of course, she wasn't interested in one either, Pandora told herself as she began to noisily pack her tools.

Another option was to cut and run. What the relatives hadn't been able to accomplish with their malice and mischief, her own heart would succeed in doing. She could get in the car, drive to the airport and fly to anywhere. Escape was the honest word. Then, she'd not only be a coward, she'd be a traitor. No, she wouldn't let Uncle Jolley down; she wouldn't run. That left her, as Pandora saw it, with one option.

She'd go on as she was. She'd stay with Michael, sleep with Michael, share with Michael—share with him everything but what was in her heart. She'd take the two months they had left together and prepare herself to walk away with no regrets.

He'd gotten to her, Pandora admitted. Gotten to her in places no other man had touched. She loved him for it. She hated him for it. With her mood as turbulent as her thoughts, she locked the shop and stomped across the lawn.

'Here she comes now.' With a new plan ready to spring, Sweeney turned away from the kitchen window and signaled to Charles.

'It's never going to work.'

'Of course it is. We're going to push those children together for their own good. Any two people who spat as much as they do should be married.'

'We're interfering where it's not our place.'

'What malarkey!' Sweeney took her seat at the kitchen table. 'Whose place is it to interfere if not ours, I'd like to know? Who'll be knocking around this big empty house if they go back to the city if not us? Now pick up that cloth and fan me. Stoop over a bit and look feeble.'

'I am feeble,' Charles muttered, but picked up the cloth.

When Pandora walked into the kitchen she saw Sweeney sprawled back in a chair, eyes closed, with Charles standing over her waving a dishcloth at her face.

'God, what's wrong? Charles, did she faint?' Before he could answer, Pandora had dashed across the room. 'Call Michael,' she ordered. 'Call Michael quickly.' She brushed Charles away and crouched. 'Sweeney, it's Pandora. Are you in pain?'

Barely suppressing a sigh of satisfaction, Sweeney let her eyes flutter open and hoped she looked pale. 'Oh, missy, don't you worry now. Just one of my spells is all. Now and then my heart starts to flutter so that I feel it's coming right out of my head.'

'I'm going to call the doctor.' Pandora had taken only one step when her hand was caught in a surprisingly strong grip.

'No need for that.' Sweeney made her voice thin and weary. 'Saw him just a few months past and he told me I'd have to expect one of these now and again.'

'I don't believe that,' Pandora said fiercely. 'You're just plain working too hard, and it's going to stop.'

A little trickle of guilt worked its way in as Sweeney saw the concern. 'Now, now, don't fret.'

'What is it?' Michael swung through the kitchen door. 'Sweeney?' He knelt down beside her and took her other hand.

'Now look at all this commotion.' Mentally she leaped up and kicked her heels. 'It's nothing but one of my little spells. The doctor said I'd have to watch for them. Just a nuisance, that's all.' She looked hard at Charles when he came in. Eventually she looked hard enough so that he remembered his cue.

'And you know what he said.'

'Now, Charles—'

'You're to have two or three days of bed rest.'

Pleased that he'd remembered his lines, Sweeney pretended to huff. 'Pack of nonsense. I'll be right as rain in a few minutes. I've dinner to cook.'

'You won't be cooking anything.' In a way Sweeney considered properly masterful, Michael picked her up. 'Into bed with you.'

'Just who'll take care of things?' Sweeney demanded. 'I'll not have Charles spreading his germs around my kitchen.'

Michael was nearly out of the room with Sweeney before Charles remembered the next step. He coughed into his hand, looked apologetic and coughed again.

'Listen to that!' Pleased, Sweeney let her head rest against Michael's shoulder. 'I won't go to bed and let him infect my kitchen.'

'How long have you had that cough?' Pandora demanded. When Charles began to mutter, she stood up. 'That's enough. Both of you into bed. Michael and I will take care of everything.' Taking Charles's arm, she began to lead him into the servants' wing. 'Into bed and no nonsense. I'll make both of you some tea. Michael, see that Charles gets settled, I'll look after Sweeney.'

Within a half hour, Sweeney had them both where she wanted them. Together.

'Well, they're all settled in and there's no fever.' Satisfied, Pandora poured herself a cup of tea. 'I suppose all they need is a few days' rest and some pampering. Tea?'

He made a face at the idea and switched on the coffee.

'Since the days of house calls are over, I'd think they'd be better off here in bed than being dragged into town. We can take turns keeping an eye on them.'

'Mmm-hmm.' Pandora opened the refrigerator and studied. 'What about meals? Can you cook?'

'Sure.' Michael rattled cups in the cupboard. 'Badly, but I can cook. Meat loaf's my specialty.' When this was met with no enthusiasm, he turned his head. 'Do you?'

'Cook?' Pandora lifted a plastic lid hopefully. 'I can broil a steak and scramble eggs. Anything else is chancy.'

'Life's nothing without a risk.' Michael joined her in her rummage through the refrigerator. 'Here's almost half an apple cobbler.'

'That's hardly a meal.'

'It'll do for me.' He took it out and went for a spoon. Pandora watched as he sat down at the table and dug in. 'Want some?'

She started to refuse on principle, then decided not to cut off her nose. Going to the cupboard, she found a bowl. 'What about the bedridden?' she asked as she scooped out cobbler.

'Soup,' Michael said between bites. 'Nothing better than hot soup. Though I'd let them rest awhile first.'

With a nod of agreement, she sat across from him. 'Michael…' She trailed off as she played with her cobbler. The steam from her tea rose up between them. She'd been thinking about how to broach the subject for days. It seemed the time had come. 'I've been thinking. In two months, the will should be final. When Fitzhugh wrote us last week, he said Uncle Carlson's lawyers were advising him to drop the probate.'

'So?'

'The house, along with everything else, will be half yours, half mine.'

'That's right.'

She took a bite of cobbler, then set down her spoon. 'What're you smiling at?'

'You're nice to look at. I find it relaxing to sit here alone in the kitchen, in the quiet, and look at you.'

It was that sort of thing, just that sort of thing, that left her light-headed and foolish. She stared at him a moment, then dropped her gaze to her bowl. 'I wish you wouldn't say things like that.'

'No, you don't. So you've been thinking,' he prompted.

'Yes.' She gave herself a moment, carefully spooning out another bite of cobbler. 'We'll have the house between us, but we won't be living here together any longer. Sweeney and Charles will be here alone. I've worried about that for a while. Now, after this, I'm more concerned than ever. They can't stay here alone.'

'No, I think you're right. Ideas?'

'I mentioned before that I was considering moving here on a semipermanent basis.' She found she had no appetite after all and switched back to her tea. 'I think I'm going to make it permanent all around.'

He heard a trace of nervousness in her voice. 'Because of Charles and Sweeney?'

'Only partly.' She drank more tea, set the cup down and toyed with her cobbler again. She wasn't accustomed to discussing her decisions with anyone. Though she found it difficult, Pandora had already resolved that she had an obligation to do so. More, she'd realized she needed to talk to him, to be, as she couldn't be on other levels, honest. 'I always felt the Folley was home, but I didn't realize just how much of a home. I need it, for myself. You see, I never had one.' She lifted her gaze and met his. 'Only here.'

To say her words surprised him was to say too little. All his life he'd seen her as the pampered pet, the golden girl with every advantage. 'But your parents—'

'Are wonderful,' Pandora said quickly. 'I adore them. There's nothing about them I'd change. But...' How could she explain? How could she not? 'We never had a kitchen like this—a place you could come back to day after day and know it'd be the same. Even if you changed the wallpaper and the paint, it would be the same. It sounds silly.' She shifted restlessly. 'You wouldn't understand.'

'Maybe I would.' He caught her hand before she could rise. 'Maybe I'd like to.'

'I want a home,' she said simply. 'The Folley's been that to me. I want to stay here after the term's up.'

He kept her hand in his, palm to palm. 'Why are you telling me this, Pandora?'

Reasons. Too many reasons. She chose the only one she could give him safely. 'In two months, the house belongs to you as much as to me. According to the terms of the will—'

He swore and released her hand. Rising, he stuck his hands in his back pockets and strode to the window. He'd thought for a moment, just for a moment, she'd been ready to give him more. By God, he'd waited long enough for only a few drops more. There'd been something in her voice, something soft and giving. Perhaps he'd just imagined it because he'd wanted to hear it. Terms of the will, he thought. It was so like her to see nothing else.

'What do you want, my permission?'

Disturbed, Pandora stayed at the table. 'I suppose I wanted you to understand and agree.'

'Fine.'

'You needn't be so curt about it. After all, you haven't any plans to use the house on a regular basis.'

'I haven't made any plans,' he murmured. 'Perhaps it's time I did.'

'I didn't mean to annoy you.'

He turned slowly, then just as slowly smiled. 'No, I'm sure you didn't. There's never any doubt when you annoy me intentionally.'

There was something wrong here, something she couldn't quite pinpoint. So she groped. 'Would you mind so much if I were to live here?'

It surprised him when she rose to come to him, offering a hand. She didn't make such gestures often or casually. 'No, why should it?'

'It would be half yours.'

'We could draw a line down the middle.'

'That might be awkward. I could buy you out.'

'No.'

He said it so fiercely, her brows shot up. 'It was only an offer.'

'Forget it.' He turned to look for soup.

Pandora stood back a moment, watching his back, the tension in the muscles. 'Michael...' With a sigh, she wrapped her arms around his waist. She felt him stiffen, but didn't realize it was from surprise. 'I seem to be saying all the wrong things. Maybe I have an easier time when we snap at each other than when I try to be considerate.'

'Maybe we both do.' He turned to frame her face with his hands. For a moment they looked like friends, like lovers. 'Pandora....' Could he tell her he found it impossible to think about leaving her or her leaving him? Would she understand if he told her he wanted to go on living with her, being with her? How could she possibly take in the fact that he'd been in love with her for years when he was just becoming able to accept it himself? Instead he kissed her forehead. 'Let's make soup.'

They couldn't work together without friction, but they discovered over the next few days that they could work together. They cooked meals, washed up, dusted furniture while the servants stayed in bed or sat, bundled up, on sofas drinking tea. True, there were times when Sweeney itched to get up and be about her business, or when Charles suffered pangs of conscience, but they were convinced they were doing their duty. Both servants felt justified when they heard laughter drift through the house.

Michael wasn't sure there had been another time in his life when he'd been so content. He was, in essence, playing house, something he'd never had the time or in-

clination for. He would write for hours, closed off in his
office, wrapped up in plots and characters and what-ifs.
Then he could break away and reality was the scent of
cooking or furniture polish. He had a home, a woman,
and was determined to keep them.

Late in the afternoon, he always laid a fire in the parlor. After dinner they had coffee there, sometimes quietly, sometimes during a hard-fought game of rummy.
It seemed ordinary, Michael admitted. It was ordinary,
unless you added Pandora. He was just setting fire to
the kindling when Bruno raced into the room and upset
a table. Knickknacks went flying.

'We're going to have to send you to charm school,' Michael declared as he rose to deal with the rubble. Though
it had been just over a month, Bruno had nearly doubled
in size already. He was, without a doubt, going to grow
into his paws. After righting the table, he saw the dog
wiggling its way under a sofa. 'What've you got there?'

Besides being large, Bruno had already earned a reputation as a clever thief. Just the day before, they'd lost a
slab of pork chops. 'All right, you devil, if that's tonight's
chicken, you're going into solitary confinement in the garage.' Getting down on all fours, Michael looked under
the couch. It wasn't chicken the dog was gnawing noisily on, but Michael's shoe.

'Damn!' Michael made a grab but the dog backed out
of reach and kept on chewing. 'That shoe's worth five
times what you are, you overgrown mutt. Give it here.'
Flattening, Michael scooted halfway under the sofa.

Bruno merely dragged the shoe away again, enjoying the game.

'Oh, how sweet.' Pandora walked into the parlor and eyed Michael from the waist down. He did, she decided, indeed have some redeeming qualities. 'Are you playing with the dog, Michael, or dusting under the sofa?'

'I'm going to make a rug out of him.'

'Dear, dear, we sound a little cross this evening. Bruno, here baby.' Carrying the shoe like a trophy, Bruno squirmed out from under the couch and pranced over to her. 'Is this what you were after?' Pandora held up the shoe while petting Bruno with her other hand. 'How clever of you to teach Bruno to fetch.'

Michael pulled himself up, then yanked the shoe out of her hand. It was unfortunately wet and covered with teeth marks. 'That's the second shoe he's ruined. And he didn't even have the courtesy to take both from one pair.'

She looked down at what had been creamy Italian leather. 'You never wear anything but tennis shoes or boots anyway.'

Michael slapped the shoe against his palm. Bruno, tongue lolling, grinned up at him. 'Obedience school.'

'Oh, Michael, we can't send our child away.' She patted his cheek. 'It's just a phase.'

'This phase has cost me two pairs of shoes, my dinner and we never did find that sweater he dragged off.'

'You shouldn't drop your clothes on the floor,' Pandora said easily. 'And that sweater was already ratty. I'm sure Bruno thought it was a rag.'

'He never chews up anything of yours.'

Pandora smiled. 'No, he doesn't, does he?'

Michael gave her a long look. 'Just what're you so happy about?'

'I had a phone call this afternoon.'

Michael saw the excitement in her eyes and decided the issue of the shoe could wait. 'And?'

'From Jacob Morison.'

'The producer?'

'*The* producer,' Pandora repeated. She'd promised herself she wouldn't overreact, but the excitement threatened to burst inside her. 'He's going to be filming a new movie. Jessica Wainwright's starring.'

Jessica Wainwright, Michael mused. Grande dame of the theater and the screen. Eccentric and brilliant, her career had spanned two generations. 'She's retired. Wainwright hasn't made a film in five years.'

'She's making this one. Billy Mitchell's directing.'

Michael tilted his head in consideration as he studied Pandora's face. It made him think of the cat and the canary. 'Sounds like they're pulling out all the stops.'

'She plays a half-mad reclusive countess who's dragged back to reality by a visit from her granddaughter. Cass Barkley's on the point of signing for the part of the granddaughter.'

'Oscar material. Now, are you going to tell me why Morison called you?'

'Wainwright's an admirer of my work. She wants me to design all her jewelry for the movie. All!' After an attempt to sound businesslike, Pandora laughed and did a quick spin. 'Morison said the only way he could talk her out of retirement was to promise her the best. She wants me.'

Michael grabbed her close and spun her around. Bruno raced around the room barking and shaking tables. 'We'll celebrate,' he decided. 'Champagne with our fried chicken.'

Pandora held on tight. 'I feel like an idiot.'

'Why?'

'I've always thought I was, well, beyond star adoration. I'm a professional.' Bubbling with excitement, she clung to Michael. 'While I was talking to Morison I told myself it was a great career opportunity, a wonderful chance to express myself in a large way. Then I hung up and all I could think was Jessica Wainwright! A Morison production! I felt as silly as any bubble-headed fan.'

'Proves you're not half the snob you think you are.' Michael cut off her retort with a kiss. 'I'm proud of you,' he murmured.

That threw her off. All of her pleasure in the assignment was dwarfed by that one sentence. No one but Jolley had ever been proud of her. Her parents loved her, patted her head and told her to do what she wanted. Pride was a valued addition to affection. 'Really?'

Surprised, Michael drew her back and kissed her again. 'Of course I am.'

'But you've never thought much of my work.'

'No, that's not true. I've never understood why people feel the need to deck themselves out in bangles, or why you seemed content to design on such a small scale. But as far as your work goes I'm not blind, Pandora. Some

of it's beautiful, some of it's extraordinary and soi.
it's incomprehensible. But it's all imaginative and ϵ
pertly crafted.'

'Well.' She let out a long breath. 'This is a red-letter
day. I always thought you felt I was playing with beads
because I didn't want to face a real job. You even said
so once.'

He grinned. 'Only because it made you furious. You're
spectacular to look at when you're furious.'

She thought about it a moment, then let out a sigh. 'I
suppose this is the best time to tell you.'

He tensed, but forced his voice to come calmly. 'To
tell me what?'

'I watch the Emmy Awards every time you're nomi-
nated.'

Tension flowed out in a laugh. There'd been guilt in
every syllable. 'What?'

'Every time,' Pandora repeated, amazed that her
cheeks were warm. 'It made me feel good to watch you
win. And…' She paused to clear her throat. 'I've watched
a few episodes of *Logan's Run.*'

Michael wondered if she realized she sounded as
though she was confessing a major social flaw. 'Why?'

'Uncle Jolley was always going on about it; I'd even
hear it discussed at parties. So I thought I'd see for myself. Naturally, it was just a matter of intellectual curiosity.'

'Naturally. And?'

She moved her shoulders. 'Of its kind—'

He stopped that line of response by twisting her ear. 'Some people only tell the truth under duress.'

'All right.' Half laughing, she reached to free herself. 'It's good!' she shouted when he held on. 'I liked it.'

'Why?'

'Michael, that hurts!'

'We have ways of making you talk.'

'I liked it because the characters are genuine, the plots are intelligent. And—' she had to swallow hard on this one '—it has style.'

When he let go of her ear to kiss her soundly, she gave him a halfhearted shove. 'If you repeat that to anyone, I'll deny it.'

'It'll be our little secret.' He kissed her again, not so playfully.

Pandora was almost becoming used to the sensation of having her muscles loosen and feeling as if her bones were dissolving. She moved closer, delighting in the feeling of having her body mold against his. When his heart thudded, she felt the pulse inside herself. When his tiny moan escaped, she tasted it on her tongue. When the need leaped forward, she saw it in his eyes.

She pressed her mouth to his again and let her own hunger rule. There would be consequences. Hadn't she already accepted it? There would be pain. She was already braced for it. She couldn't stop what would happen in the weeks ahead, but she could direct what would happen tonight and perhaps tomorrow. It had to be enough. Everything she felt, wanted, feared, went into the kiss.

It left him reeling. She was often passionate, wildly so.

She was often demanding, erotically so. But he'd never felt such pure emotion from her. There was a softness under the strength, a request under the urgency. He drew her closer, more gently than was his habit, and let her take what she wanted.

Her head tilted back, inviting, luring. His grip tightened. His fingers wound into her hair and were lost in the richness of it. He felt the need catapult through his body so that he was tense against her sudden, unexpected yielding. She never submitted, and until that moment he hadn't known how stirring it could be to have her do so. Without a thought to time and place, they lowered to the sofa.

Because she was pliant, he was tender. Because he was gentle, she was patient. In a way they'd never experienced, they made love without rush, without fire, without the whirlwind. Thoroughly, they gave to each other. A touch, a taste, a murmured request, a whispered answer. The fire sizzled gently behind them as night fell outside the windows. Fingers brushed, lips skimmed so that they learned the power of quiet arousal. Though they'd been lovers for weeks, they brought love to passion for the first time.

The room was quiet, the light dim. If she'd never looked for romance, it found her there, wrapped easily in Michael's arms. Closer they came, but comfortably. Deeper they dived, but lazily. As they came together, Pandora felt her firm line of independence crack to let him in. But the weakness she'd expected didn't follow. Only contentment.

It was contentment that followed her into that quick and final burst of pleasure.

They were still wrapped together, half dozing, when the phone rang. With a murmur of complaint, Michael reached over his head to the table and lifted the receiver.

'Hello.'

'Michael Donahue, please.'

'Yeah, this is Michael.'

'Michael, it's Penny.'

He rubbed a hand over his eyes as he tried to put a face with the name. Penny—the little blonde in the apartment next to his. Wanted to be a model. He remembered vaguely leaving her the number of the Folley in case something important was delivered to his apartment. 'Hi.' He watched Pandora's eyes flutter open.

'Michael, I hate to do this, but I had to call. I've already phoned the police. They're on their way.'

'Police?' He struggled into a half-sitting position. 'What's going on?'

'You've been robbed.'

'What?' He sat bolt upright, nearly dumping Pandora on the floor. 'When?'

'I'm not sure. I got home a few minutes ago and noticed your door wasn't closed all the way. I thought maybe you'd come back so I knocked. Anyway, I pushed the door open a bit. The place was turned upside down. I came right over here and called the cops. They asked me to contact you and told me not to go back over.'

'Thanks.' Dozens of questions ran through his mind

but there was no one to answer them. 'Look, I'll try to come in tonight.'

'Okay. Hey, Michael, I'm really sorry.'

'Yeah. I'll see you.'

'Michael?' Pandora grabbed his hand as soon as he hung up the receiver.

'Somebody broke into my apartment.'

'Oh no.' She'd known the peace couldn't last. 'Do you think it was—'

'I don't know.' He dragged a hand through his hair. 'Maybe. Or maybe it was someone who noticed no one had been home for a while.'

She felt the anger in him but knew she couldn't soothe it. 'You've got to go.'

Nodding, he took her hand. 'Come with me.'

'Michael, one of us has to be here with Sweeney and Charles.'

'I'm not leaving you alone.'

'You have to go,' she repeated. 'If it was one of the family, maybe you can find something to prove it. In any case, you have to see to this. I'll be fine.'

'Just like the last time I was away.'

Pandora lifted a brow. 'I'm not incompetent, Michael.'

'But you'll be alone.'

'I have Bruno. Don't give me that look,' she ordered. 'He may not be ferocious, but he certainly knows how to bark. I'll lock every door and window.'

He shook his head. 'Not good enough.'

'All right, we'll call the local police. They have Fitzhugh's report about trespassers. We'll explain that

I'm going to be alone for the night and ask them to keep an eye on the place.'

'Better.' But he rose to pace. 'If this is a setup...'

'Then we're prepared for it this time.'

Michael hesitated, thought it through, then nodded. 'I'll call the police.'

Chapter 10

The moment Michael left, Pandora turned the heavy bolt on the main door. Though it had taken them the better part of an hour, she was grateful he'd insisted on checking all the doors and windows with her. The house, with Pandora safely in it, was locked up tight.

It was entirely too quiet.

In defense, Pandora went to the kitchen and began rattling pots and pans. She had to be alone, but she didn't have to be idle. She wanted to be with Michael, to stand by him when he faced the break-in of his apartment. Was it as frustrating for him to go on alone, she wondered, as it was for her to stay behind? It couldn't be helped. There were two old people in the house who couldn't be left. And they needed to eat.

The chicken was to have been a joint effort and a respite from the haphazard meals they'd managed to date. Michael had claimed to know at least the basics of deep frying. While he'd volunteered to deal with the chicken, she'd been assigned to try her hand at mashing potatoes. She'd thought competition if nothing else would have improved the end result.

Pandora resigned herself to a solo and decided the effort of cooking would keep her mind off fresh trouble. Needing company, she switched on the tuner on the kitchen wall unit and fiddled with the dial until she found a country-music station. Dolly Parton bubbled out brightly. Satisfied, she pulled one of Sweeney's cookbooks from the shelf and began to search the index. Fried chicken went on picnics, she mused. How much trouble could it be?

She had two counters crowded and splattered, and flour up to her wrists when the phone rang. Using a dishcloth, Pandora plucked the receiver from the kitchen extension. Her foot was tapping to a catchy rendition of 'On the Road Again.'

'Hello.'

'Pandora McVie?'

Her mind on more immediate matters, Pandora stretched the cord to the counter and picked up a drumstick. 'Yes.'

'Listen carefully.'

'Can you speak up?' Tongue caught between her teeth, Pandora dipped the drumstick in her flour mixture. 'I can't hear you very well.'

'I have to warn you and there's not much time. You're in danger. You're not safe in that house, not alone.'

The cookbook slid to the floor and landed on her foot. 'What? Who is this?'

'Just listen. You're alone because it was arranged. Someone's going to try to break in tonight.'

'Someone?' She shifted the phone and listened hard. It wasn't malice she detected, but nervousness. Whoever was on the other end was as shaky as she was. She was certain—almost certain—it was a man's voice. 'If you're trying to frighten me—'

'I'm trying to warn you. When I found out...' Already low and indistinct, the voice became hesitant. 'You shouldn't have sent the champagne. I don't like what's going on, but it won't stop. No one was going to be hurt, do you understand? But I'm afraid of what might happen next.'

Pandora felt fear curl in her stomach. Outside the kitchen windows it was dark, pitch-dark. She was alone in the house with two old, sick servants. 'If you're afraid, tell me who you are. Help me stop what's going on.'

'I'm already risking everything by warning you. You don't understand. Get out, just get out of the house.'

It was a ploy, she told herself. A ploy to make her leave. Pandora straightened her shoulders, but her gaze shifted from blank window to blank window. 'I'm not going anywhere. If you want to help, tell me who I should be afraid of.'

'Just get out,' the voice repeated before the line went dead.

Pandora stood holding the silent receiver. The oil in the fryer had begun to sizzle, competing with the radio.

Watching the windows, listening, she hung up the phone. It was a trick, she told herself. It was only a trick to get her out of the house in hopes she'd be frightened enough to stay out. She wouldn't be shooed away by a quivering voice on the telephone.

Besides, Michael had already called the police. They knew she was alone in the house. At the first sign of trouble, she only had to pick up the phone.

Her hands weren't completely steady, but she went back to cooking with a vengeance. She slipped coated chicken into the fryer, tested the potatoes she had cooking, then decided a little glass of wine while she worked was an excellent idea. She was pouring it when Bruno raced into the room to run around her feet.

'Bruno.' Pandora crouched and gathered the dog close. He felt warm, solid. 'I'm glad you're here,' she murmured. But for a moment, she allowed herself to wish desperately for Michael.

Bruno licked her face, made a couple of clumsy leaps toward the counter, then dashed to the door. Jumping up against it, he began to bark.

'Now?' Pandora demanded. 'I don't suppose you could wait until morning.'

Bruno raced back to Pandora, circled her then raced back to the door. When he'd gone through the routine three times, she relented. The phone call had been no more than a trick, a clumsy one at that. Besides, she told herself as she turned the lock, it wouldn't hurt to open the door and take a good look outside.

The moment she opened it, Bruno jumped out and

tumbled into the snow. He began to sniff busily while Pandora stood shivering in the opening and straining her eyes against the dark. Music and the smells of cooking poured out behind her.

There was nothing. She hugged herself against the cold and decided she hadn't expected to see anything. The snow was settled, the stars bright and the woods quiet. It was as it should have been; a very ordinary evening in the country. She took a deep breath of winter air and started to call the dog back. They saw the movement at the edge of the woods at the same time.

Just a shadow, it seemed to separate slowly from a tree and take on its own shape. A human shape. Before Pandora could react, Bruno began to bark and plow through the snow.

'No, Bruno! Come back.' Without giving herself a chance to think, Pandora grabbed the old pea coat that hung beside the door and threw it on. As an afterthought, she reached for a cast-iron skillet before bolting through the door after her dog. 'Bruno!'

He was already at the edge of the woods and hot on the trail. Picking up confidence as she went, Pandora raced in pursuit. Whoever had been watching the house had run at the sight of the clumsy, overgrown puppy. She'd found she was susceptible to fear, but she refused to be frightened by a coward. With as much enthusiasm as Bruno, Pandora sprinted into the woods. Out of breath and feeling indestructible, she paused long enough to look around and listen. For a moment there was nothing, then off to the right, she heard barking and thrashing.

'Get 'em, Bruno!' she shouted, and headed toward the chaos. Excited by the chase, she called encouragement to the dog, changing direction when she heard his answering bark. As she ran, snow dropped from the branches to slide cold and wet down the back of her neck. The barking grew wilder, and in her rush, Pandora fell headlong over a downed tree. Spitting out snow and swearing, she struggled to her knees. Bruno bounded out of the woods and sent her sprawling again.

'Not me.' Flat on her back, Pandora shoved at the dog. 'Dammit, Bruno, if you don't—' She broke off when the dog stiffened and began to growl. Sprawled on the snow, Pandora looked up and saw the shadow move through the trees. She forgot she was too proud to fear a coward.

Though her hands were numb from cold, she gripped the handle of the skillet and, standing, inched her way along toward the nearest tree. Struggling to keep her breathing quiet, she braced herself for attack and defense. Relative or stranger, she'd hold her own. But her knees were shaking. Bruno tensed and hurled himself forward. The moment he did, Pandora lifted the skillet high and prepared to swing.

'What the hell's going on?'

'Michael!' The skillet landed in the snow with a plop as she followed Bruno's lead and hurled herself forward. Giddy with relief, she plastered kisses over Michael's face. 'Oh, Michael, I'm so glad it's you.'

'Yeah. You sure looked pleased when you were hefting that skillet. Run out of hair spray?'

'It was handy.' Abruptly she drew back and glared at

him. 'Dammit, Michael, you scared me to death. You're supposed to be halfway to New York, not skulking around the woods.'

'And you're supposed to be locked in the house.'

'I would've been if you hadn't been skulking in the woods. Why?'

In an offhanded gesture, he brushed snow from her face. 'I got ten miles away, and I couldn't get rid of this bad feeling. It was too pat. I decided to stop at a gas station and phone my neighbor.'

'But your apartment.'

'I talked to the police, gave them a list of my valuables. We'll both run into New York in a day or two.' Snow was scattered through her hair and matted to her coat. He thought of what might have happened and resisted the urge to shake her. 'I couldn't leave you alone.'

'I'm going to start believing you're chivalrous after all.' She kissed him. 'That explains why you're not in New York, but what were you doing in the woods?'

'Just a hunch.' He bent to retrieve the frying pan. A good whack with that, he discovered, and he'd have been down for the count.

'The next time you have a hunch, don't stand at the edge of the woods and stare at the house.'

'I wasn't.' Michael took her arm and headed back toward the house. He wanted her inside again, behind locked doors.

'I saw you.'

'I don't know who you saw.' Disgusted, Michael looked back at the dog. 'But if you hadn't let the dog out we'd

both know. I decided to check around outside before coming in, and I saw footprints. I followed them around, then
cut into the woods.' He glanced over his shoulder, still
tight with tension. 'I was just coming up behind whoever
made them when Bruno tried his attack. I started chasing.' He swore and slapped a palm against the skillet. 'I
was gaining when this hound ran between my legs and
sent me face first into the snow. About that time, you
started yelling at the dog. Whoever I was chasing had
enough time to disappear.'

Pandora swore and kicked at the snow. 'If you'd let me
know what was going on, we could've worked together.'

'I didn't know what was going on until it was already
happening. In any case, the deal was you'd stay inside
with the doors locked.'

'The dog had to go out,' Pandora muttered. 'And I had
this phone call.' She looked back over her shoulder and
sighed. 'Someone called to warn me.'

'Who?'

'I don't know. I thought it was a man's voice, but—
I'm just not sure.'

Michael's hand tightened on her arm. 'Did he threaten
you?'

'No, no it wasn't like a threat. Whoever it was certainly
seemed to know what's been going on and isn't happy
about it. That much was clear. He—she said someone was
going to try to break into the Folley, and I should get out.'

'And, of course, you handled that by running into the
woods with a skillet. Pandora.' This time he did shake
her. 'Why didn't you call the police?'

'Because I thought it was another trick and it made me mad.' She sent Michael a stubborn look. 'Yes, it frightened me at first, then it just plain made me mad. I don't like intimidation. When I looked out and saw someone near the woods, I only wanted to fight back.'

'Admirable,' he said but took her shoulders. 'Stupid.'

'You were doing the same thing.'

'It's not the same thing. You've got brains, you've got style. I'll even give you guts. But, cousin, you're not a heavyweight. What if you'd caught up with whoever was out there and they wanted to play rough?'

'I can play rough, too,' Pandora muttered.

'Fine.' With a quick move, he hooked a foot behind hers and sent her bottom first into the snow. She didn't have the opportunity to complain before he was standing over her, gesturing with the skillet. Bruno decided it was a game and leaped on top of her. 'I might've come back tomorrow and found you half-buried in the snow.' Before she could speak, he hauled her to her feet again. 'I'm not risking that.'

'You caught me off balance,' she began.

'Shut up.' He had her by the shoulders again, and this time his grip wasn't gentle. 'You're too important, Pandora, I'm through taking chances. We're going inside and calling the cops. We're going to tell them everything.'

'What can they do?'

'We'll find out.'

She let out a long breath, then leaned against him. The chase might have been exciting, but her knees had yet to

stop shaking. 'Okay, maybe you're right. We're no farther along now than when we started.'

'Calling the police isn't giving up, it's just changing
the odds. I might not have come back here tonight, Pandora. The dog may not have frightened anyone off. You'd
have been alone.' He took both her hands, pressing them
to his lips and warming them. 'I'm not going to let anything happen to you.'

Confused by the sense of pleasure his words gave her,
she tried to draw her hands away. 'I can take care of myself, Michael.'

He smiled but didn't let go. 'Maybe. But you're not
going to have the chance to find out. Let's go home. I'm
hungry.'

'Typical,' she began, needing to lighten the mood.
'You'd think of your stomach—oh my God, the chicken!'
Breaking away, Pandora loped toward the house.

'I'm not that hungry.' Michael sprinted after her. The
relief came again when he scooped her up into his arms.
When he'd heard her shout in the woods, had realized she
was outside and vulnerable, his blood had simply stopped
flowing. 'In fact,' he said as he scooped her up, 'I can
think of more pressing matters than eating.'

'Michael.' She struggled, but laughed. 'If you don't put
me down, there won't be a kitchen to eat in.'

'We'll eat somewhere else.'

'I left the pan on. There's probably nothing left of the
chicken but charred bones.'

'There's always soup.' With that, he pushed open the
kitchen door.

Rather than a smoky, splattered mess, they found a platter piled high with crisp, brown chicken. Sweeney had wiped up the spills, and had the pans soaking in the sink.

'Sweeney.' From her perch in Michael's arms, Pandora surveyed the room. 'What are you doing out of bed?'

'My job,' she said briskly, but gave them a quick sidelong look. As far as she was concerned, her plans were working perfectly. She imagined Pandora and Michael had decided to take a little air while dinner was cooking, and, as young people would, had forgotten the time.

'You're supposed to be in bed,' Pandora reminded her.

'Posh. I've been in bed long enough.' And the days of little or no activity had nearly bored her to tears. It was worth it, however, to see Pandora snug in Michael's arms. 'Feeling fit as a fiddle now, I promise you. Wash up for dinner.'

Michael and Pandora each took separate and careful studies. Sweeney's cheeks were pink and round, her eyes bright. She bustled from counter to counter in her old businesslike fashion. 'We still want you to take it easy,' Michael decided. 'No heavy work.'

'That's right. Michael and I'll take care of the washing up.' She saw him scowl, just a little, and patted his shoulder. 'We like to do it.'

At Michael and Pandora's insistence, all four ate in the kitchen. Charles, sitting next to Sweeney, was left uncertain how much he should cough and settled on a middle road, clearing his throat every so often. In an unspoken agreement, Pandora and Michael decided to keep the matter of trespassers to themselves. Both of them felt the announcement that someone was watching the house would be too upsetting for the two old people while they were recuperating.

On the surface, dinner was an easy meal, but Pandora kept wondering how soon they could nudge the servants along to bed and contact the police. More than once, Pandora caught Sweeney looking from her to Michael with a smug smile. Sweet old lady, Pandora mused, innocently believing the cook to be pleased to have her kitchen back. It made Pandora only more determined to protect her and Charles from any unpleasantness. She concentrated on cleaning up and packing them off to bed, and it was nearly nine before she was able to meet Michael in the parlor.

'Settled?'

She heard the familiar restlessness in his voice and merely nodded, pouring a brandy. 'It's a bit like cajoling children, but I managed to find a Cary Grant movie that interested them.' She sipped the brandy, waiting for her muscles to relax with it. 'I'd rather be watching it myself.'

'Another time.' Michael took a sip from her snifter. 'I've called the police. They'll be here shortly.'

She took the glass back. 'It still bothers me to take the business to outsiders. After all, anything beyond simple trespass is speculation.'

'We'll let the police speculate.'

She managed to smile. 'Your Logan always handles things on his own.'

'Someone told me once that that was just fiction.' He

poured himself a brandy and toasted her. 'I discovered I don't like having you in the middle of a story line.'

The brandy and firelight gave the evening an illusion of normalcy. Pandora took his statement with a shrug. 'You seem to have developed a protect-the-woman syndrome, Michael. It's not like you.'

'Maybe not.' He tossed back a gulp. 'It's different when it's my woman.'

She turned, brow lifted. It was ridiculous to feel pleasure at such a foolish and possessive term. 'Yours?'

'Mine.' He cupped the back of her neck with his hand. 'Got a problem with that?'

Her heart beat steadily in her throat until she managed to swallow. Maybe he meant it—now. In a few months when he was back moving in his own world, with his own people, she'd be no more than his somewhat annoying cousin. But for now, just for now, maybe he meant it. 'I'm not sure.'

'Give it some thought,' he advised before he lowered his mouth to hers. 'We'll come back to it.'

He left her flustered and went to answer the door.

When he returned, Pandora was sitting calmly enough in a high-backed chair near the fire. 'Lieutenant Randall, Pandora McVie.'

'How d'you do?' The lieutenant pulled off a wool muffler and stuck it in his coat pocket. He looked, Pandora thought, like someone's grandfather. Comfy, round and balding. 'Miserable night,' he announced, and situated himself near the fire.

'Would you like some coffee, Lieutenant?'

Randall gave Pandora a grateful look. 'Love it.'

'Please, have a seat. I'll be back in a minute.'

She took her time heating coffee and arranging cups and saucers on a tray. Not putting off, Pandora insisted, just preparing. She'd never had occasion to talk to a policeman on any subject more complex than a parking ticket. She'd come out on the short end on that one. Now, she was about to discuss her family and her relationship with Michael.

Her relationship with Michael, she thought again as she fussed with the sugar bowl. That's what really had her hiding in the kitchen. She hadn't yet been able to dull the feeling that had raced through her when he'd called her his woman. Adolescent, Pandora told herself. It was absolutely absurd to feel giddy and self-satisfied and unnerved because a man had looked at her with passion in his eyes.

But they'd been Michael's eyes.

She found linen napkins and folded them into triangles. She didn't want to be anyone's woman but her own. It had been the strain and excitement of the evening that had made her react like a sixteen-year-old being offered a school ring. She was an adult; she was self-sustaining. She was in love. Talk yourself out of that one, Pandora challenged herself. Taking a long breath, she hefted the tray and went back to the parlor.

'Gentlemen.' Pandora set the tray on a low table and stuck on a smile. 'Cream and sugar, Lieutenant?'

'Thanks. A healthy dose of both.' He set a dog-eared notepad on his knee when Pandora handed him a cup.

'Mr. Donahue's been filling me in. Seems you've had a few annoyances.'

She smiled at the term. Like his looks, his voice was comfortable. 'A few.'

'I'm not going to lecture.' But he gave them both a stern look. 'Still, you should've notified the police after the first incident. Vandalism's a crime.'

'We'd hoped by ignoring it, it would discourage repetition.' Pandora lifted her cup. 'We were wrong.'

'I'll need to take the champagne with me.' Again, he sent them a look of disapproval. 'Even though you've had it analyzed, we'll want to run it through our own lab.'

'I'll get it for you.' Michael rose and left them alone.

'Miss McVie, from what your cousin tells me, the terms of Mr. McVie's will were a bit unconventional.'

'A bit.'

'He also tells me he talked you into agreeing to them.'

'That's Michael's fantasy, Lieutenant.' She sipped her coffee. 'I'm doing exactly what I chose to do.'

Randall nodded and noted. 'You agree with Mr. Donahue's idea that these incidents are connected and one of your relatives is responsible.'

'I can't think of any reason to disagree.'

'Do you have any reason to suspect one more than another?'

Pandora thought it through as she'd thought it through before. 'No. You see, we're not at all a close family. The truth is I don't know any of them very well.'

'Except Mr. Donahue.'

'That's right. Michael and I often visited our uncle, and

we ran into each other here at the Folley.' Whether we
wanted to or not, she added to herself in her own private
joke. 'None of the others came by very often.'

'The champagne, Lieutenant.' Michael brought in the
box. 'And the report from Sanfield Laboratories.'

Randall skimmed the printout, then tucked the sheet
into the box. 'Your uncle's attorney...' He referred quickly
to his notes. 'Fitzhugh reported trespassing several weeks
ago. We've had a squad car cruise the area, but at this
point you might agree to having a man patrol the grounds
once a day.'

'I'd prefer it,' Michael told him.

'I'll contact Fitzhugh.' Seeing his cup was empty, Pandora took it and filled it again. 'I'll also need a list of the
relatives named in the will.'

Pandora frowned over her rim. Between her and Michael, they tried to fill in the lieutenant, as best as they
could. When they had finished, Pandora sent Randall an
apologetic look. 'I told you we aren't close.'

'I'll get the lawyer to fill in the details.' Randall rose
and tried not to think about the cold drive back to town.
'We'll keep the inquiries as quiet as possible. If anything
else happens, call me. One of my men will be around to
look things over.'

'Thank you, Lieutenant.' Michael helped the pudgy
man on with his coat.

Randall took another look around the room. 'Ever
think of installing a security system?'

'No.'

'Think again,' he advised, and made his way out.

'We've just been scolded,' Pandora murmured.

Michael wondered if *Logan's Run* had room for a cranky, well-padded cop. 'Seems that way.'

'You know, Michael, I have two schools of thought on bringing in the police.'

'Which are?'

'It's either going to calm things down or stir things up.'

'You pay your money and take your choice.'

She gave him a knowing look. 'You're counting on the second.'

'I came close tonight.' He bypassed the coffee and poured another brandy. 'I nearly had my hands on something. Someone.' When he looked at her, the faint amusement in his eyes had faded. The recklessness was back. 'I like my fights in the open, face-to-face.'

'It's better if we look at it as a chess game rather than a boxing match.' She came close to wrap her arms around him and press her cheek to his shoulder. It was the kind of gesture he didn't think he'd ever get used to from her. As he rested his head on her hair, he realized that the fact that he wouldn't only added to the sweetness of the feeling. When had he stopped remembering that she didn't fit into his long-established picture of the ideal woman? Her hair was too red, her body too thin, her tongue too sharp. Michael nuzzled against her and found they fit very well.

'I've never had the patience for chess.'

'Then we'll just leave it to the police.' She held him tighter. The need to protect rose as sharply as the desire to be protected. 'I've been thinking about what might have happened out there tonight. I don't want you hurt, Michael.'

With two fingers under her chin, he lifted it. 'Why not?'

'Because...' She looked into his eyes and felt her heart melt. But she wouldn't be a fool; she wouldn't risk her pride. 'Because then I'd have to do the dishes by myself.'

He smiled. No, he didn't have a great deal of patience, but he could call on it when circumstances warranted. He brushed a kiss on either side of her mouth. Sooner or later, he'd have more out of her. Then he'd just have to decide what to do with it. 'Any other reason?'

Absorbing the sensations, Pandora searched her mind for another easy answer. 'If you were hurt, you couldn't work. I'd have to live with your foul temper.'

'I thought you were already living with it.'

'I've seen it fouler.'

He kissed her eyes closed in his slow, sensuous way. 'Try one more time.'

'I care.' She opened her eyes, and her look was tense and defiant. 'Got a problem with that?'

'No.' His kiss wasn't gentle this time, it wasn't patient. He had her caught close and reeling within moments. If there was tension in her still, he couldn't feel it. 'The only problem's been dragging it out of you.'

'You're family after all—'

With a laugh, he nipped the lobe of her ear. 'Don't try to back out.'

Indignant, she stiffened. 'I never back out.'

'Unless you can rationalize it. Just remember this.'

He had her molded against him again. 'The family connection's distant.' Their lips met, urgently, then parted. 'This connection isn't.'

'I don't know what you want from me,' she whispered.

'You're usually so quick.'

'Don't joke, Michael.'

'It's no joke.' He drew her away, holding her by the shoulders. Briefly, firmly, he ran his hands down to her elbows, then back. 'No, I'm not going to spell it out for you, Pandora. I'm not going to make it easy on you. You have to be willing to admit we both want the same thing. And you will.'

'Arrogant,' she warned.

'Confident,' he corrected. He had to be, or he'd be on his knees begging. There'd come a time, he'd promised himself, when she'd drop the last of her restrictions. 'I want you.'

A tremor skipped up her spine. 'I know.'

'Yeah.' He linked his fingers with hers. 'I think you do.'

Chapter 11

Winter raged its way through February. There came a point when Pandora had to shovel her way from the house to her workshop. She found herself grateful for the physical labor. Winter was a long quiet time that provided too many hours to think.

In using this time, Pandora came to several uncomfortable realizations. Her life, as she'd known it, as she'd guided it, would never be the same. As far as her art was concerned, she felt the months of concentrated effort with dashes of excitement had only improved her crafting. In truth, she often used her jewelry to take her mind off what was happening to and around her. When that didn't work, she used what was happening to and around her in her work.

The sudden blunt understanding that her health, even

her life, had been endangered made her take a step away from her usual practical outlook. It caused her to appreciate little things she'd always taken for granted. Waking up in a warm bed, watching snow fall while a fire crackled beside her. She'd learned that every second in life was vital.

Already she was considering taking a day to drive back to New York and pack what was important to her. More than packing, it would be a time of decision making. What she kept, what she didn't, would in some ways reflect the changes she'd accepted in herself.

Both the lease on her apartment and the lease on the shop over the boutique were coming up for renewal. She'd let them lapse. Rather than living alone, she'd have the company and the responsibility of her uncle's old servants. Though she'd once been determined to be responsible only to herself and her art, Pandora made the choice without a qualm. Though she had lived in the city, in the rush, in the crowds, she'd isolated herself. No more.

Through it all wove Michael.

In a few short weeks, what they had now would be over. The long winter they'd shared would be something to think of during other winters. As she prepared for a new and different life, Pandora promised herself she'd have no regrets. But she couldn't stop herself from having wishes. Things were already changing.

The police had come, and with their arrival had been more questions. Everything in her shop had to be locked up tightly after dark, and there were no more solitary walks in the woods after a snowfall. It had become a nightly ritual to go through the Folley and check doors and windows that had once been casually ignored. Often when she walked back to the house from her shop, she'd see Michael watching from the window of his room. It should have given her a warm, comfortable feeling, but she knew he was waiting for something else to happen. She knew, as she knew him, that he wanted it. Inactivity was sitting uneasily on him.

Since they'd driven into New York to deal with the break-in at his apartment, he'd been distant, with a restlessness roiling underneath. Though they both understood the wisdom of having the grounds patrolled, she thought they felt intruded upon.

They had no sense of satisfaction from the police investigation. Each one of their relatives had alibis for one or more of the incidents. So far the investigation seemed to have twin results. Since the police had been called in, nothing else had happened. There'd been no anonymous phone calls, no shadows in the woods, no bogus messages. It had, as Pandora had also predicted, stirred things up. She'd dealt with an irate phone call from Carlson who insisted they were using the investigation in an attempt to undermine his case against the will.

On the heels of that had come a disjointed letter from Ginger who'd had the idea that the Folley was haunted. Michael had had a two-minute phone conversation with Morgan who'd muttered about private family business, overreacting and hogwash. Biff, in his usual style, had sent a short message:

Cops and robbers? Looks like you two are playing games with each other.

From Hank they heard nothing.

The police lab had confirmed the private analysis of the champagne; Randall was plodding through the investigation in his precise, quiet way. Michael and Pandora were exactly where they'd been weeks before: waiting.

He didn't know how she could stand it. As Michael made his way down the narrow path Pandora had shoveled, he wondered how she could remain so calm when he was ready to chew glass. It had only taken him a few days of hanging in limbo to realize it was worse when nothing happened. Waiting for someone else to make the next move was the most racking kind of torture. Until he was sure Pandora was safe, he couldn't relax. Until he had his hands around someone's throat, he wouldn't be satisfied. He was caught in a trap of inactivity that was slowly driving him mad. Pausing just outside her shop, he glanced around.

The house looked big and foolish with icicles hanging and dripping from eaves, gutters and shutters. It belonged in a book, he thought, some moody, misty gothic. A fairy tale—the grim sort. Perhaps one day he'd weave a story around it himself, but for now, it was just home.

With his hands in his pockets he watched smoke puff out of chimneys. Foolish it might be, but he'd always loved it. The longer he lived in it, the surer he was that he was meant to. He was far from certain how Pandora would take his decision to remain after the term was over.

His last script for the season was done. It was the only episode to be filmed before the show wrapped until fall. He could, as he often did, take a few weeks in the early spring and find a hot, noisy beach. He could fish, relax and enjoy watching women in undersize bikinis. Michael knew he wasn't going anywhere.

For the past few days, he'd been toying with a screenplay for a feature film. He'd given it some thought before, but somehow something had always interfered. He could write it here, he knew. He could perfect it here with Pandora wielding her art nearby, criticizing his work so that he was only more determined to make it better. But he was waiting. Waiting for something else to happen, waiting to find who it was who'd used fear and intimidation to try to drive them out. And most of all, he was waiting for Pandora. Until she gave him her complete trust, willingly, until she gave him her heart unrestrictedly, he had to go on waiting.

His hands curled into fists and released. He wanted action.

He tried the door and satisfied himself that she'd kept her word and locked it from the inside. 'Pandora?' He knocked with the side of his fist. She opened the door with a drill in her hand. After giving her flushed face and tousled hair a quick look, Michael lifted his hands, palms out. 'I'm unarmed.'

'And I'm busy.' But her lips curved. There was a light of pleasure in her eyes. He found it easy to notice such small things.

'I know, I've invaded scheduled working hours, but I have a valid excuse.'

'You're letting in the cold,' she complained. Once, she might have shut the door in his face without a second thought. This time she shut it behind him.

'Not a hell of a lot warmer in here.'

'It's fine when I'm working. Which I am.'

'Blame Sweeney. She's sending me in for supplies, and she insisted I take you.' He sent Pandora a bland look. "That girl holes herself up in that shed too much. Needs some sun."

'I get plenty of sun,' Pandora countered. Still, the idea of a drive into town appealed. It wouldn't hurt to talk to the jeweler in the little shopping center. She was beginning to think her work should spread out a bit, beyond the big cities. 'I suppose we should humor her, but I want to finish up here first.'

'I'm in no hurry.'

'Good. Half an hour then.' She went to exchange the drill for a jeweler's torch. Because she didn't hear the door open or shut, she turned and saw Michael examining her rolling mill. 'Michael,' she said with more than a trace of exasperation.

'Go ahead, take your time.'

'Don't you have anything to do?'

'Not a thing,' he said cheerfully.

'Not one car chase to write?'

'No. Besides, I've never seen you work.'

'Audiences make me cranky.'

'Broaden your horizons, love. Pretend I'm an apprentice.'

'I'm not sure they can get that broad.'

Undaunted, he pointed to her worktable. 'What is that thing?'

'This thing,' she began tightly, 'is a pendant. A waterfall effect made with brass wire and some scraps of silver I had left over from a bracelet.'

'No waste,' he murmured. 'Practical as ever. So what's the next step?'

With a long breath, she decided it would be simpler to play along than to throw him out. 'I've just finished adjusting the curves of the wires. I've used different thicknesses and lengths to give it a free-flowing effect. The silver scraps I've cut and filed into elongated teardrops. Now I solder them onto the ends of the wires.'

She applied the flux, shifting a bit so that he could watch. After she'd put a square of solder beside each wire, she used the torch to apply heat until the solder melted. Patient, competent, she repeated the procedure until all twelve teardrops were attached.

'Looks easy enough,' he mused.

'A child of five could do it.'

He heard the sarcasm and laughed as he took her hands. 'You want flattery? A few minutes ago I saw a pile of metal. Now I see an intriguing ornament. Ornate and exotic.'

'It's supposed to be exotic,' Pandora replied. 'Jessica Wainwright will wear it in the film. It's to have been a gift from an old lover. The countess claims he was a Turkish prince.'

Michael studied the necklace again. 'Very appropriate.'

'It'll droop down from brass and silver wires twisted together. The lowest teardrop should hang nearly to her waist.' Pleased, but knowing better than to touch the metal before the solder cooled, Pandora held up her sketch. 'Ms. Wainwright was very specific. She wants nothing ordinary, nothing even classic. Everything she wears should add to the character's mystique.'

She set the sketch down and tidied her tools. She'd solder on the hoop and fashion the neck wire when they returned from town. Then if there was time, she'd begin the next project. The gold-plated peacock pin with its three-inch filigree tail would take her the better part of two weeks.

'This thing has potential as a murder weapon,' Michael mused, picking up a burnisher to examine the curved, steel tip.

'I beg your pardon?'

He liked the way she said it, so that even with her back turned she was looking down her nose. 'For a story line.'

'Leave my tools out of your stories.' Pandora took the burnisher from him and packed it away. 'Going to buy me lunch in town?' She stripped off her apron then grabbed her coat.

'I was going to ask you the same thing.'

'I asked first.' She locked the shop and welcomed the cold. 'The snow's beginning to melt.'

'In a few weeks, the five dozen bulbs Jolley planted during his gardening stage will be starting to bloom.'

'Daffodils,' she murmured. It didn't seem possible

when you felt the air, saw the mounds of snow, but spring was closing in. 'The winter hasn't seemed so long.'

'No, it hasn't.' He slipped an arm around her shoulders. 'I never expected six months to go so quickly. I figured one of us would've attempted murder by this time.'

With a laugh, Pandora matched her step to his. 'We've still got a month to go.'

'Now we have to behave ourselves,' he reminded her. 'Lieutenant Randall has his eye on us.'

'I guess we blew our chance.' She turned to wind her arms around his neck. 'There have been times I've wanted to hit you with a blunt instrument.'

'Feeling's mutual,' he told her as he lowered his mouth. Her lips were cool and curved.

At the side window, Sweeney drew back the drape. 'Look at this!' Cackling, she gestured to Charles. 'I told you it would work. In a few more weeks, I'll be putting bells on a wedding cake.'

As Charles joined Sweeney at the window, Pandora scooped a hand into the snow and tossed it in Michael's face. 'Don't count your chickens,' he muttered.

In a desperate move to avoid retaliation, Pandora raced to the garage. She ducked seconds before snow splattered against the door. 'Your aim's still off, cousin.' Hefting the door, she sprinted inside and jumped into his car. Smug, she settled into the seat. He wouldn't, she was sure, mar his spotless interior with a snowball. Michael opened the door, slid in beside her and dumped snow over her head. She was still squealing when he turned the key.

'I'm better at close range.'

Pandora sputtered as she wiped at the snow. Because she'd appreciated the move, it was difficult to sound indignant. 'One would have thought that a man who drives an ostentatious car would be more particular with it.'

'It's only ostentatious if you buy it for status purposes.'

'And, of course, you didn't.'

'I bought it because it gets terrific gas mileage.' When she snorted, he turned to grin at her. 'And because it looks great wrapped around redheads.'

'And blondes and brunettes.'

'Redheads,' he corrected, twining her hair around his finger. 'I've developed a preference.'

It shouldn't have made her smile, but it did. She was still smiling when they started down the long, curvy road. 'We can't complain about the road crews,' she said idly. 'Except for those two weeks last month, the roads've been fairly clear.' She glanced toward the mounds of snow the plows had pushed to the side of the road.

'Too bad they won't do the driveway.'

'You know you loved riding that little tractor. Uncle Jolley always said it made him feel tough and macho.'

'So much so he'd race it like a madman over the yard.'

As they came to a curve, Michael eased on the brake and downshifted. Pandora leaned forward and fiddled with the stereo. 'Most people have equipment like this in their den.'

'I don't have a den.'

'You don't have a stereo to put in one, either,' she remembered. 'Or a television.'

He shrugged, but mentally listed what he'd lost from his apartment. 'Insurance'll cover it.'

'The police are handling that as though it were a normal break-in.' She switched channels. 'It might've been.'

'Or it might've been a smoke screen. I wish we—' He broke off as they approached another curve. He'd pressed the brake again, but this time, the pedal had gone uselessly to the floor.

'Michael, if you're trying to impress me with your skill as a driver, it's not working.' Instinctively Pandora grabbed the door handle as the car careered down the curve.

Whipping the steering wheel with one hand, Michael yanked on the emergency brake. The car continued to barrel down. He gripped the wheel in both hands and fought the next curve. 'No brakes.' As he told her, Michael glanced down to see the speedometer hover at seventy.

Pandora's knuckles turned white on the handle. 'We won't make it to the bottom without them.'

He never considered lying. 'No.' Tires squealed as he rounded the next curve. Gravel spit under the wheels as the car went wide. There was the scrape and scream of metal as the fender kissed the guardrail.

She looked at the winding road spinning in front of her. Her vision blurred then cleared. The sign before the S-turn cautioned for a safe speed of thirty. Michael took it at seventy-five. Pandora shut her eyes. When she opened them and saw the snowbank dead ahead, she screamed.

With seconds to spare, Michael yanked the car around. Snow flew skyward as the car skidded along the bank.

Eyes intense, Michael stared at the road ahead and struggled to anticipate each curve. Sweat beaded on his forehead. He knew the road, that's what terrified him. In less than three miles, the already sharp incline steepened. At high speed, the car would ram straight through the guardrail and crash on the cliffs below. The game Jolley had begun would end violently.

Michael tasted his own fear, then swallowed it. 'There's only one chance; we've got to turn off on the lane leading into the old inn. It's coming up after that curve.' He couldn't take his eyes from the road to look at her. His fingers dug into the wheel. 'Hang on.'

She was going to die. Her mind was numb from the thought of it. She heard the tires scream as Michael dragged at the wheel. The car tilted, nearly going over. She saw trees rush by as the car slid on the slippery edge of the lane. Almost, for an instant, the rubber seemed to grip the gravel beneath. But the turn was too sharp, the speed too fast. Out of control, the car spiraled toward the trees.

'I love you,' she whispered, and grabbed for him before the world went black.

He came to slowly. He hurt, and for a time didn't understand why. There was noise. Eventually he turned his head toward it. When he opened his eyes, Michael saw a boy with wide eyes and black hair gawking through the window.

'Mister, hey, mister. You okay?'

Dazed, Michael pushed open the door. 'Get help,' he managed, fighting against blacking out again. He took deep gulps of air to clear his head as the boy dashed off through the woods. 'Pandora.' Fear broke through the fog. In seconds, he was leaning over her.

His fingers shook as he reached for the pulse of her neck, but he found it. Blood from a cut on her forehead ran down her face and onto his hands. With his fingers pressed against the wound, he fumbled in the glove compartment for the first-aid kit. He'd stopped the bleeding and was checking her for broken bones when she moaned. He had to stop himself from dragging her against him and holding on.

'Take it easy,' he murmured when she began to stir. 'Don't move around.' When she opened her eyes, he saw they were glazed and unfocused. 'You're all right.' Gently he cupped her face in his hands and continued to reassure her. Her eyes focused gradually. As they did, she reached for his hand.

'The brakes....'

'Yeah.' He rested his cheek against hers a moment. 'It was a hell of a trip, but it looks like we made it.'

Confused, she looked around. The car was stopped, leaning drunkenly against a tree. It had been the deep, slushy snow that had slowed them down enough to prevent the crash from being fatal. 'We—you're all right?' The tears started when she reached out and took his face in her hands as he had with hers. 'You're all right.'

'Terrific.' His wrist throbbed like a jackhammer and his head ached unbelievably, but he was alive. When she started to move, he held her still. 'No, don't move around. I don't know how badly you're hurt. There was a kid. He's gone for help.'

'It's just my head.' She started to take his hand, and saw the blood. 'Oh God, you're bleeding. Where?' Before she could begin her frantic search, he gripped her hands together.

'It's not me. It's you. Your head's cut. You probably have a concussion.'

Shaky, she lifted her hand and touched the bandage. The wound beneath it hurt, but she drew on that. If she hurt, she was alive. 'I thought I was dead.' She closed her eyes but tears slipped through the lashes. 'I thought we were both dead.'

'We're both fine.' They heard the siren wail up the mountain road. He was silent until she opened her eyes again. 'You know what happened?'

Her head ached badly, but it was clear. 'Attempted murder.'

He nodded, not turning when the ambulance pulled into the slushy lane. 'I'm through waiting, Pandora. I'm through waiting all around.'

Lieutenant Randall found Michael in the emergency-room lounge. He unwrapped his muffler, unbuttoned his coat and sat down on the hard wooden bench. 'Looks like you've had some trouble.'

'Big time.'

Randall nodded toward the Ace bandage on Michael's wrist. 'Bad?'

'Just a sprain. Few cuts and bruises and a hell of a headache. Last time I saw it, my car looked something like an accordion.'

'We're taking it in. Anything we should look for?'

'Brake lines. It seemed I didn't have any when I started the trip down the mountain.'

'When's the last time you used your car?' Randall had his notepad in hand.

'Ten days, two weeks.' Wearily, Michael rubbed a temple. 'I drove into New York to talk to police about the robbery in my apartment.'

'Where do you keep your car?'

'In the garage.'

'Locked?'

'The garage?' Michael kept his eye on the hallway where Pandora had been wheeled away. 'No. My uncle had installed one of those remote control devices a few years back. Never worked unless you turned on the television. Anyway, he took it out again and never replaced the lock. Pandora's car's in there,' he remembered suddenly. 'If—'

'We'll check it out,' Randall said easily. 'Miss McVie was with you?'

'Yeah, she's with a doctor.' For the first time in weeks, Michael found himself craving a cigarette. 'Her head was cut.' He looked down at his hands and remembered her blood on them. 'I'm going to find out who did this, Lieutenant, and then I'm going to—'

'Don't say anything to me I might have to use later,' Randall warned. There were some people who threatened as a means to let off steam or relieve tension. Randall didn't think Michael Donahue was one of them. 'Let me do my job, Mr. Donahue.'

Michael gave him a long, steady look. 'Someone's been playing games, deadly ones, with someone very important to me. If you were in my place, would you twiddle your thumbs and wait?'

Randall smiled, just a little. 'You know, Donahue, I never miss your show. Great entertainment. Some of this business sounds just like one of your shows.'

'Like one of my shows,' Michael repeated slowly.

'Problem is, things don't work the same way out here in the world as they do on television. But it sure is a pleasure to watch. Here comes your lady.'

Michael sprang up and headed for her.

'I'm fine,' she told him before he could ask.

'Not entirely.' Behind her a young, white-coated doctor stood impatiently. 'Miss McVie has a concussion.'

'He put a few stitches in my head and wants to hold me prisoner.' She gave the doctor a sweet smile and linked arms with Michael. 'Let's go home.'

'Just a minute.' Keeping her beside him, Michael turned to the doctor. 'You want her in the hospital?'

'Michael—'

'Shut up.'

'Anyone suffering from a concussion should be routinely checked. Miss McVie would be wise to remain overnight with professional care.'

'I'm not staying in the hospital because I have a bump on the head. Good afternoon, Lieutenant.'

'Miss McVie.'

Lifting her chin, she looked back at the doctor. 'Now, Doctor...'

'Barnhouse.'

'Dr. Barnhouse,' she began. 'I will take your advice to a point. I'll rest, avoid stress. At the first sign of nausea or dizziness, I'll be on your doorstep. I can assure you, now that you've convinced Michael I'm an invalid, I'll be properly smothered and hovered over. You'll have to be satisfied with that.'

Far from satisfied, the doctor directed himself to Michael. 'I can't force her to stay, of course.'

Michael lifted a brow. 'If you think I can, you've got a lot to learn about women.'

Resigned, Barnhouse turned back to Pandora. 'I want to see you in a week, sooner if any of the symptoms we discussed show up. You're to rest for twenty-four hours. That means horizontally.'

'Yes, Doctor.' She offered a hand, which he took grudgingly. 'You were very gentle. Thank you.'

His lips twitched. 'A week,' he repeated and strode back down the hall.

'If I didn't know better,' Michael mused, 'I'd say he wanted to keep you here just to look at you.'

'Of course. I look stunning with blood running down my face and a hole in my head.'

'I thought so.' He kissed her cheek, but used the gesture to get a closer look at her wound. The stitches were small and neat, disappearing into her hairline. After counting six of them, his determination iced. 'Come on, we'll go home so I can start pampering you.'

'I'll take you myself.' Randall gestured toward the door. 'I might as well look around a bit while I'm there.'

Sweeney clucked like a mother hen and had Pandora bundled into bed five minutes after she'd walked in the door. If she'd had the strength, Pandora would have argued for form's sake. Instead she let herself be tucked under a comforter, fed soup and sweet tea, and fussed over. Though the doctor had assured her it was perfectly safe to sleep, she thought of the old wives' tale and struggled to stay awake. Armed with a sketch pad and pencil, she whiled away the time designing. But when she began to tire of that, she began to think.

Murder. It would have been nothing less than murder. Murder for gain, she mused, an impossible thing for her to understand. She'd told herself before that her life was threatened, but somehow it had seemed remote. She had only to touch her own forehead now to prove just how direct it had become.

An uncle, a cousin, an aunt? Which one wanted Jolley's fortune so badly to murder for it? Not for the first time, Pandora wished she knew them better, understood them better. She realized she'd simply followed Jolley's lead and dismissed them as boring.

And that was true enough, Pandora assured herself. She'd been to a party or two with all of them. Monroe would huff, Biff would preen, Ginger would prattle, and so on. But boring or not, one of them had slipped over the line of civilized behavior. And they were willing to step over her to do it. Slowly, from memory, she began to sketch each of her relatives. Perhaps that way, she'd see something that was buried in her subconscious.

When Michael came in, she had sketches lined in rows over her spread. 'Quite a rogues' gallery.'

He'd come straight from the garage, where he and Randall had found the still-wet brake fluid on the concrete. Not all of it, Michael mused. Whoever had tampered with the brakes had left enough fluid in so that the car would react normally for the first few miles. And then, nothing. Michael had already concluded that the police would find a hole in the lines. Just as they'd find one in the lines of Pandora's, to match the dark puddle beneath her car. It had been every bit as lethal as his.

He wasn't ready to tell Pandora that whoever had tried to kill them had been as close as the garage a day, perhaps two, before. Instead he looked at her sketches.

'What do you see?' she demanded.

'That you have tremendous talent and should give serious thought to painting.'

'I mean in their faces.' Impatient with herself, she drew her legs up cross-legged. 'There's just nothing there. No spark, no streak of anything that tells me this one's capable of killing.'

'Anyone's capable of killing. Oh yes,' Michael added when she opened her mouth to disagree. 'Anyone. It's simply that the motive has to fit the personality, the circumstances, the need. When a person's threatened, he kills. For some it's only when their lives or the lives of someone they love are threatened.'

'That's entirely different.'

'No.' He sat on the bed. 'It's a matter of different degrees. Some people kill because their home is threatened, their possessions. Some kill because a desire is threatened. Wealth, power, those are very strong desires.

'So a very ordinary, even conventional person might kill to achieve that desire.'

He gestured to her sketches. 'One of them tried. Aunt Patience with her round little face and myopic eyes.'

'You can't seriously believe—'

'She's devoted to Morgan, obsessively so. She's never married. Why? Because she's always taken care of him.'

He picked up the next sketch. 'Or there's Morgan himself, stout, blunt, hard-nosed. He thought Jolley was mad and a nuisance.'

'They all did.'

'Exactly. Carlson, straitlaced, humorless, and Jolley's only surviving son.'

'He tried contesting the will.'

'Going the conventional route. Still, he knew his father was shrewd, perhaps better than anyone. Who's to say he wouldn't cover his bases in a more direct way? Biff...' He had a laugh as he looked at the sketch. Pandora had drawn him precisely as he was. Self-absorbed.

'I can't see him getting his hands dirty.'

'For a slice of a hundred fifty million? I can. Pretty little Ginger. One wonders if she can possibly be as sweet and spacey as she appears. And Hank.' Pandora had drawn him with his arm muscle flexed. 'Would he settle for a couple of thousand when he could have millions?'

'I don't know—that's just the point.' Pandora shuffled the sketches. 'Even when I have them all lined up in front of me, I don't know.'

'Lined up,' Michael murmured. 'Maybe that is the answer. I think it's time we had a nice, family party.'

'Party? You don't mean actually invite them all here.'

'It's perfect.'

'They won't come.'

'Oh yes, they will.' He was already thinking ahead. 'You can bank on it. A little hint that things aren't going well around here, and they'll jump at the chance to give us an extra push. You see the doctor in a week. If he gives you a clean bill of health, we're going to start a little game of our own.'

'What game?'

'In a week,' he repeated, and took her face in his hands. It was narrow, dominated by the mop of hair and sharp eyes. Not beautiful, but special. It had taken him a long time to admit it. 'A bit pale.'

'I'm always pale with a concussion. Are you going to pamper me?'

'At least.' But his smile faded as he gathered her close. 'Oh God, I thought I'd lost you.'

The trace of desperation in his voice urged her to soothe. 'We'd both have been lost if you hadn't handled the car so well.' She snuggled into his shoulder. It was real and solid, like the one she'd sometimes imagined leaning on. It wouldn't hurt, just this once, to pretend it would always be there. 'I never thought we'd walk away from that one.'

'But we did.' He drew back to look at her. She looked tired and drawn, but he knew her will was as strong as ever. 'And now we're going to talk about what you said to me right before we crashed.'

'Wasn't I screaming?'

'No.'

'If I criticized your driving, I apologize.'

He tightened his grip on her chin. 'You told me you loved me.' He watched her mouth fall open in genuine surprise. Some men might have been insulted. Michael could bless his sense of humor. 'It could technically be called a deathbed confession.'

Had she? She could only remember reaching for him in those last seconds, knowing they were about to die together. 'I was hysterical,' she began, and tried to draw back.

'It didn't sound like raving to me.'

'Michael, you heard Dr. Barnhouse. I'm not supposed to have any stress. If you want to be helpful, see about some more tea.'

'I've something better for relaxing the muscles and soothing the nerves.' He laid her back against the pillows, sliding down with her. Sweetly, tenderly, he ran his lips down the lines of her cheekbones. 'I want to hear you tell me again, here.'

'Michael—'

'No, lie back.' And his hands, gentle and calm, stilled

her. 'I need to touch you, just touch you. There's plenty of time for the rest.'

He was so kind, so patient. More than once she'd wondered how such a restive, volatile man could have such comforting hands. Taking off only his shoes, he slipped into bed with her. He held her in the crook of his arm and stroked until he felt her sigh of relief. 'I'm going to take care of you,' he murmured. 'When you're well, we'll take care of each other.'

'I'll be fine tomorrow.' But her voice was thick and sleepy.

'Sure you will.' He'd keep her in bed another twenty-four hours if he had to chain her. 'You haven't told me again. Are you in love with me, Pandora?'

She was so tired, so drained. It seemed she'd reached a point where she could fight nothing. 'What if I am?' She managed to tilt her head back to stare at him. His fingers rubbed gently at her temple, easing even the dull echo of pain. 'People fall in and out of love all the time.'

'People.' He lowered his head so that he could just skim her lips with his. 'Not Pandora. It infuriates you, doesn't it?'

She wanted to glare but closed her eyes instead. 'Yes. I'm doing my best to reverse the situation.'

He snuggled down beside her, content for now. She loved him. He still had time to make her like the idea. 'Let me know how it works out,' he said, and lulled her to sleep.

Chapter 12

Michael studied the dark stains on the garage floor with a kind of grim fascination. Draining the brake fluid from an intended victim's car was a hackneyed device, one expected from time to time on any self-respecting action-adventure show. Viewers and readers alike developed a certain fondness for old, reliable angles in the same way they appreciated the new and different. Though it took on a different picture when it became personal, the car careering out of control down a steep mountain road was as old as the Model T.

He'd used it himself, just as he'd used the anonymous gift of champagne. And the bogus-message routine, he mused as an idea began to stir. Just last season one of *Logan's* heroines of the week had been locked in a cellar—left in the dark after going to investigate a window slamming in the wind. It too was a classic. Each and every one of the ploys used against himself and Pandora could have been lifted from one of his own plots. Randall had pointed it out, though he'd been joking. It didn't seem very funny.

Michael cursed himself, knowing he should have seen the pattern before. Perhaps he hadn't simply because it had been a pattern, a trite one by Hollywood standards. Whether it was accidental or planned, Michael decided he wasn't about to be outplotted. He'd make his next move taking a page from the classic mystery novels. Going into the house, Michael went to the phone and began to structure his scene.

He was just completing his last call when Pandora came down the hall toward him. 'Michael, you've got to do something about Sweeney.'

Michael leaned back against the newel post and studied her. She looked wonderful—rested, healthy and annoyed. 'Isn't it time for your afternoon nap?'

'That's just what I'm talking about.' The annoyance deepened between her brows and pleased him. 'I don't need an afternoon nap. It's been over a week since the accident.' She pulled a leather thong out of her hair and began to run it through her fingers. 'I've seen the doctor, and he said I was fine.'

'I thought it was more something along the lines of you having a head like a rock.'

She narrowed her eyes. 'He was annoyed because I healed perfectly without him. The point is, I am healed, but if Sweeney keeps nagging and hovering, I'll have a relapse.' It came out as a declaration as she stood straight in front of him, chin lifted, looking as though she'd never been ill a day in her life.

'What would you like me to do?'

'She'll listen to you. For some reason she has the idea that you're infallible. Mr. Donahue this, Mr. Donahue that.' She slapped the leather against her palm. 'For the past week all I've heard is how charming, handsome and strong you are. It's a wonder I recovered at all.'

His lips twitched, but he understood Sweeney's flattery could undo any progress he'd made. 'The woman's perceptive. However...' He stopped Pandora's retort by holding up a hand. 'Because I'd never refuse you any-thing—' when she snorted he ignored it '—and because she's been driving me crazy fussing over my wrist, I'm going to take care of it.'

Pandora tilted her head. 'How?'

'Sweeney's going to be too busy over the next few days to fuss over us. She'll have the dinner party to fuss over.'

'What dinner party?'

'The dinner party we're going to give next week for all our relatives.'

She glanced at the phone, remembering he'd been using it when she'd come down the hall. 'What have you been up to?'

'Just setting the scene, cousin.' He rocked back on his heels, already imagining. 'I think we'll have Sweeney dig out the best china, though I doubt we'll have time to use it.'

'Michael.' She didn't want to seem a coward, but the

accident had taught her something about caution and self-preservation. 'We won't just be inviting relatives. One of them tried to kill us.'

'And failed.' He took her chin in his hand. 'Don't you think he'll try again, Pandora, and again? The police can't patrol the grounds indefinitely. And,' he added with his fingers tightening, 'I'm not willing to let bygones be bygones.' His gaze skimmed up to where her hair just covered the scar on her forehead. The doctor had said it would fade, but Michael's memory of it never would. 'We're going to settle this, my way.'

'I don't like it.'

'Pandora.' He gave her a charming smile and pinched her cheek. 'Trust me.'

The fact that she did only made her more nervous. With a sigh, she took his hand. 'Let's tell Sweeney to kill the fatted calf.'

Right down to the moment the first car arrived, Pandora was certain no one would come. She'd sat through a discussion of Michael's plan, argued, disagreed, admired and ultimately she'd given up. Theatrics, she'd decided. But there was enough Jolley in her to look forward to the show, especially when she was one of the leads. And she had, as they said in the business, her part cold.

She'd dressed for the role in a slim, strapless black dress. For flair, she'd added a sterling silver necklace she'd fashioned in an exaggerated star burst. Matching earrings dripped nearly to her chin. If Michael wanted drama, who was she to argue? As the night of the dinner party had grown closer, her nerves had steeled into determination.

When he saw her at the top of the stairs, he was speechless. Had he really convinced himself all these years she had no real beauty? At the moment, poised, defiant and enjoying herself, she made every other woman he'd known look like a shadow. And if he told her so, she wouldn't believe it for a moment. Instead he merely nodded and rocked back on his heels.

'Perfect,' he told her as she walked down the main stairs. Standing at the base in a dark suit, Michael looked invincible, and ruthless. 'The sophisticated heroine.' He took her hand. 'Cool and sexy. Hitchcock would've made you a star.'

'Don't forget what happened to Janet Leigh.'

He laughed and sent one of her earrings spinning. 'Nervous?'

'Not as much as I'd thought I'd be. If this doesn't work—'

'Then we're no worse off than we are now. You know what to do.'

'We've rehearsed it a half-dozen times. I still have the bruises.'

He leaned closer to kiss both bare shoulders. 'I always thought you'd be a natural. When this is over, we have a scene of our own to finish. No, don't pull back,' he warned as she attempted to. 'It's too late to pull back.' They stood close, nearly mouth to mouth. 'It's been too late all along.'

Nerves she'd managed to quell came racing back, but

they had nothing to do with plots or plans. 'You're being dramatic.'

With a nod, he tangled his fingers in her hair. 'My sense of drama, your streak of practicality. An interesting combination.'

'An uneasy one.'

'If life's too easy you sleep through it,' Michael decided. 'It sounds like the first of our guests are arriving,' he murmured as they heard the sound of a car. He kissed her briefly. 'Break a leg.'

She wrinkled her nose at his back. 'That's what I'm afraid of.'

Within a half hour, everyone who had been at the reading of the will, except Fitzhugh, was again in the library. No one seemed any more relaxed than they'd been almost six months before. Jolley beamed down on them from the oil painting. From time to time Pandora glanced up at it almost expecting him to wink. To give everyone what they'd come for, Pandora and Michael kept arguing about whatever came to mind. Time for the game to begin, she decided.

Carlson stood with his wife near a bookshelf. He looked cross and impatient and glowered when Pandora approached.

'Uncle Carlson, I'm so glad you could make it. We don't see nearly enough of each other.'

'Don't soft-soap me.' He swirled his scotch but didn't drink. 'If you've got the idea you can talk me out of contesting this absurd will, you're mistaken.'

'I wouldn't dream of it. Fitzhugh tells me you don't

have a chance.' She smiled beautifully. 'But I have to agree the will's absurd, especially after being forced to live in the same house with Michael all these months.' She ran a finger down one of the long, flattened prongs of her necklace. 'I'll tell you, Uncle Carlson, there have been times I've seriously considered throwing in the towel. He's done everything possible to make the six months unbearable. Once he pretended his mother was ill, and he had to go to California. Next thing I knew I was locked in the basement. Childish games,' she muttered sending Michael a look of utter dislike. Out of the corner of her eye, she saw Carlson take a quick, nervous drink. 'Well, the sentence is nearly up.' She turned back with a fresh smile. 'I'm so glad we could have this little celebration. Michael's finally going to open a bottle of champagne he's been hoarding since Christmas.'

Pandora watched Carlson's wife drop her glass on the Turkish carpet. 'Dear me,' Pandora said softly. 'We'll have to get something to mop that up. Freshen your drink?'

'No, she's fine.' Carlson took his wife by the elbow. 'Excuse me.'

As they moved away, Pandora felt a quick thrill of excitement. So, it had been Carlson.

'I quit smoking about six months ago,' Michael told Hank and his wife, earning healthy approval.

'You'll never regret it,' Hank stated in his slow, deliberate way. 'You're responsible for your own body.'

'I've been giving that a lot of thought lately,' Michael said dryly. 'But living with Pandora the past few months hasn't made it easy. She's made this past winter miserable. She had someone send me a fake message so I'd go flying off to California thinking my mother was ill.' He glanced over his shoulder and scowled at Pandora's back.

'If you've gotten through six months without smoking…' Meg began, guiding the conversation back to Michael's health.

'It's a miracle I have living with that woman. But it's almost over.' He grinned at Hank. 'We're having champagne instead of carrot juice for dinner. I've been saving this bottle since Christmas for just the right occasion.'

He saw Hank's fingers whiten around his glass of Perrier and Meg's color drain. 'We don't—' Hank looked helplessly at Meg. 'We don't drink.'

'Champagne isn't drinking,' Michael said jovially. 'It's celebrating. Excuse me.' He moved to the bar as if to freshen his drink and waited for Pandora to join him. 'It's Hank.'

'No.' She added a splash of vermouth to her glass. 'It's Carlson.' Following the script, she glared at him. 'You're an insufferable bore, Michael. Putting up with you isn't worth any amount of money.'

'Intellectual snob.' He toasted her. 'I'm counting the days.'

With a sweep of her skirts, Pandora walked over to Ginger. 'I don't know how I manage to hold my temper with that man.'

Ginger checked her face in a pretty silver compact. 'I've always thought he was kind of cute.'

'You haven't had to live with him. We were hardly

together a week when he broke into my workshop and vandalized it. Then he tried to pass the whole thing off as the work of a vagrant.'

Ginger frowned and touched a bit of powder to her nose. 'It didn't seem like something he'd do to me. I told—' She caught herself and looked back at Pandora with a vague smile. 'Those are pretty earrings.'

Michael steeled himself to listen to Morgan's terse opinion on the stock market. The moment he found an opening, he broke in. 'Once everything's settled, I'll have to come to you for advice. I've been thinking about getting more actively involved with one of Jolley's chemical firms. There's a lot of money in fertilizer—and pesticides.' He watched Patience flutter her hands and subside at a glare from Morgan.

'Software,' Morgan said briefly.

Michael only smiled. 'I'll look into it.'

Pandora tried unsuccessfully to pump Ginger. The five-minute conversation left her suspicious, confused and with the beginnings of a headache. She decided to try her luck on Biff.

'You're looking well.' She smiled at him and nodded at his wife.

'You're looking a bit pale, cousin.'

'The past six months haven't been a picnic.' She cast a look at Michael. 'Of course, you've always detested him.'

'Of course,' Biff said amiably.

'I've yet to discover why Uncle Jolley was fond of him. Besides being a bore, Michael has an affection for odd practical jokes. He got a tremendous kick out of locking me in the cellar.'

Biff smiled into his glass. 'He's never quite been in our class.'

Pandora bit her tongue, then agreed. 'Do you know, he even called me one night, disguising his voice. He tried to frighten me by saying someone was trying to kill me.'

Biff's brows drew together as he stared into Pandora's eyes. 'Odd.'

'Well, things are almost settled. By the way, did you enjoy the champagne I sent you?'

Biff's fingers froze on his glass. 'Champagne?'

'Right after Christmas.'

'Oh yes.' He lifted his glass again, studying her as he drank. 'So it was you.'

'I got the idea when someone sent Michael a bottle at Christmastime. He promises to finally open it tonight. Excuse me, I want to check on dinner.'

Her eyes met Michael's briefly as she slipped from the room. They'd set his scene, she thought. Now she had to move the action along. In the kitchen she found Sweeney finishing up the final preparation for the meal.

'If they're hungry,' Sweeney began, 'they'll just have to wait ten minutes.'

'Sweeney, it's time to turn off the main power switch.'

'I know, I know. I was just finishing this ham.'

Sweeney had been instructed to, at Pandora's signal, go down to the cellar, turn off the power, then wait exactly one minute and turn it on again. She had been skeptical about the whole of Michael and Pandora's plan but had finally agreed to participate in it. Wiping her hands on her apron, the cook went to the cellar door. Pandora took a deep breath and walked back to the library.

Michael had positioned himself near the desk. He gave Pandora the slightest of nods when she entered. 'Dinner in ten minutes,' she announced brightly as she swept across the room.

'That gives us just enough time.' Michael took the stage and couldn't resist starting with a tried and true line. He didn't have to see Pandora to know she was taking her position. 'You all must be wondering why we brought you here tonight.' He lifted his glass and looked from one face to the next. 'One of you is a murderer.'

On cue, the lights went out and pandemonium struck. Glasses shattered, women screamed, a table was overturned. When the lights blinked on, everyone froze. Lying half under the desk, facedown, was Pandora. Beside her was a letter opener with a curved, ornate hilt and blood on the blade. In an instant Michael was beside her, lifting her into his arms before anyone had a chance to react. Silently, he carried her from the room. Several minutes passed before he returned, alone. He gazed, hot and hard, at every face in the room.

'A murderer,' he repeated. 'She's dead.'

'What do you mean she's dead?' Carlson pushed his way forward. 'What kind of game is this? Let's have a look at her.'

'No one's touching her.' Michael effectively blocked his way. 'No one's touching anything or leaving this room until the police get here.'

'Police?' Pale and shaken, Carlson glanced around. 'We don't want that. We'll have to handle this ourselves. She's just fainted.'

'Her blood's all over this,' Michael commented gesturing to the bloodstained letter opener.

'No!' Meg pushed forward until she'd broken through the crowd around the desk. 'No one was supposed to be hurt. Only frightened. It wasn't supposed to be like this. Hank.' She reached out, then buried her face against his chest.

'We were only going to play some tricks,' he murmured.

'First-degree murder isn't a trick.'

'We never—' He looked at Michael in shock. 'Not murder,' he managed, holding Meg as tightly as she was holding him.

'You didn't want to drink the champagne, either, did you, Hank?'

'That's when I wanted to stop.' Still sobbing, Meg turned in her husband's arms. 'I even called and tried to warn her. I thought it was wrong all along, just a mean trick, but we needed money. The gym's drained everything we have. We thought if we could make the two of you angry enough with each other, you'd break the terms of the will. But that's all. Hank and I stayed in the cabin and waited. Then he went into Pandora's shop and turned things upside down. If she thought you did it—'

'I never thought she would,' Ginger piped up. Two tears rolled down her cheeks. 'Really, it all seemed silly and—exciting.'

Michael looked at his pretty, weeping cousin. 'So you were part of it.'

'Well, I didn't really do anything. But when Aunt Patience explained it to me…'

'Patience?' There were patterns and patterns. A new one emerged.

'Morgan deserved his share.' The old woman wrung her hands and looked everywhere but at the bloodstained letter opener. She'd thought she'd done the right thing. It all sounded so simple. 'We thought we could make one of you leave, then it would all be the way it should be.'

'Message,' Morgan said, puffing wide-eyed on his cigar. 'Not murder.' He turned to Carlson. 'Your idea.'

'It's preposterous.' Carlson mopped his brow with a white silk handkerchief. 'The lawyers were incompetent. They haven't been able to do a thing. I was merely protecting my rights.'

'With murder.'

'Don't be ridiculous.' He nearly sounded staid and stuffy again. 'The plan was to get you out of the house. I did nothing more than lock—her—in the cellar. When I heard about the champagne, I had a doubt or two, but after all, it wasn't fatal.'

'Heard about the champagne.' It was what Michael had waited for. 'From whom?'

'It was Biff,' Meg told him. 'Biff set it all up, promised nothing would go wrong.'

'Just an organizer.' Biff gauged the odds, then shrugged. 'All's fair, cousin. Everyone in this room had their hand in.' He held his up, examining it. 'There's no blood on mine. I'd vote for you.' He gave Michael a cool smile. 'After all, it's no secret you couldn't abide each other.'

'You set it up.' Michael took a step closer. 'There's also a matter of tampering with my car.'

Biff moved his shoulders again, but Michael saw the sweat bead above his lips. 'Everyone in this room had a part in it. Any of you willing to turn yourselves in?' His breath came faster as he backed away. 'One of them panicked and did this. You won't find my fingerprints on that letter opener.'

'When someone's attempted murder once,' Michael said calmly, 'it's easier to prove he tried again.'

'You won't prove anything. Any of us might have drained the brake lines in your car. You can't prove I did.'

'I don't need to.' In a quick move, Michael caught him cleanly on the jaw and sent him reeling. Before he could fall, Michael had him by the collar. 'I never said anything about draining the lines.'

Feeling the trap close, Biff struck out blindly. Fists swinging, they tumbled to the floor. A Tiffany lamp shattered in a pile of color. They rolled, locked together, into a Belker table that shook from the impact. Shocked and ineffective, the rest stepped back and gave them room.

'Michael, that's quite enough.' Pandora entered the room, her hair mussed and her clothes disheveled. 'We have company.'

Panting, he dragged Biff to his feet. His wrist sang a bit, but he considered it a pleasure. Charles, looking dignified in his best suit, opened the library doors. 'Dinner is served.'

* * *

Two hours later, Pandora and Michael shared a small feast in the library. 'I never thought it would work,' Pandora said over a mouthful of ham. 'It shouldn't have.'

'The more predictable the moves, the more predictable the end.'

'Lieutenant Randall didn't seem too pleased.'

'He wanted to do it his way.' Michael moved his shoulders. 'Since he'd already discovered Biff had been visiting other members of the family and making calls to them, he was bound to find out something eventually.'

'The easy way.' She rubbed the back of her neck. 'Do you know how uncomfortable it is to play dead?'

'You were great.' He leaned over to kiss her. 'A star.'

'The letter opener with the stage blood was a nice touch. Still, if they'd all stuck together...'

'We already knew someone was weakening because of the warning call. Turned out that Meg had had enough.'

'I've been thinking about investing in their gym.'

'It wouldn't hurt.'

'What do you think's going to happen?'

'Oh, Carlson'll get off more or less along with the rest of them, excluding Biff. I don't think we have to worry about going to court over the will. As for our dear cousin—' Michael lifted a glass of champagne '—he's going to be facing tougher charges than malicious mischief or burglary. I may never get my television back, but he isn't going to be wearing any Brooks Brothers suits for a while. Only prison blues.'

'You gave him another black eye,' Pandora mused.

'Yeah.' With a grin, Michael drank the wine. 'Now you and I only have to cruise through the next two weeks.'

'Then it's over.'

'No.' He took her hand before she could rise. 'Then it begins.' He slipped the glass from her other hand and pressed her back against the cushions. 'How long?'

Pandora struggled to keep the tension from showing. 'How long what?'

'Have you been in love with me?'

She jerked, then was frustrated when he held her back. 'I'm not sitting here feeding your ego.'

'All right, we'll start with me.' He leaned back companionably and boxed her in. 'I think I fell in love with you when you came back from the Canary Islands and walked into the parlor. You had legs all the way to your waist and you looked down your nose at me. I've never been the same.'

'I've had enough games, Michael,' she said stiffly.

'So've I.' He traced a finger down her cheek. 'You said you loved me, Pandora.'

'Under duress.'

'Then I'll just have to keep you under duress because I'm not giving you up now. Why don't we get married right here?'

She'd started to give him a hefty shove and stopped with her hands pressed against his chest. 'What?'

'Right here in the library.' He glanced around, ignoring the overturned tables and broken china. 'It'd be a nice touch.'

'I don't know what you're talking about.'

'It's very simple. Here's the plot. You love me, I love you.'

'That's not simple,' she managed. 'I've just been accessible. Once you get back to your blond dancers and busty starlets, you'll—'

'What blond dancers? I can't stand blond dancers.'

'Michael, this isn't anything I can joke about.'

'Just wait. You buy a nice white dress, maybe a veil. A veil would suit you. We get a minister, lots of flowers and have a very traditional marriage ceremony. After that, we settle into the Folley, each pursuing our respective careers. In a year, two at the most, we give Charles and Sweeney a baby to fuss over. See?' He kissed her ear.

'People's lives aren't screenplays,' she began.

'I'm crazy about you, Pandora. Look at me.' He took her chin and held it so that their faces were close. 'As an artist, you're supposed to be able to see below the surface. That should be easy since you've always told me I'm shallow.'

'I was wrong.' She wanted to believe. Her heart already did. 'Michael, if you're playing games with me, I'll kill you myself.'

'Games are over. I love you, it's that simple.'

'Simple,' she murmured, surprised she could speak at all. 'You want to get married?'

'Living together's too easy.'

She was more surprised that she could laugh. 'Easy?'

'That's right.' He shifted her until she was lying flat on the sofa, his body pressed into hers. When his mouth came down, it wasn't patient, wasn't gentle, and everything he thought, everything he felt, communicated itself through that one contact. As she did rarely, as he asked rarely, she went limp and pliant. Her arms went around him. Perhaps it was easy after all.

'I love you, Michael.'

'We're getting married.'

'It looks that way.'

His eyes were intense when he lifted his head. 'I'm going to make life tough on you, Pandora. That's just to pay you back for the fact that you'll be the most exasperating wife on record. Do we understand each other?'

Her smile bloomed slowly. 'I suppose we always have.'

Michael pressed a kiss to her forehead, to the tip of her nose, then to her lips. 'He understood both of us.'

She followed his gaze to Jolley's portrait. 'Crazy old goat has us right where he wants us. I imagine he's having a good laugh.' She rubbed her cheek against Michael's. 'I just wish he could be here to see us married.'

Michael lifted a brow. 'Who says he won't be?' He pulled her up and picked up both glasses. 'To Maximillian Jolley McVie.'

'To Uncle Jolley.' Pandora clinked her glass to Michael's. 'To us.'

* * * * *

The Return of
Rafe MacKade

To bad boys everywhere

Prologue

The MacKade brothers were looking for trouble. They usually were. In the small town of Antietam, Maryland, it wasn't always easy to find, but then, looking was half the fun.

When they piled into Jared's secondhand Chevy, they'd squabbled over who would take the wheel. It was Jared's car, and he was the eldest, but that didn't carry much weight with his three brothers.

Rafe had wanted to drive. He'd had a need for speed, a thirst to zip along those dark, winding roads, with his foot hard on the gas and his foul and reckless mood chasing behind him. He thought perhaps he could outdistance it, or perhaps meet it head-on. If he met it, bloodied it, conquered it, he knew he would just keep driving until he was somewhere else.

Anywhere else.

They had buried their mother two weeks ago.

Perhaps because his dangerous mood showed so clearly in Rafe's jade eyes and in the cold set of his mouth, he'd been outvoted. In the end, Devin had taken the wheel, with Jared riding shotgun. Rafe brooded in the back seat with his youngest brother, Shane, beside him.

They were a rough and dangerous group, the MacKade boys. All of them tall and rangy as wild stallions, with fists ready and often too eager to find a target. Their eyes, MacKade eyes, all varying shades of green, could carve a man into pieces at ten paces. When the dark mood was on them, a wise man stayed back eleven or more.

They settled on pool and beer, though Shane complained, as he was still shy of twenty-one and wouldn't be served in Duff's Tavern.

Still, the dim, smoke-choked bar suited them. The slam and crack of the balls had just enough of a violent edge, the gaze of the scrawny-shouldered Duff Dempsey was just uneasy enough. The wariness in the eyes of the other customers, gossiping over their beers, was just flattering enough.

Nobody doubted the MacKade boys were out for trouble. In the end, they found what they were looking for.

While a cigarette dangled from the corner of his mouth, Rafe squinted against the smoke and eyed his shot. He hadn't bothered to shave in a couple of days, and the rough stubble mirrored his mood. With a solid smack, a follow-through smooth as silk, he banked the cue ball, kissed it off the seven and made his pocket.

'Good thing you're lucky at something.' At the bar, Joe Dolin tipped back his beer. He was, as usual after sundown, mostly drunk, and mean with it. He'd once been the star of the high school football team, had competed with the MacKades for the favors of pretty young girls. Now, at barely twenty-one, his face had begun to bloat and his body to sag.

The black eye he'd given his young wife before leaving the house hadn't really satisfied him.

Rafe chalked his cue and barely spared Joe a glance.

'Going to take more than hustling pool, MacKade, to keep that farm going, now that your mama's gone.' Dangling his bottle from two fingers, Joe grinned. 'Heard you're going to have to start selling off for back taxes.'

'Heard wrong.' Coolly Rafe circled the table to calculate his next shot.

'Oh, I heard right. You MacKades've always been fools, and liars.'

Before Shane could leap forward, Rafe shot out his cue to block the way. 'He's talking to me,' he said quietly. He held his brother's gaze another moment before he turned. 'Isn't that right, Joe? You're talking to me?'

'I'm talking to any of you.' As he lifted his beer again, Joe's gaze skimmed over the four of them. At twenty, Shane was tough from farm work, but still more boy than man. Then Devin, whose cool, thoughtful gaze revealed little. Over Jared, who was leaning negligently against the jukebox, waiting for the next move.

He looked back at Rafe. There was temper, hot and

ready. Recklessness worn like a second skin. 'But you'll do. Always figured you for the biggest loser of the lot, Rafe.'

'That so?' Rafe crushed out his cigarette, lifted his own beer. He drank as they completed the ritual before battle, and customers shifted in their chairs to watch. 'How're things going at the factory, Joe?'

'Least I get a paycheck,' Joe shot back. 'I got money in my pocket. Ain't nobody going to take my house from over me.'

'Not as long as your wife keeps putting in twelve-hour shifts working tables to pay the rent.'

'Shut your mouth about my wife. I earn the money in my house. I don't need no woman paying my way, like your mama had to do for your old man. Went through her inheritance like it was water, then up and died on her.'

'Yeah, he died on her.' Anger and guilt and grief welled up inside him. 'But he never laid a hand on her. She never had to come into town hiding behind scarves and dark glasses, and saying how she took a fall. Only thing your mother ever fell over, Joe, was your father's fist.'

Joe slammed his beer onto the bar, shattering the glass. 'That's a lie. I'm going to ram that lie down your throat.'

'Try it.'

'He's drunk, Rafe,' Jared murmured.

Those lethal green eyes sliced toward his brother. 'So?'

'So there isn't much point in breaking his face when he's drunk.' Jared moved a shoulder. 'He's not worth it.'

But Rafe didn't need a point. He just needed action. He lifted his cue, studied it, then laid it across the table. 'You want to take me on, Joe?'

'Don't you start in here.' Though he knew it was already too late, Duff jerked a thumb toward the wall phone. 'You make any trouble in here, I'm calling the sheriff, and the lot of you can cool off in jail.'

'Keep your damn hand off the phone,' Rafe warned him. His eyes were hard enough to have the bartender backing off. 'Outside,' he said simply.

'You and me.' Curling his fists, Joe stared at the MacKades. 'I ain't having your brothers jumping in on me while I whip your butt.'

'I don't need any help with you.' To prove it, the moment they cleared the door Rafe pivoted to avoid Joe's swing, rammed his fist into Joe's face and felt the first satisfying spill of blood.

He couldn't even have said why he was fighting. Joe meant less to him than the dust in the street. But it felt good. Even when Joe got past his guard and connected, it felt good. Fists and blood were the only clear solution. When he felt the satisfying crack of knuckles against bone, he could forget everything else.

Devin winced, then tucked his hands philosophically in his pockets when blood spurted from his brother's mouth. 'I give it five minutes.'

'Hell, Rafe'll take him down in three.' Grinning, Shane watched the grunting opponents wrestle to the ground. 'Ten bucks.'

'You're on. Come on, Rafe!' Shane shouted. 'Whip his sorry butt!'

It took three minutes, plus thirty nasty seconds with Rafe straddling Joe and methodically pumping a fist into his face. Since Joe's eyes had rolled up white and his arms were limp at his sides, Jared stepped forward to drag his brother away.

'He's finished.' To decide the matter, Jared rammed Rafe up against the brick wall of the bar. 'He's finished,' he repeated. 'Let it go.'

The vicious rage drained slowly, fading from Rafe's eyes, uncurling his fists. Emptying him. 'Let go, Jare. I'm not going to hit him again.'

Rafe looked to where Joe lay moaning, half-unconscious. Over his battered body, Devin counted out bills for Shane. 'I should have factored in how drunk he was,' Devin commented. 'If he'd been sober, it would've taken Rafe the five.'

'Rafe would never waste five full minutes on a punk like that.'

Jared shook his head. The arm that was restraining Rafe slipped companionably around Rafe's shoulders. 'Want another beer?'

'No.' He glanced toward the window of the bar, where most of the patrons had gathered to watch. Absently he swiped blood from his face. 'Somebody better pick him up and haul him home,' he called out. 'Let's get out of here.'

When he settled in the car again, the aches and bruises began to make themselves known. With half an ear, he listened to Shane's enthusiastic play-by-play of the bout and used Devin's bandanna to mop more blood from his mouth.

He was going nowhere, he thought. Doing nothing.

Being nothing. The only difference between him and Joe Dolin was that Joe was a drunk on top of it.

He hated the damn farm, the damn town, the damn trap he could feel himself sinking into with every day that passed.

Jared had his books and studies, Devin his odd and ponderous thoughts, Shane the land that seemed to delight him.

He had nothing.

On the edge of town, where the land began to climb and the trees to thicken, he saw a house. The old Barlow place. Dark, deserted and haunted, so it was said. It stood alone, unwanted, with a reputation that caused most of the townspeople to ignore it or eye it warily.

Just as they did Rafe MacKade.

'Pull over.'

'Hell, Rafe, you going to be sick?' Not concerned so much as apprehensive, Shane gripped his own door handle.

'No. Pull over, damn it, Jared.'

The minute the car stopped, Rafe was out and climbing the rocky slope. Brambles thick with thorns and summer growth tore at his jeans. He didn't need to look behind or hear the curses and mutters to know that his brothers were following him.

He stood, looking up at three stories of local stone. Mined, he supposed, from the quarry a few miles out of town. Some of the windows were broken and boarded, and the double porches sagged like an old woman's back. What had once been a lawn was overgrown with wild blackberries, thistles and witchgrass. A dead oak rose from it, gnarled and leafless.

But as the moon wheeled overhead and the breeze sang chants through the trees and tall grass, there was something compelling about the place. The way it stood two hundred years after its foundation had been laid. The way it continued to stand against time, weather and neglect. And most of all, he thought, the way it stood against the distrust and gossip of the town it overlooked.

'Going to look for ghosts, Rafe?' Shane stood beside him, eyes gleaming against the dark.

'Maybe.'

'Remember when we spent the night there, on a dare?' Absently Devin plucked a blade of grass, rolled it between his fingers. 'Ten years ago, I guess it was. Jared snuck upstairs and started creaking doors. Shane wet his pants.'

'Hell I did.'

'Hell you didn't.'

This incited the predictable shoving match, which the older brothers ignored.

'When are you leaving?' Jared said quietly. He'd known it, saw it now in the way Rafe looked at the house, into it, beyond it.

'Tonight. I've got to get away from here, Jare. Do something away from here. If I don't, I'm going to be like Dolin. Maybe worse. Mom's gone. She doesn't need me anymore. Hell, she never needed anybody.'

'Got any idea where you're going?'

'No. South, maybe. To start.' He couldn't take his eyes

off the house. He would have sworn it was watching him, judging him. Waiting. 'I'll send money when I can.'

Though he felt as though someone were wrenching off one of his limbs, Jared merely shrugged. 'We'll get by.'

'You have to finish law school. Mom wanted that.' Rafe glanced behind, to where the shoving match had progressed to wrestling in the weeds. 'They'll handle themselves okay once they figure out what they want.'

'Shane knows what he wants. The farm.'

'Yeah.' With a thin smile, Rafe took out a cigarette. 'Go figure. Sell off some of the land, if you have to, but don't let them take it. We have to keep what's ours. Before it's over, this town's going to remember the MacKades meant something.'

Rafe's smile widened. For the first time in weeks, the gnawing ache inside him eased. His brothers were sitting on the ground, covered with dirt and scratches and laughing like loons.

He was going to remember them that way, he promised himself, just that way. The MacKades, holding together on rocky ground no one wanted.

Chapter 1

The bad boy was back. The town of Antietam was buzzing over it, passing fact, rumor and innuendo from one to another, the way the guests at a boardinghouse passed bowls of steaming stew.

It was a rich broth, spiced with scandal, sex and secrets. Rafe MacKade had come back after ten years.

Some said there would be trouble. Bound to be. Trouble hung around Rafe MacKade like a bell around a bull's neck. Wasn't it Rafe MacKade who'd decked the high school principal one spring morning and gotten himself expelled? Wasn't it Rafe MacKade who'd wrecked his dead daddy's Ford pickup before he was old enough to drive?

And surely it was Rafe MacKade who'd tossed a table—and that fool Manny Johnson—through the plate-glass window of Duff's Tavern one hot summer night.

Now he'd come back, a-riding into town in some fancy sports car and parking, bold as you please, right in front of the sheriff's office.

Of course, his brother Devin was sheriff now, had been for five years last November. But there'd been a time—and most remembered—when Rafe MacKade spent more than a night or two in one of the two cells in the back.

Oh, he was as handsome as ever—so the women said. With those devil's good looks the MacKades were gifted—or cursed—with. If a female had breath in her body, she'd look twice, maybe even sigh over that long, wiry build, that loose-legged stride that seemed to dare anyone to get in the way.

Then there was that thick black hair, those eyes, as green and hard as the ones in that little Chinese statue in the window of the Past Times antique store. They did nothing to soften that tough, sharp-jawed face, with that little scar along the left eye. God knew where he'd gotten that.

But when he smiled, when he curved that beautiful mouth up and that little dimple winked at the corner, a woman's heart was bound to flutter. That sentiment came directly from Sharilyn Fenniman who'd taken that smile, and his twenty dollars for gas, at the Gas and Go, just outside of town.

Before Rafe had his car in gear again, Sharilyn had been burning up the phone wires to announce the return.

'So Sharilyn called her mama, and Mrs. Metz got right on her horse and told Mrs. Hawbaker down at the general store that Rafe maybe plans to stay.'

As she spoke, Cassandra Dolin topped off Regan's coffee. The way snow was spitting out of the January sky and clogging streets and sidewalks, there was little business at Ed's Café that afternoon. Slowly Cassie straightened her back and tried to ignore the ache in her hip where it had struck the floor after Joe knocked her down.

'Why shouldn't he?' Smiling, Regan Bishop loitered over her mulligan stew and coffee. 'He was born here, wasn't he?'

Even after three years as a resident and shopkeeper of Antietam, Regan still didn't understand the town's fascination with comings and goings. It appealed to and amused her, but she didn't understand it.

'Well, yeah, but he's been gone so long. Only came back for a day or so at a time, once or twice in ten whole years.' Cassie looked out the window, where the snow fell thin and constant. And wondered where he had gone, what he had seen, what he had done. Oh, she wondered what there was out there.

'You look tired, Cassie,' Regan murmured.

'Hmm? No, just daydreaming. This keeps up, they're going to call school early. I told the kids to come straight here if they did, but...'

'Then that's what they'll do. They're great kids.'

'They are.' When she smiled, some of the weariness lifted from her eyes.

'Why don't you get a cup? Have some coffee with me?' A scan of the café showed Regan there was a customer in a back booth, dozing over his coffee, a couple at the counter chatting over the stew special. 'You're not exactly overrun with business.' Seeing Cassie hesitate, Regan pulled out her trump. 'You could fill me in on this Rafe character.'

'Well.' Cassie nibbled on her lip. 'Ed, I'm going to take a break, okay?'

At the call, a bony woman with a frizzed ball of red hair stuck her head out of the kitchen. Sparkling-framed glasses rested on her scrawny chest, above her bib apron. 'You go ahead, honey.' Her low voice rasped from two packs of cigarettes a day. Her face was carefully painted from red lips to red eyebrows, and glowed from the heat of the stove. 'Hey there, Regan. You're fifteen minutes over your lunch hour.'

'I closed at noon,' Regan told her, well aware that her clocklike schedule amused Edwina Crump. 'People aren't looking for antiques in this kind of weather.'

'It's been a hard winter.' Cassie brought a cup to the table and poured coffee for herself. 'We're not even through January, and the kids are already getting tired of sledding and making snowmen.' She sighed, careful not to wince when the bruise on her hip ached when she sat. She was twenty-seven, a year younger than Regan. She felt ancient.

After three years of friendship, Regan recognized the signs. 'Are things bad, Cassie?' Keeping her voice low, she laid a hand over Cassie's. 'Did he hurt you again?'

'I'm fine.' But Cassie kept her eyes on her cup. Guilt, humiliation, fear, stung as much as a backhand slap. 'I don't want to talk about Joe.'

'Did you read the pamphlets I got you, about spousal abuse, the women's shelter in Hagerstown?'

'I looked at them. Regan, I have two children. I have to think of them first.'

'But—'

'Please.' Cassie lifted her gaze. 'I don't want to talk about it.'

'All right.' Struggling to hold back the impatience, Regan squeezed her hand. 'Tell me about bad boy Mac-Kade.'

'Rafe.' Cassie's face cleared. 'I always had a soft spot for him. All of them. There wasn't a girl in town who didn't moon a few nights over the MacKade brothers.'

'I like Devin.' Regan sipped at her coffee. 'He seems solid, a little mysterious at times, but dependable.'

'You can count on Devin,' Cassie agreed. 'Nobody thought any of them would turn out, but Devin makes a fine sheriff. He's fair. Jared has that fancy law practice in the city. And Shane, well, he's rough around the edges, but he works that farm like two mules. When they were younger and they came barreling into town, mothers locked up their daughters, and men kept their backs to the wall.'

'Real upstanding citizens, huh?'

'They were young, and always seemed angry at something. Rafe most of all. The night he left town, Rafe and Joe got into it over something. Rafe broke Joe's nose and knocked out a couple of his teeth.'

'Really?' Regan decided she might like this Rafe after all.

'He was always looking for a fight, Rafe was. Their father died when they were kids. I'd have been about ten,' she mused. 'Then their mama passed on, right before Rafe left town. She'd been sick nearly a year. That's how things at the farm got so bad around then. Most people thought the MacKades would have to sell out, but they held on.'

'Well, three of them did.'

'Mmm…' Cassie savored the coffee. It was so rare to have a moment just to sit. 'They were barely more than boys. Jared would have been right about twenty-three, and Rafe's just ten months behind him. Devin's about four years older than me, and Shane's a year behind him.'

'Sounds like Mrs. MacKade was a busy woman.'

'She was wonderful. Strong. She held everything together, no matter how bad it got. I always admired her.'

'Sometimes you need to be strong to let things go,' Regan murmured. She shook her head. She'd promised herself she wouldn't push. 'So, what do you think he's come back for?'

'I don't know. They say he's rich now. Made a pile buying land and houses and selling them again. He's supposed to have a company and everything. MacKade. That's what he calls it. Just MacKade. My mother always said he'd end up dead or in jail, but…'

Her voice trailed off as she looked through the window. 'Oh, my,' she murmured. 'Sharilyn was right.'

'Hmm?'

'He looks better than ever.'

Curious, Regan turned her head just as the door jingled open. As black sheep went, she was forced to admit, this one was a prime specimen.

He shook snow from thick hair the color of coal dust

and shrugged off a black leather bomber jacket that wasn't meant for East Coast winters. Regan thought he had a warrior's face—the little scar, the unshaven chin, the slightly crooked nose that kept that mouth-watering face from being too pretty.

His body looked hard as granite, and his eyes, sharp green, were no softer.

In worn flannel, torn jeans and scarred boots, he didn't look rich and successful. But he sure looked dangerous.

It amused and pleased Rafe to see Ed's place was so much the same. Those could be the same stools at the counter that he'd warmed his seat on as a child, anticipating a sundae or a fountain drink. Surely those were the same smells—grease, frying onions, the haze from Ed's constant cigarettes, an undertone of pine cleaner.

He was sure Ed would be back in the kitchen, flipping burgers or stirring pots. And sure as hell that was old man Tidas snoring in the back booth while his coffee went cold. Just as he'd always done.

His eyes, cool, assessing, skimmed over the painfully white counter, with its clear-plastic-topped plates of pies and cakes, over the walls, with their black-and-white photos of Civil War battles, to a booth where two women sat over coffee.

He saw a stranger. An impressive one. Honey brown hair cut in a smooth chin-length swing that framed a face of soft curves and creamy skin. Long lashes over dark and coolly curious blue eyes. And a sassy little mole right at the corner of a full and unsmiling mouth.

Picture-perfect, he thought. Just like something cut out of a glossy magazine.

They studied each other, assessed each other as a man or woman might assess a particularly attractive trinket in a shop window. Then his gaze shifted to land on the fragile little blonde with the haunted eyes and the hesitant smile.

'Son of a bitch.' His grin flashed and upped the temperature by twenty degrees. 'Little Cassie Connor.'

'Rafe. I heard you were back.' The sound of her giggle as Rafe plucked her from the booth had Regan's brow lifting. It was rare to hear Cassie laugh so freely.

'Pretty as ever,' he said, and kissed her full on the lips. 'Tell me you kicked that idiot out and left the path clear for me.'

She eased back, always fearful of wagging tongues. 'I've got two kids now.'

'A boy and a girl. I heard.' He tugged the strap of her bib apron, and thought with some concern that she'd lost too much weight. 'You're still working here?'

'Yeah. Ed's in the back.'

'I'll go see her in a minute.' Resting a hand casually on Cassie's shoulder, he looked back at Regan. 'Who's your pal?'

'Oh, sorry. This is Regan Bishop. She owns Past Times, an antique and decorating store a couple doors down. Regan, this is Rafe MacKade.'

'Of the MacKade brothers.' She offered a hand. 'Word's already traveled.'

'I'm sure it has.' He took her hand, held it, as his eyes

held hers. 'Antiques? That's a coincidence. I'm in the market.'

'Are you?' She'd risk her dignity if she tugged her hand from his. From the gleam in his eye, she was sure he knew it. 'Any particular era?'

'Mid-to-late-1800s—everything from soup to nuts. I've got a three-story house, about twelve hundred square feet to furnish. Think you can handle it?'

It took a lot of willpower for her to keep her jaw from dropping. She did well enough with tourists and towns-people, but a commission like this would easily triple her usual income.

'I'm sure I can.'

'You bought a house?' Cassie said interrupting them. 'I thought you'd be staying out at the farm.'

'For now. The house isn't for living in, not for me. After some remodeling, restoring, I'll be opening it up as a bed-and-breakfast. I bought the old Barlow place.'

Stunned, Cassie bobbled the coffeepot she'd fetched. 'The Barlow place? But it's—'

'Haunted?' A reckless light glinted in his eyes. 'Damn right it is. How about a piece of that pie to go with the coffee, Cassie? I've worked up an appetite.'

Regan had left but Rafe had loitered for an hour, entertained when Cassie's kids burst in out of the snow. He watched her fuss over them, scold the boy for forgetting to put on his gloves, listened to the big-eyed little girl solemnly relate the adventures of the day.

There was something sad, and somehow soothing,

about watching the girl he remembered settling her two children at a booth with crayons and books.

A lot had stayed the same over a decade. But a lot had changed. He was well aware that news of his arrival was even now singing over telephone wires. It pleased him. He wanted the town to know he was back—and not with his tail between his legs, as many had predicted.

He had money in his pocket now, and plans for the future.

The Barlow place was the heart of his plans. He didn't subscribe to ghosts, under most circumstances, but the house had certainly haunted him. Now it belonged to him, every old stone and bramble—and whatever else it held. He was going to rebuild it, as he had rebuilt himself.

One day he would stand at the top window and look down on the town. He would prove to everyone—even to Rafe MacKade—that he was somebody.

He tucked a generous tip under his cup, careful to keep the amount just shy of one that would embarrass Cassie. She was too thin, he thought, and her eyes were too guarded. That weary fragility had been thrown into sharp relief when she sat with Regan.

Now there was a woman, he mused, who knew how to handle herself. Steady eyes, stubborn chin, soft hands. She hadn't so much as blinked when he offered her a shot at furnishing an entire inn. Oh, he imagined her insides had jolted, but she hadn't blinked.

As a man who'd earned his keep on the wheel and deal, he had to admire her for it. Time would tell if she'd hold up to the challenge.

And there was no time like the present.

'That antique place, two doors down?'

'That's right.' Cassie kept one eye on her children as she brewed a fresh pot of coffee. 'On the left. I don't think she's open, though.'

Rafe shrugged into his jacket and grinned. 'Oh, I bet she is.'

He strolled out, hatless, jacket open, his footsteps muffled by the cushioning snow. As he'd expected, the lights were on inside Past Times. Instead of seeking shelter inside, he studied her window display and found it clever and effective.

A sweep of blue brocade like a pool of shimmering water flowed over varying levels. A bright-eyed porcelain doll sat on a child-size ladder-back rocker, an artful tumble of antique toys at her feet. A snarling jade dragon curled on a pedestal. A glossy mahogany jewelry box stood open, glittery baubles spilling out of its drawers as though a woman's hands had slid through them in search of just the right piece.

Perfume bottles were arranged in pretty sunbursts of color on an enameled shelf.

Put the sparkles up front, he thought with a nod, and rope the customers in.

Sleigh bells hung on the door tinkled musically when he opened it. The air inside was spiced with cinnamon and cloves and apples. And, he realized after a deep breath of it, of Regan Bishop. The subtle and sultry perfume he'd noted in the café just teased the air.

He took his time wandering. Furniture was meticulously arranged for traffic patterns. A settee here, an occasional table there. Lamps, bowls, vases, all doing double duty as display and decoration. A dining room table was gracefully set with china and glassware, candles and flowers, as if guests were expected any moment. An old Victrola stood open beside a cabinet filled with 78s.

There were three rooms, each as polished and organized as the last. Nowhere in her inventory did he notice a single speck of dust. He paused by a kitchen hutch filled with white stoneware dishes and blue-tinted mason jars.

'It's a nice piece,' Regan said from behind him.

'We have one like this in the kitchen at the farm.' He didn't turn. He'd known she was there. 'My mother kept the everyday dishes in it. White ones, like these. And glasses. Thick ones that didn't break easy. She threw one at me once when I sassed her.'

'Did she hit you?'

'No. Would have if she'd meant to.' Now he turned and flashed that killer grin. 'She had a hell of an arm. What are you doing in the middle of nowhere, Regan Bishop?'

'Selling my wares, Rafe MacKade.'

'Your wares aren't half-bad. How much for the dragon in the window?'

'You have excellent taste. It's five-fifty.'

'That's steep, Regan.' Reaching out, he slipped open the single gold button of her navy blazer.

She found the little gesture oddly intimate, but refused to comment on it. 'You get what you pay for.'

'If you're smart, you can get more.' He tucked his

thumbs in the front pockets of his jeans and began to wander again. 'How long have you been in town?'

'Three years last summer.'

'From?' When she didn't answer, he glanced back, lifted one of those sexy black brows. 'Just making conversation, darling. I like to get a handle on the people I'm doing business with.'

'We haven't done any business, yet.' She tucked her hair behind her ear and smiled. 'Darling.'

His laugh erupted, quick and charming. Little ripples of response skidded up her spine. He was, she was sure, the man every mother had ever warned her daughter about. As tempting as it was, business was business. And it always came first.

'I think I'm going to like you, Regan.' He tilted his head. 'You sure are a looker.'

'Making conversation again?'

'An observation.' With a smile hovering around his mouth, he glanced down at her hands. She wore rings, pretty, glittery stones and twists of gold. 'Any of those mean anything that's going to get in my way?'

Her stomach fluttered. Her spine stiffened. 'I'd say that depends on which way you're heading.'

'Nope,' he declared. 'You're not married. You'd have tossed that in my face. So.' Satisfied, he sat on a red velvet love seat, tossed his arm over the curved back. 'Want to sit down?'

'No, thanks. Did you come in to do business, or to talk me into bed?'

'I never talk women into bed.' He smiled at her.

No, she thought, he'd just have to flash that smile and crook his finger.

'Business, Regan.' Relaxed, he crossed his booted feet. 'For now, just business.'

'All right. Then I'll offer you some hot cider.'

'I'll take it.'

She moved through a doorway, into the back. Alone, Rafe brooded for a moment. He hadn't meant to be so obvious, hadn't realized he was quite so attracted. There had been something about the way she stood there, in her tailored blazer and tasteful jewelry, her eyes so cool and amused, her scent just short of hot.

If he'd ever seen a woman who announced a thorny road, it was Regan Bishop. Though he rarely chose the smooth path, he had too much on his plate to take the challenge.

Then she came back in on those long, glamorous legs, that pretty swing of hair half curtaining her face.

What the hell, he thought, he could always make room on his plate.

'Thanks.' He took the steaming enameled mug she offered. 'I figured on hiring a firm out of D.C. or Baltimore, maybe taking some time to hunt through some shops myself.'

'I can acquire anything a firm in D.C. or Baltimore can, and offer a better price.' She hoped.

'Maybe. The thing is, I like the idea of keeping the business close to home. We'll see what you can do.' He sipped the cider, found it hot and pungent. 'What do you know about the Barlow place?'

'It's falling apart. I think it's a crime that nothing's been done to preserve it. This part of the country is usually careful with its historic areas and buildings. But the town ignores that place. If I had the means, I'd have bought it myself.'

'And you'd have gotten more than you bargained for. The house is solid as rock. If it wasn't so well built, it'd be rubble by now. But, it needs work…' he mused, and began to picture it all in his head. 'Floors to be leveled and sanded and sealed, walls to be plastered or taken down, windows replaced. The roof's a mess.'

He brought himself back, shrugged. 'That's just time and money. When it's ready, I want to put it back the way it looked in 1862, when the Barlows lived there and watched the Battle of Antietam from their parlor window.'

'Did they?' Regan asked with a smile. 'I'd have thought they'd have been cowering in the root cellar.'

'Not the way I imagine it. The rich and privileged watching the show, maybe annoyed when cannon fire cracked a window or the screams of the dead and dying woke the baby from its nap.'

'You're a cynical one. Being rich wouldn't mean you wouldn't feel horror if you had to watch men dying on your front lawn.'

'The heart of the battle didn't get quite that close. Anyway, that's what I want—the right colors, trim, wallpaper, furnishings, doodads. The works.' He had an urge for a cigarette and banked it. 'How do you feel about redoing a haunted house?'

'Interested.' She eyed him over the rim of her mug. 'Besides, I don't believe in ghosts.'

'You will before it's done. I spent the night there once, as a kid, with my brothers.'

'Creaking doors, rattling chains?'

'No.' He didn't smile now. 'Except the ones Jared arranged to scare the guts out of the rest of us. There's a spot on the stairway that'll turn your skin to ice. You can smell smoke near the living room hearth. And you can feel something looking over your shoulder when you walk down the hallways. If it's quiet enough, and you're listening, you can hear sabers clash.'

Despite herself, she couldn't quite suppress a shudder. 'If you're trying to scare me off the commission, you won't.'

'Just laying out the blueprint. I'll want you to take a look at the place, go through the rooms with me. We'll see what kind of ideas you have. Tomorrow afternoon suit you? About two?'

'That'll be fine. I'll need to take measurements.'

'Good.' He set his mug aside, rose. 'Nice doing business with you.'

Again she accepted his hand. 'Welcome home.'

'You're the first one who's said it.' Enjoying the irony, he lifted her hand to his lips, watching her. 'Then again, you don't know any better. See you tomorrow. And, Regan,' he added on his way to the door, 'take the dragon out of the window. I want it.'

On the way out of town, he pulled his car to the side of the road and stopped. Ignoring the snow and the icy fingers of the wind, he studied the house on the rise of the hill.

Its broken windows and sagging porches revealed nothing, just as Rafe's shadowed eyes revealed nothing. Ghosts, he mused, while snow drifted silently around him. Maybe. But he was beginning to realize that the only ghosts he was trying to put to rest were inside him.

Chapter 2

The beauty of owning your own shop, as far as Regan was concerned, was that you could buy and sell what you chose, your hours were your own to make, and the atmosphere was your own to create.

Still, being the sole proprietor and sole employee of Past Times didn't mean Regan Bishop tolerated any slack. As her own boss, she was tough, often intolerant, and expected the best from her staff. As that staff, she worked hard and rarely complained.

She had exactly what she'd always wanted—a home and business in a small rural town, away from the pressures and headaches of the city where she'd lived the first twenty-five years of her life.

Moving to Antietam and starting her own business had been part of her five-year plan after she graduated from American University. She had degrees in history and business management tucked under her belt, and by the time she donned cap and gown she'd already earned five years experience in antiques.

Working for someone else.

Now she was the boss. Every inch of the shop and the cozy apartment atop it was hers—and the bank's. The MacKade commission was going to go a long way toward making her share a great deal larger.

The minute Rafe left the afternoon before, Regan had locked up and dashed to the library. She'd checked out an armload of books to supplement her own research volumes.

By midnight, when her eyes had threatened to cross, she had read and taken notes on every detail of life as it applied to the Civil War era in Maryland.

She knew every aspect of the Battle of Antietam, from Lee's march to his retreat across the river, from McClellan's waffling to President Lincoln's visit to a farm outside Sharpsburg. She knew the number of dead and wounded, the bloody progress over hill and through cornfield.

It was sad and standard information, and she'd studied it before. Indeed, her fascination with the battle and the quiet area into which it had exploded had influenced her choice of a home.

But this time she'd been able to find bits and pieces on the Barlows—both fact and speculation. The family had lived in the house on the hill for almost a hundred years before that horrible day in September of 1862. Prosperous landowners and businessmen, they had lived like lords.

Their balls and dinners had enticed guests from as far as Washington and Virginia.

She knew how they had dressed—the frock coats and lace and the hooped skirts. Silk hats and satin slippers. She knew how they had lived, with servants pouring wine into crystal goblets, their home decorated with hothouse flowers, their furniture glowing with bee's wax polish.

Now, negotiating snowy, windy roads under sparkling sunlight, she could see exactly the colors and fabrics, the furnishings and knickknacks that would have surrounded them.

Chiffoniers of rosewood, she mused. Wedgwood china and horsehair settees. The fine Chippendale chest-on-chest for the master, the graceful cherrywood-and-beveled-glass secretaire for his lady. Brocade portieres and rich Colonial blue for the walls in the parlor.

Rafe MacKade was going to get his money's worth. And, oh, she hoped his pockets were deep.

The narrow, broken lane leading up to the house was deep in snow. No tire tracks or handy plow had marred its pretty, pristine—and very inconvenient—white blanket.

Annoyed that Rafe hadn't taken care of that detail, Regan eased her car onto the shoulder.

Armed with her briefcase, she began the long trudge up.

At least she'd thought to wear boots, she told herself as the snow crept past her ankles. She'd very nearly worn a suit and heels—before she remembered that impressing Rafe MacKade wasn't on her agenda. The gray trousers, tailored blazer and black turtleneck were acceptable business wear for an assignment such as this. And, as she doubted the place was heated, the red wool coat would come in handy, inside, as well as out.

It was a fabulous and intriguing place, she decided as she crested the hill. All those flecks of mica in the stone, glinting like glass in the sunlight, made up for the boarded windows. The porches sagged, but the building itself rose up tall and proud against the bitter blue sky.

She liked the way the east wing jutted off at a stern angle. The way the trio of chimneys speared from the roof as if waiting to belch smoke. She even liked the way the broken shutters hung drunkenly.

It needed tending, she thought, with an affection that surprised her. Someone to love it, and accept its character for what it was. Someone who would appreciate its strengths and understand its weaknesses.

She shook her head and laughed at herself. It sounded as though she were thinking of a man—one, perhaps, like Rafe MacKade—rather than a house.

She walked closer, through the deep, powdery drifts. Rocks and overgrown brush made uneven lumps in the snow, like children under blankets waiting to do mischief. Brambles were sneaky enough to grab at her trousers with sharp, wiry fingers. But once the lawn had been lush and green and vivid with flowers.

If Rafe had any vision, it would be again.

Reminding herself that the landscaping was his problem, she puffed her way to the broken front porch.

He was, she thought with a scowl, late.

Regan looked around, stomped her feet for warmth and

glanced at her watch. The man could hardly expect her to stand out in the cold and the wind and wait. Ten minutes, tops, she told herself. Then she would leave him a note, a very firm note on the value of keeping appointments, and leave.

But it wouldn't hurt to take a peek in the window.

Maneuvering carefully, she inched her way up the steps, avoided broken planks. There should be wisteria or morning glories climbing up the side arbor, she mused, and for a moment she almost believed she could catch the faint, sweet scent of spring.

She caught herself moving to the door, closing her hand over the knob before she realized that had been her intention all along. Surely it was locked, she thought. Even small towns weren't immune to vandals. But even as she thought it, the knob turned freely in her hand.

It was only sensible to go in, out of the wind, begin to site the job. Yet she pulled her hand back with a jerk. Her breath was coming in gasps, shockingly loud on the silent air. Inside her neat leather gloves, her hands were icy and trembling.

Out of breath from the climb, she told herself. Shivering from the wind. That was all. But the fear was on her like a cat, hissing through her blood.

Embarrassed, she looked uneasily around. There was no one to see her ridiculous reaction. Only snow and trees.

She took a deep breath, laughed at herself, and opened the door.

It creaked, of course. That was to be expected. The wide main hall gave her such a rush of pleasure, she forgot everything else. Closing the door, she leaned back against it and sighed.

There was dust and mold, damp patches on the walls, baseboards ruined by gnawing mice, spiderwebs draped like filthy gauze. She saw rich, deep green paint, creamy ivory trim, the buff and shine of waxed pine floors under her feet, a runner blooming with cabbage roses.

And there, she thought a hunt table, with a Dresden bowl spilling more roses, flanked by silver candlesticks. A little walnut hall chair with a pierced back, a hammered brass umbrella stand, a gilded mirror.

How it had been, and could be, spun through her mind, and she didn't feel the cold that sent her breath ahead of her in clouds as she wandered.

In the parlor, she marveled over the Adam fireplace. The marble was filthy, but undamaged. She had twin vases in the shop that would be perfect for the mantel. And a needlepoint footstool that was meant for weary feet in front of this very hearth.

Delighted, she pulled out her notebook and got to work.

Cobwebs dragged through her hair, dirt smudged her cheek, dust covered her boots, as she measured and plotted. She was in heaven. Her mood was so high that when she heard the footsteps, she turned with a smile instead of a complaint.

'It's wonderful. I can hardly—' She was talking to thin air.

Frowning, she walked out of the parlor and into the hall. She started to call out, then noted that there were no footprints in the dust but her own.

Imagining things, she told herself, and shuddered. Big, empty houses made all sorts of noises. Settling wood, wind against the windows…rodents, she thought with a grimace. She wasn't afraid of mice or spiders or creaking boards.

But when the floor groaned over her head, she couldn't muffle the shriek. Her heart flew straight to her throat and beat like a bird's. Before she'd managed to compose herself again, she heard the unmistakable sound of a door closing.

She was across the hall in a dash, fumbling for the knob when it hit her.

Rafe MacKade.

Oh, he thought he was clever, she thought furiously. Sneaking into the house ahead of her, creeping through the back, she imagined. He was up there right now, doubled over at the idea of her bolting from the house like some idiotic Gothic heroine with a heaving bosom.

Not on your life, she thought determinedly, and straightened her shoulders. She thrust her chin up and marched to the curving stairs.

'You're not funny, MacKade,' she called out. 'Now, if you've finished your pathetic little joke, I'd like to get some work done.'

When the cold spot hit her, she was too shocked to move. The hand she'd gripped on the rail went numb with it, her face froze with it. There, halfway up the graceful sweep of stairs, she swayed. It was her own whimper that broke her free. She was up to the first landing in four effortless strides.

A draft, she told herself, cursing her own sobbing breaths. Just a nasty draft.

'Rafe.' Her voice broke, infuriating her. Biting her lip, she stared down the long hallway, at the closed and secretive doors that lined it. 'Rafe,' she said again, and struggled to put irritation in her voice, rather than nerves. 'I have a schedule to keep, even if you don't, so can we get on with this?'

The sound of wood scraping wood, the violent slam of a door, and a woman's heartbroken weeping. Pride forgotten, Regan flew down the stairs. She'd nearly reached the bottom when she heard the shot.

Then the door she'd rushed to meet groaned slowly open.

The room whirled once, twice, then vanished.

'Come on, darling, snap out of it.'

Regan turned her head, moaned, shivered.

'All the way out, pal. Open those big blue eyes for me.'

The voice was so coaxing, she did. And found herself looking into Rafe's.

'It wasn't funny.'

A bit dizzy with relief, he smiled and stroked her cheek. 'What wasn't?'

'Hiding upstairs to scare me.' She blinked to bring the world back into sharp focus and discovered she was cradled on his lap on the window seat in the parlor. 'Let me up.'

'I don't think so. You're still a little shaky on your pins.

Just relax a minute.' He shifted her expertly so that her head rested in the crook of his arm.

'I'm fine.'

'You're white as a sheet. If I had a flask, I'd pour some brandy into you. Never saw a woman faint as gracefully, though. You sort of drifted down, gave me a chance to catch you before your head knocked against the floor.'

'If you expect me to thank you, forget it.' She shoved, found him unmovable. 'It's your fault.'

'Thanks. It's flattering to think the sight of me has a woman dropping at my feet. There.' He traced a finger down her cheek again. 'That brought some color back.'

'If this is the way you do business, you can take your job and—' She ground her teeth. 'Let me up.'

'Let's try this.' Lifting her, he plopped her down on the seat beside him. 'Hands off,' he added, lifting his. 'Now why don't you tell me why you're ticked off at me?'

Pouting, she brushed at her smudged trousers. 'You know very well.'

'All I know is, I walked in the door and saw you doing a swan dive.'

'I've never fainted in my life.' And she was thoroughly mortified that she had done so now—in front of him. 'If you want me to work on this house, scaring me into unconsciousness isn't the way to do it.'

He studied her, reached into his pocket for the cigarettes he'd given up exactly eight days before. 'How did I scare you?'

'By walking around upstairs, opening and closing doors, making those ridiculous noises.'

'Maybe I should start off by telling you I got held up at the farm. I didn't leave until fifteen minutes ago.'

'I don't believe you.'

'I don't blame you.' If he wasn't going to smoke, he had to move. Rising, he strolled over to the hearth. He thought he caught a whiff of smoke, as from a fire that had recently died. 'Shane was there—and so was Cy Martin. He's mayor now.'

'I know who Cy Martin is,' she said testily.

'You should have known him in high school,' Rafe mused. 'He was a complete ass. Anyway, Cy dropped by to see if Shane could plow his lane. He was still there when I left. Fifteen minutes ago. I borrowed Shane's four-wheel to make the hill. Parked it and came to the door in time to see your eyes roll back in your head.'

He walked back to her, stripped off his coat and tucked it over her legs. 'By the way, how'd you get in?'

'I—' She stared at him, swallowed. 'I opened the door.'

'It was locked.'

'No, it wasn't.'

Lifting a brow, he jingled the keys in his pocket. 'That's interesting.'

'You're not lying,' she said after a moment.

'Not this time. Why don't you tell me what you heard?'

'Footsteps. But there was no one there.' To warm them, she tucked her hands under his coat. 'Boards creaking upstairs. I started up. It was cold, bitterly cold, and it frightened me, so I went to the landing.'

'You were scared, so you went up instead of out?'

'I thought you were up there. I was going to yell at you.'

Her smile was weak, but it was there. 'I was furious that you'd managed to make me jump. Then I looked down the hallway. I guess I knew you weren't there. I heard wood scrape, and a door slam hard and someone crying. Then I bolted.'

He sat beside her again, put his arm around her shoulders in a friendly squeeze. 'Who wouldn't?'

'A shot,' she remembered. 'I was almost down the stairs when I heard a gunshot. It made my ears ring. Then the door opened, and lights-out.'

'I shouldn't have been late.' Unexpectedly, he leaned over and gave her a quick, casual kiss. 'Sorry.'

'That's hardly the point.'

'The thing is, some people feel things in this place, some don't. You struck me as the cool, practical type.'

She folded her arms over her chest. 'Oh, really?'

'Single-minded,' he added with a grin. 'It seems you have more imagination than I expected. Feeling better now?'

'I'm fine.'

'Sure you don't want to sit on my lap again?'

'Quite sure, thank you.'

With his eyes on hers, he brushed a cobweb from her hair. 'Want to get out of here?'

'Absolutely.'

He picked up his coat. 'I'd like to take you somewhere.'

'That isn't necessary. I said I was…' She stood and, as he held his ground, bumped into his chest. 'Fine,' she managed.

'Business, darling.' He tucked her hair behind her ear,

flicked a finger over the square-cut aquamarine at the lobe. 'For the moment. I think we can find someplace a little warmer and more hospitable to hash out the details.'

That was reasonable, she decided. Perfectly sensible. 'All right.'

She picked up her briefcase and walked ahead of him to the door.

'Regan?'

'Yes?'

'Your face is dirty.' He laughed at the smoldering look she shot at him, then scooped her up in his arms. Even as she stuttered a protest, he carried her over the broken porch. 'Got to watch your step,' he told her, setting her on her feet next to a Jeep.

'I make a habit of it.'

'I bet you do,' he murmured as he rounded the hood.

He maneuvered his way down the lane, circled around her car and kept going.

'I thought I'd follow you,' she began.

'Since I don't think you mean to the ends of the earth, let's just take one car. I'll bring you back.'

'From?'

'Home, sweet home, darling.'

In the snow, with the sun glazing the white fields, the MacKade farm was Currier and Ives pretty. A stone house with covered porch, an arched roof on the red barn, weathered outbuildings and a pair of golden dogs, barking and yipping and kicking up snow completed the scene—one that appealed to Regan.

She'd driven past the MacKade place countless times—when the fields were brown and furrowed from the plow, when they were high with hay and corn. She'd even stopped once or twice when Shane was riding his tractor, and thought how completely suited he seemed to be to the land.

She couldn't picture Rafe MacKade in the same scene.

'You didn't come back to farm, I imagine.'

'Hell, no. Shane loves it, Devin tolerates it. Jared looks on it as an ongoing enterprise.'

She tilted her head as he parked the Jeep beside his car. 'And you?'

'Hate it.'

'No ties to the land?'

'I didn't say that. I said I hated farming.' Rafe hopped out of the Jeep, clucking at the leaping golden retrievers. Before Regan could step down into the foot-deep snow, he'd plucked her up.

'I wish you'd stop that. I'm perfectly capable of walking through a little snow.'

'City boots. Pretty enough, though,' he commented as he carried her onto the porch. 'You've got little feet. Stay out,' he ordered the dogs. Smoothly he opened the door, elbowed it aside and carried her in.

'Hey, Rafe, what you got there?'

Grinning, Rafe shifted Regan in his arms and winked at Shane. 'Got me a female.'

'Good-looking one, too.' Shane tossed the log he held onto the fire, straightened. His eyes, the color of fog over seawater, warmed in appreciation. 'Hi there, Regan.'

'Shane.'

'Any coffee hot?' Rafe asked.

'Sure.' Shane kicked the log into place with his boot. 'Kitchen's never closed.'

'Fine. Now get lost.'

'Well, that was certainly rude.' Regan blew her hair out of her eyes as Rafe carted her down the hall and into the kitchen.

'You're an only child, right?'

'Yes, but—'

'Figured.' He dropped her into one of the cane chairs at the kitchen table. 'What do you take in your coffee?'

'Nothing—black.'

'What a woman.' He stripped off his coat, tossed it over a peg by the back door, where his brother's heavy work jacket already hung. From a glass-fronted cupboard, he chose two glossy white mugs. 'Want anything to go with it? Some hopeful woman's always baking Shane cookies. It's that pretty, innocent face of his.'

'Pretty, maybe. You're all pretty.' She shrugged out of her coat with a murmur of appreciation for the warmth of the room. 'And I'll pass on the cookies.'

He set a steaming mug in front of her. Out of habit, he turned a chair around and straddled it. 'So, are you going to pass on the house, too?'

Biding her time, she studied her coffee, sampled it, and found it superb. 'I have a number of pieces in stock that I think you'll find more than suitable when you're ready to furnish. I also did some research on the traditional color schemes and fabrics from that era.'

'Is that a yes or a no, Regan?'

'No, I'm not going to pass.' She lifted her gaze to his. 'And it's going to cost you.'

'You're not worried?'

'I didn't say that, exactly. But now I know what to expect. I can guarantee I won't be fainting at your feet a second time.'

'I'd just as soon you didn't. You scared the life out of me.' He reached over to play with the fingers of the hand she'd laid on the table. He liked the delicacy of them, and the glint of stones and gold. 'In your research, did you dig up anything on the two corporals?'

'The two corporals?'

'You should have asked old lady Metz. She loves telling the story. What kind of watch is this?' Curious, Rafe flicked a finger under the twin black elastic bands.

'Circa 1920. Elastic and marcasite. What about the corporals?'

'It seems these two soldiers got separated from their regiments during the battle. The cornfield east of here was thick with smoke, black powder exploding. Some of the troops were engaged in the trees, others just lost or dying there.'

'Some of the battle took place here, on your fields?' she asked.

'Some of it. The park service has markers up. Anyway, these two, one Union, one Confederate, got separated. They were just boys, probably terrified. Bad luck brought them together in the woods that form the boundary between MacKade land and Barlow.'

'Oh.' Thoughtful, she dragged her hair back. 'I'd forgotten the properties border each other.'

'It's less than a half mile from this house to the Barlow place through the trees. Anyway, they came face-to-face. If either of them had had any sense, they'd have run for cover and counted their blessings. But they didn't.' He lifted his mug again. 'They managed to put holes in each other. Nobody can say who crawled off first. The Reb made it as far as the Barlow house. Odds are he was half-dead already, but he managed to crawl onto the porch. One of the servants saw him and, being a Southern sympathizer, pulled him inside. Or maybe she just saw a kid bleeding to death and did what she thought was right.'

'And he died in the house,' Regan murmured, wishing she couldn't see it so clearly.

'Yeah. The servant ran off to get her mistress. That was Abigail O'Brian Barlow, of the Carolina O'Brians. Abigail had just given orders for the boy to be taken upstairs, where she could treat his wounds. Her husband came out. He shot the kid, right there on the stairway.'

Sadness jolted straight into horror. 'Oh, my God! Why?'

'No wife of his was going to lay her hands on a Reb. She herself died two years later, in her room. Story is that she never spoke a word to her husband again—not that they had much to say to each other before. It was supposed to be one of those arranged marriages. Rumor was he liked to knock her around.'

'In other words,' Regan said tightly, 'he was a prince among men.'

'That's the story. She was delicate, and she was miserable.'

'And trapped,' Regan murmured, thinking of Cassie.

'I don't suppose people talked much about abuse back then. Divorce…' He shrugged. 'Probably not an option in her circumstances. Anyway, shooting that boy right in front of her must have been the straw, you know. The last cruelty she could take. But that's only half of it. The half the town knows.'

'There's more.' She let out a sigh and rose. 'I think I need more coffee.'

'The Yank stumbled off in the opposite direction,' Rafe continued, murmuring a thank you when she poured him a second cup. 'My great-grandfather found him passed out by the smokehouse. My great-grandfather lost his oldest son at Bull Run—he'd died wearing Confederate gray.'

Regan shut her eyes. 'He killed the boy.'

'No. Maybe he thought about it, maybe he thought about just leaving him there to bleed to death. But he picked him up and brought him into the kitchen. He and his wife, their daughters, doctored him on the table. Not this one,' Rafe added with a small smile.

'That's reassuring.'

'He came around a few times, tried to tell them something. But he was too weak. He lasted the rest of that day and most of the night, but he was dead by morning.'

'They'd done everything they could.'

'Yeah, but now they had a dead Union soldier in their kitchen, his blood on their floor. Everyone who knew them knew that they were staunch Southern sympathizers who'd already lost one son to the cause and had two more still fighting for it. They were afraid, so they hid the body. When it was dark, they buried him, with his uniform, his weapon, and a letter from his mother in his pocket.'

He looked at her then, his eyes cool and steady. 'That's why this house is haunted, too. I thought you'd be interested.'

She didn't speak for a moment, set her coffee aside. 'Your house is haunted?'

'The house, the woods, the fields. You get used to it, the little noises, the little feelings. We never talked about it much; it was just there. Maybe you'd get a sense of something in the woods at night, or in the fields, when the morning was misty and too quiet.' He smiled a little at the curiosity in her eyes. 'Even cynics feel something when they're standing on a battlefield. After my mother died, even the house seemed…restless. Or maybe it was just me.'

'Is that why you left?'

'I had lots of reasons for leaving.'

'And for coming back?'

'One or two. I told you the first part of the story because I figured you should understand the Barlow place, since you're going to be involved with it. And I told you the rest…' He reached over and loosened the duo of black buttons on her blazer. 'Because I'm going to be staying at the farm for a while. Now you can decide if you want me to bring you here, or if you'd rather I come to your place.'

'My inventory's at the shop, so—'

'I'm not talking about your inventory.' He cupped her chin in his hand, kept his eyes open and on hers when he kissed her.

Softly at first, testing. Then with a murmur of satisfaction, deeper, so that her lips parted and warmed. He watched her lashes flutter, felt her breath sigh out and into his mouth, felt the pulse just under her jaw, just under his fingers, throb. The smoky scent of her skin was a seductive contrast to her cool-water taste.

Regan kept her hands gripped tight in her lap. It was shocking how much she wanted to use them on him. To drag them through his hair, to test the muscles under that faded flannel shirt. But she didn't. Her mind might have blurred for just an instant with astonished pleasure, even more astonishing greed, but she managed to hold on to her focus.

When he leaned back, she kept her hands where they were and gave herself time to level her voice. 'We're business associates, not playmates.'

'We have business,' he agreed.

'Would you have pulled that maneuver if I'd been a man?'

He stared at her. The chuckle started low, bloomed into a full laugh while she squirmed at the ridiculous way she'd phrased the question.

'I can give you a definite no on that one. I figure in that case you probably wouldn't have kissed me back, either.'

'Look, let's clear this up. I've heard all about the MacKade brothers and how they're irresistible to women.'

'It's been a curse all our lives.'

She would not smile—even if she had to clamp her teeth together. 'The point is, I'm not interested in a quick roll, an affair, or a relationship—which should cover any and all possibilities.'

Damned if she wasn't even more alluring when she went prim. 'I'm going to enjoy changing your mind. Why don't we start with the quick roll and work our way up from there?'

She rose sharply and pulled her coat on. 'In your dreams.'

'You're right about that. Why don't I take you out to dinner?'

'Why don't you take me back to my car?'

'All right.' Unoffended, he got up to pluck his coat from the peg. After he'd shrugged it on, he reached out and flipped her hair out from the collar of hers. 'Nights are long and cold this time of year.'

'Get a book,' she suggested on her way down the hall. 'Sit by the fire.'

'Is that what you do?' He shook his head. 'I'm going to have to add a little excitement to your life.'

'I like my life just fine, thanks. Don't pick me—' The order ended with an oath as he scooped her up. 'Mac-Kade,' she said with a sigh as he carried her to the Jeep, 'I'm beginning to think you're as bad as everyone says.'

'Count on it.'

Chapter 3

It was a good sound. The thud of hammers, the buzz of saws, the whir of drills. Through it came the jingle of a radio set to country music, so that Wynonna wailed over the clomp of boots and male voices.

It was a noise, the music of labor, that Rafe had known all of his life. This was different from the clatter of the milking barn, the hum of a tractor in the field. He preferred it. He'd chosen it the day he left Antietam.

Construction work had probably saved him. He had no problem admitting he'd been looking to rumble when he roared out of Washington County a decade before on his secondhand Harley. But he'd needed to eat, so he'd needed to work.

He'd strapped on a tool belt and sweated out the worst of the frustration.

He still remembered when he'd stepped back and looked at the first house he'd had a part in building. It had come to him in a flash that he could make something that mattered. And that he could make something of himself.

So he'd saved, and he'd sweated, and he'd learned.

The first place he'd bought, in central Florida, was little more than a shack. He'd choked on drywall dust, hammered until his muscles wept with the strain. But he'd made a profit, and used that to buy again. To sell again.

In four years, the tiny shoestring company called MacKade had earned a reputation for reliable, quality work.

Still, he'd never stopped looking back. Now, standing in the parlor of the Barlow place, he understood he'd come full circle.

He was going to make something in the town he'd been so hell-bent to escape from. Whether he stayed or not after he was done was undecided. But he would, at least, have left his mark.

Hunkered down in front of the fireplace, Rafe studied the stone hearth. He'd already gone to work on the chimney, and was covered with soot and grime. She'd draw, he thought with satisfaction. The first thing he was going to do, when the new lining was installed to bring it up to code, was build a fire. He wanted to watch the flames and warm his hands on them.

He wanted just the right andirons, the right screen. He could depend on Regan for that.

With a little smile, he picked up his trowel to mix a

bucket of mortar. He had a feeling Regan could be depended on for most anything.

With care, precision and enjoyment, he began to re-point the stone.

'I figured the boss would be sitting at a desk, running figures.'

Rafe glanced back and lifted a brow. Jared stood in the center of the room, his gleaming black shoes resting on a spattered drop cloth. For some reason, his black Wayfarer shades didn't look out of place with his gray pin-striped three-piece suit.

'That stuff's for lawyers and bookkeepers.'

Jared took off the sunglasses and tucked them into the pocket of his suit jacket. 'And think what the world would be without them.'

'Simpler.' Rafe stuck his trowel in the mortar and gave his brother a once-over. 'On your way to a funeral?'

'I had business in town, thought I'd drop by and see how things are going.' He glanced around the room, then back toward the hall when something crashed, someone cursed. 'So, how's it going?'

'Steady.' Rafe sighed when Jared took out a slim cigar. 'Blow some of that over here, will you? I quit ten really long days ago.'

'Reforming yourself?' Obligingly, Jared walked over, crouched. He smoked lazily as he and Rafe frowned meaningfully at the stone. 'Not too shabby.'

Rafe knocked a fist against the rose-grained marble. 'An Adam, pal.'

Jared grunted, clamped the cigar between his teeth. 'Need a hand around here?'

Blandly Rafe looked down. 'You're wearing your lawyer shoes.'

'I meant over the weekend.'

'I can always use another back.' Pleased with the offer, Rafe picked up the trowel again. 'How's yours?'

'As good as yours.'

'Still working out?' He gave Jared's biceps a testing punch. 'I still say gyms are for sissies.'

Jared blew out a stream of smoke. 'Want to go a round, bro?'

'Sure, when you're not dressed so pretty.' To torture himself, Rafe sucked in secondhand smoke. 'I appreciate you handling the settlement on this place for me.'

'You haven't got my bill, yet.' Grinning, Jared straightened. 'I thought you were crazy when you called and told me to go after it. Then I did a walk-through.' He turned, still grinning. 'And I knew you were crazy. You practically stole the place, but I figure it's got to cost you two times the purchase price to make it livable.'

'Three times,' Rafe said mildly, 'to make it the way I want it.'

'How do you want it?'

'The way it was.' Rafe scraped the edge of his trowel over stone, leveling his mortar.

'That's always a tough one,' Jared murmured. 'You don't seem to be having a problem with labor. I wondered if you would, considering the place's rep.'

'Money talks. Lost a plumber's assistant this morning,

though.' Wicked amusement sparkled in his eyes. 'They were checking pipes in one of the second-floor johns. This guy claims someone clamped a hand on his shoulder. He was still running when he made it to the road. Don't guess he'll be back.'

'Any other problems?'

'Nothing I need a lawyer for. Did you hear the one about the lawyer and the rattlesnake?'

'I've heard them all,' Jared said dryly. 'I keep a file.'

With a chuckle, Rafe wiped his hands on his jeans. 'You did good, Jare. Mom would've liked seeing you duded up like that.' For a moment, he said nothing. There was only the scrape of trowel on stone. 'It's weird, staying at the farm. Mostly just me and Shane. Devin spends half his nights on a cot in the sheriff's office. You're in that fancy little town house in the city. When I hear Shane get up in the morning, it's still dark. The idiot's whistling, like going out to milk in January's just a boatload of laughs.'

'He's always loved it. He's kept that place alive.'

'I know.'

He recognized the tone, shook his head at it. 'You did your part, Rafe. The money you sent back made a difference.' Eyes shadowed, Jared stared out the grimy window. 'I'm thinking of selling the place in Hagerstown.' When Rafe said nothing, Jared moved his shoulders. 'It seemed practical to keep it after the divorce. The market was soft, and we'd only built up a couple years' equity. Barbara didn't want it.'

'Still sore?'

'No. The divorce is three years past, and God knows it was civilized. We just didn't like each other anymore.'

'I never liked her.'

Jared's lips quirked. 'I know. Anyway, I'm thinking of selling, hanging out at the farm for a while, until I find the right place.'

'Shane would like that. So would I. I missed you.' Rafe swiped a grimy hand over his grimy chin. 'I didn't realize how much until I got back.' Satisfied with the repointing, he scraped his trowel on the edge of the bucket. 'So, you want to put in some honest labor on Saturday?'

'You buy the beer.'

Rafe nodded, rose. 'Let's see your hands, city boy.'

Jared's response was crude, simple, and uttered just as Regan stepped into the room.

'Nice mouth, Counselor,' Rafe said with an easy smile. 'Hello, darling.'

'I'm interrupting.'

'No. The guy from the gutter here's my brother Jared.'

'I know. He's my lawyer. Hello, Jared.'

'Regan.' Jared found an empty can of soda and doused the stub of his cigar. 'How's business?'

'Picking up, thanks to your little brother. I have some estimates, figures, suggestions, paint and fabric samples,' she said to Rafe. 'I thought you'd like to look them over.'

'You've been busy.' He crouched again, flipped over the top of a small cooler. 'Want a drink?'

'No, thanks.'

'Jare?'

'One for the road. I've got another appointment.' Jared

caught the canned soft drink on the fly, then took his sunglasses out of his pocket. 'I'll let you two get down to business. Nice to see you again, Regan.'

'Saturday,' Rafe called out as Jared left the room. 'Seven-thirty. That's a.m., pal. And lose the suit.'

'I didn't mean to chase him off,' Regan began.

'You didn't. Want to sit down?'

'Where?'

He patted an overturned bucket.

'That's very gracious of you, but I can't stay. I'm on my lunch hour.'

'The boss isn't going to dock you.'

'She certainly will.' Opening her briefcase, Regan took out two thick folders. 'Everything's in here. Once you have a chance to look through it, let me know.' For lack of anywhere better, she set the files across two saw-horses. She looked back over her shoulder, toward the hall. 'You've certainly jumped right in.'

'When you know what you want, there's no point in wasting time. So how about dinner?'

She looked back, narrowed her eyes. 'Dinner?'

'Tonight. We can go over your files.' He tapped a finger against them, left a smudge of soot. 'Save time.'

'Oh.' Still frowning, she combed her fingers through her hair. 'I suppose.'

'How's seven? We'll go to the Lamplighter.'

'The where?'

'The Lamplighter. The little place off of Main, at Church Street.'

She tilted her head as she visualized the town. 'There's a video store at Main and Church.'

He jammed his hands in his pockets with an oath. 'Used to be a restaurant. Your place used to be a hardware store.'

'I guess even small towns have their changes.'

'Yeah.' He couldn't have said why it annoyed him. 'Like Italian?'

'Yes. But the closest Italian place is across the river, into West Virginia. We can just meet at Ed's.'

'No. Italian. I'll come by about six-thirty.' Needing to gauge his time, he pulled a watch from his pocket. 'Yeah, I can do six-thirty.'

'That's a nice one.' Without thinking, she crossed over, took his wrist gingerly in two fingers to get a better look at the pocket watch. 'Hmm… American Watch Company, mid-1800s.' Already appraising, she turned the watch over to study the case. 'Sterling, good condition. I'll give you seventy-five for it.'

'I paid ninety.'

She laughed and shook back her hair. 'Then you got a hell of a bargain. It's worth a hundred and fifty.' Her gaze danced up to his. 'You don't look like the pocket-watch type.'

'Wear one on your wrist on the job, they end up smashed.' He wanted to touch her. She looked so neat and tidy that the idea of mussing her up was enormously appealing. 'Damn shame my hands are filthy.'

Alerted, she released his wrist, brushed one hand against the other. 'So's your face. But you're still pretty.'

After shifting her briefcase strap more comfortably on her shoulder, she stepped back. 'Six-thirty, then. Don't forget the files.'

She'd changed three times before she caught herself. A business dinner, Regan thought as she dropped down on the padded stool of her vanity, was a business dinner. Her appearance was certainly important, but it was secondary.

She bit her lip and wondered if she should have gone with the little black dress, after all.

No, no, no. Annoyed with herself, she snatched up her brush. Simplicity was best. The restaurant in West Virginia was casual, family-style. The purpose was professional. The blazer, slacks and silk blouse in forest green were right. There was no harm in jazzing it up with the moonstone lapel pin. But maybe the earrings were wrong. She could go with plain gold hoops instead of the more dramatic dangles.

The hell with it. She dropped her brush, then tugged on her suede ankle boots. She would not fall into the trap of thinking of this as a date. She didn't want to date Rafe MacKade. Just now, with her business showing real promise, she didn't want to date anyone.

A relationship, if indeed she decided to cultivate one, was three years down the road. Minimum. She would never make the mistake her mother had and depend on someone else for emotional and financial support. First, she would make certain she was solvent, solid and secure. And then, if and when she chose, she would think about sharing her life.

No one was going to tell her if she could work or not. She would never have to cajole an extra few dollars out of a man to buy a new dress. Maybe it suited her parents to live that way—and they'd certainly always seemed happy enough. But that wasn't the life Regan Bishop wanted.

It was just too damned bad that Rafe was so dangerously attractive. And, she noted when she heard the knock on the door, prompt.

Confident again after the quick pep talk, she walked out of the bedroom, through the small, cozily furnished living room, and opened the door.

And, oh, she thought one last time, it was really too bad.

He flashed that grin at her, and those wonderful green eyes swept down, then up. 'Looking good.' Before she could think to avoid it, his mouth brushed hers.

'I'll get my coat,' she began, then stopped, the door still open to the wind. 'What are those?'

'These?' He jostled the bags he carried. 'These are dinner. Where's your kitchen?'

'I—' He was already in, kicking the door behind him. 'I thought we were going out.'

'No, I said we were having Italian.' He took quick stock of the room. Lady chairs, gleaming tables, pretty little knickknacks and fresh flowers. All female, he mused. And the portrait of a gloomy-faced cow above the sofa added wit. 'Nice place.'

'Are you telling me you're cooking me dinner?'

'It's the quickest way, without physical contact, to get a woman into bed. The kitchen through there?'

When she'd managed to close her mouth, she followed him into the galley-style kitchen off the dining el. 'Doesn't that depend on how well you cook?'

Appreciating her response, he smiled as he began pulling ingredients out of the bags. 'You'll have to tell me. Got a skillet?'

'Yes, I have a skillet.' She took a large cast-iron pan from its cupboard, then lips pursed, tapped it against her palm.

'You conk me with it, you'll miss out on my ziti with tomato and basil.'

'Ziti?' After running her tongue around her teeth, she set the skillet on a burner. 'I'll wait until after I eat.' She got out a second pot for the pasta and handed it to him.

Once he'd added water and set it to boil, she watched him wash greens for a salad.

'Where'd you learn to cook?'

'We all cook. Chef's knife? My mother didn't believe there was women's work and men's work. Thanks,' he added and began chopping with a quick, negligent flair that had Regan lifting her brows. 'There was just work,' he continued.

'Ziti doesn't sound like farm food.'

'She had an Italian grandmother. Can you stand a little closer?'

'Hmm?'

'You smell good. I like to smell you.'

Ignoring that, and the little twist in her stomach, she picked up the wine he'd brought along. 'Why don't I open this?'

'Why don't you?'

After she'd set it on the counter to breathe, she scooted behind him to reach the cupboard to get a salad bowl. When he asked for music, she slipped back into the living room and put Count Basie on low. Why, she wondered, did a man look so sexy with his sleeves rolled up, grating carrots into a salad?

'Don't open that olive oil,' she told him. 'I have some.'

'Extra virgin?'

'Of course.' She tapped a long-spouted copper pitcher on the counter.

'Count Basie, your own olive oil.' His eyes met hers, laughed. 'Want to get married?'

'Sure. I've got time on Saturday.' Amused that he didn't have such a quick comeback for that, she reached overhead for wineglasses.

'I was planning on working Saturday.' Watching her, he set the salad aside.

'That's what they all say.'

Lord, she was one terrific piece of work. He moved closer as she poured the wine. 'Tell me you like watching baseball on TV on hot summer nights, and we've got a deal.'

'Sorry. I hate sports.'

He moved closer still, and with a wineglass in either hand, she moved back. 'It's a good thing I found this flaw now, before we had five or six kids and a dog.'

'You're a lucky guy.' Heart jittering, she backed up again.

'I like this,' he murmured, and traced a finger over the

little mole beside her mouth. Inching closer, he ran his finger down to flip open the buttons of her blazer.

'Why are you always doing that?'

'Doing what?'

'Fooling with my buttons.'

'Just practicing.' The grin was quick as lightning, and just as bold. 'Besides, you always look so tidy, I can't resist loosening you up.'

Her retreat ended with her back between the side of the refrigerator and the wall.

'Looks like you've backed yourself into a corner, darling.'

He moved in slowly, slipping his hands around her waist, fitting his mouth to hers. He took his time sampling, his fingers spread over her rib cage, stopping just short of the curve of her breasts.

She couldn't stop her breath from quickening or her lips from responding. His tongue flicked over them, between them, met hers. His taste was dark, and rabidly male, and streaked straight to her center like an arrow on target.

The small part of her mind that could still function warned her that he knew exactly how he affected women. All women. Any woman. But her body didn't seem to give a damn.

Her blood began to pound, her skin to vibrate, from the shock of dozens of tiny explosions. She was certain she could feel her own bones melt.

She was exciting to watch. His eyes were open as he changed the angle of the kiss, deepened it, degree by painfully slow degree. He found the flutter of her lashes arousing, the faint flush desire brought to her cheeks seductive. And that helpless hitch of breath, that quick shiver when his fingers skimmed lightly over the tips of her breasts, utterly thrilling.

With an effort, he stopped himself from taking more. 'God. It gets better every time.' Gently he nuzzled his way to her ear. 'Let's try it again.'

'No.' It surprised her that what she said and what she wanted were entirely different. In defense, she pressed a wineglass against his chest.

He glanced down at the glass, then back at her face. His eyes weren't smiling now, weren't gently amused. There was an edge in them now, dark and potentially deadly. Despite all common sense, she found herself drawn to this man who would take, and damn all consequences.

'Your hand's shaking, Regan.'

'I'm aware of that.'

She spoke carefully, knowing that the wrong word, the wrong move, and what was in his eyes would leap out and devour her. And she would let it. She would love it.

That was something she definitely had to think over.

'Take the wine, Rafe. It's red. It'll leave a nasty stain on that shirt.'

For one humming moment, he said nothing. A need he hadn't understood or counted on had him by the throat with rusty little claws. She was afraid of him, he noted, deciding she was smart to be afraid. A woman like her didn't have a clue what a man like him was really capable of.

Taking the glass, he tapped it against hers, making the crystal ring, then turned back to the stove.

She felt as though she'd barely avoided a tumble from a cliff. And realized she already regretted not taking the plunge. 'I think I should say something. I, um...' She took a deep breath, then an even deeper gulp of wine. 'I'm not going to pretend I'm not attracted to you, or that I didn't enjoy that, when obviously I am, and I did.'

Trying to relax, he leaned back against the counter, studied her over the rim of his glass. 'And?'

'And.' She scooped back her hair. 'And I think complications are...complicated,' she said lamely. 'I don't want—that is, I don't think...' She shut her eyes and drank again. 'I'm stuttering.'

'I noticed. It's a nice boost to the ego.'

'Your ego doesn't need any boosting.' She blew out a breath, cleared her throat. 'You're very potent. I have no doubt sex would be memorable— Don't smile at me that way.'

'Sorry.' But the smile didn't dim. 'It must have been your choice of words. *Memorable*'s good. I like it. Why don't we save time here? I get your point. You want to mull the idea over, make the next move when you're ready.'

She considered, then nodded slowly. 'That's close enough.'

'Okay. Now here's my point.' He turned on the burner under the skillet and added oil. 'I really want you, Regan. It hit me right off, when I walked into Ed's and you were sitting there with little Cassie, looking so pressed and polished.'

She fought to ignore the flutters in her stomach. 'Is that why you offered me the job on the Barlow place?'

'You're too smart to ask a question like that. This is sex. Sex is personal.'

'All right.' She nodded again. 'All right.'

He picked up a plump roma tomato, examined it. 'The problem here, as I see it, is that I don't much care for mulling over things like this. No matter how you fancy it up, sex is still the animal. Smell, touch, taste.'

His eyes were dark again, reckless. He picked up the knife, tested its point. 'Take,' he added. 'But that's just me, and there are two of us here. So you go on ahead with your mulling.'

Baffled, she stared at him as he chose a clove of garlic. 'I'm trying to decide if you expect me to thank you for that.'

'Nope.' Expertly he laid the flat of his knife over the garlic, gave one quick pound of his fist to crush it. 'You're just supposed to understand it, like I'm understanding you.'

'You're a real nineties man, MacKade.'

'No, I'm not. And I'm going to make you stutter again. You can count on that.'

Challenged, she picked up the wine, topped off their glasses. 'Well, you count on this. If and when I decide to make my move, you'll do some stuttering of your own.'

He scooped the minced garlic into the oil, where it sizzled. 'I like your style, darling. I really like your style.'

Chapter 4

Sunny skies and a southerly breeze brought in a welcome end-of-January thaw. Icicles dripped prettily from eaves and shone with rainbows. In front yards and fallow fields, snowmen began to lose weight. Regan spent a pleasant week earmarking stock for the Barlow place and hunting up additions to her supply at auction.

When business was slow, she revised and honed her room-by-room decorating scheme for what was going to be the MacKade Inn at Antietam.

Even now, as she described the attributes of a walnut credenza to a pair of very interested buyers, her mind was on the house. Though she hadn't realized it, yet, she was as haunted by it as Rafe had been.

The front bedroom, second floor, she mused, should have the four-poster with canopy, the rosebud wallpaper and the satinwood armoire. A romantic and traditional bridal suite, complete with little bowls of potpourri and vases of fresh flowers.

And what had been the gathering room, on the main level, had that wonderful southern exposure. Of course, Rafe had to pick the right windows, but it would be spectacular in sunny colors with a trio of ficus trees, hanging ferns in glazed pots, and pretty little conversation groups of boldly floral love seats and wingback chairs.

It was perfect for a conservatory, a place to gaze through the glass into the woods and gardens, with forced narcissi and hyacinths brightening midwinter gloom.

She couldn't wait to get her hands on the place, add those tiny, perfect details that would make it a home again.

An inn, she reminded herself. A business. Comfortable, charming, but temporary. And it wasn't hers. With an effort, she shook her head clear and concentrated on the sale at hand.

'You can see the marquetry is high-quality,' she continued, keeping her sales pitch moderate and pleasant. 'The bowfront cupboards on the side are the original glass.'

The woman fingered the discreet tag longingly, and Regan's sharp eye caught the hopeful glance she sent her less enthusiastic husband.

'It really is lovely. But it's just a little more than we had in mind.'

'I understand. But in this condition—'

She broke off when the door opened, furious with herself for the quick leap, then the quick disappointment when it wasn't Rafe who came in. Before she could smile a welcome at Cassie, she saw the livid bruises on the side of her friend's face.

'If you'd excuse me for just a moment, I'll give you time to talk it over.'

An antique bangle jingling on her wrist, sensible shoes clacking, she moved swiftly through the shop. Saying nothing, she took Cassie's arm and led her into the back room.

'Sit down. Come on.' Gently, she eased Cassie into a chair at the tiny iron table. 'How bad are you hurt?'

'It's nothing. I just—'

'Shut up.' Grinding back the spurt of temper, Regan slammed a kettle on the hot plate. 'I'm sorry. I'm going to make some tea.' She needed a moment, she realized, before she could deal with this rationally. 'While the water's boiling, I'll go finish up with my customers. You sit here and relax for a minute.'

Shame swimming in her eyes, Cassie stared down at her hands. 'Thanks.'

Ten minutes later, after ruthlessly hacking the price of the credenza to move the customers along, Regan hurried back. She told herself she'd gotten the anger under control. She promised herself she would be supportive, sympathetic.

One look at Cassie, slumped in the chair while the kettle belched steam, had her exploding.

'Why in the hell do you let him do this to you? When are you going to get tired of being that sadistic bastard's punching bag? Does he have to put you in the hospital before you walk away?'

In utter defeat, Cassie folded her arms on the table, then dropped her head on them and wept.

Her own eyes stinging, Regan dropped to her knees beside the chair. In the tidy little office, with its ice-cream-parlor chairs and neat rolltop desk, she struggled to face the reality of battering.

'Cassie, I'm sorry. I'm so sorry, Cass. I shouldn't be yelling at you.'

'I shouldn't have come here.' Lifting her head, Cassie covered her face with her hand and fought to get her breath back. 'I shouldn't have come. But I just needed somebody to talk to.'

'Of course you should have come here. This is exactly where you should have come. Let me see,' Regan murmured, easing Cassie's hand away. The bruises ran from temple to jaw, in ugly purple. One of Cassie's lovely smoke gray eyes was swollen nearly shut.

'Oh, Cassie, what happened? Can you tell me?'

'He… Joe…he hasn't been feeling well. This flu that's been going around.' Cassie's voice hitched and jittered. 'He missed a lot of work, being sick, and yesterday they laid him off.'

Avoiding Regan's eyes, she fumbled in her bag for a tissue. 'He was upset—he's worked there almost twelve years now, on and off. The bills. I just bought a new washing machine on credit, and Connor wanted these new tennis shoes. I knew they were too expensive, but—'

'Stop,' Regan said quietly, and laid a hand over Cassie's. 'Please stop blaming yourself. I can't bear it when you do.'

'I know I'm making excuses.' With a long, shuddering breath, Cassie shut her eyes. To Regan, at least, she could be honest. Because Regan, in the three years they had known each other, had always been there. 'He hasn't had the flu. He's been drunk almost day and night for a week. They didn't lay him off, they fired him because he went to work drunk and mouthed off to his supervisor.'

'And then he came home and took it out on you.' Rising, Regan took the kettle off the hot plate and began to make the tea. 'Where are the kids?'

'At my mother's. I went there last night, after. He hurt me pretty bad this time.'

Unconsciously she touched her hand to her throat. Beneath the turtleneck there were more bruises, where Joe's hands had held and choked her until she accepted that he would kill her. Almost wished for it.

'I got the kids out, and I went to Mama, because I needed some place to stay.'

'Okay, that's good.' Ready to move step-by-step now, Regan brought two china cups to the table. 'That's the best way to start.'

'No.' Very carefully, Cassie wrapped both hands around her cup. 'She expects me to go back today. She won't let us stay another night.'

'After you told her, after she saw you, what he'd done, she expects you to go back?'

'A woman belongs with her husband,' Cassie said simply. 'I married him for better or for worse.'

Regan had never understood her own mother, the easy subservience, the catering. But, while it had infuriated her often, it had never appalled her like this.

'That's monstrous, Cassie.'

'It's just Mama,' Cassie murmured, wincing as the tea stung her puffy lip. 'She believes a woman should make a marriage work. It's her duty to make it work.'

'Do you believe that? That it's your responsibility to take this? Do you believe that means you are supposed to stay for better or worse, even if worse means being beaten whenever he has the whim?'

'I used to. I tried to. I took vows, Regan.' She took a shuddering breath, because to her that had always been the bottom line. She had promised. 'Maybe I was too young when I married Joe. Maybe I made a mistake, but I still took the vows. He didn't keep them. There were those other women, he didn't even care if I knew who they were. He was never faithful, never kind. But I took vows and I wanted to keep them.'

She began to cry again, quietly now, because she had failed. 'We've been married ten years. We have children together. I make so many mistakes—using my tip money to buy those shoes for Connor, and letting Emma play dress-up with my lipstick. And we couldn't afford that washing machine. I was never any good in bed, not like those other women he'd go to. I knew—'

She broke off when Regan only continued to watch her.

'Are you hearing yourself this time?' Regan said quietly. 'Are you listening to yourself, Cassie?'

'I can't stay with him anymore.' Her voice broke, shattering like thin, fragile glass. 'He's hitting me in front of the kids. He used to wait until they were in bed, and that was bad. But now he hits me in front of them, and he says terrible things. Things they shouldn't hear. It's not right. It makes them part of it, and it's not right.'

'No, Cass, it's not right. You need help now.'

'I thought about it all night.' She hesitated, then slowly eased down the neck of her sweater.

At the sight of the raw marks scoring that pale, innocent flesh, Regan's face went white and cold. 'Oh, dear God—he tried to strangle you.'

'I don't think he meant to at first. I was crying, and he wanted me to stop. But then he did.' Cassie lowered her hand again. 'I could see it in his eyes. It wasn't just the drinking, or the money, or the other women he seems to want. He hated me just for being there. He'll hurt me again if he gets the chance, and I have to think about the kids. I have to go to Devin and file charges.'

'Thank God.'

'I had to come here first, to get up my nerve.' Knowing there was no more point in them, Cassie wiped at the tears. 'It's hard, being it's Devin. I've known him all my life. It's not like it's a secret. He's been out to the house I don't know how many times when the neighbors called in. But it's hard.' She sighed. 'Being it's Devin.'

'I'll go with you.'

Cassie closed her eyes. That was why she had come here, to have someone stand with her. No, she admitted, ashamed all over again. To have someone hold her up.

'No, I need to do it myself. I haven't thought about after,' she said, and soothed her raw throat with a sip of tea. 'I can't take the kids back to the house until I know what's going to happen.'

'The shelter—'

Stubbornly, Cassie shook her head. 'I know it's pride, Regan, but I can't go there. I can't take my kids there. Not yet, anyway.'

'All right, then you'll stay here. Here,' Regan repeated as Cassie protested. 'I only have one extra bedroom, so you and the kids will have to rough it.'

'We can't pile in on you that way.'

'You were the first friend I made when I moved here. I want to help. So let me help.'

'I could never ask you that, Regan. I've saved some tip and overtime money. Enough for a motel for a couple of days.'

'You wouldn't want to hurt my feelings that way. You're going to stay at my place. For the kids,' Regan murmured, knowing that nothing would tilt the scales as heavily.

'I'll go get them after I see Devin.' She had no pride when it came to her children. 'I'm awfully grateful, Regan.'

'So am I. Now.'

'What's this? Tea party during business hours?' Because his eyes were on Regan, Rafe had stepped into the office and tossed his coat over the back of a chair before he saw Cassie's face.

Regan was stunned to watch charm metamorphize into pure violence in a split second. The quick, potent grin sharpened into a snarl. His eyes fired. Her first startled thought, as that lean body tensed to spring, was *wolf.*

When his hand shot out, Cassie flinched, and Regan leapt to her feet. Before Regan could step between them with some wild idea of protecting Cassie, Rafe's fingers stroked, gentle as a kiss, over the battered face.

'Joe?'

'It—it was an accident,' Cassie stammered.

His opinion of that was one vicious word. He swung around, blood in his eye. Cassie was on her feet and racing after him.

'No, Rafe, please don't do anything.' Desperate, she pulled at his arm, all but jumped on his back. 'Please don't go after him.'

He could have knocked her aside with a shrug. It was that knowledge that added bitter fuel to the fire. 'You stay here. Stay with Regan.'

'No, please.' Cassie began to weep again, helplessly, as she pulled at him. 'Please. Don't make me any more ashamed than I already am.'

'The bastard's going to pay this time.' He bit the words out, started to set her aside and looked down. The tears did what fists and threats could never have done. They stopped him cold. 'Cassie.' Undone, he wrapped his arms around her and cradled her against his chest. 'Don't cry, baby. Come on now, it's going to be all right.'

From the doorway of the office, Regan watched him. How could there be such tenderness, she wondered, side by side with such savagery? He was holding Cassie as though she were a child, his head close to hers as he murmured to her.

Regan's own throat burned, and her own cheeks were wet when he lifted his head and looked at her.

Yes, the violence was still there, alive and restless in his eyes. Vital and fierce enough to steal her breath from her throat and make her stomach muscles quiver. She swallowed hard before she spoke.

'Bring her back in here, Rafe. Please.'

Every nerve inside him was tensed for battle. He craved the hunt, the fight, the blood. But the woman in his arms was trembling. And the one who watched him with shocked, frightened eyes was quietly pleading.

'Come on, baby.' As if she were a fretful child, Rafe tucked Cassie under his arm. 'Come on, let's go sit down.'

'I'm sorry.'

'Don't apologize to me.' It took every ounce of control to lead her back into the office, to keep his voice easy on the words. 'Don't apologize to anyone.'

'She's going to Devin.' Because her hands were shaking, Regan busied them with the tea and cups. 'She's going to file charges. That's the right way to handle it.'

'That's one way.' He preferred his own, but he eased Cassie into a chair, brushed her hair way from her damp face. 'Have you got a place to stay?'

Cassie nodded, took the tissues Regan handed her. 'We're going to stay with Regan for a little while. Just until...'

'The kids okay?'

She nodded again. 'I'm going to get them as soon as I see Devin.'

'You tell me what you need, and I'll go by the house and pick it up for you.'

'I... I don't know. I didn't take anything.'

'You tell me later. Why don't I walk you down to the sheriff's office?'

She shuddered out a breath, mopped her face. 'No, I need to do it by myself. I should go now.'

'Here.' Regan pulled open a drawer in her desk. 'Here's a key to the door upstairs. You and the kids settle in.' She put the key in Cassie's hand, closed her fingers over it. 'And lock it, Cassie.'

'I will. I'll go now.' It was the hardest thing she'd ever done, just standing, walking to the door. 'I always thought it would get better,' she said, almost to herself. 'I always hoped it would.' She left, with her head bowed and her shoulders hunched.

'Do you know where he is?' Rafe murmured.

'No, I don't.'

'Well, I'll find him.' As he reached for his coat, Regan put her hand over his. His eyes lifted slowly to hers and burned. 'Don't get in my way.'

Instinct had her laying her other hand on his cheek, her mouth on his. The kiss was soft, soothing them both.

'What was that for?'

'A couple of things.' She took a deep breath, then put both hands on his shoulders. 'For wanting to kick the bastard's face in.' She kissed him again. 'For not doing it because Cassie asked you.' And again. 'And last, for showing her that most men, real men, are kind.'

'Damn.' Defeated, he laid his brow on hers. 'That's a hell of a way to keep me from killing him.'

'Part of me would like you to. I'm not proud of it.' As the anger stirred again, she turned back to the hot plate.

'Part of me would like to watch while you beat him sense-less. Even worse, I'd like a shot at him myself.'

Rafe stepped over, uncurled the hand she'd balled into a fist. Thoughtfully, he lifted it, pressed his lips to the palm. 'Well, well... And I figured you for a cream puff.'

'I said I'm not proud of it.' But she smiled a little. 'It's not what she needs now. Violence is just what she needs to get away from. Even if it's justified.'

'I've known her since she was a kid.' Rafe glanced down at the tea Regan poured him, shook his head at it. It smelled like a meadow at springtime, and would un-doubtedly taste the same.

'She was always little, pretty and shy. All this sweet-ness.' At Regan's curious look, he shook his head again. 'No. I never made any moves in that direction. Sweet's never been my type.'

'Thanks.'

'Don't mention it.' He stroked a hand over her hair, let his fingers drift into it, through it. 'You're taking on a lot, letting her and the kids stay with you. I can take them out to the farm. We've got plenty of room.'

'She needs a woman, Rafe, not a bunch of men—how-ever well-intentioned. Devin will find him, won't he? And take care of it?'

'You can count on it.'

Satisfied, she picked up her own tea. 'Then I will, and so should you.' Now that the step had been taken, she eyed him over her cup. 'You must have come by for a reason.'

'I wanted to look at you for a while.' Her bland gaze had his lips curving. 'And I figured to go over some of the wall treatments—and the parlor furniture. I want to complete that one room, give me a feel for the rest.'

'That's a nice idea. I—' She broke off at the sound of movement and voices from the shop. 'I've got customers. Everything's here—the paint samples and fabrics, itemized lists of furnishings.'

'I picked up some samples of my own.'

'Oh, well, then…' She crossed to the desk, booted up her computer. 'I have a room-by-room rundown here. Why don't you go over it? Several of the pieces I've suggested are here. You can take a look at them when you've finished here.'

'All right.'

Thirty minutes later, flush with three sales, Regan stepped back into the office. He looked so big, she thought, so…male, sitting at her lovely little Chippendale desk. She could smell him—wood dust, soot, oil.

His boots were scarred, his shirt was ripped at the shoulder. There were traces of plaster or drywall dust in his hair.

She thought he was the most magnificent animal she had ever seen. And she wanted him with a kind of primal, mindless lust.

Whoa! To steady herself, she pressed a hand to her jumpy stomach, took three deep breaths.

'Well, what do you think?'

'You're an efficient woman, Regan.' Without turning, he flipped open a file with printouts of her lists. 'It doesn't look like you've missed a trick.'

Flattered, she walked over to look over his shoulder.

'I'm sure we'll need to adjust, add a few details after we see one of the rooms completed.'

'I've already made some adjustments.'

She straightened again. 'Oh, really?'

'This color's out.' Briskly he tapped the paint chip, then located the page on-screen where her colors were listed. 'I ditched this pea green here for—what's it called? Yeah. Loden.'

'The original color is accurate.'

'It's ugly.'

Yes, it was, but— 'It's accurate,' she insisted. 'I researched very carefully. The one you've chosen is entirely too modern for the 1800s.'

'Maybe. But it won't spoil anyone's appetite. Don't get your panties in a twist, darling.' When her breath hissed out at that, he chuckled and turned around in the chair. 'Listen, you're doing a hell of a job here. I have to admit, I didn't expect this much detail, certainly not so fast. You've got a real feel for it.'

She didn't care to be placated. 'You hired me to help you reconstruct a particular era, and that's what I'm doing. It was your choice to make the house look the way it did in the past.'

'And it's my choice to make adjustments. We've got to make some room here for aesthetics and modern taste. I've had a look at your place upstairs, Regan. It's a little too much on the female side for me—'

'Fortunately, that's hardly the issue here,' she told him, stiffening all over again.

'And so neat a man'd be afraid to put his feet up,' Rafe

continued smoothly. 'But you've got taste. I'm just asking you to use it, along with research and accuracy.'

'It seems to me we're talking about your taste. If you're going to change the guidelines, at least make them clear.'

'Are you always so rigid, or is it just with me?'

She refused to stoop to answering such an insulting question. 'You asked for accuracy. I don't care to have rules changed in midstream.'

Considering, Rafe picked up the paint chip that had started the ball rolling. 'One question. Do you like this color?'

'That's not the point—'

'Simple question. Do you like it?'

Her breath whistled between her teeth. 'Of course not. It's hideous.'

'There you go. Guidelines are, if you don't like it, it doesn't fly.'

'I can't take the responsibility.'

'I'm paying you to take it.' Since that settled the matter as far as he was concerned, he turned back to the screen, and scanned down the displays. 'You got this what-do-you-call-it in stock, right? Isn't that what this I.S. stands for?'

'Yes. The double chairback settee.' Her heart dropped to her feet. She'd bought it the week before at auction, with his parlor in mind. If he rejected it, her books were going straight into the red. 'It's in the shop,' she continued, keeping her voice coolly professional. 'I've put a hold on it.'

'So, let's take a look. I want to see this fire-screen and these tables.'

'You're the boss,' she muttered under her breath, and led the way.

Her nerves strained as she stopped by the settee. It was a gorgeous piece, and it had had a price to match. However much she coveted it, she would never have made the bid if she hadn't had a customer in the wings.

Now, she thought of that customer—the scarred boots, the ripped shirt, the potent aura of man. What had she been thinking of, she wondered frantically, imagining Rafe MacKade approving of an elegant, curvy, and decidedly feminine piece such as this?

'Ah, it's walnut…' she began, running a suddenly icy hand over the carved arm. 'Around 1850. It's been reupholstered, of course, but the material is very much in keeping with the era. You can see the double-shaped backs are centered by a circular upholstered panel. The workmanship is first-rate, and the seat is surprisingly comfortable.'

He grunted and crouched down to peer under the seat. 'Pricey little thing.'

'It's sixty-nine inches wide, and well worth the expense.'

'Okay.'

She blinked. 'Okay?'

'Yeah. If I stay on schedule, I should have the parlor ready by the weekend. I could take delivery on this by Monday, unless I tell you different.' He glanced up at her. 'That suit you?'

'Yes.' She realized she'd lost all feeling below the knees. 'Of course.'

'C.O.D. all right? I don't have my checkbook on me.'

'That'll be fine.'

'Let's see the Pembroke table.'

'The Pembroke table.' She looked dizzily around the shop. 'Over here.'

He straightened, holding back a grin. He wondered if she had any idea that, for a few minutes there, she'd been clear as glass. He doubted it.

'What's this?'

Distracted, she stopped. 'Oh, that's a display table. Satinwood and mahogany.'

'I like it.'

'You like it,' she repeated.

'It'd look good in the parlor, wouldn't it?'

'Yes, I had it down as a possibility.'

'Send it over with the couch thing. Is this the Pembroke here?'

All she could do was nod weakly. When he left, an hour later, she was still nodding.

Rafe headed straight to the sheriff's office. He'd have to put in a couple of hours overtime on the job, but he wasn't leaving town until he knew Joe Dolin was in a cage.

When he stepped inside, he found Devin tilted back in his chair, his feet propped on his battered metal desk. Devin's uniform consisted of a cotton shirt, faded jeans and boots worn down at the heel. His only concession to his position was the star on his chest.

He was reading a dog-eared copy of *The Grapes of Wrath*.

'And you're responsible for law and order in this town.'

In his slow, deliberate way, Devin marked his place and set the book aside. 'That's what they tell me. Always got a cell waiting for you.'

'If you've got Dolin in one, I wouldn't mind you putting me in with him for five minutes or so.'

'He's back there.'

With a nod, Rafe walked to the coffeemaker. 'Have any trouble with him?'

Devin's lips curved in a lazy and wicked smile. 'Just enough to make it fun. I'll have a cup of that.'

'How long can you keep him in there?'

'That's not up to me.'

Devin reached out for the chipped mug Rafe offered. Since he insisted on making the coffee himself, it was the MacKade brew. Hot, strong and black as night.

'We'll transfer him to Hagerstown,' Devin went on. 'He'll get himself a public defender. If Cassie doesn't back down, he'll have his day in court.'

Rafe sat on the corner of the cluttered desk. 'You think she'll back down?'

Fighting frustration, Devin shrugged. 'This is the closest she's ever come to doing anything about things. The son of a bitch has been pounding on her for years. Probably started on her on their wedding night. She can't weigh more than a hundred pounds. Got bones like a bird.' His usually calm eyes went molten. 'She's got bruises around her throat where he choked her.'

'I didn't see that.'

'I got pictures.'

After rubbing a hand over his face, Devin dropped his

feet to the floor. Tussling with Joe, slapping cuffs on him, along with a few bruises—in the line of duty—hadn't taken the edge off.

'I had to take her statement, and pictures for evidence, and she sat there looking at me like she was getting beat up all over again. God knows how she'll handle it if she has to go to court and lay it all out.'

Abruptly he pushed away from his desk, paced to the window, where he could look out on the town. He'd given his word to serve the town, protect its citizens. Not to relieve his own bitter frustrations by pummeling one of them into the ground.

'I gave her the standard lines,' he continued. 'Therapy, counseling, shelters. And I put just enough pressure on when she started to waffle, so she'd sign the complaint. She just sat there crying, and I felt like scum.'

Rafe studied his coffee, frowned. 'You still have a thing for her, Dev?'

'That was high school,' Devin snapped. With an effort, he uncurled his fist, turned back to his brother.

They might have been twins, with barely a year separating them. The same bold, dark looks, rangy build. Only Devin's eyes were cooler, more like moss than jade. And the scars he carried were on his heart.

'Sure I care about her,' he said, calm again. 'Hell, Rafe, we've known her all our lives. I've hated watching what he's been doing to her, not being able to stop it. Every time I got called out to their place, every time she had a fresh bruise, she'd just say it was an accident.'

'Not this time.'

'No, not this time. I sent my deputy with her to get the kids, whatever stuff she needs.'

'You know she's going to stay with Regan Bishop.'

'She told me.' He drained his coffee, went back for more. 'Well, she's taken the first step. It's probably the hardest.'

Since there was nothing more he could do, Devin sat behind his desk again and put the matter in the corner of his mind. 'Speaking of Regan Bishop, word is you've been sniffing around her.'

'There a law against it?'

'If there is, it wouldn't be one you haven't broken before.' Devin rose again, rooted through the side drawer of his deputy's desk. He confiscated two candy bars, tossed one to Rafe. 'She's not your usual type.'

'I'm upgrading my taste.'

''Bout time.' Devin bit into chocolate. 'Serious?'

'Getting a woman into bed's always serious, bro.'

Mumbling an agreement over candy, Devin kicked back again. 'So is that all there is?'

'I don't know. But I've got a feeling it'll be a hell of a start.' He glanced over and grinned as Regan came through the door.

She stopped short, as any woman might when faced with two gorgeous men smiling at her. 'I'm sorry. I'm interrupting.'

'No, ma'am.' All quiet country charm, Devin unfolded himself and stood. 'It's always a pleasure to see you.'

Angling his head, Rafe put a hand on Regan's shoulder. 'Dibs,' he said in a mild warning.

'Excuse me?' Regan stepped back and gaped. 'I beg your pardon, but did you just say 'Dibs'?'

'Yeah.' Rafe bit off candy, offered her the rest of the bar. When she smacked his hand away, he only shrugged and ate it himself.

'Of all the ridiculous, outrageous— You're a grown man, and you're standing there eating candy and saying 'Dibs' as if I were the last ice-cream bar in the freezer.'

'The way I grew up, it was real important to stake your claim quick.' To prove it, he cupped her elbows, lifted her to her toes and kissed her long and hard. 'Gotta go,' he said, releasing her just as arrogantly. 'See you, Dev.'

'Yeah.' Too wise to let the laugh loose, Devin cleared his throat. Seconds passed, and Regan continued to stare at the door Rafe had slammed at his back. 'You want me to go after him, haul him into the back room?'

'Have you got a rubber hose back there?'

'Afraid not. But I broke his finger once, when we were kids. I could probably do it again.'

'Never mind.' She shook herself. She'd deal with Rafe later, personally. 'I came here to see if you'd arrested Joe Dolin.'

'So did Rafe.'

'I should have known he would.'

'Want some coffee, Regan?'

'No, I can't stay. I just came to see if you had, and to ask, since Cassie and the children are going to be staying with me, if there are any precautions I should take.'

Quietly he measured her. He'd known her casually for three years, admired her looks, enjoyed a few conversations with her at the café or on the street. Now he saw what had attracted his brother. Spine, good sense, compassion.

He wondered if Rafe understood the difference the combination could make in his life.

'Why don't you sit down,' he told her. 'We'll go over some things.'

Chapter 5

On Monday morning, Regan was up early, a song on her lips. In a few hours, the first furnishings would be delivered to the house on the hill. With her payment deposited, she would dash to an auction in Pennsylvania scheduled for that afternoon.

It would be well worth closing the shop for the day.

She put the coffee on, popped bread into the toaster. Then turned and nearly jumped out of her slippers.

'Oh, Connor.' Laughing, she pressed a hand to her speeding heart. 'You scared me.'

'I'm sorry.' The boy was thin, pale, with big eyes the color of shadows. His mother's eyes, Regan thought as she smiled at him.

'It's okay. I didn't know anyone was up. It's early, even for a school day. Want some breakfast?'

'No, thank you.'

She bit back a sigh. No eight-year-old boy should be so apologetically polite. She lifted a brow and took out a box of the cereal she'd learned was his favorite. With a wink, she gave it a shake.

'How about joining me for a bowl?'

He smiled then, so sweetly shy it broke her heart. 'I guess if you're having some.'

'Why don't you get the milk out, put it on the table?' Because it hurt to see how carefully, how deliberately, he performed the simple chore, she made her voice bright. 'I heard on the radio we're in for some more snow. Maybe a big one.'

She carried out bowls and spoons, set them down. When she lifted a hand to brush it over his tousled hair, he went very still. Cursing Joe Dolin, she kept the smile on her face. 'I bet they close school tomorrow.'

'I like school,' he said then bit his lip.

'I always did, too.' Brisk and determinedly cheerful, she breezed into the kitchen again for her coffee. 'I never minded a day off now and again, but I really liked school. What's your favorite subject?'

'English class. I like to write things.'

'Really? What kind of things?'

'Stories.' He hunched his shoulders, looking down. 'Just stupid stuff.'

'I bet it's not.' She could only hope she wasn't making a mistake, moving into territory best left to the experts. But her heart simply moved her hand. She cupped it under Connor's chin and lifted it gently as she sat beside him.

'You should be proud. I know your mother's proud of you. She told me you won a prize in your English class for a story you wrote.'

'She did?' He was torn between wanting to smile and wanting to let his head drop again. But Regan had her hand on his face. It felt good there, warm. The tears were in his eyes before he could stop them. 'She cries at night.'

'I know, baby.'

'He was always hitting her. I knew it. I could hear them. But I never did anything to stop it. I never did anything to help her.'

'You're not to blame.' Letting instinct rule, she lifted him onto her lap, cuddling him close. 'You're not to blame, Connor. And there was nothing you could have done. But now you and your mother and your little sister are safe. You're all going to look after each other.'

'I hate him.'

'Shh…' Jolted by how such fierceness could spurt from someone so small, so young, Regan pressed her lips to his hair and rocked.

In the hallway, Cassie stepped back. Torn in a dozen different directions, she swayed there a moment, a hand over her mouth. Then she went back into the little spare bedroom to wake her daughter for school.

Regan arrived at the Barlow place just ahead of the van and movers she'd hired. The cheerful noise of construction blasted her the minute she opened the door. Nothing could have lifted her mood higher.

The hallway was draped with tarps and drop cloths.

But the spiderwebs and the mustiness were gone. The dust that lay now was fresh, and somehow clean.

She supposed it was a kind of exorcism. Amused by the thought, she studied the stairway. As a kind of test, she walked toward it, started up.

The cold slapped her like a fist, sending her back two steps. She stood, one hand gripping the rail, the other pressed to her stomach as she struggled to get back the breath the icy air had stolen.

'You've got guts,' Rafe murmured from behind her.

Though her eyes were still wide in shock, she looked down and met his levelly. 'I wondered if it had just been my imagination. How do the laborers go up and down these steps without—?'

'Not everyone feels it. I'd say the ones who do grit their teeth and think about their paycheck.' He walked up the steps to take her hand. 'How about you?'

'I'd never have believed it if I hadn't experienced it.' Without protest, she let him lead her down to the main level. 'It should make for some interesting breakfast conversation among the guests, once you're open.'

'Darling, I'm counting on it. Give me your coat. We've got the heat for this part of the house up and running.' He slipped her coat off himself. 'It's on low, but it takes the edge off.'

'You're telling me.' Pleased that it seemed warm enough to make shivering unnecessary, she flipped back her hair. 'What's going on upstairs?'

'A little bit of everything. I'm putting in an extra bath. I want you to dig up one of those claw-foot tubs, a pedestal sink. Reproductions'll do, if you don't have any luck finding originals.'

'Give me a few days. Well.' She rubbed her hands together, not from cold, but nerves. 'Are you going to show me, or do I have to beg?'

'I'm going to show you.' He'd been itching to, looking out the window every five minutes to watch for her. But now that she was here, he was nervous. He'd slaved for more than a week, twelve-and fourteen-hour days, to make that one room, that one spot, that one step, perfect.

'I think the paint turned out.' Rather than reach for her hand, he tucked his in his pockets and walked into the parlor ahead of her. 'It's a nice contrast with the trim and the floor, I think. Had a little trouble with the windows, but I just had to diddle with the framing.'

She didn't speak. For a moment, she merely stood in the doorway. Then, quietly, her boots clicking on the floor, she stepped inside.

It gleamed. The tall, elegant windows, with their graceful arches sent sun streaming over the newly polished floor of lovely old pine. The walls were a deep, warm blue against creamy carved trim in the most delicate of ivories.

He'd turned the window seat into a charming alcove, scrubbed the marble on the fireplace until it shone like glass. The molding along the ceiling bloomed with delicately carved florets that had been smothered and choked by the grime of decades.

'It needs furniture, drapes, and that mirror you picked out for over the mantel.' He wished she would say something, anything. 'I have to replace the pocket doors, yet.'

Scowling, he jammed his hands deeper into his pocket. 'Well, what's the problem? Did I miss some vital, authentic detail?'

'It's absolutely wonderful.' Enchanted, she ran a finger down the glossy trim of a window. 'Absolutely perfect. I didn't realize you were this good.' With a quick laugh, she glanced back at him. 'That wasn't meant as an insult.'

'It wasn't taken as one. I was pretty surprised myself, the first time I realized I had a talent for putting something together.'

'It's more than that. It's bringing something to life. You must be proud.'

He was, he realized, moved, and just a little embarrassed. 'It's a job. Hammer and nails and a good eye.'

She angled her head, and he watched the sun beam through the window and glow golden on her hair. His mouth watered, then went bone dry.

'You're the last man I'd expect to be modest about anything. You must have killed yourself to get so much accomplished in so little time.'

'It was mostly cosmetic in here.'

'You've done something,' she murmured, and looked around, turning a slow, graceful circle. 'You've really done something.'

Before he could comment, she was on her hands and knees, running her hands over the floor.

'It's like glass.' She all but crooned over the golden planks. 'Oh, look at the grain in this wood! What did you use? How many coats?' When he didn't answer, she tossed her head and sat back on her heels. The dazzled smile faded when he only stared at her. 'What is it? What's wrong?'

'Stand up.'

His voice was raw. As she rose to her feet, he kept his distance. He didn't dare touch her now. If he did, he'd simply never be able to stop.

'You look right in here. You should see yourself, how right you look. You're as polished and perfect as this room. I want you so much I can't see anything else but you.'

Her heart did a long, unsteady cartwheel in her chest. 'You're going to make me stutter again, Rafe.' She had to make a conscious effort to pump air in and out of her lungs.

'How long are you going to make me wait?' he demanded. 'We're not kids. We know what we feel and what we want.'

'That's exactly the point. We're not kids, and we should be adult enough to be sensible.'

'Sensible's for old lady's shoes. Sex may have to be responsible, but it sure as hell doesn't have to be sensible.'

The thought of wicked, completely insensible sex with him numbed every nerve ending in her body. 'I don't know how to handle you. I don't know how to handle the way you make me feel. I'm usually good at handling things. I guess we need to talk about this.'

'I guess you need to. I just said what I needed to say.' Unbelievably frustrated, irrationally angry at his own helpless response to her, he turned to the window. 'Your truck's here. I've got work upstairs. Put the stuff wherever the hell you want it.'

'Rafe—'

He stopped her, froze her before her hand could reach his arm. 'You wouldn't want to touch me right now.' His voice was quiet, very controlled. 'It'd be a mistake. You don't like to make them.'

'That's not fair.'

'What the hell makes you think I'm fair?' His eyes slashed her to ribbons. 'Ask anybody who knows me. Your check's on the mantel.'

With her own temper sizzling, she stomped into the hall after him. 'MacKade.'

He stopped on the steps, turned back. 'Yeah?'

'I'm not interested in what anyone else thinks or says. If I were, you'd never have gotten within three feet of me.'

She glanced up as an interested laborer poked his head into the stairway. 'Beat it,' she snapped, and had Rafe's lips twitching reluctantly. 'I make up my own mind, in my own time,' she continued and turned on her heel to open the front door for the movers. '*You* ask anybody.'

When she looked back, he was gone, like one of his ghosts.

Nearly blew it, Rafe thought later. He wasn't entirely sure why he'd reacted that way. Anger and demands weren't his usual style with women. Maybe that, he mused as he troweled drywall compound on a seam, was the problem.

Women had always come easily.

He liked them, always had. The way they looked, thought, smelled, spoke. Soft, warm, fragrant, they were one of the more interesting aspects of life. Frowning, he slapped on more compound, smoothed it.

Women were important. He enjoyed cultivating them, the companionship they offered. And the sex, he acknowledged with a thin smile, he enjoyed that, too.

Hell, he was human.

Houses were important, he reflected, coating another seam of drywall. Repairing them was satisfying, using your own hands and sweat to turn them into something that lasted. And the money that came from the end result was satisfying, too.

A man had to eat.

But there'd never been a single house that was specifically important, as this one had come to be.

And there'd never been a single woman who was specifically important, as Regan had now become.

And he calculated that she would slice him into dog meat if she knew he was comparing her to stone and wood.

He doubted she would understand that it was the first time in his life he'd ever focused on something, and someone, so entirely.

The house had haunted him for a lifetime. He hadn't set eyes on her a month before. Yet they were both in his blood. He hadn't been exaggerating when he told her that he couldn't see anything but her. She was haunting him, just as the restless ghosts haunted these rooms and hallways.

Seeing her there that morning had turned him on his head, set his hormones raging, and he'd fumbled. He supposed he could make up ground. But this was the first time he could remember being tackled by emotion— emotion double-teamed with desire—and he wasn't at all sure of his moves.

Back off, MacKade, he told himself, and scooped more compound out of the bucket. She wants room, give her room. It wasn't as though he didn't have time—or as though she were some sort of life-altering encounter. Maybe she was unique, maybe she was more intriguing than he'd counted on. But she was still just a woman.

He heard the weeping, felt the stir of chilled air. With barely a hesitation, he leveled his seam.

'Yeah, yeah, I hear you,' he muttered. 'You might as well get used to company, 'cause I'm not going anywhere.'

A door slammed. It amused him now, these endless little dramas. Footsteps and creaks, whispers and weeping. It was almost as though he were part of it all. A caretaker, he decided. Making the house livable for those who could never leave.

He thought it was too bad none of the permanent residents ever made an appearance. It would be quite an experience to see, as well as hear. An involuntary shudder worked up his back, as if fingers had trailed along his spine.

And feel, he thought.

Footsteps echoed down the hall outside as he moved to the next sheet of drywall. To his surprise and curiosity, they stopped just outside the door. He watched the knob turn, just as the work lamp behind him went out, plunging the room into darkness.

He'd have suffered torments from hell before admitting that his heart skipped several beats. To cover the lapse, he muttered oaths under his breath, rubbed his suddenly damp palms on his spattered jeans. From memory, he fumbled his way toward the door. It swung open fast and caught him full in the face.

He wasn't muttering oaths now, but spewing them. Stars were revolving in front of his eyes. And, with disgust, he felt blood trickle from his nose.

He heard the hoarse scream, saw the ghostly figure in the shadows of the hall, and didn't hesitate. Pain and fury had him shooting forward like a bullet. Ghost or not, anything that gave him a bloody nose was going to pay.

It took him several furious seconds to realize he had warm flesh wriggling in his arms, and little more to recognize the scent.

She was haunting him all right, he thought bitterly.

'What the hell are you doing?'

'Rafe?' Her voice squeaked out. In the dark, she threw up her arms, one flailing hand catching him sharply on the chin before she managed the wholehearted embrace. 'Oh, my God, you scared me to death. I thought— I don't know. I heard… I came up. Oh, it's you.'

'What's left of me.' Swearing, he set her firmly aside. There was enough light from the lamp hooked at the top of the stairs for him to see her pale face and huge eyes. 'What are you doing here?'

'I picked up some things at auction and thought I'd put them— You're bleeding.'

'No kidding.' Scowling at her, he swiped a hand under his nose. 'I don't think you broke it again. Quite.'

'I—' She rubbed a hand over her heart to make sure it hadn't exploded from her chest. 'Did I hit you with the door? I'm sorry. Here.' She dug in the pocket of her jacket and found a tissue. 'I'm really sorry,' she repeated, and began to dab at the blood herself. 'I was just…' Helpless, she tried to disguise a laugh as a hiccup. 'I didn't realize.' She gave up, wrapped her arms around her aching stomach, and slid to the floor.

'It's a real laugh riot.'

'I'm sorry. I can't stop. I thought—I don't know what I thought. I heard them, or it, or whatever. I just had to come up and see, well, if I could see. Then you came barreling out.'

'You're lucky I didn't punch you,' he said, with relish.

'I know. I know.'

His eyes narrowed as he watched her fold with mirth. 'I still could.'

'Oh, help me up.' Still chuckling, she wiped at her eyes. 'Let's get some ice on that nose.'

'I can take care of it myself.' But he took hold of her wrist and hauled her, none too gently, to her feet.

'Did I scare you?' She tried to keep her voice meek and apologetic as she followed him to the stairs.

'Get real.'

'But you heard—you heard it, didn't you?' She braced, held her breath as they passed through the cold spot.

'Sure, I heard it. Goes on every night. A couple times during the day.'

'And it doesn't…bother you?'

It boosted his ego to be able to flick a disdainful glance over his shoulder. 'Why should it bother me? It's their house, too.'

'I suppose.' She looked around the kitchen. It was all but bare, and still grimy. There was a small, dented re-frigerator, a stove that was down to two working burners, and an old door propped on sawhorses that served as a table. Rafe went directly to the pitted cast-iron sink and ran cold water. 'Do you have a clean rag?'

In lieu of an answer, he bent over and scooped icy water onto his face. Adopting a shamed pose, Regan folded her hands.

'I'm really terribly sorry, Rafe. Does it hurt?'

'Yes.'

He snatched up a frayed towel and dried his face. With-out another word, he strode to the refrigerator and pulled out a beer.

'It's stopped bleeding.'

He twisted off the top, tossed it aside, then downed a third of the bottle. Regan decided that, under the circum-stances, she could try again.

'I didn't see your car. That's why I didn't think any-one was here.'

'Devin dropped me off.' He decided that, under the circumstances, he could give her a break. 'I've been put-ting in some extra time at night, camping out here. We're supposed to get hit with a snowstorm tonight, so it didn't make any sense to have the car. I can walk into town if I need to.'

'Oh. Well. That explains it.'

'Want a beer?'

'No thanks, I don't drink beer.'

'Fresh out of champagne.'

'Well, then, I really should be getting back. Actually, it's already starting to snow.' Feeling awkward now, she pushed at her hair. 'Ah, there were these candlesticks, and a really wonderful set of fire irons I bought today. I just wanted to bring them by, see how they looked.'

He lifted the beer again, watching her. 'So, how do they look?'

'I don't know. I set everything down in the hall when I came in and heard the, ah, evening performance.'

'You decided to go ghost hunting instead of decorating.'

'Looks that way. Well, why don't I set them up now, before I take off?'

Taking the beer along, he went with her. 'I guess you've cooled off since this morning.'

'Not exactly.' She spared him a brief look as she headed to the main hall. 'Though giving you a bloody nose, even inadvertently, was satisfying. You acted like a jerk.'

His eyes narrowed as she picked up the box she'd left in the hall and sailed into the parlor. 'I was giving it to you straight. Some women appreciate honesty.'

'Some women like jerks.' She set the box on a drum table she'd had the movers place at the window. 'I don't. I like simplicity, manners, tact. Which, of course, you're completely without.' Then she turned, and smiled. 'But I think, under the circumstances, a truce is in order. Who broke your nose before?'

'Jared, when we were kids and fighting in the hayloft. He got lucky.'

'Hmm…' She supposed she would never understand why brotherly affection meant bloody noses to the Mac-Kades. 'So this is where you're camping out.' She gestured toward the sleeping bag tossed in front of the fire.

'It's the warmest room in the house right now. And the cleanest. What circumstances equal a truce?'

'Don't set that bottle down without a coaster.' Heaving a sigh, she walked over, took one from the silver-plated basket and offered it. 'You can't treat antiques like…'

'Furniture?' he finished, but he used the coaster. 'What circumstances, Regan?'

'Our ongoing business relationship, for one.' Because her fingers were tense again, she busied them by unbuttoning her coat as she walked back to the window. 'We're both trying to accomplish the same thing with this house, so it doesn't make sense to be at odds. These are nice, aren't they?' She took the fire irons from the box, stroked a finger over the curved handle of the coal shovel. 'They could use some polish.'

'It ought to work better than the crowbar I've been using.' Tucking his thumbs in his pockets, he watched her carry the irons to the fire, set them carefully and individually in their stand on the stone hearth.

'Whatever you used, it's a nice fire.' Torn between courage and doubt, she stared at the flames. 'I'm still looking for the right screen. This one doesn't really suit.

It would be better in one of the rooms upstairs. I imagine you'll have them all working. The fireplaces.'

'Eventually.'

He'd only known her for a few weeks, he realized. How could he be so sure she was arguing with herself? With the firelight flickering over her, her back so straight, that sweep of hair curtaining half her face, she looked relaxed, confident, perfectly at ease. Maybe it was the way she had her fingers linked together, or the way she wasn't looking at him. But he was certain some small inner war was being waged.

'Why are you here, Regan?'

'I told you.' Dragging her fingers apart, she went back to the box. 'I have some other stuff from the auction in my car, but you're not ready for it. But these...' With care, she unwrapped heavy crystal candlesticks. 'I could see them in here, right on this table. You'll want flowers for this vase. Even in the winter.'

She fussed with the arrangement, placing the candlesticks just so on one side of the Doulton vase she'd already sold him.

'Tulips would be lovely, when you can get them,' she continued, carefully unwrapping the two white tapers she'd brought along. 'But mums would do, and roses, of course.' She put a smile on her face again and turned. 'There, what do you think?'

Saying nothing, he took a box of wooden matches from the mantel and walked over to light the tapers. And watched her over the delicate twin flames. 'They work.'

'I meant the whole effect, the room.' It was a good excuse to move away from him, wandering the space, running a finger along the curved back of the settee.

'It's perfect. I didn't expect any less from you.'

'I'm not perfect.' The words burst out of her, unexpected on both sides. 'You make me nervous when you say so. I was always expected to be perfect, and I'm just not. I'm not carefully arranged, like this room, with every piece in place, no matter how much I want to be. I'm a mess.' She dragged nervous fingers through her hair. 'And I wasn't, before. I wasn't. No, stay over there.' She backed up quickly when he stepped forward. 'Just stay over there.'

Frustrated, she waved her hands to ward him off, then paced. 'You scared me this morning. You made me angry, but more, you scared me.'

It wasn't easy for Rafe to keep his hands to himself. 'How?'

'Because no one's ever wanted me the way you do. I know you do.' She stopped, rubbing her hands over her arms. 'You look at me as though you already know how it's going to be with us. And I have no control over it.'

'I figured I was giving you control, laying it out for you.'

'No. No,' she repeated, flinging up her arms. 'I don't have any control over the way I'm feeling. You have to know that. You know exactly the way you affect people.'

'We're not talking about people.'

'You know exactly the way you affect *me*.' She almost shouted it before she fisted her hands and fought for composure. 'You know I want you. Why wouldn't I? It's just as you said, we're adults who know what we want. And the more I backpedal, the more stupid I feel.'

His eyes were shadowed in the shifting light. 'You're going to stand there and say these things to me and expect me to do nothing about it?'

'I expect to be able to make a sane and rational decision. I don't expect my glands to overwhelm my brain.' She blew out a breath. 'Then I look at you and I want to rip your clothes off.'

He had to laugh. It was the safest way to defuse the bomb ticking inside of him. 'Don't expect me to stop you.' When he stepped forward, she jumped back like a spring. 'Just the beer,' he muttered, lifting the bottle. 'I need it.' He took a long, deep gulp, but it didn't do much to put out the fire. 'So, what have we got here, Regan? Two unattached, healthy adults who want pretty much the same thing from each other.'

'Who barely know each other,' she added. 'Who've barely scratched the surface of any sort of relationship. Who should have more sense than to jump into sex as if it was a swimming pool.'

'I never bother testing the water.'

'I do. An inch at a time.' Ordering herself to be calm, she linked her hands again. 'It's important to me to know exactly what I'm getting into, exactly where I'm going.'

'No detours?'

'No. When I plan something, I stick to it. That works for me.' She was calmer now, she told herself. Rational now. 'I had a lot of time to think, driving to Pennsylvania and back. We need to slow down, take a look at the whole picture.'

If she was calm, why couldn't she stop fiddling with her blazer, twisting her rings?

'It's like this house,' she continued quickly. 'You've finished one room, and it's beautiful, it's wonderful. But you didn't start this project without a complete plan in mind for the rest of it. I think intimacy should certainly be as carefully thought out as the renovation of a house.'

'Makes sense.'

'Good.' She drew in a breath, released it. 'So, we'll take a few steps back, get a clearer view of things.' Her hand was still unsteady when she reached for her coat. 'That's the sensible, the responsible route to take.'

'Yeah.' He set down his beer. 'Regan?'

She gripped her coat like a lifeline. 'Yes.'

'Stay.'

Her fingers went numb. Her breath came out in a long, shuddering sigh. 'I thought you'd never ask.'

With a jittery laugh, she threw herself into his arms.

Chapter 6

'This is crazy.' Already breathless, she curled her fingers into his hair to drag his mouth to hers. Everything in her strained into the kiss, the heat of it, the danger, the promise. 'I wasn't going to do this.'

'That's okay.' He dragged his lips from hers to race over her face. 'I'll do it.'

'I'd thought it all through.' When her knees trembled, she gave a quick, helpless laugh. 'I had. Everything I just said made perfect sense. This is just chemistry. It's just superficial attraction.'

'Yeah.' In one fluid movement, he yanked her blazer down her shoulders, locking her arms, trapping her body to his. Her gasp of alarm stirred his blood. The huge, wary eyes tightened his loins. 'Stop thinking.'

A smile curved his lips as he tugged the bunched material, pressing her against him. He watched her eyes glaze, heard the ragged moan when his mouth fed on hers. Then his lips rushed down over the line of her throat. It was as smooth, as scented, as he'd imagined it. So he feasted.

Her hands clutched at his hips, her head falling back to offer him whatever he chose to take. All the while the heat coursed through her painfully, forcing her breath out in harsh, ragged moans.

With a jerk, he freed her arms. Before she could reach out, his hands, his wide, clever hands, streaked under her sweater to mold, to possess.

Flesh and lace, curves and shudders. He found everything he wanted, and wanted more. His mouth continued its relentless assault, while his fingers tortured her skin, and her skin tortured him.

With a flick of his wrist, he unsnapped her trousers, then skimmed the tips of his fingers along her quivering belly, under the edge of more lace. She moved against him, pressed urgently against him, her teeth scraping along his neck in greedy bites.

He could take her now, fast and hot, where they stood. The speed would release this terrible pressure that burned inside him.

But he wanted more.

He dragged the sweater over her head, tossed it aside and filled his palms with her breasts. The lace covering was smooth, delicate, and the flesh beneath already flushed and warm with desire. Ruthlessly controlling the pounding need to rush, Rafe watched her face, the flicker of light and shadow over it, while he rubbed his work-roughened thumbs over the points of her breasts.

'I've imagined you like this.'

'I know.'

His lips curved again, and his eyes were focused keenly on hers when he nudged a slim strap down her shoulder. 'I don't think you've imagined what I've thought of doing to you. I don't think you could. So I'm going to show you.'

His eyes stayed on hers, watching, measuring, as he skimmed a finger along the valley between her breasts, up over the curve, then back to flick open the center clasp.

So he saw that lovely sky blue gaze darken with the storm he set off inside her. And he felt it quake, in both of them.

Her breath caught in her throat when he jerked her off her feet and set his hungry mouth to work. Shocked, she arched back, her hands fumbling in his hair, over his shoulders, tugging desperately at his shirt. His teeth nipped into her, just short of savage, just short of pain. His tongue tormented, and aroused needs too violent to bear.

Wild, frantic, she clawed at him. Even as she felt herself falling, she tore and ripped at his shirt. She was on her back, on the thin cushion of the sleeping bag, and bucking desperately beneath him.

Finally she tugged his shirt away, cursing when she found yet another layer separating them. She wanted flesh, craved it with a mindless hunger. The moment he'd dragged the thin undershirt aside, she sank her teeth into his shoulder.

'Touch me.' Her words were raw and urgent. 'I want your hands on me.'

They were, everywhere at once. Her world became primitive, dangerously exciting, pumped full to bursting with unspeakable sensations. Each rough, impatient caress sent fresh shocks erupting, until her body was nothing but sweaty flesh over sparking nerves.

Beside her, the fire shot hissing embers against the screen. Inside her, flames leapt and burned.

She could see him through the haze that blurred her vision. The dark hair, the fierce eyes, the muscles that glistened with sweat in the dance of light. Her moan of protest when his mouth left hers turned to one of giddy pleasure as his lips streaked down over throat, over breasts and torso.

He levered back and, blind with need, she reared up, her arms circling possessively, her lips searching for each new taste.

His oath was brief and vicious. 'Boots,' he managed, fighting to pry hers off while his blood screamed. She was draped around him, that wonderful body sliding over his, her hands... Those incredible elegant hands.

Boots thudded where he heaved them aside, then, quick as a snake, turned to take her.

She was tangled around him, all long, silky limbs. He wanted her naked and writhing beneath him. He wanted to hear her scream his name and watch the jolts and shocks of pleasure glaze her eyes. Breath ragged, he dragged the slacks down her hips. In one reckless swipe, he tore the lace to shreds. Even as her gasp echoed off the walls, he shoved her back. And used his mouth.

The climax slammed into her, a bare-knuckled punch that knocked her senseless. Reeling from it, she sobbed out his name. And, shuddering, shuddering, hungered for more.

He gave her more. And took more. Each time she thought he would end it, must end it, he found some new way to batter her senses. There was only him, the taste, the feel, the smell of him. They rolled over the floor in a wild, glorious combat, her nails digging ruthlessly into his back, his mouth searing hers.

Nearly blinded by need, he gripped her hands, fingers vised. He thought his own breathing must tear his lungs apart. Her face was all he could see as he drove himself into her. Twin groans mixed. A log shattered thunderously in the grate.

They trembled, watching each other as they savored that timeless instant of mating.

Muscles straining, he lowered his head, covered her mouth. When the kiss was at its deepest, when her flavor filled him as intimately as he was filling her, they began to move together.

It was the cold that finally roused Regan. Though it seemed impossible, she thought she must have fallen asleep. As she struggled to orient herself, she discovered her back was against the cold, hard wood of the floor, pressed firmly against it by the weight of Rafe's body.

She looked around dazedly. Somehow or other, they'd gotten themselves several feet from the fire.

'You awake now?' Rafe's voice was thick, a little sleepy.

'I guess.' She tried a deep breath, was relieved to find she could accomplish it. 'I can't really tell.'

He shifted his head, skimmed his lips over the curve of her breast. Her exhausted body quivered in response.

'I guess I can tell after all,' she said.

'You're cold.' He shifted, hauled her up and put her back on the sleeping bag. Wished, for her, that it was a feather bed. 'Better?'

'Yeah.' Not quite sure of her moves, she tugged a corner of the bag up to her chin. She'd never been so exposed, so completely naked, body and soul, before anyone. 'I must have dozed off.'

'Just a couple minutes.' He grinned at her. He felt as though he'd climbed a mountain. And could climb ten more. 'I'll put another log on.'

Naked and easy, he rose to go to the woodbox. The scratches scoring his shoulders had Regan's mouth falling open. She'd done that. She'd actually... Good God. 'I, ah, should go. Cassie'll be worried.'

Rafe set the screen back in place. Without a word, he reached into the duffel bag beside the woodbox and took out a cell phone. 'Call her.'

'I...didn't realize you had a phone.'

'It's a tool on a job like this.' He handed it to her, then sat down beside her. 'Call her,' he repeated. 'And stay.'

She was sure there were reasons why she should go.

But she dialed her own number, watching Rafe as the phone rang.

'Cassie, it's Regan. Yes, everything's fine. Snow?' Baffled for a moment, she pushed her hair away from her face. 'Oh, yes, it's really coming down. That's why I'm calling. I got, um, involved, and I think...'

She trailed off as Rafe tugged the corner of the bag out of her hand, as his fingers trailed down the curve of her breast.

'What?' She swallowed, then bit back a moan. His mouth had replaced his fingers. She slid bonelessly to her back. 'Pennsylvania?' she murmured. 'No, I'm not in Pennsylvania.'

Rafe took the phone from her limp fingers. 'She's with me. She's staying with me. No kidding? She'll call you tomorrow. Right.'

He clicked the phone off, set it aside. 'Cassie says we've got over a foot out there, the streets are a mess, and you should stay put.'

'Oh.' She closed her eyes, lifted her arms. 'That's very sensible.'

The candles had guttered out and the fire had burned to embers when she awoke. The house was so still, so quiet, she could hear her own heartbeat. The room was filled with shadows and darkness, but it was oddly peaceful. Perhaps the ghosts slept, she mused. Or perhaps she felt at ease with them because Rafe slept beside her.

She turned her head and studied his face in the dying firelight. Asleep or not, she mused, there was no innocent-little-boy look about him. All that power, and the potential for violence, were still there, carved into his face.

She knew he could be gentle, caring. She'd seen that in the way he was with Cassie. But as a lover, he was demanding, relentless and rough.

And, for the first time in her life, she'd been the same.

Now, with the quiet like a blanket over her, she found it hard to believe she had done what she'd done, had allowed him—wanted him—to do what he had done.

Her body ached from bruises, and she wondered if in the full light of day she would wince at the memory of how she'd come by them. Of how she'd ached and trembled and hungered under those big, hard hands.

Even more, of how she'd used her own.

Of how, she realized with a jolt, she wanted to use them now.

Taking a shallow breath, she eased out from under Rafe's possessive arm. She moved as quietly as she could, settled on slipping on his flannel shirt for covering. Buttoning it as she went, she padded toward the kitchen.

A cold drink of water, she told herself. A few moments to evaluate the situation.

At the sink, she filled a glass. As her eyes adjusted, she watched the drift of snow falling outside the window.

She didn't regret. That, she mused, would be foolish. Fate had placed an extraordinary lover in her path. The kind of man few women ever knew. She could, and would, be content with the physical thrill of it. She could, and would, prevent it, and him, from complicating her life.

They were both adults, as he had said. They both

knew what they wanted. When the house was finished, he would probably grow restless and move on. Meanwhile they would enjoy each other. And when it was over, it would end with mutual understanding, and, she hoped, affection.

It would probably be wise to discuss those expectations, or the lack of them, before things went any further. But she found herself torn at the very idea of voicing them.

From the doorway, Rafe studied her, the way she stood, leaning a little on the counter, her eyes on the window. Her face reflected in it. His shirt skimmed her thighs, worn flannel against creamy skin.

It struck him, hard, that he'd never in his life seen anything more beautiful. He had the words to tell her; he was good with them. But he found there were none this time, none good enough to show how much she mattered.

So he chose easy ones, casual ones, and ignored the ache just looking at her had spreading around his heart.

'I like your dress, darling.'

She jolted, nearly bobbled the glass before she turned. He'd tugged on jeans, but hadn't bothered to fasten them. Grinning, he leaned against the unframed doorway.

'It was handy,' she said, matching his tone.

'That old shirt's never had it so good. Restless?'

'I was thirsty.' But she set the glass down without taking so much as a sip. 'I guess the quiet woke me. It's odd, don't you think, how quiet it is?'

'The snow always makes it quiet.'

'No, I mean the house. It seems different. Settled.'

'Even dead soldiers and unhappy women have to sleep

sometime.' He crossed the room to pick up the glass and drink himself. 'It's almost dawn,' he murmured. 'My brothers and I spent the night here once when we were kids. I guess I told you that already.'

'Jared rattling chains. And all of you telling ghost stories and smoking stolen cigarettes.'

'You got it. I came into this room then, too. It was just about this time of day, but it was late summer. Everything was so green, and the woods were so dense and thick they made you wonder what was in them. There was a mist over the ground like a river. It was beautiful, and I thought—' He broke off, shrugged.

'No.' She laid a hand on his arm. 'Tell me.'

'I thought I could hear the drums, slowly, the sounds of camps breaking to prepare for battle. I could smell the fear, the excitement, the dread. I thought I could hear the house waking around me, the whispers and creaks. I was petrified, paralyzed. If I could have moved, I'd have hauled my butt out of here. The guys would've rubbed my nose in it for years, but I'd have run like a rabbit if my legs had moved.'

'You were just a boy.'

'You've never been a boy, so you don't know that made it ten times worse. I'd gotten through the night, even gotten a kick out of it. And here it was morning, dawn breaking, and I stood here with my teeth chattering. When it passed, I just stood looking out this window. And I thought, no damn house is going to get the better of me. Nothing's going to get the better of me. I'll own this house before I'm finished.'

He smiled then, set the glass down. 'I don't know how many times I came back here, alone, after that. Waiting for something to happen, wishing it would, just so I could stand up to it. I crept through every room of this place at one time or another. I heard things, saw things, felt things. The night I left town, I promised myself I'd come back.'

'Now you have it,' she said quietly.

'Yeah.' Faintly embarrassed, he looked down at her. 'I never told anyone that.'

'Then neither will I.' She lifted a hand, touched his cheek. 'Whatever your reasons, you're doing something important. This house has been neglected too long.'

'Were you frightened, staying here through the night?'

'No. Not of the house.'

His brow lifted. 'Of me?'

'Yes. I'm frightened of you.'

The humor faded from his eyes. 'I was rough with you,' he said carefully.

'I don't mean that.' She turned away. Out of habit, she set a kettle on the stove, flicked on the burner. 'I've never been the way I was last night, with anyone. So out of control. So…needy. I'm a little surprised when I think back and… Well.' She let out a shaky breath, searched out a filter for the drip cone.

'Surprised? Or sorry?'

'Not sorry, Rafe.' Making the effort, she turned back and met his eyes. 'No, not sorry at all. Uneasy, because I know now exactly what you can do to me. I knew making love with you would be exciting. I didn't know it would be so shattering. Nothing about you is tidy or predictable. The way I like things to be.'

'I want you now. That should be predictable.'

'My heart jumps,' she managed. 'Literally, when you say things like that. But I do need things to be tidy.' Opening the can of coffee, she deliberately measured out scoops. 'I imagine your men will be coming along in an hour or so. This probably isn't the best time to talk this out.'

'Nobody's coming today. There's better than two feet of snow out there, on top of what we already had.'

'Oh.' Her hand faltered, spilling ground coffee on the stove.

'We're snowbound for a while, darling. You can talk all you want.'

'Well.' After clearing her throat, she faced him again. 'I just think it's best if we both understood things.'

'What things?'

'Things.' She bit the word off, furious at herself for hesitating. 'Things that we didn't quite finish outlining last night. That what we're having is a mutual satisfying and physical affair, no strings, no entanglements, no...'

'Complications?'

'Yes.' Relieved, she nodded. 'Exactly.'

Surprised to find himself annoyed with her coolheaded description—one that should have mirrored his own wishes—he scratched his head. 'That's tidy enough. But if that means you're planning on seeing somebody else, it'll get messy when I break him in half.'

'Oh, of all the ridiculous—'

'And cut off his—'

'Stop that.' She blew out a heated breath. 'I have no intention of seeing someone else while we're involved, but if I—'

'Smarter to stop there,' he said quietly. 'Let's just say we have a mutually satisfying and exclusive physical relationship. That suit you?'

Calmer, she turned back to pour boiling water through the filter. 'Yes, I can agree to that.'

'You're a piece of work, Regan. You want the contract in triplicate?'

'I only want to make sure we expect the same things.' She concentrated hard on covering the grounds with water, on being sure not to pour too much water, or too little. 'We haven't taken time to really get to know each other. Now we're lovers. I don't want you to think I'm looking for any more than that.'

'And if I'm looking for more?'

Her fingers whitened on the handle of the kettle. 'Are you?'

He looked away from her, toward the window and the softly falling snow. 'No.'

She closed her eyes, telling herself it was relief she felt at his answer. Only relief. 'Well, then there's no problem.'

'No, everything's dandy.' His voice was as cool and detached as hers. 'You don't want romance, saves me the trouble. You don't want promises, I don't have to lie. We want each other in bed.' He reached for two mugs. 'That keeps it simple.'

'I want you in bed.' Pleased with her casual tone, she

took the mugs from him. 'But if I didn't like who you are, we wouldn't have gotten there. I've wanted other men.'

In a deceptively calm gesture, he flicked her hair behind her ear. 'Now you're trying to make me mad.'

The fact that he couldn't see how difficult it was for her to be so open, to keep things simple, made it easier. Oddly enough, this kind of openness seemed completely natural with him. 'I'm trying to give you a compliment. I wouldn't have come here last night, hoping you'd be here, if I hadn't cared about you.'

'You came to drop off candlesticks.'

'You're an idiot.' Amused at both of them, she poured coffee. She hadn't realized sexual frankness could be fun. 'You didn't really buy that, did you?'

Intrigued, he took the mug she offered. 'Yeah, I did.'

She sipped, smiled. 'Sucker.'

'Maybe I don't like sneaky, aggressive women.'

'Yes, you do. In fact, you're hoping I'll seduce you right now.'

'Think so?'

'I know so. But I want my coffee first.'

He watched her take another delicate sip. 'Maybe I want my shirt back. You didn't ask if you could borrow it.'

'Fine.' With one hand, she undid the buttons. 'Take it.'

He nipped the coffee from her hand, set both mugs aside. Her smug smile had him scooping her off her feet. She was laughing and assaulting his ear as he carried her back down the hall. The front door swung open, letting in cold and blowing snow and a figure crusted with white.

Shane dragged off his cap and shook himself like a

dog. 'Hey.' Casually he kicked the door closed. 'Your car's buried to the wheel wells, Regan.'

'Oh.' With a fumbling hand, she clutched the shirt together and tried to mirror his easy tone. 'We got a lot of snow.'

'Over two feet.' Unabashed, he grinned at his brother. 'Figured you'd need someone to plow you out.'

'Does it look like I want you to rescue me?' Disgusted, Rafe strode into the parlor and dumped Regan on the settee. 'Stay right there.'

'Rafe!' Futilely she tried to tug the hem of the shirt down over her legs. 'For heaven's sake!'

'Right there,' he repeated, and headed back into the hall.

'That coffee I smell?' Shane asked conversationally. 'I could use some.'

'Give me one reason why I shouldn't break your neck.'

Shane took off his gloves, blew on his chilled fingers. ''Cause I rode over here in a blizzard to save yours.' He leaned forward, but couldn't quite see into the parlor. 'She's sure got legs.'

'Where do you want to die?'

'Just an observation.' His grin only widened, the MacKade dimple flashing. 'Hey, who knew? I figured you were stuck here, without transportation. Alone. Then, when I saw her car, I thought maybe she needed a lift into town.' Again he inched forward, hopeful. 'Maybe I should ask her.'

'One more step and they won't find your body till spring.'

'If I win, can I keep her?' When Rafe snarled, Shane

erupted with laughter. 'Don't hit me, I'm frozen. I'll break.'

Muttering threats, Rafe grabbed Shane by the collar and dragged him down the hall. 'Eyes front, MacKade.' In the kitchen, he found a thermos, filled it with coffee. 'Now beat it.'

'I'm going.' But Shane drank straight from the thermos. 'The wind's a bitch.' Grateful for the heat, he drank again. 'Look, I didn't mean to horn in on your little love nest,' he began, then stopped, lowered the thermos when he read quick fury in Rafe's eyes. 'Hey, are you serious about her?'

'Mind your own damn business.'

Shane whistled out a breath, screwed the top on the thermos. 'You've always been my business. Regan's a real lady. I mean that.'

'So?'

'So nothing.' Embarrassed now, Shane shifted position. 'I like her, always have. I thought about…' Realizing he'd taken a wrong turn, he pulled out his gloves again and whistled a cheerful tune.

'Thought about what?'

Cautious, Shane ran his tongue around his teeth. He really wanted to keep all of them. 'Just what you think I thought. Hell, look at her. A man's bound to think.' Agile, he evaded Rafe's lunging arm. 'Think is all I did. I'm not going to fight you over thinking.' In a gesture of peace, he threw up his hands. 'What I'm saying is, it's great. You hit the jackpot.'

Temper vanished. Rafe reached for the pot again. 'We're sleeping together. That's all.'

'You gotta start somewhere.'

'She's different, Shane.' He hadn't been able to admit it to himself, but it came easily brother to brother. 'I haven't sorted it out, but she's different. She matters a lot.'

'Everybody's got to take the big fall sometime.' Shane slapped a hand on Rafe's bare shoulder. 'Even you.'

'I didn't say anything about falling,' Rafe muttered. He knew the implications of that. Falling in love. Being in love.

'You didn't have to. Look, I'll plow the lane, just in case. You got any food around here?'

'Yeah, there's enough.'

'I'll take off, then. It's supposed to let up by midmorning. I have animals to tend to, so if you need something, try Devin first. I might be out.'

'Thanks. Shane?' He turned, eyeing his brother. 'If you so much as glance in that parlor on your way out, I'll have to kill you.'

'I already got a good look at her legs.' Whistling cheerfully, Shane ambled down the hall. 'See you, Regan.' It cost him, but he kept his eyes averted on his way to the door.

The minute she heard it slam, Regan pressed her face on her updrawn knees. Stepping into the parlor, Rafe winced at her defensive posture, her trembling shoulders.

'Look, darling, I'm sorry. I should have locked the damn door.' Gently he patted her shoulder and sat down beside her. 'Shane doesn't mean to be an idiot. He was born that way. He doesn't mean any harm. Don't be upset.'

She made a strangled sound, and when she lifted her face, it was wet with tears. Her laughter bubbled out like wine. 'Can you imagine what we looked like, the three of us, in that hall?' She pressed her hand over her mouth and rocked. 'The two of us half-naked, Shane looking like the abominable snowman.'

'You think that's funny?'

'No, I think it's hysterical.' Weak with laughter, she collapsed against him. 'The MacKade brothers. Oh, God, what have I gotten myself into?'

Delighted with her, he hauled her into his lap. 'Give me back my shirt, darling, and I'll show you.'

Chapter 7

Cozy in the sleeping bag, Regan dozed by the fire. It sizzled, logs crackling, and brushed heat over her face and her outflung arm. She sighed, cruising with the dream, shifting toward her lover.

Her dreams were nearly as erotic as the reality of the past hours, vivid enough to have her stirring, and yearning. When she reached out and found herself alone, she sighed again, in disappointment.

The fire was lively, so she knew Rafe had built it up once more before he left her. The room was quiet enough that she could hear the ticking of the mantel clock marking time. Evidence of the night's activities was all around her, in the hastily strewn clothes littering the floor, the torn bits of lace and the jumbled boots. And the evidence was within her as she stretched, feeling the warm glow of desire.

She wished he was there, so that he could stoke it as he had stoked the fire.

Still, it was a wonderful shock to realize she could lay claim to such a bottomless well of passion.

It had never been so before, she reflected, sitting up to exercise her stiff and sore muscles. Physical relationships had always been far down on her list of priorities. She wondered if, after her recent behavior, Rafe would be surprised to know that before him, she had considered herself hesitant, even a little shy, when it came to intimacy.

With a yawn, she reached for her sweater and pulled it over her head.

Knowing him, she decided, he'd just be smug.

It was a pity she couldn't blame her celibacy of the past few years for her wildfire response to him. It felt as though her libido had been nothing more than dry timber set to the torch the moment he put his hands on her. But using abstinence as the major reason for her response would be far from honest.

Whatever her life had been before, he'd changed it just by stepping into her path. It was certain she would never look at cozy nights by a fire in the same way again. It was doubtful she would look at anything in quite the same way again, she mused, now that she knew what she was capable of with the right...mate.

Just how, she wondered, did a woman go back to a quiet, settled life once she'd had a taste of Rafe MacKade?

That was something she was going to have to deal with, one cautious day at a time.

At the moment, the only thing she wanted was to find him.

In her stocking feet, she began to wander the house. He could be anywhere, and the challenge of hunting him down, finding him busy with some chore—one she was determined to distract him from—amused her.

The chill of the bare floors seeped through and had her rubbing her hands together for a little warmth. But curiosity far overweighed a little discomfort.

She'd been through the first-floor rooms only twice before. First on her initial viewing to take notes and measurements. The second time to recheck them. But there were no workmen now, no sounds of voices or hammering.

She slipped into the room beyond the parlor, dreaming a bit.

This would be the library—glossy shelves filled with books, deep-cushioned chairs inviting a guest to curl up to read. A library table would stand there, she mused, a Sheraton if she could find one, with a decanter of brandy, a vase of seasonal flowers, an old pewter inkwell.

Library steps, of course, she continued visualizing, seeing it all perfectly, almost to the grain of wood. And the wide-backed chairs near the crackling fire would need cozy footstools.

She wanted a reading stand in the far corner, one with a cabriole base. She'd set a big, old Bible with gilt-edged pages open on it.

*Abigail O'Brian, married to Charles Richard Bar-
low, April 10, 1856*
Catherine Anne Barlow, born June 5, 1857
*Charles Richard Barlow, Junior, born November
22, 1859*
Robert Michael Barlow, born February 9, 1861
Abigail Barlow, died September 18, 1864

Regan shivered, swayed. She came back to herself
slowly, her arms wrapped tight to ward off the sudden,
bitter cold, her heart pounding as the vision faded from
in front of her eyes.

How had she known that? she wondered, running a
shaky hand over her face. Where had those names and
dates come from?

She'd read them somewhere, she assured herself, but
shuddered again. All the research she'd done, of course
she'd read them. Very slowly, she backed out of the room
and stood in the hall to catch her breath.

Of course she'd known the Barlows of that time had
had three children. She'd looked it up. The dates must
have been there, as well—she'd retained them for some
reason, that was all.

Not for anything would she have admitted that she had
thought, just for a moment, that she'd actually seen the
thick white page of a Bible opened, and the names and
dates written there in a carefully formal hand.

She walked to the stairs and climbed them.

He'd left the door open this time. When she reached

the landing, she heard the scrape of his trowel against the wall. Letting out a relieved breath, she crossed the hall.

And was warm again, just looking at him.

'Need a hand?'

He glanced back, saw her standing there in her classic sweater and pleated trousers. 'Not in that outfit. I just wanted to get this coat finished, and I thought you needed some sleep.'

She contented herself with leaning against the doorway to watch him. 'Why is it that manual labor is so attractive on some men?'

'Some women like to see guys sweat.'

'Apparently I do.' Thoughtfully she studied his technique, the slide of the trowel, the flick of the wrist. 'You know, you're better at this than the guy who did my place over the shop. Very tidy.'

'I hate drywall work.'

'Then why are you doing it?'

'I like when it's finished. And I'm faster than the team I hired.'

'How did you learn?'

'We were always having to fix something out at the farm.' He twisted his neck, cracking out kinks. 'When I left, I did a lot of handyman stuff.'

'Then started your own company.'

'I don't like working for somebody else.'

'Neither do I.' She hesitated, waiting while he scraped off his tools. 'Where did you go? When you left?'

'South.' He stooped to bang the top back on the bucket of compound. 'Picked up some jobs here and there. Figured out I was better at swinging a hammer than running a plow.' Out of habit, he reached into his shirt pocket, found it empty. Swore. 'Quit smoking,' he muttered.

'Good for you.'

'It's driving me nuts.' To keep himself busy, he walked over to check a seam he'd finished the night before.

'You went to Florida,' she said prompting him.

'Yeah, that's where I ended up. Lots of construction work in Florida. I started buying houses—dumps—fixing them up, turning them over. Did pretty well. So I came back.' He turned to her. 'That's about it.'

'I wasn't prying,' she began.

'I didn't say you were. There just isn't much to it, Regan. I had a rep when I left here. Spent my last night in town in a bar fight. With Joe Dolin.'

'I wondered if there was history there,' she murmured.

'Not much of one.' He slipped off the bandanna he'd twisted at his forehead to keep the hair out of his eyes, stuffed it in his pocket. 'We just hated each other's guts.'

'I'd say your taste in enemies is excellent.'

Restless again, he moved his shoulders. 'If it hadn't been him, it would have been somebody else. I was in the mood that night.' His grin flashed, but there wasn't much humor in it. 'Hell, I was usually in the mood to cause trouble. Nobody ever figured I'd amount to anything, not even me.'

If he was trying to tell her something, she wasn't sure she quite understood it. 'It looks as though they were wrong. Even you.'

'People are going to talk, about us.' He'd thought about

it, as he watched her sleep, finding himself restless and edgy and needing to move. 'You're going to walk into Ed's or Kingston's Market, and conversation's going to take a hitch. And when you walk out again, people are going to start talking about what that nice Bishop woman is doing with that troublemaker Rafe MacKade.'

'I've been here three years, Rafe. I know how it works.'

He needed something to do with his hands, so he picked up sandpaper and attacked the first dry seam. 'I don't imagine you've given them much to gossip about up to now.'

He worked as if the devil were looking over his shoulder, she thought. It seemed he did everything with that controlled urgency just under the surface.

'I was pretty hot news when I opened the shop. What's this flatlander doing taking over old Leroy's place, selling antiques instead of screws and pipe fittings?' She smiled a little. 'That got me a lot of browsers, and a good many browsers became customers.' She angled her head, watching him. 'Something like this should pick business up dramatically for a few weeks.'

'I want you to understand what you're getting into.'

'It's a little late for that.' Because she sensed he needed some prodding, she obliged. 'Maybe you're worried about your reputation.'

'Right.' Dust flew as he sanded. 'I was thinking of running for mayor.'

'No, your bad-boy rep. 'MacKade must be getting soft, hanging around that nice Bishop woman. Next thing you know, he'll be buying flowers instead of a six-pack. Bet she'll whip him into shape.''

Curious, he tossed the sandpaper aside, tucked his thumbs in his front pockets and turned to look at her. 'Is that what you're going to try to do, Regan? Whip me into shape?'

'Is that what you're worried about, MacKade? That I could?'

It wasn't a comfortable thought. 'Legions have tried.' He walked over, skimmed a dusty finger down her cheek. 'It'd be easier for me to corrupt you, darling. I could have you playing nine-ball at Duff's Tavern in no time.'

'I could have you quoting Shelley.'

'Shelley who?'

With a chuckle, she rose on her toes to give him a friendly kiss. 'Percy Bysshe Shelley. Better watch yourself.'

The idea of that was so ridiculous, his tensed shoulders relaxed. 'Darling, the day I start spouting poetry's the day Shane's prize hog sprouts wings and flies down Main Street.'

She smiled again, kissed him again. 'You don't want to make it a bet. Come on, I'd like to take a look at the work in progress.'

He snatched her hand. 'What kind of bet?'

She laughed, tugged him into the hall. 'Rafe, I'm joking. Give me a tour.'

'Just hold on. MacKades never back down from a dare.'

'I'm daring you to quote Shelley?' She sighed, shook her head. 'Okay, I dare you.'

'No, that's not how it works.' Considering, he lifted her hand, nibbled on her fingers. The flicker of arousal in her eyes inspired him. 'I say I can have you so crazy about me within a month that you'll wiggle into a leather miniskirt. A red one. Walk into the tavern for beer and nine-ball.'

Arousal turned quickly into amusement. 'What odd fantasies you have, MacKade. Can you actually see me in some tarty little skirt, playing pool?'

The smile turned wicked. 'Oh, yeah. I can see that just fine. Make sure you wear those really high heels, too. The skinny ones.'

'I never wear leather without stilettos. Anything less would be tacky.'

'And no bra.'

Her laughed puffed out. 'Really into this, aren't you?'

'I'm getting there. You'll do it, too.' He cupped a hand on her hip to nudge her closer. 'Because you'll be crazy about me.'

'It's obvious one of us has already lost his mind. Okay.' Not one to refuse a challenge, she put a hand on his chest, pushed him back. 'I say within that same period of time, I'll have you on your knees, clutching a bouquet of… ah…lilacs—'

'Lilacs?'

'Yes, I'm very fond of lilacs. You'll quote Shelley like a champ.'

'What's the winner get?'

'Satisfaction.'

He had to smile. 'That ought to be enough. Deal.'

They shook hands on it. 'Am I going to get that tour now?'

'Sure.' He draped an arm around her shoulders and

entertained himself with the vision of those very fine legs beneath a tight red skirt. 'We went with your idea of a kind of bridal suite.' He led the way down the hall, opened a six-paneled door. 'Just about ready for trim work in here.'

'Rafe.' Delighted, she stepped inside.

The delicate floral wallpaper was nearly all hung. The coffered ceiling gleamed with fresh paint. French doors were in place, and would one day open onto the wide porch, overlook gardens in riotous bloom. The floor was covered with drop cloths, but she could imagine it glossy and accented with a lovely faded tapestry rug.

She stepped around buckets and ladders, already arranging furniture in her head. 'It's going to be beautiful,' she murmured.

'It's coming along.' He lifted a tarp from the fireplace. 'The mantel was shot. I couldn't fix it. Found a good piece of yellow pine, though. The woodworker's using the original as a guide.'

'That rose-colored trim is going to be wonderful in here.' She looked through an adjoining doorway. 'And this is the bath.'

'Mmm…' He studied the room over her shoulder. It was good-sized, and the plumbers had roughed it in. 'Used to be a dressing room.'

She reached for his hand, gripped it. 'Can you smell it?'

'Roses.' Absently he rubbed his cheek over her hair. 'It always smells like roses in here. One of the paper hangers accused his partner of wearing perfume.'

'This was her room, wasn't it? Abigail's. She died in here.'

'Probably. Hey.' He tipped up her face, watched uncomfortably as a tear trailed down her cheek. 'Don't.'

'It's so sad. She must have been terribly unhappy. Knowing the man she'd married, the father of her children, was capable of such cold-blooded cruelty. How did he treat her, Rafe? Did he love her, or did he only own her?'

'There's no way to know. Don't cry.' Awkward, he brushed the tear away. 'It makes me feel like I have six thumbs. I mean it.' For lack of something better to do, he patted her head. 'There's no use crying over something that happened more than a hundred years ago.'

'But she's still here.' Wrapping her arms around him, Regan snuggled into his chest. 'I feel so sorry for her, for all of them.'

'You're not going to do yourself, or me, any good if you get tangled up every time you come in here.'

'I know.' She sighed, comforted by the way his heart beat strong and steady against her. 'It's odd how you get used to it, a little bit at a time. Rafe, when I was downstairs alone...'

'What?' Uneasy, he tilted her face toward his again.

'It's nothing.'

'What?' he repeated, giving her chin a little shake.

'Well, I walked into the library. What was the library,' she went on, torn between the need to tell him and embarrassment. 'What will be the library. And I— Rafe, I could see it.'

His eyes were sharp, narrowed, totally concentrated. 'See what?'

'The room. Not the stained floors and the new wiring you've put in. The room. Books on the wall, flowers on the table, drapes at the windows. I could really see it,' she repeated, her own brow creasing. 'Not the way I do in my head when I'm planning things out. Not exactly like that. I was thinking to myself, sort of projecting, I suppose. I imagined this, well, I thought I was imagining a Bible stand, with an old family Bible opened on it. And I could read the page, almost touch it. Marriage and births and death.'

She took time to catch her breath. 'You're not saying anything.'

'Because I'm listening to you.'

'I know it sounds crazy.'

'Not in this house, it doesn't.'

'It was so real, so sad. The way the scent of roses in this room is real, and sad. Then it was so cold, bitter, like a window had been flung open to the weather.'

She moved her shoulders, laid her head on his chest again. 'That's all.'

'That's a lot for one day.' Wanting to soothe, he stroked his hand over her hair. 'I can give Devin a call, have him come get you.'

'No, I don't want to leave. It shook me for a moment, but it's just as I said before. You get to accept it. I can handle it.'

'I shouldn't have left you alone.'

'Don't be silly. I don't need to be guarded against grieving ghosts.'

But he wanted to guard her. He wished she had called for him. It surprised him just how much he wished she had needed him enough to call out for him.

'Next time you want to go in the library, let me know. I'll go with you.'

'The house is already changing,' she said quietly. 'You've done that by caring for it. I like feeling I've had a part in that, too.'

'You have.' He pressed his lips to her hair.

'When people live in it, make love in it, laugh in it, it'll change again. The house needs people.'

She shifted, lifted her mouth to his. 'Make love with me.'

He cupped her face in his hands, deepened the kiss. When he picked her up, carried her from the room, the scent of roses followed. She looped her arms around him, pressed her lips to his throat. Already her blood was heating, already her pulse was pounding.

'It's like a drug,' she murmured.

'I know.' He stopped at the top of the stairs, found her mouth again.

'I've never been like this before.' Swamped with emotions, she turned her face into his shoulder.

Neither had he, he thought.

As he carried her down, neither noticed that the air had remained warm and calm.

He laid her in front of the fire. Levering himself up on his elbow, he traced the shape of her face with a fingertip. Something kindled inside her, simmered with desire and flamed around her heart.

'Rafe.'

'Shh…'

To quiet her, he brushed his lips over her brow. She didn't know what she would have said, was grateful he'd stopped her. The wanting was more than enough. She could be relieved that neither of them needed words.

She should have been relieved.

Her mouth was ready for his, and it warmed beautifully under the pressure of lips and tongue. Though desire remained, poised and trembling, everything in her seemed to soften.

Here was tenderness, so sweet, so unexpected. Her sigh whispered out like a secret.

He felt the change, in her, in himself. Marveled at it. Why had they always been in such a hurry? he wondered. Why had he hesitated to savor, and be savored, when there was so much here?

He loved the flavor of her, that quietly seductive taste that clung to her skin. The feel of her, soft curves, long lines. The smell of her hair, her clothes, her shoulders.

So he savored it now, all of it, with long, slow kisses that clouded his mind and made him forget there was anything beyond this room for either of them.

His hands were careful this time as he drew her sweater off, slipped the trousers down her hips. Rather than touch, rather than take, he kissed her again, drawing out the simple meeting of lips until her body went limp.

'Let me.' With a dreamy murmur, she shifted until they

were both kneeling. Already clouded, her eyes stayed on his while she unbuttoned his shirt. Trapped in the silky mood, she slipped it away and, with her hands resting lightly on his shoulders, swayed to him.

They held each other, moving only for quiet, sipping tastes, soft, gentle caresses. She smiled when his lips brushed her shoulder, sighed when hers tasted his throat.

When they were naked, he drew her down so that she lay over him, so that her hair fell to curtain them both.

She could have floated on this whisper-thin cloud of sensations endlessly, with the winter sun slanting cold light through the windows, the fire crackling, his body strong and hard beneath hers.

The feel of his hands on her, stroking, soothing even as they aroused, was like a gift. She felt the wonder of it in every pore, in every nerve, with every pulse.

There was no clash and fury now, no desperation, no vicious drive to mate. Now she was aware of everything—the dust motes spinning in the sunbeam that rayed over the floor, the sedate hiss of flame on wood, the scent of roses and man.

She could count his heartbeats, quicker, stronger, as her lips trailed over his chest. The bunching and quivering of a muscle beneath her hand, the sound of her own thickening breath.

With a sigh that caught in her throat, she wrapped around him as he rolled her to her back.

Time spun out, stretched, quivered. The clock on the mantel ticked the seconds away, and the minutes. But that was another world. Here there were only needs lazily satisfied, and hearts quietly lost.

For pleasure—his as well as hers—he eased her gently to the edge and over. His name was only a murmur on her lips as she arched, tensed, softened to silk. She opened for him, drawing him close with a velvety moan as he slipped into her.

Overwhelmed by her, by the simplicity of it, he burrowed his face in her hair. The tenderness shattered them both.

They didn't speak of it. When they parted in the morning, both of them were determinedly casual. But they thought of it. And they worried.

Rafe watched her drive off as the sun struggled over the mountains to the east. When she was gone, when there was no one to see, he rubbed the heel of his hand over his heart.

There was an ache there that he couldn't quite will away. He had a very bad feeling that she was the cause of it, and that somehow, in a matter of hours, he'd gotten in over his head.

God, he missed her already.

He swore at himself for that, then swore again for reaching like a trained dog for the cigarettes that weren't there. Both were just habits, he assured himself. If he wanted, he could just go buy a pack of cigarettes and smoke his brains out. Just as he could snatch her back anytime.

Sex was a powerful bond. It wasn't surprising it had caught him, as well.

It didn't have to be any more than that. They'd tidied that up, hadn't they? A man was entitled to be a little shaky after thirty-odd hours of sex and solitude with a gorgeous woman.

He didn't want anything more. Neither did she.

It was a relief and a pleasure to find a lover who wanted no more and no less than he did himself. A woman who didn't expect him to play games, make promises neither expected to be kept, say words that were only words, after all.

Scowling, he grabbed a shovel and began to deal with the snow that piled the walk. The sun was strengthening, and he worked fast, so that even with the bite of the northern wind he sweated satisfactorily under his coat.

She'd probably head straight for the shower, he mused, tossing heavy snow off the path. Wash that pretty doe-colored hair of hers.

He wondered what it looked like wet.

She'd dig some of those neat, classy clothes out of her closet. Nope, he thought, correcting himself. Regan would never dig. She'd select. Quiet colors, simple lines. One of those professional-woman's jackets, with a pin on the lapel.

She'd fix her face, nothing too obvious. Just hints of blush along the cheekbones, a touch of color above those ridiculously long lashes. Then lipstick—not red, not pink, a kind of rose that accented those full lips and that sassy little mole beside them.

Halfway down the walk, he stopped, leaned against the shovel and wondered if he was losing his mind. He was actually thinking about her makeup.

What the hell did he care what paint she slapped on before she went down to open the shop?

She'd put on the kettle for tea, or have cider simmering so that the place smelled of apples and spices. Then she'd go through the day without giving him a thought.

Snow flew as he attacked it. Well, he had plenty to do himself, and no time to brood about her.

He'd reached the end of the walk, and the end of his patience, when Devin rattled up the lane in the sheriff's cruiser.

'What the hell do you want?' Rafe shouted. 'Haven't you got somebody to arrest?'

'Funny how a little blizzard quiets things down.' Leaning on the open car door, Devin watched his brother with amusement. 'Saw Regan's car was gone, figured it was safe to drop by.'

'I've got men due any minute. I don't have time to chat.'

'In that case, I'll take my doughnuts and go.'

Rafe swiped a hand over his chilled face. 'What kind?'

'Apple and brown sugar.'

Some things were sacred, and an apple doughnut on a cold morning topped the list.

'Well, are you going to stand there all morning with that idiot grin on your face? Give me a damn doughnut.'

Obligingly, Devin took the bag out of the car and sauntered over. 'Had three fender benders in town yesterday from people not smart enough to stay put.'

'Antietam's a wild town, all right. Have to shoot any-body?'

'Not lately.' Devin took out a doughnut for himself before passing the bag to Rafe. 'Broke up a fistfight, though.'

'Down at the tavern?'

'Nope, at the market. Millie Yeader and Mrs. Metz were going at it over the last pack of toilet paper.'

Rafe's lips twitched. 'People get a little nervous over necessities when a big snow hits.'

'Tell me about it. Miz Metz conked Millie with a bunch of bananas. Took a lot of diplomacy to keep Millie from filing charges.'

'Assault with tropical fruit. Could've done hard time for that.' Calm again, Rafe licked apple from his thumb. 'Did you come by to give me the latest trials and tribula-tions of Antietam?'

'That's just a bonus.' Devin polished off his doughnut, reached for a cigarette. His grin was wide and unsympa-thetic when Rafe groaned. He lit it, inhaled lavishly. 'I hear food tastes better when you quit.'

'Nothing's better,' Rafe shot back. 'But some of us have real willpower. Blow it over here, you bastard.'

'Secondhand smoke's the real killer,' Devin told him, and blew a stream in Rafe's direction. 'You look a little out of sorts, Rafe. Trouble in paradise?'

Rafe gave some thought to beating his brother to death with the snow shovel and stealing all his cigarettes. Re-minding himself it was all a matter of self-control, he leaned on the shovel, instead.

'How long did it take Shane to open his big mouth?'

'Let's see.' Considering, Devin smoked and studied the landscape. 'The way the roads were yesterday, I'd say it took him, oh, about seven minutes to get from here to my office.' He flicked ash aside. 'Let's say seven minutes and ten seconds.'

'Now you're here to offer your sage advice?'

'Hey, it was pretty sage to talk those two snarling women into splitting the six-pack of pink toilet paper. But no.' With a self-deprecating smile, he took a last drag, then flicked the cigarette away.

Rafe watched it wistfully as it hissed in the snow.

'I'm not exactly the expert on romance in the MacKade family.' Devin's grin was crooked, and didn't last long. 'I thought you might like the latest on Joe Dolin.'

'He's locked up.'

'For now. I got word he's copping to second-degree assault. If he listens to his lawyer, he'll agree to alcohol counseling. He'll get a fine, suspended sentence with probation, and a stern warning not to hit his wife again.'

'What the hell kind of deal is that?'

'Prisons are crowded. Domestic disputes don't usually equal tough sentencing. He says 'Yeah, I did it, I'm sorry. I lost my temper, I was drunk, I lost my job. My self-esteem is really low.' The judge says 'Get yourself into counseling, my boy, and sin no more.''

Rafe studied his brother's face. Beneath the calm, he caught the twitches of fury and frustration. 'You're just going to let it go at that?'

'I don't sentence.' Devin struggled to bite back on his

sense of anger and impotence. 'There's nothing I can do except talk Cassie into letting me issue a restraining order, and make sure he doesn't get near her or the kids.'

'Meanwhile, they're bunked down at Regan's. That puts her in the middle.'

'I don't like it any better than you do. I've got the law to work around.'

'I don't.'

Devin's gaze was cool and level. 'No, you don't. But you start something with Dolin, and it's going to come down in his favor. He'll make a mistake, Rafe. All it takes is one, and I'll have him caged again. Until I do... I don't know where things stand between you and Regan, but if you were staying there, it'd hold a lot more weight with me than some useless restraining order.'

'You want me to ask Regan to let me move in with her?'

'And Cassie, and the kids.'

The idea was surprisingly appealing. Waking up beside her, sharing that first cup of coffee. 'You going to deputize me, Dev?'

'Not on your life.'

'Too bad. Well, I'll run it by Regan and let you know.'

Chapter 8

'Absolutely not.' Regan planted her feet, folded her arms over her chest. 'You are not sleeping in my bed with two little children in the next room.'

'This isn't about sex,' Rafe said patiently. 'That's just a bonus. I'm telling you, this is an official request from the sheriff.'

'Who just happens to be your brother. No.' She turned away to set glassware back on the shelf she'd been dusting. 'It would make Cassie uncomfortable and set a poor example for the children.'

And if they weren't there? He found the question leaping to the tip of his tongue like a frog. He was barely in time to prevent himself from letting it jump out.

'It's Cassie and the kids who are the issue,' he insisted.

'You think Dolin's just going to leave them alone because Cassie signs some paper telling him to?'

'I have no idea what he'll do, but he'll have to get past me first.'

The thought of it, just the thought of it, had his blood icing over. 'Now you listen...'

She jerked his hand from her shoulder and whirled back. 'No, *you* listen. The man is a bully and a drunk. I'm not afraid of drunken bullies. I offered Cassie my home, and she's welcome to stay there as long as she wants. I have a good solid lock on the door, which I'll use. I know the number for the sheriff's office, which I'll use, as well, if it's necessary.'

'There's no lock on that door.' Rafe jerked a thumb toward the front of the shop. 'What's to stop him from walking in here during business hours and harassing you? Or worse.'

'I am.'

'Right.' He wondered if shaking her would rattle her brains back into place. 'Putting Dolin on the receiving end of that stubborn chin of yours isn't going to stop him. In case you haven't figured it out, he likes hurting women.'

'I'll take a moment to remind you that for the past three years I've been here and you haven't. I've seen exactly what he's done to Cassie.'

'And you figure because you're not married to him, you're safe?' He did shake her. 'You can't be that stupid.'

'I'm not stupid,' she shot back. 'I'm competent. I don't need or want you for a bodyguard.'

His eyes changed, going from full heat to slow burn. On her shoulders, his hands tensed, then lifted away.

'I guess that's the bottom line, isn't it? You don't need or want my help.'

Ego, she thought with a muffled sigh. There was no monster so fierce or so vulnerable as a man's ego. 'The sheriff's office is five minutes away, if I need to call out troops.' Hoping to calm them both, Regan put her hands on his shoulders. 'Rafe, I appreciate your concern, really I do. But I can take care of myself, and Cassie, too, if it comes to that.'

'I bet you can.'

'I worked a shop in D.C. for years. One memorable evening, I was robbed at gunpoint. I know how to be sensible, how not to take chances and how to defend myself. I appreciate the fact that you're worried, but I'm not Cassie. He can't frighten or intimidate me.'

'Regan—'

'Wait, let me finish. Cassie is so fragile right now, and the children are too quiet. I'm not sure how they would handle having a man around. The kids don't know you.'

He jammed his hands in his pockets. 'I'm not going to kick them around.'

'They don't know that. Little Emma sits at Cassie's feet with her doll and barely says a word. And the boy— God, Rafe, he breaks my heart. They need time to feel safe again. You're too big, you're too strong, you're too…male.'

Stubbornly he ignored the fact that she'd hurt him— that he could be hurt—and concentrated on the situation at hand. 'You're being pigheaded.'

'I'm doing what seems right to me. That's the only way I know how to handle things. Believe me, I've thought this through, weighed the options. Having you move in just isn't one of them.'

'Invite me to dinner,' he said abruptly.

'You want to come to dinner?'

'Ask me to dinner, so I can get to know the kids, so they'll get used to me being around.'

'Now who's pigheaded?' But she sighed. It was a reasonable compromise. 'All right, seven-thirty, and you're out by ten.'

'Can we neck on the couch after the kids go to bed?'

'Maybe. Now go away.'

'Aren't you going to kiss me goodbye?'

She huffed out a breath, then kissed him primly on the cheek. 'Business hours,' she said, then laughed when he grabbed her. 'Rafe, we're right in front of the window. I—'

The rest was lost as he crushed his mouth to hers. 'Might as well give them something to talk about.' And give her something to think about, he told himself. She was damn well going to do a lot of thinking about Rafe MacKade.

He nipped her lip, let her go, then sauntered out the door.

A block away, Cassie sat in Devin's office, twisting her hands together. She knew it should be easier because it was Devin, someone she'd known all her life. But it only made the shame worse.

'I'm sorry, we got busy, and I couldn't take my break until now.'

'That's all right, Cassie.' It had become habit to keep his voice quiet when he spoke to her, as a man might speak to a wounded bird. 'I've got the paperwork filled out for you. You just have to sign it.'

'He's not going to go to jail.'

A fist squeezed his heart at the emptiness in her tone. 'No.'

'Is it because I let him hit me?'

'No.' He wished he could reach out to soothe those nervous hands. But the desk was between them, an official barrier. 'He admitted that he hurt you, but the court took other things into consideration. His drinking problem, his loss of a longtime job. He'll have to go into counseling, report to his probation officer. Stay out of trouble.'

'It could be good for him.' She looked up, then, just as quickly, down again. 'The counseling. If he stops drinking, maybe everything would be all right.'

'Yeah.' And he could run a Popsicle stand in hell, Devin thought. 'In the meantime, you need to protect yourself. That's what the restraining order's for.'

She lifted her gaze again, and this time her eyes held his. 'That paper is going to keep him from coming back?'

Devin grabbed a cigarette out of his pack, then tossed it down. When he spoke, his voice was cool and official. 'This bars him from coming near you. He can't come into the diner when you're working there. He can't approach you on the street, or come to Regan's house as long as you're staying there. If he breaks any one of the regulations set down here, he'll void his parole and serve the eighteen months.'

'He knows about this?'

'He's been notified.'

She moistened her lips. He couldn't come near her. The idea whirled around in her head. If he couldn't come near her, he couldn't hit her.

'I only have to sign it.'

'Yes, you only have to sign it.' Devin rose then, came around the desk to offer her a pen. When she made no move to take it, he bit back an oath. 'Cassie, what do you want? Can you just tell me what you want?'

She shook her head, took the pen. She signed her name quickly, as though it hurt. 'I know I've put you through a lot of trouble, Devin.'

'It's my job,' he said shortly.

'You're a good sheriff.' When he glanced back, obviously surprised, she tried to smile. 'You are quiet and competent and good with people. Everyone knows they can count on you. My mother always said you and your brothers would end up behind bars.' She flushed and stared down at the floor. 'I'm sorry. That was stupid.'

'No, it wasn't. I used to think the same myself.' He smiled then, because just for a moment she'd sounded like the girl he remembered. 'You know, Cass, that's about the longest little speech I've heard out of you in close to ten years.'

'I'm always putting my foot in my mouth.'

'Don't do that.' He'd taken her chin to lift her head before he realized he meant to—before she flinched like a startled doe. Moving with care, he dropped his hand, eased a hip on the corner of the desk. 'How are the kids?'

'They're all right. Better.'

'Getting along all right at Regan's?'

'She's wonderful. I forget I'm imposing, because she makes everything so normal. She and Rafe—' She broke off, her color rising again. 'You've got better things to do than listen to me gossip.'

'No, I don't.' He'd have done anything to keep her talking. To keep her there. 'What do you think about them? Regan and Rafe?'

'I— She looked happy when she came home this morning.'

'He looked miserable when I dropped by the house this morning.'

Her smile was slow and shy. 'That's a good sign. Rafe always needed a woman who could make him unhappy. It was always too easy for him. For all of you.'

'Was it?' Thoughtful, he picked up his cigarette again, ran it through his fingers. 'I remember you turned me down.'

'Oh.' Fumbling, she rose. 'That was a hundred years ago.'

'Not quite twelve. You were sweet sixteen.'

'I was going with Joe.' As she tugged on her coat, she wondered if she'd really ever been sixteen. 'I can't even remember who we were then, or what we were looking for. Thanks, Devin, for taking care of this.'

'That's what I'm here for, to take care of things.'

At the door, she paused, but didn't look back. It was

easier to speak if she didn't have to look into those cool, pitying eyes. 'You asked me what I wanted, Devin. I just want to feel safe.' She said it so quietly, he barely heard. 'That's really all.'

In a coat that was too thin to fight off the biting wind, she walked back to the café.

Rafe arrived ten minutes early for dinner and squirmed on Regan's doorstep like a nervous suitor. He had a bottle of wine in one hand and a bakery box of cookies designed to win the kids over in the other.

He wished he'd remembered before his brainstorm that he knew nothing about people under the age of sixteen.

As a test, he turned the knob. It was somewhat satisfying to find it locked tight. He knocked sharply, stepped back. It was Regan who opened it, as far as the thick security chain allowed.

'Okay, so far you're passing. But you should have asked who it was first.'

'I looked out the window.' She shut the door in his face, then, after a rattle of chain, opened it. 'I had the feeling there'd be a quiz.' Smiling, she studied the offerings. 'No lilacs?'

'No chance.' He would have kissed her if he hadn't noticed the solemn gray eyes watching him from the cushions of the sofa. 'Looks like you've got a mouse in the house.'

Regan jerked, then smiled when she saw Emma. 'She's quiet as one, but prettier. Emma, this is Mr. MacKade.

You met him at Ed's, remember?' Regan held out a hand. Eyeing him warily, Emma slipped from the couch.

She was five, Rafe knew, and tiny as a fairy princess, with her mother's pale hair and smoky eyes.

'I knew your mama when she was your age,' he told her.

Emma darted behind Regan's legs and peered up at him.

Knowing it was a shameless bribe, he shook the bakery box. 'Want a cookie, honey?'

That earned him the faintest of smiles, but Regan took the box out of his hands. 'Not before dinner.'

'Spoilsport. But dinner smells good.'

'Cassie's chicken and dumplings. I had to practically tie her down to keep her from taking the kids and eating at the diner. We compromised and had her cook dinner. Come on, Emma, we'll take the cookies in the kitchen.'

With one hand clutching Regan's slacks, Emma darted looks over her shoulder.

She thought he was big, but his eyes weren't mean. She'd already learned how to read eyes. And he looked a lot like the sheriff, who sometimes picked her up and gave her lemon drops.

But Emma watched her mother carefully to gauge her reaction to the man.

Cassie looked up from the stove and smiled. 'Hi, Rafe.'

He moved to her, lightly kissed her bruised cheek. 'How's it going?'

'Fine, everything's fine.' She laid a hand on the shoulder of the boy beside her. 'Connor, you remember Mr. MacKade.'

'Nice to see you again, Connor.' Rafe offered a hand. The little boy with the pale hair and the dusky blue eyes shook hands hesitantly. 'You'd be, what, in third, fourth grade?'

'Third, yes, sir.'

Rafe lifted a brow and passed the bottle of wine to Regan. That would make him about eight, Rafe figured, and the kid spoke as quietly as an old priest. 'Miz Witt still teaching there?'

'Yes, sir.'

'We used to call her Miz Dimwit.' When the boy's eyes widened, Rafe plucked a carrot from beside the salad bowl. 'Bet you still do.'

'Yes, sir,' Connor mumbled, slanting a look at his mother. 'Sometimes.' Screwing up the courage he'd worked on building ever since he'd been told Rafe Mac-Kade was coming, Connor drew in his breath. 'You bought the Barlow Place.'

'That's right.'

'It's haunted.'

Rafe bit off some carrot and grinned. 'You bet.'

'I know all about the battle and everything,' Connor said in one quick burst. 'It was the bloodiest day of the Civil War, and nobody really won, because—' He broke off, embarrassed. This, he thought miserably, was why some of the kids called him nerdhead in school.

'Because nobody went for the final push,' Rafe finished for him. 'Maybe you'd like to come by the house sometime, take a look. I could use somebody who knows all about the battle.'

'I've got a book. With pictures.'

'Yeah?' Rafe took the wine Regan offered him. 'Let's see.'

It was simple enough to draw the boy out, as long as they were discussing McClellan's flawed strategy or the Battle of Burnside Bridge. Rafe saw a bright, needy boy, too bookish to fit neatly with his contemporaries, too shy to showcase his own brain.

The girl, a miniature of her mother, never strayed far from Cassie or Regan, ate her dinner in small, neat bites. And watched him like a baby hawk.

'Ed would be better off having you in the kitchen than waiting tables,' Rafe commented after he'd polished off a second helping. 'Her business would double in a month.'

Off guard, Cassie blinked at him. No one had complimented her cooking in too many years to count. 'I'm glad you liked it. I could put some of the leftovers in a dish for you. You'd just have to heat them up.'

'I'll take them.'

When Cassie rose and began to clear, Regan held up a hand. 'No, you don't. You cooked, I clear.'

'But—'

'That was the deal. And since Rafe ate enough for two growing boys, he can help.'

The Dolins looked on, awed, as Rafe cheerfully stacked plates. The men they knew would have belched, loosened their belts and plopped down in front of the TV with a six-pack.

'Daddy says girls and sissies do dishes,' Emma announced, in a surprisingly clear voice.

'Emma!' Paling, Cassie stared at Rafe and waited for the retribution.

He considered making a comment about her father's brains but decided against it. 'My mama always said a meal has to be earned.' He said it lightly and winked at her. 'And if I do the dishes with Regan, I'll probably be able to kiss her.'

'Why?'

'Because she tastes almost as good as your mama's chicken and dumplings.'

Satisfied with that, Emma nibbled solemnly on her cookie.

'I'll just give Emma her bath, then.' Flustered, Cassie shooed her children along. 'I have to turn in early. I have the breakfast shift in the morning.'

'Thanks for dinner, Cassie.'

'You handled that very well,' Regan murmured. 'That's probably the first time in years they've sat at the dinner table with a man and had a civilized conversation.'

'Dolin's not only a swine, he's a fool.' Rafe set stacked plates on the kitchen counter. 'Sweet woman like that, beautiful kids. Any man would be lucky to have them.'

A home of your own, Rafe mused. A woman who loved you. Kids racing out to meet you at the end of the day. Family meals around a table. Noise in the kitchen.

Funny, he'd never thought that was something he'd wanted, or needed.

'You made an impression,' Regan went on as she filled

the sink with hot, soapy water. 'A good one. I can't think of anything better for all of them than seeing a strong, intelligent man behaving in a strong, intelligent way.'

She glanced back, and her smile faltered at the look in his eye. She was used to the way he stared at her, or she nearly was. But this was different, deeper.

'What is it?'

'Hmm?' He caught himself, realized he felt like a man who had nearly skidded hard and landed on very thin ice. 'Nothing. It's nothing.' Good God, he'd actually been thinking about marriage and kids and picket fences. 'The boy, Connor. He's awfully bright, isn't he?'

'Straight *A*s,' Regan said, as proudly as if he were her own. 'He's bright, sensitive and sweet—which made him a perfect target for Joe. The man bullied the poor kid mercilessly.'

'He hit him?' The question was mild, but the fire was already burning.

'No, I don't think so. Cassie's fiercely protective of her children. But emotional abuse doesn't leave bruises.' She shrugged. 'Well, they're out of it now.' She handed him a plate to dry. 'Did your father do dishes?'

'Only on Thanksgiving.' Rafe polished off the plate, set it aside. 'Buck MacKade was a man's man.'

'Buck?' Impressed, Regan pursed her lips. 'Sounds formidable.'

'He was tough. Had eyes that could drill holes in you if you messed up. Devin got his eyes. I got his hands.' Bemused, Rafe stared down at his palms, flexed his fingers.

'It was a hell of a surprise to me when I looked down one day and saw my father's hands on the end of my arms.'

She couldn't have said why it touched her so to see him smiling down at his hands, a dishcloth tossed over his shoulder. 'You were close to him?'

'Not close enough. Not for long enough.'

'When did you lose him?'

'I was fifteen. Tractor rolled on him. It took him a week to die.'

She plunged her hands into the water again, struggled with tears. 'Is that why you hate the farm?'

'Yeah, I guess it is.' Odd, he'd never realized it was that simple, that direct. The farm had taken his father, so he had to hate the farm. 'He loved it, every rocky acre. The way Shane does.'

'What did Jared get from him?'

'The mouth—Jared can horse-trade just like the old man, and make you think you got the best end of the deal.'

'Then I'm relieved he's my lawyer.' She offered another plate. 'My father never did a dish in his life. I'm sure my mother would be horrified if he tried. The kitchen is a woman's domain,' she said dryly. 'They agree on that completely. She brings him his first cup of coffee every morning before he goes to the hospital. He's a surgeon.'

'Hard feelings?'

'I used to have them,' she admitted. 'She made herself into exactly the woman he wanted her to be. If she was ever anything else, wanted to be anything else, anything more, it doesn't show. She's Dr. Bishop's wife, and that's all.'

He began to see just why she was so set on marking her own boundaries, taking her own stands. 'Maybe that's all she wants to be.'

'Apparently. It just infuriated me to see the way she catered to him, the way he patted her on the head. He actually gives her an allowance and calls her 'the little woman.''

It still made her grit her teeth. 'She loved living in D.C., but a few years ago when he decided that he wanted to relocate to Arizona, she packed up without a murmur.' Regan sighed. 'But they're blissfully happy. I baffle them as much as they baffle me.'

'Because you don't have a rich husband, a big house and a membership at the country club.'

'Exactly.' Surprised and amused, she glanced at him. 'Have you met them?'

'I think I just did.' And, in doing so, caught a fresh new glimpse of her. 'So, darling, why don't you have a rich husband, a big house and a membership at the country club?'

'Because I like independence, my own space and my golf game is dreadful.' She shook back her hair. 'Actually, my mother had high hopes for me when she met Jared.'

The bowl he was drying clattered when he set it down. 'Run through that again.'

'They came to visit right after the settlement. He took us out to dinner.'

'Jared,' Rafe said carefully, 'took you out to dinner.'

'Mmm-hmm… A couple of times. My mother really

liked the idea that I was seeing a lawyer. Next-best thing to a doctor, in her mind.'

'Seeing. As in dating. You dated Jared?'

'We went out a few times. It was right after his divorce.' She held out another bowl, lifting a brow when he made no move to take it. 'Is there a problem?'

'You dated my brother?'

'I believe we just established that.' She decided it was a better idea to bite the inside of her lip than to let it curve. 'Didn't he mention it?'

'No. I think I'd like your definition of *date*.'

'You mean, did I sleep with him?' Struggling to keep her face composed, she tilted her head. 'Are you going to go beat him up, big guy? Can I come watch?'

Obviously she didn't know how close she was to having her pretty face dumped in dishwater. 'It's a simple question.'

'You've got a muscle twitching in your jaw, Rafe. It looks good on you. No,' she said, and then she did laugh. 'Of course I didn't sleep with him.' Enjoying herself, she shoved the bowl into his hands. 'I did kiss him good-night. A couple of times. I'm now in the position to state, un-equivocally, that at least fifty percent of the MacKade brothers are champion kissers.'

'Think twice before you try for a hundred percent—or even seventy-five.' He set the bowl aside, picked up his wine. 'Why didn't you sleep with him?'

'Really, Rafe.' She rolled her eyes. 'In the first place, he didn't ask me. And in the second, I didn't ask him. We were more comfortable being friends. Satisfied?'

'Maybe I'll beat him up anyway. On principle.'

After setting his wine aside, he took her by the shoulders, turned her to face him. Even as she grinned at him, he pressed her back into the sink.

Hard, possessive, his mouth covered hers. The little purr that sounded in her throat enticed him to draw the kiss out, soften it, until all points of pleasure narrowed and centered just there.

When her head fell back in surrender, her hands slid limply down his arms, he eased back.

'That's so you remember which MacKade you're with now.'

She had to remind herself to breathe. 'What was your name again?'

He grinned, then closed his teeth over her sensitized bottom lip. 'Tell you what. Why don't we skip necking on the couch and go try out the back seat of my car?'

'That's quite an offer.' It was fascinating to feel her own head spin. 'I think I'll take you up on it.'

Rafe let himself into the Barlow house at midnight. He'd recognized the car at the top of the lane, and he wasn't surprised to find Jared in the parlor, brooding over a beer.

'Foreclosing already, Lawyer MacKade?'

Instead of rising to the bait, Jared stared down at his beer. 'I put my house on the market today. Didn't feel like staying there.'

Rafe grunted, sat down on his sleeping bag to pull off his boots. He knew the dark moods, often had them himself. Either he'd manage to shake Jared out of it, or they'd both ride through it.

'Never liked that house, no personality. Just like your ex-wife.'

It was so cold, and so true, Jared had to laugh. 'Decent investment, though. I'll make a profit.'

Rafe shook his head at the beer Jared held out. 'They don't taste the same without a smoke. Besides, I gotta be up in six and a half hours. I was going to come look for you,' he added.

'Oh? Why?'

'To beat the hell out of you.' With a yawn, Rafe lay back. 'It'll have to wait till tomorrow. I'm too relaxed.'

'Okay. Any particular reason?'

'You kissed my woman.' Rafe figured he had just about enough energy to strip off his pants.

'I did?' Jared tossed his legs up over the settee. A slow smile curved his lips. 'Oh, yeah. Oh, *yeah*...' he said again, with more feeling. 'It's all coming back to me. When'd she get to be your woman?'

Rafe heaved his jeans aside, started on his shirt. 'That's what comes from living in the city. You're out of the loop, bro. She's mine now.'

'Does she know that?'

'*I* know.' With his eyes closed, he dragged the sleeping bag over him. 'I'm thinking about keeping her.'

Jared choked on his beer. 'You mean like a wife?'

'I mean like keeping her,' Rafe repeated. No way was he going to try to get his tongue around a word like *wife*. 'Keeping things the way they are now.'

This was interesting, Jared mused. And even more fun than brooding. 'And how are things now?'

'Things are good.' Rafe could smell her on the quilted material of the sleeping bag. 'I'm still going to have to break your face. It's the principle.'

'Understood.' Jared stretched out, settled back. 'Then again, I never did pay you back for talking Sharilyn Bester, now Fenniman, into riding out to the quarry with you to skinny-dip.'

'I was just easing her broken heart after you'd dumped her.'

'Yeah. But it's the principle.'

Considering, Rafe scratched his face. 'You got a point. But Sharilyn, pretty as she is, is no Regan Bishop.'

'I never got to see Regan naked.'

'That's why you're still breathing.' Rafe shifted, folded his arms under his head. 'Maybe we'll call it even.'

'I can sleep easy now.'

Rafe's lips twitched at the dry tone. 'I'm sorry about your house, Jared, if you are.'

'I'm not sorry about it, really. It just brought a lot of things back. I screwed up as much as Barbara did, Rafe. It would have been easier if we'd yelled at each other, threw things.' He took a last swig and set the empty bottle on the floor. 'There's nothing more demoralizing than a civilized divorce between two people who couldn't care less about each other.'

'It's got to be better than getting your heart broken.'

'I don't know. I kind of wish I'd had the chance.'

They were both silent as the sound of weeping drifted down the stairs.

'Ask her,' Rafe suggested. 'I'd bet she'd tell you you're better off.'

'Maybe you should start thinking exorcism,' Jake said, smiling at the idea as his eyes drooped and he settled himself for sleep.

'No. I like having them around. I've had plenty of time to be alone.'

Chapter 9

It was rare for Rafe to dream. He preferred his fantasies during waking hours, so that his consciousness could appreciate them.

But he dreamed that night, as the fire burned low and the moon rose over drifts of snow, if you could call it a dream...

He was running, terror and smoke at his heels. His eyes were burning from fatigue, and from the horror he'd already seen.

Men blown apart before they could scream from the shock and agony. The ground exploding, hacked by mortar fire, drenched with blood. The smell of death was in his nostrils, and he knew he'd never be free of it.

Oh, and he longed for the scent of magnolias and roses, for the lush green hills and rich brown fields of his home.

If he had had tears left, he would have wept them for the quiet gurgling of the river that wound through his family's plantation, the bright laughter of his sisters, the crooning songs of the field hands.

He was afraid, mortally afraid, that everything he'd known and treasured was already gone. His most desperate wish was to get back, to see it again.

He wanted to see his father again, to tell him his son had tried to be a man.

The battle raged everywhere. In the fields, through the corn, in his heart. So many of his comrades lay dead on these godforsaken rocky hills of Maryland.

He'd lost his way. He hadn't been able to see through the choking smoke, or hear through the thunder of guns and the horrible shrieks of men. Suddenly he was running, running as a coward runs for any hole to crawl in.

Mixed with the horror now was a shame just as terrible. He'd forgotten his duty, and lost his honor. Now, somehow, he must find them both again.

The woods were thick, carpeted with the dying leaves that fell, brilliant in golds and russets, from the trees. He had never been so far north, seen such color, or smelled the poignant decay of autumn.

He was only seventeen.

A movement ahead had him fumbling his rifle onto his shoulder. The blue uniform was all he could see, and he fired too quickly, and poorly. The answering shot had fire singeing his arm. Driven by pain and terror, he gave a wild Rebel yell and charged.

He wished he hadn't seen the eyes, the eyes of the

enemy, as wide and terror-glazed and young as his own. Their bayonets crashed, point to point. He smelled the blood, and the stinking scent of fear.

He felt the steel of his blade slice into flesh, and his stomach roiled. He felt the rip of his own, and cried out in agony. He fought, blindly, bitterly, recklessly, until there was nothing inside him but the battle. And when they both lay in their own blood, he wondered why.

He was crawling, delirious with pain. He needed to get home for supper, he thought. Had to get home. There was the house, he could see it now. He dragged himself over rocks and dying summer flowers, leaving his blood staining the grass.

Hands were lifting him. Soft voices. He saw her standing over him, an angel. Her hair like a halo, her eyes warm, her voice filled with the music of the South he yearned for.

Her face was so beautiful, so gentle, so sad.

She stroked his head, held his hand, walking beside him as others carried him up curving steps.

I'm going home, he told her. *I have to go home.*

You'll be all right, she promised. *You'll go home as soon as you're well again.*

She looked away from him, up, and her lovely face went pale as a ghost's.

No. He's hurt. He's just a boy. Charles, you can't.

He saw the man, saw the gun, heard the words.

I'll have no Confederate scum in my house. No wife of mine will put her hands on a Rebel.

Rafe jolted awake with the sound of a gunshot ringing

in his ears. He sat where he was while it echoed away, until all that was left was his brother's quiet breathing.

Chilled, he rose, added logs to the fire. Then he sat, watching the flames and waiting for dawn.

Regan slept like a baby. With the kids off to school and Cassie taking the early shift at the diner, she indulged herself with a second cup of coffee. She still prized her privacy, but she'd discovered she liked having the company.

It was nice having the children pad around the house in the morning, having Emma offer one of her solemn kisses or Connor one of his rare smiles.

She liked beating Cassie to the kitchen so that she could fix breakfast and smooth down pale, sleep-tousled hair.

Motherhood had never been one of her ambitions, but she was beginning to wonder if she wouldn't be good at it.

She picked up a crayon Emma had left on the table. She smelled it, and smiled. It was funny, she thought, how quickly a house could smell like children. Crayons and white paste, hot chocolate and soggy cereal.

And it was funny how quickly she'd come to look forward to finding them there after work.

Absently she tucked the crayon in her pocket. Work was exactly where she had to go.

Out of habit, she rinsed her coffee cup in the sink, set it on the drain. After a last glance around, she opened the door in the kitchen and headed down the stairs to open the shop for the day.

She'd barely turned the Open sign around, unlocked

the door and moved behind the counter to unlock the till when Joe Dolin walked in.

The quick spurt of alarm came first. Then she soothed it by reminding herself that he was here, and Cassie wasn't.

He'd put on weight even in the three years she'd known him. There was muscle there still, but it was cushioned by too many six-packs. She imagined he'd been an attractive man once, before his square face had bloated and his moody brown eyes had sunken behind bags.

He had a chipped front tooth she didn't know was courtesy of a younger Rafe's fist, and a nose that had been broken by Rafe, and several others.

With disgust, she remembered that he had tried, once or twice, to touch her. Had watched her, more than once or twice, with greedy eyes and a knowing smile.

Regan hadn't even told Cassie that. And never would.

She braced herself for the altercation, but he shut the door quietly, took off his billed cap and held it humbly in his hands, like a peasant before the queen.

'Regan. I'm sorry to bother you.'

The penitent sound of his voice and bowed head almost softened her. But she remembered the bruises on Cassie's neck. 'What do you want, Joe?'

'I heard Cassie's staying with you.'

Just Cassie, she noted. Nothing about his children. 'That's right.'

'I guess you know about the trouble.'

'Yes, I know. You beat her, and you were arrested.'

'I was awful drunk.'

'The court may find that an excuse. I don't.'

His eyes narrowed and flashed, but he kept his head down. 'I feel terrible about it. Done nothing but worry about her for days. Now they've fixed it so I can't even go near her to tell her so. I come to ask you a favor.'

He lifted his head then, and his eyes were moist. 'Cassie sets a lot of store by you.'

'I set a lot of store by her,' Regan said evenly. She would not let the sight of a man's tears blur her judgment.

'Yeah, well. I was hoping you'd talk to her for me. See that she gives me another chance. I can't ask her myself, long as there's that damn restraining order. But she'll listen to you.'

'You're giving me credit for influence over Cassie I don't have, Joe.'

'No, she'll listen to you,' he insisted. 'She's always running off at the mouth about how smart you are. You tell her to come on home, and she'll do it.'

Very slowly, Regan placed her palms on the countertop. 'If she'd listened to me, she would have left you years ago.'

His unshaven jaw tightened. 'Now, you look. A man's got a right—'

'To beat his wife?' she snapped. 'Not in my book, he doesn't, and not in the law's. No, I won't tell her to come back to you, Joe. And if that's all you came in for, you'll have to leave.'

His lips peeled back, showing clenched teeth, his eyes hardened like marbles. 'Still all high-and-mighty. You think you're better than me.'

'No, I don't. I *know* I'm better than you. Get out of my

shop or I'll have Sheriff MacKade throw you in jail for harassment.'

'A woman belongs to her husband.' He crashed his fist on the counter, hard enough to have a crack splitting through the glass. 'You tell her to get her skinny butt home, if she knows what's good for her. And what's good for you.'

Fear trembled in Regan's throat, and was swallowed, hard. As if it were a talisman, she closed a hand around the crayon in her pocket. 'Is that a threat?' she asked coolly. 'I don't believe your parole officer would approve. Shall I call him and ask?'

'Bitch. You're nothing but a frigid, dried-up bitch who can't get herself a real man.' He wanted to hit her, to feel his fist pound into that ice-queen face. 'You get between me and my wife and both of you'll find out what it's like. When I finish with her, I'll come after you. We'll see if you're so high and mighty when I'm finished.'

He jammed his hat back on his head, spun to the door. 'You tell her what I said. You tell her I'm waiting. She'd better have that bastard MacKade tear up those papers and be home by suppertime.'

The instant the door slammed behind him, Regan slumped against the counter. Her hands were shaking, and she hated it, hated being afraid, hated being vulnerable. She grabbed the phone, had nearly followed through on her first instinct to call Rafe when she stopped herself.

That was wrong, she thought, carefully replacing the receiver. For so many reasons it was wrong. Wouldn't his first reaction be to hunt Joe down, to fight? He'd probably get hurt and certainly more fighting wasn't going to solve anything.

She straightened and drew a few calming breaths. Where was her pride, her sense of control? She had always handled herself and any situation that came her way. Her feelings for Rafe shouldn't—couldn't change that intrinsic part of her. She wouldn't allow it. So, she would do what was right, what was practical, and what was necessary. Regan picked up the phone and dialed the sheriff's office.

'He was almost pitiful at first.' The tea sloshed in her cup. With a grimace, Regan set it down again. 'I guess he spooked me more than I'd thought.'

'Shake all you want,' Devin told her, and frowned at the crack in her counter. It could have been worse, he thought grimly. A lot worse. 'I have to say, I didn't think he was fool enough to pull a stunt like this.'

'I don't think he'd been drinking.' Regan cleared her throat. 'At least he wasn't drunk. He got steadily more angry, steadily more abusive.' She reached for her tea again. 'I don't have any witnesses. It was just him and me.'

'You file charges, I'll go after him.'

Her lips trembled upward. 'It sounds like you're looking forward to it.'

'You don't know the half of it.'

'I'll file charges. Cassie?'

'I had one of my deputies go to the diner as soon as you called. He'll hang out there and get paid for drinking coffee and flirting with Ed. I've got another one driving by the school.'

'The kids.' Her blood ran cold. 'You don't think he'd go after the kids?'

'No, I don't think he gives two damns about them.'

'You're right.' She tried to feel relieved. 'He never said a word about them. Only Cassie. It was as if his children didn't exist. Well, I'll lock up and go with you now, if that's all right.'

'The sooner the better. Odds are he's at home, knocking back a bottle and waiting for her.'

Once the complaint was official, Regan detoured to the market. She had a feeling both she and Cassie were going to need a lift that evening. Comfort food was in order. Spaghetti and meatballs, she decided, and double-fudge brownies.

While she waited for her purchases to be bagged, she tried not to chuckle at the darting looks and whispers. The gossip brigade, she thought, was in full march.

Mrs. Metz, all two hundred and twenty pounds of her, waddled over. 'Why, Regan Bishop, I thought that was you.'

'Hello, Mrs. Metz.' Here, Regan thought, was the brigade's head scout. 'Do you think we're going to get hit with snow again?'

'Ice storm,' she said with a shake of her head. 'Heard on the radio. Into February now, and don't look like this winter's ever going to end. Surprised to see you in here this time of day.'

'Business is slow.' Regan counted out bills for the groceries. 'Everybody's hibernating.'

'Know what you mean. Still, you got yourself some business over at the old Barlow place, don't you?'

'Yes, indeed.' Willing to play, Regan set the bag on her hip. 'It's really coming along, too. It'll be a showplace when it's finished.'

'Never thought to see the day anybody'd bother fixing her up. Never thought to see Rafe MacKade come riding back into town, neither.' Her curious eyes brightened. 'Guess he did pretty well for himself down South.'

'Apparently.'

'You can't tell about those MacKade boys. They fool you every time. You know that Rafe crashed his daddy's Ford pickup on Marble Quarry Road before he so much as had a license. That was right after Buck died, as I recall. He was wild as wild can be, that Rafe. Chasing girls, picking fights, flying around on the back roads on that noisy motorcycle of his. Time was, when you found trouble, there was always a MacKade boy in the middle of it.'

'Times change, I suppose.'

'Not that much, they don't.' Her chins wagged as she chuckled. 'I seen him around town. He's still got that look in his eye. Little bird told me he had that eye on you.'

'Well, your little bird's right. And I've got mine right back on him.'

Mrs. Metz laughed so hard she had to put down her box of Ho-Hos to hold her belly. 'With a boy like that, you'd better keep it there. He'd be harder to keep down than spit on a hot griddle. He was a bad one, Regan. Bad boys turn into dangerous men.'

'I know.' Regan winked. 'That's why I like him. You come in and browse real soon, Mrs. Metz.'

'I'll do that.' Chuckling to herself, she emptied her cart. 'Stop gawking, boy,' she snapped at the skinny clerk, who was still watching Regan's retreat, 'and ring me up here. You ain't never going to be dangerous enough to reel in that kind of woman.'

Amused by the encounter, Regan strolled down the sidewalk. It was a good town, she thought, lifting a hand in response to a greeting from across the street. The sidewalks were uneven, heaved up by tree roots and frost, the library was only open three days a week, and the post office was closed for a full hour every afternoon.

But despite that, or perhaps because of it, it was a good town. She didn't think Rafe realized he'd been welcomed home.

No fatted calf, she mused, crossing at the corner and turning down Main. That wasn't their style. The prodigal son just slipped back into the town's rhythm with neither a hitch nor fanfare.

When he left again, his departure would be just as unheralded. A few comments over the counter at the post office, some speculation at the diner. Then the town would move along, as easy as ever.

She hoped she would.

Shifting her bag, she circled around the side of the shop. Enjoy the moment, she reminded herself. Don't project into the future. Those were the rules; she'd stated them herself. All she had to do was follow them.

And if she found an excuse to slip by his house later, steal an hour with him, so much the better.

Bolstered by the idea, she took her keys from her pocket. She jingled them as she climbed the stairs with her groceries.

If she'd been paying attention, if she hadn't been thinking about Rafe, perhaps she would have noticed sooner. But her hand was already reaching for the door when she saw that it wasn't on its hinges, but was propped there.

Her mind stayed blank for an instant too long.

Even as she spun around to run, Joe hauled the door aside. The crash dragged a shriek from her. It was choked off to a gurgle when his arm jerked around her neck.

'Wondered which one of you'd come first. This is good.' His breath panted out, sour with whiskey and excitement. 'Been wanting to get my hands on you for a long time.'

He pressed his mouth to her ear, excited by the way she tried to curl away from him. 'I'm going to show you what a real man's all about. Going to get you out of those prim and proper clothes and show you real good.'

He panted as his free hand came around to squeeze hard on her breast. Her skin crawled, and for one hideous moment the fear was so bright it blinded her eyes, and her reason.

'I'm going to get me some of what I hear that bastard Rafe MacKade's been getting. Then I'm going to fix your face so nobody thinks it's so pretty anymore.'

As he started to drag her over the broken door and inside, the horror of what he would do flashed through her. She swung back. Groceries flew, smashing into the little alley below. Her heels skidded back over the door.

'Cassie gets here, I'm going to give her the same. But first I'm going to enjoy taking you down a few pegs.' With his free hand, he yanked her hair, darkly pleased when she whimpered.

Then she remembered the keys that were still gripped in her frozen fist. With prayers screaming in her head, she flung her hand back, hacking with the point she'd pushed between her clenched fingers.

He howled like a wild dog, and the vicious grip released. Dragging in air, she flew down the steps, certain he would be on her again in an instant. At the bottom, she stumbled, went down hard on her hands and knees. Prepared to scream, she looked back.

And saw him crumpled on the landing, holding a hand to his face, while blood dripped through his fingers. Like a woman in a trance, she rose to her feet, put one foot slowly in front of the other until she reached the diner. The buzzing in her ears warned her to take deep, careful breaths.

She stepped inside, closed the door behind her, unaware that her coat was hanging by one sleeve and the knees of her slacks were torn and bloody.

Cassie dropped the tray she was holding, shattering dishes. 'Regan! My God!'

'I think you should call Devin,' Regan said, testing each word as she spoke it. 'Joe's on the landing of my apartment. I think I hurt him.' When the room revolved, she braced a hand on the back of a booth. 'I have to sit down now.'

'Go call Devin,' Ed snapped, and rushed over to ease Regan into a booth. 'Head down.' In a quick movement, she had Regan's head between her knees. 'Long, deep breaths, that's a girl.' Eyes sharp, she scanned the room, where a half a dozen customers sat staring. 'Well, what are you waiting for? One of you big strong men get on over there and hold that son of a bitch for the sheriff. You, Horace, get up off your lard butt and get this girl a glass of water.'

Ed's rasped orders had everyone moving at once. Satisfied, she eased Regan up again. 'Got a little color back,' she declared, and sat back on her haunches. She took a cigarette from the pack in her apron pocket, lit it with a wooden match. After one long drag, she smiled. 'Hope to hell you hurt him bad, honey. Real bad.'

Sitting in Devin's office, with the coffee Shane had poured for her warming her hands, Regan was sure she was over the worst of it. Everything had happened too fast for anything but pure emotion. But the rabbity fear had passed now, and she could think.

Beside her, Cassie sat saying nothing. Shane paced, like a boxer revving up for a match. At his desk, Devin coolly filled out a report.

'I'm sorry to ask you to go through it again, Regan,' he began. 'The clearer your statement, the easier it'll be to close it all up.'

'That's all right. I'm fine now, really.' Absently she picked at her torn slacks. The knees beneath still burned. As much, she thought, from Ed's liberal application of antiseptic as from their abrupt meeting with asphalt. 'I'd like to get it over with. I can—'

She broke off when the door burst open. For an instant, she saw nothing but Rafe's face—pale, hard as rock, lit with eyes green enough, sharp enough, to murder in one vicious slice.

The rabbit pulse pounded in her throat. Before she could get to her feet, he was on her, dragging her up, crushing her in an embrace that bruised ribs.

'You're all right? Are you hurt?' His voice was raw, brittle as broken glass. He couldn't think. There'd been nothing inside him but bright terror from the moment he got word of the attack. His body was ice, enveloping hers as he buried his face in her hair.

Perhaps that was why she began to tremble helplessly. 'I'm okay. Really, I'm—' But her voice shuddered off. If she could have burrowed inside him, she would have.

'Did he hurt you?' With a hand he was fighting to steady, he stroked her hair, eased her face back so that he could see for himself. 'Did he touch you?'

She could only shake her head and press her face against his shoulder.

With his arms tight, as possessive as they were protective, he stared at Devin over Regan's head. His eyes fired like torches. 'Where is he?'

'He's in custody.'

Rafe's gaze whipped toward the cells in the back.

'He's not here, Rafe.' Though his voice was calm, Devin was braced for the attack. 'You're not going to be able to get to him.'

'You think you can stop me?'

From behind, where he'd stood since he'd followed Rafe in, Jared laid a hand on his brother's shoulder. 'Why don't you sit down?'

With a snarl humming in his throat, Rafe jerked the restraining hand aside. 'Back off.'

'This is the law's problem now,' Devin told him, rising slowly.

'The hell with the law, and you with it. I want to know where he is.'

'You find him, Rafe, I'll hold your coat.' Primed for action, Shane smiled thinly. 'If you had a coat. Always hated the son of a bitch.'

'Shut up,' Jared muttered, glancing down at the silent Cassie.

'You can stick your lawyer talk,' Shane told him, fists already bunched. 'I'm with Rafe on this.'

'I don't need you or anybody else with me. Don't get in my way, Devin.'

'I'm already in your way. Now sit down, or I'll throw your ass in a cell.'

He moved so fast, Regan had time only to squeak while Rafe lunged over the desk and had Devin by the shirt-front. She'd never considered herself sheltered, but the things they shouted at each other, the echo of the sentiments from the two MacKades behind her, had her already shocked system shuddering.

There was no doubt in her mind that blood would flow any moment.

'Stop it,' she said, but the order was shaky and weak under the vicious words hurling through the room. 'I said stop it,' she repeated, hugging herself. Something crashed behind her, and shot her pulse to critical. 'Stop it this minute!' she bellowed.

The surprising power in her voice halted Rafe's fist and put a stop to the shoving match behind her. Four hard-eyed men stared at her, like statues frozen in battle.

'You're acting like children. *Worse* than children. What good is it going to do anyone for the four of you to punch each other out? It's just typical,' she said, more disgusted now than frightened. 'Just the sort of typical behavior I'd expect from a bunch of boneheaded baboons. Real heroes.' With a sniff, she grabbed her coat. 'Well, I'm certainly not going to stand here and watch the four of you beat one another to a pulp.'

'Sit down, Regan.' When she continued toward the door, Rafe swore and went after her. 'Sit down,' he repeated, holding back his rage and turning her gently. 'God, look at your hands.'

Shaken all over again, he gathered them carefully in his, pressed his lips to the abraded palms. It was a gesture that had the remaining MacKades shifting in embarrassment.

'What do you expect me to do?' The rest of the anger drained and left him helpless. 'What do you expect me to feel?'

'I don't know.' She no longer knew exactly what she

was feeling herself, not with those eyes so concentrated on her face. 'I just want to get this over with, Rafe. Please, let me tell Devin what he needs to know, so I can get this over with.'

'Fine.' He let her go, stepped back. 'Do what you have to do.'

She walked back to her chair, accepted the fresh mug Jared offered. Devin questioned, she answered. Rafe listened. Then he left, without a word.

She tried not to be hurt by it, tried to understand it. 'Devin, can you tell me what to expect now?'

'My deputy will call in once they're finished with Joe at the hospital. He'll be transferred. He broke parole, and the restraining order, so he'll serve his full time on the earlier charges.'

It was a small satisfaction, Devin thought with a quick look at Cassie. She hadn't moved or spoken in thirty minutes.

'Now he'll face additional charges,' Devin went on. 'Breaking and entering, assault, attempted rape. We'll toss in the property damage. There may be a trial, and you'd have to testify.'

'I'm prepared for that.'

'Under the circumstances, his lawyer may advise him to deal and plead guilty.'

At Devin's questioning glance, Jared nodded. 'That's what I'd do.'

'Yeah, well.' It was hard not to hate the system, Devin mused, when it got personal. 'Either way, he's going away for a good while. I figure three to five. He won't be bothering you again. Either of you.'

'Well, then.' Regan drew in a deep breath. 'It's done. Cassie and I can go home now?'

'Sure. I'll be in touch.'

'I can't go home with you.' For the first time since she'd come into the office, Cassie tried her voice. It was small and rusty.

'Of course you can.'

'How can I?' She stared at the lovely smoke gray slacks Regan wore, at the nasty tears in the soft material. 'How could you even want me after what he's done to you?'

'What *he's* done,' Regan said quietly. 'Not you, Cassie. You're not responsible.'

'Of course I am.' It cost Cassie to lift her head, to look into Regan's eyes. 'I know what he might have done to you if you hadn't been strong enough to stop him. Done to you to get to me, Regan. You're the best friend I've ever had.'

'Then let me keep being your friend.'

'I want that, and I know you've already forgiven me.'

'Cassie, there's nothing to forgive. Don't take this on,' Regan murmured, covering Cassie's hands with hers.

'I have to, because I have to start figuring out how to forgive myself now. I'm going to start by taking my kids home and finding a way to make the kind of life for them they deserve. I need to start taking care of myself and them. I need to do that.'

'In a few more days,' Regan protested.

'No, now.' She closed her eyes, steadied herself, then

opened them and looked at Jared. 'Can you help me, Jared?'

'Of course I can. Whatever you need, honey. There are plenty of programs—'

'No.' She pressed her lips together hard. It was time, she told herself, long past time, that she took a stand. 'I want to file for divorce. Today. I need you to tell me what to do.'

'All right.' He took her hand to help her up, then slipped an arm gently around her shoulders. 'Why don't you come with me now? We'll take care of everything.'

''Bout time,' Shane muttered, the minute the door closed behind them. He shrugged at the blazing look Devin aimed at him. 'Hey, we all know she should have ditched that bastard years ago.'

'You won't get any argument there.' Regan rose, surprised she wasn't as steady as she'd believed. 'But that was hard for her. It's going to be hard for her to follow through.'

'She wouldn't have done it if he hadn't hurt somebody else,' Devin mumbled. 'That's the kind of thing it would take for her.'

'Then I'm glad he did. And I'm glad I hurt him right back.' Regan took a deep breath, then asked the question that had been hovering in a corner of her mind. 'His eye, Devin?'

'I can let you know when I find out. If you want me to.'

'I think I have to know.' She held out a hand for his, not to shake, but to hold. 'You've been wonderful. I know Rafe was upset, but he was wrong in the things he said to you. You did everything you could. You did everything right.'

'If I'd done everything right, it wouldn't have happened.'

'You know better than that.' She squeezed, then winced as her hand throbbed. 'I'm going home, take a bottle of aspirin, and crawl into bed for a few hours. Please call when you hear anything.'

'I will. Shane?'

'Ahead of you, like always.' He already had Regan's coat, and he helped her into it. 'I'll drive you home and fix that door for you.'

'Thanks.' With a smile, she kissed his cheek. 'Baboons or not, the MacKade brothers aren't half-bad.'

'Baby—' he put an arm around her waist to lead her out '—we're all bad. Later, Dev.' When he'd helped her into his truck, he paused. 'Rafe'll come around. He just needs to go punch something.'

'That's the answer?'

'Hey, it works.' He slammed her door, then circled the truck to climb behind the wheel.

'You'd have gone with him. After Joe.'

'We'd have all gone with him.' Shane glanced in the rearview, then whipped the truck into a quick and illegal U-turn. 'Dev and Jared would have spouted off for a while about law and order. We'd have shoved each other around. Then we'd have gone with him.' With some regret, he shook his head. 'It would've been fun.'

'Fun.' She could almost laugh as she let her head sink back on the seat.

'Nobody messes with a MacKade woman.'

'Oh, really? And is that my status at this point?'

He caught the tone, and then, with a wary glance, the martial look in her eyes. 'I just meant…seeing as you and Rafe… That is, the way he's…' Even a MacKade knew the value of retreat. 'I ain't touching this one.'

He pulled up at the base of her stairs and looked up to study the door. 'Looks like somebody beat me to it.'

'What?' She was still simmering.

'I'll check it, but it looks from here like it's already been fixed.' He got out of the truck, climbed the stairs. 'Yep. Few nicks and scratches, but it's back on its hinges.' As a precaution, he tried the lock, gave it a good shove. 'Solid. Rafe probably took care of it.'

'I see.' It did nothing to appease her. 'I'll have to be sure to thank him, won't I?'

'Yeah.' Shane retreated again, backing down the stairs. 'Are you going to be all right? Want me to get you anything, or hang around?'

'No, no, I'm fine. Just fine.' It wasn't pleasant to take out her keys, but she did it, turned the lock. 'I appreciate the ride.'

'No problem.' As he hurried back to his truck, Shane decided Rafe had a problem. A big one. It gave him a reason to smile all the way through town.

Chapter 10

It felt good to beat on something. Even if it was only a nail. To prevent himself beating on something, or someone else, Rafe had closed himself inside the east-wing bedroom. The look in his eye had warned any and all of his men to keep their distance—if they wanted to keep their teeth.

The sounds of construction bumped against the walls, a sound just violent enough to suit his black mood. Rafe ignored the nail gun at his disposal and beat in nails with hammer and muscle. Every new stud that he secured with nails and a swing of his arm was Joe Dolin's face.

When the door opened behind him, Rafe bared his teeth without looking around. 'Get the hell out. Stay out or you're fired.'

'Go ahead and fire me.' Regan slammed the door at her

back. 'Then I can say what I have to say to you without damaging our professional relationship.'

He looked over his shoulder now, briefly. She'd changed, he noted. Not just the slacks, but everything— shirt, blazer, jewelry. From her hair to her shoes, she was neat as a pin.

But he remembered exactly how she'd looked, frazzled, pale, with blood on her clothes.

'You don't want to be here right now.' He set another nail, shot it home.

'You couldn't be more accurate on that, MacKade, but I'm here.'

She'd had to shower first, had to scrub herself every-where and throw out every stitch she'd been wearing when Joe touched her. But she was steady again, and ready to deal with Rafe MacKade.

'I want to know what the hell is wrong with you.'

If he told her, she was liable to laugh in his face. And that, he was dead sure, would push him over that final edge.

'I'm busy, Regan. Weather's cost me a full day.'

'Don't hand me that. Look at me when I'm talking to you, damn it.' When he didn't, just kept battering nails into wood, she fisted her hands on her hips. 'Why did you leave Devin's office that way? Just leave?'

'I had things to do.'

To illustrate her opinion of that, she kicked at a tool-box. 'I suppose I'm to thank you now for fixing my door.'

'I'll bill you.'

'Why are you mad at me?' she demanded. 'I didn't do anything to—'

Her breath sucked in as the hammer sailed across the room and crashed into a newly framed wall.

'No, you didn't do a damn thing. You just got your-self tossed around, bruised, bloodied up and damn near raped. Why the hell should that bother me?'

Someone had to be calm, she told herself. Obviously, the way his eyes were glowing, it was going to have to be her. 'I know you're upset about what happened.'

'Yeah, I'm upset.' He picked up the toolbox, heaved it, because it made more sense than throwing her around. Metal and steel crashed and scattered like small bombs. 'I'm just a little upset. Now get out.'

'I won't.' Instead she angled her chin. 'Go ahead, big guy, throw something else. When you've got it out of your system, we'll have a civilized conversation.'

'You'd better get it through that thick head that there's nothing civilized about me.'

'Oh, that's coming through loud and clear,' she tossed back. 'What's next? You want to take a shot at me? That should prove you're a bigger man than Joe Dolin.'

His eyes went black. For an instant, a heartbeat, she thought she saw hurt mixed with the rage. And it shamed her. 'I'm sorry.' Fumbling, she lifted her hands. 'You didn't deserve that. I didn't mean that.'

Now there was only rage, viciously controlled. 'You usually say what you mean.' He held up a hand before she could speak again. 'You want to have a conversation, fine. We'll have a damn conversation.'

He strode to the door, simmering when she flinched. Yanking it open, he bellowed to every corner of the rambling house. 'Out! Everybody out, now!'

He slammed the door again, satisfied by the scramble of feet and the clatter of tools.

'There's no need for the work to stop,' she began. 'I'm sure this will only take a few minutes.'

'Sometimes it just can't be your way.'

'I don't know what you mean.'

'No, I don't guess you do.' Disgusted, he hauled open the door again. 'Somebody give me a damn cigarette,' he shouted. But as there was no one brave enough to approach, he ended up slamming the door again.

Regan watched, quietly fascinated, while he paced and swore. His shirt was shoved up to the elbows, a tool belt was slung at his hips like a holster. He'd wrapped a bandanna around his forehead to catch the sweat. He looked, she thought, like a bandit who would just as soon kill as steal.

And it was certainly ridiculous to be aroused.

'I could make coffee,' she began, then let out a breath at the razor-edged look he shot her. 'Maybe not. Rafe—'

'Just shut up.'

Her back jammed straight as a poker. 'I don't care to be spoken to that way.'

'Get used to it. I've held back long enough with you.'

'Held back?' Her eyes went wide. If he hadn't looked like a maniac, she might have laughed. 'You've been holding back? I'd like to see what you consider cutting loose.'

'You're about to.' He gnawed off the words like stringy

meat from a bone. 'You're ticked off that I left? Well, now you're going to be treated to what would have happened if I'd stayed.'

'Don't you touch me.' Her arms shot up, hands fisted like those of a boxer ready to spar. 'Don't you dare.'

Eyes simmering, he closed a hand over her fist and used his leverage to push her back to the door. 'Same goes, darling. I gave you a chance to walk, you didn't take it.'

'Don't call me darling in that tone of voice.'

The way his lips peeled back, she wouldn't have been surprised to see fangs. 'God, you're a piece of work.' He tossed her hand down and walked away, because it was safer for both of them. 'You want to know why I left. That's the big, burning question, isn't it? That's what had you coming over here? Coming to me?'

'Yes.'

'But you didn't come to me this morning when he threatened you. You didn't come to me when he hurt you.' And that, Rafe thought, however it devastated him, was that.

'I had to tell Devin,' she began.

'Yeah. You had to tell Devin.' Bitterly calm now, he turned back. 'You know what I heard in that nice and de-tailed statement you made, Regan? Dolin came into your place this morning, just like I thought he would.'

'And I handled it,' she countered. 'Just like I told you I would.'

'Sure, you're great at handling things. He threatened you. He scared you.'

'Yes, all right, he scared me.' And she was scared now,

too, she realized, of where this was leading. 'That's why I called Devin.'

'But not me. You went down to Devin's office, filed your charges.'

'Yes, of course. I wanted Joe arrested.'

'Nice and tidy. Then you went *grocery* shopping.'

'I…' She linked her hands together, pulled them apart. 'I thought—I knew Cassie was going to be upset, and I wanted… I just thought if I fixed a meal it would make us both feel better.'

'And in all that time, going to Devin's, to the market, walking there and back, you never stopped to call me. It never even occurred to you, did it?'

'I was—' She opened her mouth, closed it again. 'All right, yes. It was my first reaction, but I calmed down and decided against it.'

'You calmed down?'

'Yes, I realized it was my problem, and my responsibility to handle it.'

Her simple honesty sliced through him like a blade. He could almost see himself split in half, one part rage, one part misery. 'And after he had you, after he had his hands on you, and hurt you, tried to—'

He couldn't say it. If he did, he'd fall to pieces.

'You didn't think to call me then, either. I only heard it from Shane because he was in with Devin when the call came through, and he figured I'd be interested.'

Somehow, she realized, she *had* hurt him. She'd never meant to. Hadn't known he could be hurt. 'Rafe, I wasn't thinking at all.' She started forward, stopped, knowing it would do no good to go farther. 'I was numb. By the time I could really think again, I was in Devin's office. It all happened so fast,' she said hurriedly, desperate now to make him see. To understand. 'And part of the time it seemed as if I wasn't really there at all.'

'You were handling it.'

'I had to. It wouldn't have done any good to fall apart.'

'You're real good at keeping yourself together.' He walked over, picked up the hammer. 'All by yourself.'

'I have to be. I expect myself to be, because—'

'You don't want to be like your mother,' he finished for her.

It sounded so callous, and so foolish. 'All right, yes, that's partially true. It's important for me to be a certain way, but that really doesn't apply to this. If I didn't call you, it was only because...'

'You didn't need me.' His eyes were level, and no longer hot. He had very little heat left inside him. 'You don't need me.'

A new kind of panic was twisting through her. 'That's not true.'

'Oh, the sex is great.' He smiled then, coolly, humorlessly. 'That's a need we handle together real well. It's my problem that I let it get personal. I won't make the mistake again.'

'It's not about sex.'

'Sure it is.' He plucked a nail out of his pouch, set it in place. 'It's been about sex right from the get-go. That's all we've got. It's plenty.' He rammed the nail home. 'You know where to find me when you've got the itch.'

The blood drained from her cheeks and froze around her heart. 'That's a horrible thing to say.'

'Your rules, darling. Why complicate a good thing, right?'

'I don't want things to be this way between us, Rafe.'

'Well, now I do. Take it or leave it.' He rammed another nail into wood. She wasn't going to get the chance to hurt him again, he told himself. No woman hurt him like this.

She opened her mouth, primed to tell him she'd leave it. Leave him. And couldn't. Tears burned in her eyes, in her throat. Could there have been a worse possible time, she wondered, for her to realize she was in love with him?

'Is that the way you really feel?'

'I try to say what I mean, too.'

Unwilling to humiliate herself, she swallowed the tears. 'And all this is because you're angry about what happened. About how I dealt with it.'

'Let's just say it made everything clear. You don't want to clutter up your life, right?'

'No, I—'

'Hell, neither do I. Call it ego— I've got one. I didn't like you running to my brother instead of me. Like you said, I've got it out of my system. We can just go back to the way things were. The way things are.'

She hadn't realized how much she could prefer that lethal temper over this calculated disinterest. 'I'm not sure that's possible. I can't give you an answer right at the moment.'

'You mull it over, Regan. You do that real well, too.'

'Would you rather—' She pressed a hand to her lips,

waited until she could steady her voice. 'If you'd rather suspend our business relationship, I can give you the names of some other dealers in the area.'

'No reason for that. I'm already behind.' When he turned to her, all he saw was that her eyes were dry, her face was composed. 'I can take shipment on this room in about a week, if you've got a problem with storage.'

'That'll be fine. I'll make the arrangements.' She turned and reached blindly for the doorknob. Terrified she'd crumble, she walked away quickly. She didn't start to run until she was outside, with the wind slapping her wet cheeks.

When he heard the door close below, Rafe sat down on the floor. At the sound of weeping shimmering in the air, he rubbed his hands hard over his face.

'I know just how you feel,' he muttered.

It was the first time in his checkered career that anyone had managed to break his heart. His only solace was that he'd make damn sure it was the last.

The predicted ice storm raged through, glazing the snow, turning the streets to glass. It was days before the temperature inched up enough to soften it. Each night the thermometer would plunge again, hardening and slickening every coated surface.

It didn't mean a damn thing to Rafe. The lousy weather gave him an excuse to stay just where he was, work twenty out of every twenty-four hours. With every nail he hammered, every wall he sanded, the house became more his.

When he couldn't sleep, even after exhausting himself, he wandered the house with the other ghosts.

He was too busy to think about Regan. Or so he tried to convince himself.

Whenever he did, whenever she snuck through his well-fortified defenses, he just worked harder, longer.

'You look a little ragged, pal.' Devin lit a cigarette and watched Rafe hammer freshly painted baseboard into place. 'Remember that book—*Dorian Gray?* The way it's starting to look, you're the picture in the closet, and this house is old Dorian.'

'Pick up a hammer, or beat it.'

Instead, Devin crouched, ran a fingertip over the wide, carved trim. 'Sure is pretty as a picture. What'd you call this color?'

'Rose dust.' He framed the words like a dare.

'Yep, sure is pretty.' Devin used an empty coffee can as an ashtray. 'If you're into pink.'

Rafe spared him a look. 'You trying to start something?'

'Nope, just making conversation. They transferred Joe from the hospital today.'

Rafe's eyes iced over before he turned away. 'None of my business.'

'He didn't lose his eye,' Devin went on easily. 'Be wearing a patch for a while though. They can't tell yet if there'll be permanent damage.'

'She should have aimed between his legs.'

'Yeah, too bad about that. Well, I thought you'd want to know, he pleaded guilty to the B and E, the assault, on advice of counsel. They dumped the attempted rape charges to get the guilty plea and avoid trial, but he's not going to pass Go.'

Rafe didn't want to care. 'How long?'

'My guess is three, solid. Before you say it's not enough, I'm going to the sentencing tomorrow myself, and adding weight. When he's up for parole, in a year or so, I'll go back and add more.'

'I said it's none of my business.' Rafe toed in the last piece of baseboard. 'How's Cassie holding up?'

'Okay, I guess. Jared's pushing through the divorce. With the spousal abuse and adultery, it won't take the usual year. Joe's not in much of a position to contest it. The quicker it's done, the quicker she and the kids can get on with things.'

Thoughtfully he tapped his cigarette out in the can. 'Aren't you going to ask how Regan's holding up?'

'No.'

'Well, I'll tell you.' Ignoring Rafe's snarl, Devin folded his legs and sat. 'She doesn't look like she's been getting a lot of sleep, if you ask me.'

'I didn't.'

'Ed says she hasn't been coming in for lunch, so I guess her appetite's off, too. I could figure that experience with Joe shook her up enough to interfere with her sleeping and eating. But I got a hunch it's something else.'

'She'll handle it. She's good at taking care of herself.'

'Good thing, too. Odds are, if Joe had managed to drag her inside that day, somebody would've seen the door quick enough, heard the ruckus. Still, he could've done a lot of damage in a short time.'

'Don't you think I know that?' Rafe shot out. 'Do you think I don't know what he could have done to her?'

'Yeah, I think you know it. I think it's eating at you, and I'm sorry. Are you ready to listen to me?'

'No.'

But there wasn't any heat behind the denial, so Devin prepared to say his piece. 'Witnesses in the diner said they thought she was drunk at first when she came in, the way she was walking. She'd have passed out if Ed hadn't gotten her down first.'

'I don't need to hear this.'

'Yeah,' Devin murmured, watching Rafe's knuckles whiten on the hilt of the hammer, 'you do. When I got to her, Rafe, she was in shock. Are you getting this? Her pupils were as narrow as the point of one of those nails. I was set to have her taken into Emergency, but she pulled herself together. I watched her do it. It was impressive.'

'So she's tough.' The image projecting into his mind scraped him raw. 'Tell me something I don't know.'

'Okay. I don't figure you were in any shape to see the way she looked at you when you walked into my office. She'd pulled herself together because she had to, because that's the way she's made, I guess. Then you walked in. A man could go his whole life without having a woman look at him the way she looked at you.'

'She doesn't need me.'

'That's bull. You may be stupid, but you should know that.'

'I know I was stupid enough to let her matter. To let what she thought of me, what she wanted from me, matter. I'm not doing it again.' He rose, hooked his hammer in his tool belt. 'I don't need her, either.'

With a sigh, Devin unfolded himself and stood. 'You're cross-eyed in love with her.'

'No, I'm not. I got soft on her for a while, then I got over it.'

Devin pursed his lips. There was one quick, potentially painful way to handle this. 'You're sure?'

'I just said so, didn't I?'

'Good.' Devin smiled. 'That clears the way. When I thought you had a thing for her, I didn't want to muscle in. Since you don't, I'll go see if I can…stimulate her appetite.'

He was expecting the punch, and took the fist on the jaw philosophically. It was always satisfying to make a point. He lifted a hand, wiggled his jaw, mildly relieved it wasn't broken.

'Yeah, I can see how you got over it.'

'I ought to hit you again,' Rafe said between his teeth. It was infuriating, humiliating, to know how neatly he'd been conned.

'I wouldn't. That one was free.' Cautious, Devin moved his jaw again. 'Damn, Rafe, you've still got a nice right jab.'

Almost amused, Rafe flexed his aching fingers. 'You've still got a face like a rock. You son of a bitch.'

'I love you, too.' Cheered, Devin draped an arm over his brother's shoulders. 'Feel better now?'

'No.' Then he paused. 'Maybe.'

'You want to go find her and straighten this mess out?'

'I'm not crawling after some woman,' Rafe mumbled.

You will, Devin thought. Sooner or later. 'Well then, I got the night off. Want to get drunk and disorderly?'

'Yeah.' They walked into the hall, started down the steps. 'Why don't I meet you at the tavern? Ten o'clock.'

'Suits me. I'll see if I can round up Shane and Jared.'

'Just like old times. When Duff sees us coming, it'll scare the—' Rafe broke off, felt his heart skip. Regan stood straight-backed and cool-eyed at the base of the stairs.

'I've got your delivery.' She'd worked very hard on being able to speak without inflection. 'Your message said you'd be ready for it by three.'

'Just.' His stomach quivered, infuriating him. 'You can have it hauled up.'

'All right. Hello, Devin.'

'Hello, Regan. I'm just on my way out. See you tonight, Rafe.'

'Yeah.' Rafe kept his eyes on Regan's as he came down the last few steps. 'Have any trouble on the roads?'

'No. They're mostly clear now.' She wondered that he couldn't see her heart bleeding. 'I was able to get that feather mattress you wanted for the four-poster. I'll be happy to set it up so you can be sure you want to go with it.'

'Appreciate it. I'll get out of your way. I've got—' Nothing, he realized. He had nothing. 'Work,' he said finally. 'Give a yell when you're ready. I'll have your check.'

She wanted to say something, anything, but he was

already walking away. Squaring her shoulders, she went back to the door to instruct the movers.

It was nearly five when she finished arranging things exactly as she wanted them. She hadn't noticed the quiet that drifted in to replace the steady bang and buzz of labor. But as the light changed, she switched on the rose-patterned globe lamp by the button-backed chair she'd angled toward the fireplace.

There was no mantel there yet, no flames crackling. Faintly the scent of paint stirred in the air. But she thought the room was waiting to be lived in.

And the scent of roses hung like tears in the air.

A wedding-ring quilt, she mused, running her hand over one of the posts of the bed. A few pillows edged with lace to match the canopy that would drape overhead. A cedar chest, a hope chest, at the foot of the bed, filled with sweet-smelling linens and net bags of lavender sachet.

Yes, she thought, those would be just the right touches to finish it off. Perhaps some Irish lace at the windows, a silver-backed brush for the vanity.

It would be beautiful. It would be perfect.

She wished to God she'd never seen the room, the house, or Rafe MacKade.

He stood in the doorway, saying nothing, watching her move through the room, as graceful as any ghost.

Then her back stiffened. She turned and faced him. Seconds passed, though it could have been eons for both of them.

'I was just finishing up,' she managed to say.

'So I see.' He stayed where he was, tore his gaze from hers and scanned the room. 'It looks terrific.'

'I have some tintypes and antique silver frames. I think they'd add a nice touch to the mantel when it's in place.'

'Great.'

The strain of manners was tearing at her stomach. 'I noticed you've made a lot of progress on the next bedroom.'

'It's coming along. I've got a couple more ready for drywall.'

'You work fast.'

'Yeah, that's what they always say.' He pulled a check out of his pocket, stepped forward. 'Payment on delivery.'

'Thank you.' Very deliberately, she opened the purse she'd set on a table, slipped the check inside. And damned him to hell. 'I'll be going, then,' she said briskly. She turned back and bumped solidly into him. 'Excuse me.' She took a step around. He shifted, blocked her. Made her heart pound like a drum. 'You're in my way.'

'That's right.' And since he was, he took a good long look. 'You look lousy.'

'Thank you so much.'

'You've got shadows under your eyes.'

So much for cosmetics, she thought in disgust. 'It's been a long day. I'm tired.'

'How come you haven't been eating over at Ed's?'

She wondered why she'd ever thought she liked small towns. 'Despite what you and the Antietam grapevine might think, what I do on my lunch hour is my business.'

'Dolin's locked up. He's not going to bother you again.'

'I'm not afraid of Joe Dolin.' She tossed back her hair, proud of her own bravado. 'I'm thinking about buying a gun.'

'Think again.'

She hadn't really thought of it the first time, but it grated to have him dictate to her. 'That's right, you're the only one who can defend himself, or anyone else. Back off, MacKade. I'm finished here.'

When he grabbed her arm, she swung out without thinking. Her hand cracked against his cheek before she could stop it. Appalled, she stumbled back.

'Now look what you've made me do.' Enraged and close to tears, she tossed down her purse. 'I can't believe you goaded me into that. I've never struck anyone in my life.'

'You did a pretty good job on your debut.' Watching her, he ran his tongue over the inside of his stinging cheek. 'You want to put your shoulder into it next time. Not much of a crack if you swing from the wrist.'

'There won't be a next time. Unlike you, I don't have to hit people to make a point.' She took a steadying breath. 'I apologize.'

'If you head for the door again, I'm going to get in your way again, and we're going to start this all over.'

'All right.' She left her purse where it lay. 'Obviously there's something you want to say.'

'If you keep aiming that chin at me, you're going to make me mad. I'm being civilized, asking how you are. Civilized is how you like it, isn't it?'

'I'm fine.' She bit the words off. 'And how are you?'

'Good enough. You want some coffee, a beer?'

'No, thank you so much.' Who the hell was this man, she thought, making uselessly polite conversation while her insides tangled into dozens of frayed knots? 'I don't want coffee or beer.'

'What do you want, Regan?'

Now she recognized him. It took only that sharp, impatient tone to bring him back. And to make her yearn. 'I want you to leave me alone.'

He said nothing at all, just stepped out of her way.

Once more she picked up her purse. Once more she set it down again. 'That's not true.' The hell with her pride, with sense, even with her heart. It couldn't be any more battered than it already was.

'You'd never have made it to the door,' he said quietly. 'You probably knew that.'

'I don't know anything except I'm tired of fighting with you.'

'I'm not fighting. I'm waiting.'

She nodded, sure she understood. If it was all he was willing to give her now, she would accept that. And she would make it enough. She stepped out of her shoes, unbuttoned her blazer.

'What are you doing?'

'Answering your ultimatum of last week.' She tossed the blazer on the chair and unbuttoned her blouse. 'You said take it or leave it. I'm taking it.'

Chapter 11

It was a curve he hadn't been expecting. By the time he could speak, she was wearing nothing but two scraps of black silk. And all the blood had drained out of his head.

'Just like that?'

'It was always just like that, wasn't it, Rafe? Chemistry, pure and simple?'

He'd want her, she promised herself. By God, when she was done with him, he'd never stop wanting her. Keeping her eyes locked on his, she walked slowly toward him.

'Take it or leave it, MacKade.' She put her hands on his shirt and stunned them both by ripping it open and sending buttons flying. 'Because I'm about to take you.'

Her mouth was fire on his, burning, flashing, shooting dozens of wild blazes into him. Rocked to the core, he gripped her hips, fingers digging through silk to flesh.

'Put your hands on me.' She sank her teeth into his shoulder. 'I want your hands on me.' Hers were dragging at his jeans, closing around him.

'Wait.' But the bombs erupting inside him drowned out everything but pulsing, grappling need. With only his wounded heart as a pitiful weapon, he was defenseless against the spear thrust of desire. Against her.

He kicked himself free of clothes, lifted her off the floor.

He was deep inside her before they fell onto the bed.

It was all sweat and speed and blind sex. The hard slap of flesh against flesh, the raspy gasps of labored breathing. Teeth and nails and tangled tongues drove them both over the sumptuous mattress, rolling and riding.

It was a battle both had already surrendered to. Hot and hard and hurried, fast and frenzied and frantic, they pounded together. Wanting more, accepting less. The scent of roses choked the air with strong, sad perfume.

She straddled him, bowed back as his hands streaked over her. She wanted him to take her to that tenuous edge between pleasure and pain. There she would be alive, as she hadn't been since he'd turned from her.

She had to know that here, at least here, he was as helpless as she, as unable to resist, as pathetically needy. She could feel that need riot through him, taste it each time he dragged her mouth back to his with a ravenous hunger.

While her heart screamed at him to love her, just a little, her quivering body greedily devoured, fueling itself with whatever scraps he would give.

No room for pride, no time for tenderness.

When she sank toward him, limp as water, he rolled her ruthlessly onto her back and drove her on.

He couldn't breathe, didn't think, just battered himself into her. He had to fill her, to empty her, to claim her in the only way he knew she would accept. With a jerk of his head, he tossed the hair out of his eyes. It was vital that he see her, every flicker of shock and pleasure on her face, every tremble of her lips.

Love for her swamped him. All but destroyed him.

'Look at me.' He grated the words out. 'You look at me.'

Her eyes opened, but remained blind with passion. He felt her body quake under his, saw those eyes glaze as her head fell back.

He was powerless to stop himself from following her recklessly over the edge. But he cursed her, then himself, as he fell.

It didn't seem possible to have been so completely aroused, and to feel so utterly empty. He'd never understood how vitally entwined the heart and the body were, until now. And now, staring at the ceiling, with Regan silent beside him, he understood it would never be possible to separate his again.

Not with her.

And he wanted only her.

She'd taken something from him that he'd struggled for years to build. His self-respect. How odd that he hadn't realized that, either, until this moment.

He wasn't sure he could forgive either of them for it.

She desperately wanted him to reach out to her, to fold

her to him as he had in the past. It was miserable to be left like this, so cold, so alone, even as she was still quivering from him.

Yet how could she reach out for him, when she was the one who had taken the step, made the stand, and agreed to take him on his own terms? His own terms, she thought, closing her eyes against the lovely rosy glow of the lamp. Bad Rafe MacKade had returned, she thought bitterly, and taken it all.

'Well, we managed to have sex in a bed for a change.' She sat up, kept her back to him. She could control her voice, but was certain her face would show him that she was shattered. 'It's always firsts with us, isn't it, Mac-Kade?'

'Yeah.' He wanted to stroke that back, but it was so stiff and straight. 'We'll have to try it with sheets sometime.'

'Why not?' Her hands trembled as she slid off the bed, reached down for her underwear. 'We could even throw in a couple of pillows, and a pretense of affection. Just for a change of pace.'

His eyes sharpened, narrowed, as she snapped her bra into place. Hurt and fury bubbled together in a messy stew. Rising, he snatched his jeans, jammed his legs in them.

'I don't like pretenses much.'

'Oh, that's right.' She grabbed her shirt. Silk whipped through the air and onto her back. 'Everything's up-front with you. No frills, no spills.'

'What the hell's wrong with you? You got what you wanted.'

'You don't know diddly about what I want.' Terrified she might weep, she jerked on her slacks. 'Apparently neither do I.'

'You're the one who took off your clothes, darling.' His voice was entirely too smooth. 'You're the one putting them right back on so you can move right along.'

'And you're the one who rolled off me the minute you were done, as if your twenty bucks was up.' Rushing now, she jammed her feet into her shoes.

She might have had a chance if she'd been looking at him. A slim one. But he moved fast, and she was six inches off the ground, his hands like a vise on her, his eyes drilling holes in hers before she drew a second breath.

'Don't say that. I've never treated you that way. I've never thought that way.'

'You're right.' Oddly enough, it was the lash of his temper that calmed her. Stopped her, she hoped, from being a perfect fool. 'I'm sorry, Rafe. That was unfair and untrue.'

Very slowly, he set her back on her feet. He realized his fingers were digging hard enough into her flesh to meet bone, and dropped his hands. 'Maybe I moved too fast, but you caught me off guard.'

'No.' Yes, she felt very calm, she thought as she turned to pick up her blazer. Very calm, and very, very fragile. If he touched her again, she would crack like flawed glass. 'I initiated things, and I agreed to your terms.'

'My terms—'

'Are clear,' she said, finishing for him. 'And acceptable. I suppose the problem is that we're both volatile personalities under the right circumstances. Any circumstances, as far as you're concerned. And as for me, the past few days have been difficult. That doesn't mean I should take it out on you.'

'Do you have to be reasonable, Regan?'

'No, but I'm going to be.' Though her lips curved brightly, she couldn't move the smile into her eyes. 'I don't know what we're fighting about, when we've found the perfect solution. A simple, physical relationship. It's perfect, because the rest of our common ground is narrow to nonexistent. So, I'll apologize again for picking a fight. I'm just a little tired and out of sorts.'

She made herself rise on her toes and kiss him lightly. 'If you'd like to come by tomorrow after work, I'll make it up to you.'

'Yeah, maybe.' Why the hell couldn't he read her eyes? He could always read her eyes if he looked hard enough. 'I'll take you home.'

'No, really.' She had to will herself not to run to the door and escape. Instead, she picked up her purse. 'I've got my car,' she added. 'And I really am tired. I could use an early night.'

He just wanted to hold her, to fold her into his arms and keep her there. 'Whatever you say. I'm supposed to meet my brothers at the tavern in a few hours, anyway.'

'Good, then we'll try for tomorrow.' She made it to the door without stumbling. He didn't offer a goodbye, and neither did she. Her coat was a bright red slash over the newel post, or she might have walked outside without it. She put in on, buttoned it carefully.

Outside, she got into her car, turned the key in the ignition. She concentrated on backing down the lane as if her life depended on it. She took the turn toward town, drove a half mile.

Then she pulled over to the side of the road, carefully put the car in gear, turned the engine off. And cried like a baby.

Twenty minutes later, exhausted, she let her head fall back against the seat. It was freezing, but she didn't have the energy to turn the car on again and pump up the heater.

She was a competent woman, Regan thought. Everyone said so. She was bright, well-organized, moderately successful, and levelheaded.

So why, if she was indeed all of those fine, admirable things, had she managed to mess up her life so miserably?

Rafe MacKade was responsible, of course. She hadn't had a full day's easy running since he'd swaggered back into town. He was messy, arrogant, angry. Oh, so angry. And charming, she thought with a sigh, with all those unexpected sweet spots mixed with the rough.

She should never have fallen for him. She certainly shouldn't have deluded herself that she could have an affair with him and stay objective.

He hadn't been completely objective, either, she remembered. He'd had feelings tangling him up, too. Before she'd ruined it. If she had been just a little more of what he needed, if she hadn't been so dead set on doing it all her way, he might have stayed tangled. Until he'd fallen in love.

Oh, that was wrong, she thought, and banged her fist

against the steering wheel. That was her mother's kind of thinking. Make everything pretty, everything perfect for the man. Stroke his ego, cater to his whims. Play the game and win the prize.

Well, she wouldn't. She was appalled she'd even considered it. She would not squash her own needs, her own personality, her own ego, to lure a man into love.

But hadn't she just done that? She shuddered, but not from the cold. Hadn't she just done that, up in that bedroom?

At a loss, she braced her elbows on the wheel, her head in her hands. She wasn't sure of anything any longer. Except that she loved him. She loved him, and in her stubborn stance against luring him into love with her, she had blocked, perhaps even rejected his feelings. And humiliated herself in the bargain.

That, Regan concluded, made her an idiot.

So what if she had to make some changes in herself? Hadn't he, in his way, done the same?

He'd been hurt, she remembered. She had hurt him, infuriated him. Yet he had gone off to pound nails, instead of picking a fight. It was she who was the coward, who had been unwilling to trust, refusing to bend. He'd never tried to run her life, or her thoughts, or tried to change her. No, he'd given her room, he'd given her affection, and he'd given her the kind of passion a woman dreamed of.

But she'd held back anyway, foolishly, in a knee-jerk response rooted in her upbringing.

Why hadn't she thought of his needs, his pride? Wasn't it time she did so? She could be flexible, couldn't she? Compromise wasn't capitulation. It couldn't be too late to show him she was willing. She wouldn't let it be too late to...

The thought that came into her mind was so simple, and so ridiculous, she knew it had to be right. Without giving herself a moment to think it through, she revved up the car and hit the gas. In minutes, she was on Cassie's doorstep, banging.

'Regan.' With Emma on her hip, Cassie dragged a hand through her tousled hair. 'I was just—you've been crying.' Alarm sprinted through her. 'Joe—'

'No, no. I'm sorry. I didn't mean to scare you. I need help.'

'What is it?' In a flash, Cassie had closed the door and locked it. 'What's wrong?'

'What's nine-ball?'

'What—?' Baffled, Cassie set Emma down, gave her a little pat on the bottom to send her along. 'What's nine-ball?'

'Yes. And where am I going to find a red leather miniskirt at this hour?'

Cassie thought for a moment, brushing a hand over the wet spot on her sweater that was courtesy of Emma's bath. 'If that's what you want, we'll have to call Ed.'

'Suck it in, sweetie.'

'I am.' Valiantly Regan gritted her teeth and held her breath as Ed tugged at the zipper of a skirt the size of a place mat.

'Trouble is, you've got a figure. I've got bones.' Mouth clamped tight in determination, Ed hauled, and tugged.

Then, with a wheeze of triumph, sat back on Cassie's bed. 'She's on, but I wouldn't make any sudden moves.'

'I don't think I can make *any* moves.' Testing, Regan took a step. The skirt, already dangerously high, snuck up another fraction.

'You got a little height on me, too,' Ed announced, and pulled out a cigarette. Her eyes sparkled with amusement as she let her rhinestone glasses fall to her chest. 'If it was much shorter on you, Devin would have to arrest you.'

'I can't see.' Though she rose on her toes and turned carefully, Cassie's mirror offered nothing but a view from the waist up.

'You don't have to, honey. Take my word, he will.'

'I got the kids settled,' Cassie said as she walked in. She stopped short, her mouth forming a shocked circle. 'Oh, my…'

'It's a hot little number,' Ed agreed. When she'd worn it last time, at the Legion dance, eyes had popped loose. The way Regan was filling it out, Ed imagined they'd not only pop, but go flying across the room.

'Try those shoes with it now,' she ordered. 'I stuffed some tissue in the toes to bring 'em down to size.'

Regan braced a hand on Cassie's dresser, stepped gingerly into the four-inch spikes. 'I'll get a nosebleed in these.'

'Honey, you'll cause nosebleeds.' Ed gave a raspy laugh. 'Now let's try some war paint.' Happily she up-ended her enormous purse onto the bed.

'I'm not sure I can go through with this. It's a crazy idea.'

'Don't go chicken on me now.' Ed riffled her hand

through a department-store array of cosmetics. 'You want that man, don't you?'

'Yes, but—'

'Then sit down here on the bed and let me buff you up. This here red's a killer,' she murmured fondly as she unscrewed a lipstick.

'I can't sit,' Regan stated after a single attempt. 'I'd damage an internal organ.'

'Then stand.' After making her choices, Ed rose and went to work. 'Now, you said nine-ball, right?'

'Yeah.'

In her forty-two years—forty-five, if God was listening—she'd never seen a woman less likely to chalk a stick than Regan Bishop. 'Ever play pool, honey?'

'Billiards.' Regan uttered a silent prayer as Ed advanced with eyeliner. 'With my father. Several times.'

'Hell, honey, billiards ain't nothing. Why, nine-ball's the second-best thing you can do on a pool table.' She cackled when Cassie flushed scarlet. 'Now listen up while I explain how it works.'

Balls smacked and clattered when Rafe shot his cue. The five ball thumped satisfactorily into the corner pocket.

'Luck,' Jared said, and lazily chalked his cue.

Rafe only snorted. 'Six off the nine and in the side.' He made his shot, lined up the next.

'Never could beat Rafe at nine-ball.' More interested in the little redhead at the bar than the game, Shane leaned on the juke. She was all alone, and looked as cuddly as a new down pillow. 'Seen her around before, Dev?'

Devin glanced up, over. 'Holloway's niece, from up on Mountain View. She's got a boyfriend the size of a semi who'll break you in half if you breathe on her.'

It was all the challenge Shane needed. He sauntered over, leaned on the bar and turned on the charm.

Devin gave a resigned smile. If the boyfriend came in, Devin would have to use his badge. And that would blow his night.

'My game.' Rafe held out his hand for the ten dollars Jared owed him. 'You're up, Dev.'

'I need a beer.'

'Jared's buying.' Rafe grinned at his older brother. 'Right, bro?'

'I bought last round.'

'You lost the last game.'

'So be a gracious winner. His tab,' Jared told the bartender, and held up three fingers.

'Hey, what about me?'

Jared flicked a glance at Shane. The redhead was clutching his arm like a fast-growing vine. 'You're driving, kid.'

'Flip for it.'

Obligingly, Jared took a coin from his pocket. 'Call it.'

'Heads.'

He flipped the coin, caught it neatly. 'Tails. You're driving.'

With a philosophical shrug, Shane turned back to the redhead.

'Does he have to hit on everything in a skirt?' Rafe muttered while Devin racked the balls.

'Yep. Somebody had to take up where you left off.' Devin stepped back, chose his cue. 'And since you're spoken for…'

'Nobody said I was spoken for.' Rafe gave the curvy redhead a long look, felt nothing more than a low-level tug of basic appreciation. And thought of Regan, just thought of her and his heart shattered. 'We've got an understanding.' He bit the words off, but still tasted bitterness. 'Nothing serious.'

'He's hooked.' Jared grinned and lifted his beer. 'And his heart looks so pretty, right there on his sleeve.'

No way he was going to take the bait, Rafe thought. It was bad enough having your heart broken without having your family watch you fumble with the pieces. 'You want to eat this cue?' Rafe executed his break, smugly pleased when two balls rolled into pockets.

'She came into the house today,' Devin said conversationally, 'and that hook in his mouth dragged him right down the stairs like a trout on a fly. I think there were stars in his eyes, too.' Devin met Rafe's steely look equably. 'Yep, I'm sure of it.'

'Pretty soon he's going to start shaving regular and wearing clean shirts.' Jared shook his head, as if in mourning. 'Then we'll know we've lost him.'

'Then it'll be antique shows and ballets.' Devin heaved a heavy sigh. 'Poetry readings.'

Because that hit entirely too close to home, Rafe jerked the cue and missed his shot. He wasn't going to think of her. Damn it, he wasn't going to give Regan or the hole in his gut a single thought. 'Keep it up and I'll take both of you on.'

'Well, I'm shaking.' After lining up his shot, Devin leaned over the table. He made his ball cleanly. As he circled the table, he sniffed at Rafe. 'That cologne, lover-boy?'

'I'm not wearing any damn—' Rafe hissed out a breath. 'You're just jealous 'cause you're sleeping alone on some cot outside a cell every night.'

'You got me there.'

Enjoying himself, Jared plugged coins into the jukebox. 'What time do you have to be home, Rafe? We wouldn't want you getting conked with a rolling pin for missing curfew.'

'How long have you been a practicing ass?' It was some small satisfaction to note that Duff was shooting them uneasy glances. A man didn't like to lose his touch. 'What's the fine for breaking up a couple of chairs?'

Nostalgia swam sweetly along with the beer in Devin's bloodstream. Unless he counted breaking his brothers up, and you could hardly count that, he hadn't been in a decent fight in years.

'Can't let you do it,' he said, with mildly drunk regret. 'I carry a badge.'

'Take it off.' Rafe grinned. 'And let's beat hell out of Shane. For old times' sake.'

Jared tapped his fingers on the juke in time to the music. He eyed their youngest brother, who was definitely making progress with the redhead. That alone was reason enough to punch him a few times.

'I've got enough on me to post bond,' Jared told them. 'And a little extra to bribe the sheriff, if we have to.'

Devin sighed, straightened from the table. With brotherly affection, he studied the unsuspecting Shane. 'Hell, he's going to get his butt whipped before the night's over, anyway, if he keeps playing with that girl. We might as well do it first.'

'We'll be more humane,' Jared agreed.

The bartender watched them move together, recognized, with despair, the look in each eye. 'Not in here. Come on now, Devin, you're the law.'

'Just doing my brotherly duty.'

'What's the idea?' Scenting trouble, Shane danced back from the bar. He scanned his brothers, shifted as they moved to flank him. 'Three against one?' His mouth curved in a wide, reckless grin as other customers moved to safety. 'Come on, then.'

He crouched, braced, then made the mistake of glancing over as the door opened. His mouth had already fallen open in surprise when Rafe caught him low and sent them both crashing into a table.

'You make it too easy.' Laughing, Rafe turned and caught him in a cheerful headlock. Then he went numb, right down to his toes.

The skirt barely made it past the legal limit. It wasn't tight. It went beyond tight as it squeezed possessively over curvy hips in an eye-popping fire-engine red. The legs went on. And on. Rafe's dazzled gape followed them down to the razor-sharp skyscraper heels in that same bold color.

When he managed to lift his gaze, he saw that the skinny black top was as snug as the skirt, and dipped down low over firm, unfettered breasts. It took him a full ten seconds to get to her face.

Her mouth was red and wet and curved. Beside it, the little mole was a bold exclamation of sex. Her hair was tousled, and her eyes were shadowed and heavy. She looked like a woman who'd just climbed out of bed, and was willing to climb right back in.

'Holy hell.' It was Shane's strained muttering that jolted him out of shock. 'Is that Regan in there? She is *hot*.'

Rafe didn't have the strength to put much behind the punch. When he gained his feet and moved to the door, his head was still buzzing, as if he'd been the one to take the blow.

'What are you doing?'

She moved a shoulder, causing the excuse for a blouse to follow her stretch. 'I thought I'd play a little nine-ball.'

There was something stuck in his throat. 'Nine-ball?'

'Yeah.' She sauntered over to the bar, leaned an elbow on it. 'Going to buy me a beer, MacKade?'

Chapter 12

If he kept staring at her, she was going to lose it, Regan thought. She was already so nervous that if her clothes hadn't been girdled on, she'd have jumped out of them.

Because she'd wanted to make an entrance, she'd left her coat in the car. Only the heat of possible humiliation kept her teeth from chattering.

Her feet were killing her.

When Rafe didn't answer, she scanned the room and tried not to swallow audibly at the stares. Gathering courage, she flashed a smile at the bartender. Even the weary-eyed Duff was goggling at her.

'I'll have what he's having.' When she had the beer in her hand, she turned back. No one had moved a muscle. It was either run or play it out, Regan told herself, taking a quick swallow of beer.

She hated beer.

'Are you going to rack them, MacKade, or am I?'

'I'll rack them,' Jared interjected helpfully. His hands were still a little sweaty, but he'd gotten over the worst of the shock. Rafe's face was almost as much of a pleasure to watch as the sway of Regan's hips, as she sauntered over to study the arsenal of cues.

Rafe heard the clatter of balls, and blinked. 'You said you wanted an early night.'

'Changed my mind.' Her voice was breathy from necessity, rather than design. The leather and Spandex were cutting off her air supply. 'I had all this…energy all of a sudden.' She walked slowly to the table, resisting the urge to tug at the hem of the skirt. 'Who wants to play?'

Half a dozen men moved with scraping chairs and clattering boots. Rafe's snarl was the low, vicious sound of a wild dog guarding his bone. Half a dozen men decided they weren't in the mood for pool after all.

'This is a joke, right?'

Regan took the cue Devin offered, smiled and stroked her fingertips from the tip down the shaft. Someone moaned. 'I felt like some action, that's all.'

With her confidence building, she passed the bottle of beer to Jared. This, at least, she thought, she knew how to do. Planting her feet, bending one knee for balance, she leaned over the table. Leather strained.

Rafe's elbow plowed into Shane's gut. 'Keep looking where you're looking, and you'll be blind for a week.'

'Jeez, Rafe.' Shane tucked his hands in his pockets and prepared to watch the show. 'Where's a guy supposed to look?'

She broke cleanly, even managed to sink a ball. With the rules of the game Ed had drilled into her flipping through her head, she circled the table. She had to stop, smile, as Devin was still rooted in her path.

'You're blocking the table, Sheriff.'

'Oh. Yeah, right. Sorry.' When she draped herself over the felt this time, his eyes met Jared's. They grinned at each other like two kids over a shiny new bike.

She managed to sink one more. That made her cocky enough to try a complicated shot that required a little English. Her hips wiggled as she set her position. From behind her, Jared stuck a hand under his shirt and mimed a thumping heart.

'You think what you're thinking again, and I'll rip your lungs out,' Rafe muttered.

As the ball missed the pocket by a good six inches, Regan pouted with that red-slicked mouth. 'Oops.' She straightened, batted thickly mascaraed eyes at Rafe. 'Your turn.' She put her weight on one foot and ran a hand down his shirtfront. 'Want me to…chalk your cue?'

The room exploded with whoops and whistles. Some brave soul made a suggestion that had Rafe's lips peeling back in a growl. 'That does it.'

He grabbed her cue, tossed it at Devin, then clamped a hand over hers to drag her toward the door.

'But we haven't finished the game,' she protested, forced to scramble on the skinny heels to keep up with him.

He yanked his jacket from the hook by the door and bundled it around her. 'Put this on before I have to kill somebody.' She was still struggling with it when he shoved her through the door.

Devin let out a long, appreciative sigh. 'He's a dead man.'

'Yeah.' Shane rubbed a hand over his stomach. 'Did you ever notice her—'

In Rafe's stead, Jared rapped him with a cue.

'I have my car,' Regan began, while Rafe towed her along.

He dragged open the door of his own. 'Get in. Now.'

'I could follow you.'

'Now.'

'All right.' It wasn't a simple operation to get into his car. Snug red leather rode higher as she tried for graceful and dignified as she lowered herself into the seat. Rafe ground his teeth audibly. 'Where are we going?'

'I'm taking you home.' He slammed her door, stormed around the hood, then slammed his own hard enough to rock the car. 'And if you're smart, you won't talk to me.'

She was smart. When his brakes squealed at the base of her steps, she stayed where she was. There was no possible way she could maneuver herself out of the tiny sports car without help.

He gave it to her, though no one would have called the hard yank a gentlemanly gesture. 'Keys,' he snapped, then snatched them out of her hand and unlocked the door himself.

Miffed, she strode in ahead of him. 'I assume you're coming in, so—'

She was rapped back against the door, his mouth hotly

devouring hers. The heels put them head-to-head, heat to heat, with a pressure that fried his already overheated brain. Both his mouth and his hands were hard, possessive. He could only think of branding her his.

His breath was ragged when he jerked back. He'd be damned if she'd work him this way again, make him a victim of his own needs.

He tugged his jacket off her shoulders, tossed it aside. 'Get out of those clothes.'

Something in her sank. With her lashes lowered, she reached around for the zipper of the skirt.

'No, I didn't mean— God.' If she peeled herself out of that leather in front of him, he was lost. It was the confusion in her eyes that had him leveling his voice. 'I meant I'd appreciate it if you changed into something else. Please.'

'I thought you—'

'I know what you thought.' He was dying here. 'Just change, so I can talk to you.'

'All right.'

He knew it was a mistake to watch her walk toward the bedroom. But he was only human.

Inside, Regan stepped out of the ankle-breaking shoes, stripped off the red leather. It was good to breathe again. She wanted to be amused, at both of them, but she felt so incredibly stupid. She'd made a spectacle of herself, thrown aside every scrap of dignity. For nothing.

No, she thought as she fastened on pleated trousers. For him. She'd done it for him, and he didn't even have the sense to appreciate it.

When she came back in, face washed, her hair brushed back into place, an ivory sweater tucked neatly into the waistband of black slacks, he was pacing.

'I want to know what you were thinking of,' he said without preamble. 'Just what you were thinking of, walking into a bar dressed like that?'

'It was your idea,' she tossed back, but he was too busy clenching his jaw and muttering to himself to listen.

'Five more minutes in there, and we'd have had a riot. I'd have started it myself. I've seen you naked, and I'm not sure I knew you were built like that. Now everybody in town's going to know.'

'You said you wanted—'

'I don't give a damn what they say about me, but nobody's going to talk behind their hands about you. Where the hell did you get that skirt?' he exploded. 'Tarts R Us?'

'Well, really…'

'Yeah, really. And leaning over the pool table that way, so everyone was looking at your—'

Her eyes narrowed to slits. 'Watch it, MacKade.'

'Now I'm going to have to go bash all of my brothers' brains in for what they were thinking.'

'You like bashing their brains in,' she retorted.

'That's beside the point.'

'I'll give you a point.'

She picked up her favorite Milton vase and tossed it to the floor. Rather than smashing satisfactorily, it bounced and rolled on the dainty floral rug. But the gesture shut him up.

'I humiliated myself for you. It nearly took a crowbar

to get me into that ridiculous skirt, and I think I bruised my intestines. I'll probably never get all this makeup out of my pores, my arches are screaming, and I have not an ounce of dignity left. I hope you're satisfied.'

'I—'

'Shut up. This time you just *shut up*. You wanted me to be that way, so I tried. I was willing to be what you wanted, and now all you can do is stand there and criticize and worry about gossip. Well, go to hell!'

She plopped down in a chair, because her feet were cramping painfully.

He waited until he was sure she'd run down, watched her sniffle and rub her bare feet. 'You did that for me?'

'No, I did it because I like teetering on four-inch heels and going around half-naked in the middle of winter. I live for it,' she said nastily.

'You did it to get to me.'

The bout of temper had drained her. She sat back, closed her eyes. 'I did it because I'm crazy about you. Just like you said I'd be. Now go away and leave me alone. You'll have to wait till tomorrow to beat your chest and drag me off by the hair. I'm too tired.'

He studied her a moment, then walked to the door and shut it quietly behind him.

She didn't bother to get up, or even to move. She didn't feel like crying. If she'd been ridiculous, she would weather it. She'd given him everything now, and there was no taking it back. Why should she bother? She'd never stop loving him.

She heard the door open again, and kept her eyes closed. 'I really am tired, Rafe. Can't you gloat tomorrow?'

Something fell into her lap. Regan blinked her eyes open and stared at the bouquet of lilacs.

'They're not real,' he told her. 'You can't get them in February. I've had them in the trunk of my car for a few days, so they're cold.'

'They're lovely.' Slowly she ran her fingers over the chilly silk blooms. 'A few days,' she murmured, and looked up again.

'Yeah, so?' He scowled, jammed his hands in his pockets, shifted. 'Man.' He thought facing a noose would be easier than what he was about to do. It certainly couldn't burn his throat any less.

He got down on his knees.

'What are you doing?'

'Just keep quiet,' he warned her. 'And if you laugh, you pay.' Mortified, he swore under his breath, dragged a hand through his hair. And bit the bullet.

' "When I arose and saw the dawn, I sighed for thee." '

'Rafe...'

'Don't interrupt me.' Miserably embarrassed, he glared at her. 'Now I have to start over.'

'But you don't have to—'

'Regan.'

She drew in a breath, wondered if there was another woman in the world who had ever had Shelley quoted to her with eyes that threatened murder. 'Sorry. You were saying?'

He shifted his weight. 'Okay. 'When I arose and saw

the dawn, I sighed for thee; When the light rode high, and the dew was gone, and…' Oh, hell.' He raked his fingers through his hair and tried to concentrate. 'I got it. 'And noon lay heavy on flower and tree, And the weary Day turned to her rest, lingering like an unloved guest, I sighed for thee.''

His breath came out on a huff of tremendous relief. 'That's all I've got. It took me more than a week to memorize it. If you mention this to anyone—'

'I wouldn't dream of it.' Incredibly moved, she laid a hand on his cheek. 'That was very sweet of you.'

'It kind of fits the way I feel about you.' And now that it was over—thank God—it hadn't been as bad as he'd feared. 'I think about you, Regan, all day. Every day. So if you want poetry—'

'No.' With a quick shake of her head, she reached out and laid her cheek on his shoulder. 'No, I don't need poetry, Rafe.'

'I haven't bothered to give you much romance.' And he knew now, by the way her eyes had gone soft and dreamy, that he should have. 'Now it's fake flowers and somebody else's words.'

She had to cry now, but they were lovely tears, soothing ones. 'I love the flowers, and I loved the words. But I don't need them. I don't want you to change for me, Rafe. There's nothing about you I'd want to change. I said I'd take you as you are and I mean it.'

'I like you the way you are, Regan, all neat and tidy. Not that I didn't appreciate the way you filled out that leather.'

'I'm sure I could borrow it from Ed again.'

'Ed?' He rolled his eyes and chuckled weakly. 'No wonder it fit you like skin.' Then he felt the warm drops on his neck. 'Oh, don't do that, baby. Please don't.'

'I'm not really crying. I'm just touched that you'd memorize Shelley for me. That you'd care enough.' She gave him a hard squeeze before leaning back. 'I guess we both won the bet, or lost it, depending on your viewpoint.' She dried off her cheeks with the back of her hand. 'Of course, you didn't lose yours in public.'

'If you think you can talk me into giving that little recital down at the tavern, you really are crazy. I'd never get out alive.'

She drew in a deep breath. 'I think we should both stick with who and what we are. I do like who and what you are, Rafe. And I need you more than you think. I needed you when Joe came into the shop and frightened me. I just didn't want you to know it. I was afraid to let you know how much I count on you.'

He picked up her hand, kissed it, and felt dozens of wounds heal. 'You didn't have to be.'

'I figured that out for myself. I like figuring things out for myself.'

'Tell me about it.' He smiled and no longer felt foolish being on his knees. 'I like the way you figure things out for yourself. The way you handle yourself, Regan. Even when it ticks me off, I like your style.'

'I like yours, too.' She leaned forward and kissed him lightly. 'I'm going to get something to put these in.'

He reached behind him and picked up the vase she'd thrown. 'How about this?'

'That'll be fine.' She took it from him and rose to arrange the silk bouquet on the table. 'I can't believe I actually threw it.'

'It's been an eventful evening. So far.'

She glanced back, smiled. 'It certainly has. Would you like to stay, and see what happens next?'

'There we are, on the same wavelength again. You know, Regan, I think we've got more common ground than either one of us realized. You shoot decent pool, I like antiques.' He stood, moving restlessly, picked up a china cat in suddenly nerveless fingers, then set it down again. 'So, you want to get married?'

She tucked a sprig of lilacs into place. 'Hmm… You asked me that before, as I remember. And never took me up on it, because I won't watch baseball.'

'I mean it.'

She twirled to face him, and her limp hand knocked against the table. 'Excuse me?'

'Look, we haven't known each other very long.' He stepped toward her, stopped cold. She was staring at him as though he'd lost his mind. He was certain he had. 'But we've got something going here. I know we said it was just going to be sex, and we've just finished deciding we really like each other.'

'Rafe, I can't—'

'If you'd just let me fumble through this.' His tone went from quiet to testy in an instant. 'I know how you are with having to weigh your options and think things through. But the least you can do is look at this from my perspective for one damn minute. It's not just sex for me, and it never was. I'm in love with you.'

She stared into those sharp, angry eyes, heard the treasured phrase delivered in a furious snarl. And felt her heart swell like a rose blooming in her chest. 'You're in love with me,' she repeated.

It had always been easy to say the words when it didn't count—when they were just words, and not these tiny, razor-edged little pellets in his throat. 'I'm in love with you,' he said again. 'It probably happened five minutes after I met you, maybe five minutes before. I don't know. It's never happened to me before.'

'Me, either,' she murmured.

He didn't hear her, didn't hear anything but the roaring in his head. 'No one's ever needed me. I've never wanted anyone to need me. It gets in the way. But I want that from you. I have to ask that from you.' He paused, fought to steady himself. 'I don't like asking.'

'I know. You don't have to.' She walked to him, framed his face in her hands. 'Rafe, you don't have to ask.'

'If you'd give me a chance—' he gripped her wrists '—I could make it work. We could make it work. Come on, Regan, take a risk. Live dangerously.'

'Yes.'

His grip on her wrists went lax. 'Yes, what?'

'Why do we have such a hard time hearing each other?' she asked. 'Listen up,' she ordered, and kissed him firmly. 'Yes, I'll marry you.'

'Just like that? You're not going to think about it?'

'Nope.'

'Good. Great.' A little dazed, he stepped back. 'We could, ah, t-take care of…it. Take care of it tomorrow. The license. Whatever. You want a ring…or something?'

'Yes, I do. Rafe, you're stuttering.'

'No, I'm not.' He stepped back when she stepped forward. 'I just didn't expect you to take the jump so quick.'

'If you're trying to change your mind, forget it. Was it the skirt?'

His eyes went blank and baffled. 'What skirt?'

No answer could have pleased her more. 'I think you should tell me you love me again.' Before he could evade her, she wrapped her arms around his neck, linked her fingers. 'I think you should get used to saying it.'

'I do love you.'

'And you were in love with me that first night, when we were alone, in the house on the hill?'

'I guess I was.'

'I didn't know, didn't have a clue. I wonder if the house did. I remember how quiet it got that night—how settled it all seemed. Would you like to go back there, tonight?'

'Yes.' He rested his brow on hers. 'I would.'

'There's something I should tell you first, Rafe. Something I think we should clear up between us.'

'Regan, if you're going to slap down more rules and parameters—'

'I think I should tell you,' she said interrupting him,

'that as attracted as I was to you, as aroused as I was by you, I could have slept with you without loving you.'

'I know.' He refused to be hurt by it. 'It's okay.'

'I could have done that because you're the most incredibly attractive man I've ever met, all the way through. But there's no way I would have squeezed myself into that ridiculous outfit tonight unless I'd been wildly, stupidly and completely in love with you.' Her eyes shimmered and smiled. 'Is that okay?'

'Say it again.' He took her face in his hands. 'Look at me straight-on and say it again.'

'I love you. I'm so very much in love with you, Rafe. There's nothing I want more than to go on loving you, and needing you for the rest of my life.'

The thrill of it sprinted through him, then settled, warm and easy. 'You could get used to saying it, too.'

'I'm a very quick study. I love you,' she murmured against his mouth, then poured the words into the kiss.

'It's going to get complicated.' He gathered her close and held her. Just held her. 'Life's going to be messy.'

'I hope so.' Eyes closed, she pressed her cheek against his. 'Oh, I hope so. Why was I so scared?' she whispered. 'Why was I so afraid to let you know?'

'Probably for the same reason I was.' He tilted her head back. 'It happened so fast, and it matters so much. And it always will.'

'It always will,' she agreed.

Later, when they were curled together in the deep feather bed, she laid her hand on his heart and smiled.

'I'm awfully glad you came back to town, MacKade. Welcome home.'

The house was quiet around them, and slept as they slept.

* * * * *

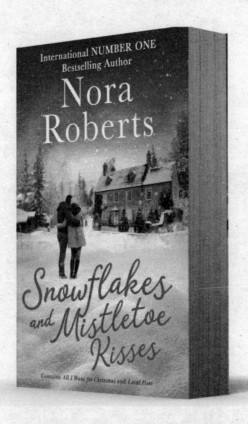